Our Unbound Firsts titles are inspired by Unbound's mission to discover fresh voices, new talent, and amazing stories. As part of our commitment to amplifying diverse voices, Unbound Firsts is an annual opportunity for writers of colour to have their debut book published by an award-winning, crowd-leading publishing house.

Zahra Barri is an Irish-Egyptian writer and stand-up comedian. She has featured on Channel 4's *Jokes Only A Muslim Can Tell*, BBC Radio and BBC Asian Network. In 2020, Zahra was named a runner-up in the Comedy Women in Print Unpublished Prize and she is currently doing a PhD in Creative Writing at the University of Hertfordshire. Her work is supported by the Society of Authors. She lives in Kent. @ZahraBarri1

DAUGHTERS OF THE NILE
ZAHRA BARRI

unbound

First published in 2024

Unbound
c/o TC Group, 6th Floor King's House,
9-10 Haymarket, London, SW1Y 4BP
www.unbound.com

Text design by Jouve (UK), Milton Keynes

A CIP record for this book is available from the British Library

ISBN 978-1-80018-312-4 (paperback)
ISBN 978-1-80018-313-1 (ebook)

Printed in Great Britain by Clays Ltd, Elcograf S.p.A.

1 3 5 7 9 8 6 4 2

For my Mum, Teresa.
Thank you for encouraging my naughtiness.

History repeats itself, first as tragedy, second as farce.
— Karl Marx

Yasminah

CAIRO, 1966

ي

I planned to do it while everyone was at Mosque.

'Mama,' I said, stumbling into her office and clutching my stomach, 'I can't go to Friday prayers because I have my period.'

My mother put her policy papers into her drawer before looking at me. She opened her mouth to speak, then closed it again.

'Stay home and rest, habibbti,' Baba called out from the hall. Mama slammed her thick diary shut and sighed. She gazed out her small window onto the side street where we went for ice cream on days when the heat was the thickest. I could hear Baba coming towards us, reciting Abu Dawud's hadith under his breath. He kissed my forehead before looking at my mother wide eyed and shrugging.

'Yallah, Usman, Aziz!' he called out, clapping his hands as he walked, rallying my brothers who were on the balcony that overlooked a hectic Heliopolis. My thoughts were as loud and fast as Osman Ibn Affan Street. I twiddled the door handle. My

I

mother's eyebrows rose, and her lips swished from side to side. I gulped and followed my father through the apartment and out onto the balcony. The sun was setting and squares of orange were interspersing with squares of grey, turning our large balcony into a chess board. Usman, the Knight, was in a section of shade, kicking his football against the dusty wall. Aziz, the Rook, was squinting, leaning on the balustrade, ogling the girls in the apartment below.

Watching my brothers both pursuing their passions, I sat on the wobbly wooden chair. It was the one that Uncle Jeddy broke last Eid and that Baba had done his best to fix. I tried to relax. They'd be out for hours after Mosque. Mama would go for coffee with Naila and reminisce about the 'glory days' at *Bint Al Nil*, and Baba would go for shisha with Naila's husband, Dyab, and be thankful that the 'glory days' at *Bint Al Nil* were over.

'Now that she is not protesting, she is cooking!' Dyab would say, as if he hadn't made the joke a thousand times.

Baba would laugh, slapping Dyab on the back, as if he hadn't heard it a thousand times.

Usman would put his balcony practice to the test and play with his friends on the street. Meanwhile, Aziz would go to his nightclub to leer at more women. He was thankful that his latest entrepreneurial venture placated Mama and Baba, blurring the lines between business and pleasure. He'd end the night entwined between Maggie and Eleanor. No doubt not the only man in Cairo who enjoyed the aftermath of colonisation.

'Alibi's, habibbti, my club is called Alibi's, you girls must come . . . How about tonight?' Aziz shouted down to the sisters.

I could hear the girls giggling in response before their father, Mr Yaghoubi, in his deep, abrasive voice from years of tobacco smoking, called them in from his armchair.

2

Aziz tutted. He took a mirror out of his pocket and loudly spat on his hand before mopping his thick black hair and adjusting his jacket. I heard my mother's boots striding into the living room. I turned around and the chair creaked and slid to the side, almost toppling me over. She had her headscarf on now and was putting her gloves on.

'Yallah, Usman, Aziz . . . let's go!' Baba whistled.

I joined them, as we all walked towards Mama. She looked at me and my eyes wandered.

'This is not the word of Aisha but the word of Abu Dawud, what did I tell you, some of the hadiths, the word of Mohammed, peace be upon him, is transcribed from unreliable narrators. Written by men with an agenda . . .' she began.

'Nashit nisayiyun . . .' Baba hissed as she ranted, '. . . nashit nisayiyun . . . feminist,' he whispered it as if it were a swear word. He made a face while tying his shoelaces.

'It's my belief, Mama, and Baba thinks it too,' I said, 'the hadith of Abu Dawud said that the Prophet (peace and blessings be upon him) asked Aisha to give him something while he was at Mosque and she declined, saying that she was menstruating.'

My mother crossed her arms and bit her fat bottom lip. She tutted and walked towards the door. She knew I often used the Quran to my advantage. But then again, so did she.

'Bismillah,' Mama hissed to herself, looking me up and down one last time, as if scanning my body for clues of my deceit.

'Usman, Aziz, Ali!' Mama roared and pointed at the door.

'Hey! What about Yasminah?' Aziz grumbled.

My mother raised her brows at him, pushing her eyeballs almost cartoonishly out of their sockets.

'OK,' he said, 'I am *also* on my period!'

Usman clutched a cushion to his stomach and fell onto the sofa laughing.

'Wallahi!' my mother shouted and her voice echoed above the high ceiling. All three of them flinched. Usman shot up from the sofa, Baba opened the door, mumbling to Aziz about respecting a woman's monthly pain and Mama clipped her eldest most outspoken son over the head. The door slammed behind them.

'Don't be so childish, your sister is in pain!' I heard Mama hiss as they galloped down the five flights of stairs. Each clip quieter than the last until there were only the sounds of cars beeping.

Alone, I sat in the armchair, turned the fan on beside the telephone and for a while I listened to its rhythmic beat somewhat subduing the traffic below. Then I turned the radio on. Umm Kulthum's 'Inta Omri' was playing.

This is the song I told my best friend Mona we had danced to. I closed my eyes.

'Let's dance,' he had said as he took my hand and kissed me. At first his lips felt like rose petals. Yet, later, all I could feel were the sharp thorns of his stubble as his head buried itself into my neck. It felt both tremendous and torturous, it was like someone was tickling me to death.

I switched the radio off and then the fan and walked towards the dining room. I opened Mama's cabinet, where she now displayed her wine like trophies. When I was a little girl I used to find the bottles stashed away in her wardrobe, but the more Islamic poets she consumed, the bolder she grew.

'Shall I spurn it, when Allah himself hasn't and our own caliph shows its veneration?' she would always utter as she opened the bottle, '. . . superlative wine, radiant and bright. Rivalling the sun's scintillation. While we may not know Heaven in this life, still we have paradise's libation.' Then she'd say to

4

Baba or whoever she felt might be judging her before taking the first sip, 'The poetry of Abu Nawas, alhamdulillah.'

My fingers touched each bottle, making lines in the dust, recalling my mother's ritual. I clicked the glass cabinet closed again and found my hands wandering to the wooden cupboard below, where she hid her spirits like dirty secrets. She was yet to find an Islamic poet who heralded the spiritual qualities of a gin and tonic.

I took an unopened bottle from Mama's cupboard and brought it back into the living room. Was this all the medicine I needed to right someone else's wrong? The girl at my school had warned me that it wasn't guaranteed but it was at least worth a try. I sat back down again on the armchair and unscrewed the top. It cracked like the sound a pistol makes before a race. With sudden speed, I poured it down my throat. I could feel the sting attacking the parasite inside me. I drank some more. Tremendous and torturous. I flicked the radio on then flicked it off again before taking another big swig. This time I had taken more than I could swallow; my cheeks expanded, and I was forced to let some dribble out of my mouth and onto the fabric of the chair. I could feel my world blurring; looming over the coffee table, I saw a clock like the one I'd seen in a painting, melting in a desert, bending to the dimensions of time and space. I drank more, before bringing the bottle tightly to my chest. I was a child again, hugging my teddy bear, scared of the monster within. I drank again and again and again, each sip, swig, gulp, swallow less potent than the last. It was only when the spirit turned sweet that my hearing slowed and my vision sped. I fell onto the ceramic floor and I heard the bottle smashing like the crescendo of an orchestral piece before going quiet. The tiles underneath me were soft clouds and I dozed into a dream.

I lost parts of that night to the spirit. When I woke on the floor, I felt a warmness between my legs. I opened my eyes and yelped like a small dog being trod on. I saw the blood streaming down the floor. I followed it, flowing like the Nile. The blood river fusing into the smashed glass. The alcohol distilling the redness, turning an acrylic painting into a watercolour. I picked myself up, carelessly stepping over the tragic masterpiece.

Then I raided Mama's cabinet for another bottle, as I heard the call to prayer.

Nadia

BRISTOL, 2011

ن

I had woken up to herpes again. Heavy, bulbous sores seemed to protrude from my knickers. Thick gunky pus was oozing out of one of them with the same viscosity of PVA glue, sealing the fabric of my underwear to my skin. Its colour was the muddy brown that emerges when mucus and blood meet. I groaned, chastising both the two suspects I presumed had afflicted me with this sodden disease, all those years ago: Zain from Saudi or the bikini I had tried on in Primark. This was a particularly bad flare-up. I had been burning the candles at both ends and by the looks of things, the wax was now seeping into my nether regions.

I hobbled into the hall, feeling an unusual weight between my legs. I had never had this many sores before. The package of pimples pulsated and throbbed. Was this what it felt like to be a man? A mixture of disgust and pride at what was between my legs.

I somehow mustered up the energy to battle the obstacle course of our hallway. The shabby, grotty corridor was riddled with street signs and orange road cones and the no smoking sign from the Princess Victoria pub. Memorabilia which we had thought indicative of a successful night out failed to induce a smile as usual. The clutter only made me feel more disoriented as I reached my final destination. I leaned my head on the bathroom door as if I'd just summitted Everest or at the very least Machu Pichu.

A hint of a scream came from the bathroom, followed by a thunderous groan – the dehumidifier somewhat muting my flatmate's shower sex. I thumped on the door unashamedly.

'I need the toilet!' I croaked. I was now resting my entire body on the bathroom door, which I held for several seconds before succumbing to it all, sliding down to the ground like a distressed soap opera actor. *Stop. Having. Sex*, I thought. I tasted salt and touched my cheeks like I would a heated pan, surprised to find them hot with tears.

I tried bashing my head on the door systematically, hoping the proverbial sense would be knocked into me. This proved futile. However, the thumps to my head and the door did serve to remind my housemate that there were other people in this flat who needed to use the bathroom as it was designed for. To shit and shower and to sit on the toilet and wince in agony as urine and tears stung both sets of lips simultaneously.

The door clicked open and with it my head and torso fell into the steam, the condensation only adding to my discombobulation. Angela and Mr Tennis stepped over my sprawled body. They often saw me in such a state. It was not uncommon for any of our household to be rolling around on the bathroom floor in agony of any given morning.

But today wasn't a hangover. I very rarely got hangovers these days. I admit a night of carnage caused me to shake the next day, mix up my words, inflict a headache so banging it defied the laws of physics and made the earth implode, but that was nothing a few shots of vodka and a paracetamol couldn't sort. Besides, I suspected, by how little I cared that Mr Tennis could now see the cheeks of my arse, that I was still a little bit drunk. Not only my naked buttocks but quite possibly the yellow pus that was migrating north from my vagina to my arse-hole. Settling in like cement between two bricks. Either that or the pain had numbed my sense of humility. I enjoyed the destruction of the ego that the intense physical pain and alcohol accommodated in me.

'Do you want to walk in together?' Angela asked as I heard Mr Tennis move into our shared kitchen-cum-living room grunting inaudible niceties at my sister Kadijah who was trans-fixed by Lorraine Kelly interviewing a *Big Brother* contestant.

'Uergh . . .' I grunted, still on the floor. 'Herpes is really bad today, not sure I can walk, let alone run.'

Angela crouched down to my level and rubbed my back. For the first time in a long while I felt mothered. I lifted my head up onto her knees and she held it, stroking my hair, which made me further recoil into the nest of her bosom. She smelt of lemon-grass and tea tree oil and out of the corner of my eye I could see its roots: the luminous yellow Original Source shower gel. I imagined the almighty sting that would arise if I douched my calloused vagina with it. Perhaps it would burn them all off, I wondered.

'Babe, you have to come into work today, Fitty McHotty is in Edit Suite 5.'

A sudden energy seemed to vibrate from my chest causing me to sit up. It felt as though there was a butterfly on my heart. I told myself it was caused by the romance of Fitty McHotty

9

when, really, I knew they were the heart palpitations I often had after rigorous drinking sessions.

'Really?'

'Yes, really!' she said, getting up and unravelling her towel from her hair and using it to dry her golden mane as if she was drying a wet Labrador, roughly with love. She had her usual spark in her sapphire blue eyes. And her cheekbones shone with an unadulterated zest for life. Angela seemed to never tire of life.

'He's in Edit Suite 5 alone all day, which means you will be his own personal runner. You have to go in! If you don't, Lydia will get her claws into him.'

Suddenly the thought of this other woman made me put aside the pain between my legs. I had to go in. I had to make Fitty McHotty, the most eligible bachelor in Bristol, fall in love with me. Fuck the herpes, I thought.

∾

I didn't walk in with Angela as I needed extra time to sort myself out. She would be walking half the way with Mr Tennis anyway and I didn't fancy being a third wheel. Especially when they approached the tennis courts where he worked, as they normally started doing tennis puns about love and game and how great his backhand was while they smothered each other in kisses and slobbers and gropes. I mean, I was already feeling sick from all the sores that were in my pants.

I'd put the prescribed cream onto my genitals and the sores were fizzing in delight. I then strapped on a sanitary towel as if it were a gigantic bandage to absorb any remaining pus or excess cream. Then I did my face. I worked like Dalí, turning everything sexual. I turned my lips into his infamous red plump sofa. It was as if I were inviting men to sit on them. I brushed red onto my cheeks, flushing them with hints of orgasm, and I outlined my eyes in the thick black kohl eyeliner, complete with Cleopatra flicks at the corners. I loved telling men I was Egyptian as I knew they automatically thought of this wanton sexual figure. It was far sexier than simply saying you were Arab.

I looked at my now unrecognisable face and felt a kinship with both my western and Middle Eastern roots. My grandma Teta was right: every woman regardless of religion covers her face for a man in some way.

As I walked out of the flat, I was still a little shaky on my legs, but it hurt less if I walked slower. I texted Angela as I locked up asking if she could cover for me as I was no doubt going to be late, having only the capacity to walk half as fast as usual.

Upon sending the text, my phone instantly beeped back, not with a text from Angela but from Pamela. It read:

Uncle Aziz is getting married again.

I called her instantly. I loved it when my mother casually revealed titillating secrets about members of our family during our phone calls to each other. I figured the gossip would distract me from the pain as it so often did in our family. Our almost daily conversations covered mostly three topics: our bowel movements, Pamela's prolapse, and family drama. And although I was fascinated by her pelvic problems (and somewhat sorry that I had caused them) as well as being a long-standing sufferer of irritable bowel syndrome (I had the Bristol Stool Chart memorised as if it was the Periodic Table), it was the family drama that always invigorated me the most.

'Which cousin is he cavorting with now, Pam?' I asked, dodging the sea of dead-eyed commuters trudging up the steep slope of Park Street towards their office jobs. I was envious of them all. They got to sit down all day. At desks with internet access.

Some of these lucky bastards even had desks where their bosses couldn't see their screens. If I could sit down all day, my herpes sores would clear up at double the rate. Instead, I had to run up and down stairs all day, making tea and getting lunch for all the edit suites in the hope that I'd meet a director who could give me a leg-up and get me a job on an actual TV set, not an edit suite. Where I would also spend the day running around all day, making tea and fetching lunches in the hope that I would meet a producer who would give me a job in an actual TV production office, and only then would I finally achieve my dream of sitting down all day. Oh, to sit down all day, with internet access at a desk where my screen could not be seen by either my boss or my colleagues! Then I would finally be free.

'Which cousin, Pam?' I said again.

I felt her roll her eyes and wince. The rolling of the eyes, no doubt for calling her 'Pam' and not 'Pamela', and the wince was because I no longer called her 'Mum'.

'Well,' she said, starting to narrate the latest event. I tuned out for a minute, recalling the scandalous affair between Uncle Aziz and his cousin Reem. Scandalous, to our family, because Reem was twelve years his senior, rather than the fact that she was his blood relative. The fact that Reem and Aziz used to play together because their dads are brothers was not cause for concern. A sizeable percentage of our Egyptian family had not only fraternised but indeed married their cousins, including my paternal grandparents, Teta and Dodo. But according to hearsay that was only because no man outside the family could handle 'Fatiha's outspoken disposition'.

'It's time to accept that we are from a long line of cousin fuckers,' Kadijah had once told me gravely. Perhaps it was a testament to my innate optimism that I chose this to signify that my family were not dissimilar to the British royal family rather than fret about any potential medical morbidities.

'Uncle Aziz is always marrying some new woman; can't he ever keep it in his pants?' I was approaching my favourite part of Bristol; a refreshing change from the lull of Park Street: White-ladies Road. Not that I advocated the post-colonial subtext, but I did enjoy the hubbub of it. It was the sort of road that in the cold light of day always felt like the morning after. It emitted real hangover vibes, but not a deflated or depressed hangover. The sort of hangover where you feel the alcohol has possessed you. (I think that's why they call it a spirit.) You have a hyper sort of clarity where you feel like you can do anything. The last time I felt this sort of hangover I felt so profoundly moved by it, in a Tracey-Emin-Unmade-Bed kind of way, I wondered if it was possible to nominate a hangover for the Turner Prize.

Whiteladies Road of a morning was a personification of this. Quite simply, the hangover it emanated was not really a hangover at all. For it was still drunk. The road was awash with people either doing the walk of shame or dodging people they had sincerely regretted sleeping with from the night before.

As if to prove my point, I found myself smiling as I passed a girl with hair like a barrel of hay in both colour and texture. The result of rolling around in the proverbial sack of it all night. Although the sores were still throbbing, I was laughing to myself and feeling a deep surge of happiness. Never had I lived some-where where such hedonism was the norm. It was refreshing not to have to hide parts of myself. I finally had found a place I truly belonged.

I passed the Esso petrol station opposite the BBC, breathing in its glorious toxicity. Petroleum, tar, smoke and Krispy Kreme doughnuts filled my lungs. There was a man texting while stuffing his face with the sugary, sinful pastry as he filled up his car. Perhaps I had douched too much of the medicated cream onto myself causing such philosophical pontifications, but the man seemed to evoke to me the spirit of this very road. He just didn't give a fuck. The rules of life, don't use your phone at a petrol station, don't eat doughnuts, don't inhale toxic fumes, he was doing all three and all the happier for it by the looks of his face. The man in front of him, however, did not evoke such a feeling. His face was sullen and pale in comparison to the brightness of his lime green baseball cap. He scratched his crotch, as all men do with no apparent shame, while furiously texting. It was only then that I took a closer look at his face and it dawned on me who it was. I could feel the throbbing fizz in my underwear again, which had been somewhat subdued by my feeling of belonging. Hot, painful panic rushed through me, like a high-speed train passing through a quaint village station. I instinctively dodged behind a car. I had to hide myself. It was Giles Jeppo, a local TV newsreader that I had been having one-night stands with for several months.

'He has always struggled with social moralities.' Pamela began her usual monologue about Uncle Aziz while I found myself on a side street, having escaped Giles's eyeline. 'If he's not screwing around with other women who are not his wife, he's screwing around with the law . . . It's like when he came to the UK and . . .'

'. . . paid his friend to pass his driving test for him,' I said, finishing my mother's sentence. While my dad – the obedient immigrant – had studiously followed the laws of the land when he came to the UK in the seventies, his brother had not. Ever the conscientious student, my dad had learned about roundabouts, theorised as well as practised the three-point turn and how to master the parallel park. However, my uncle Aziz had decided it was far easier to 'pay someone as brown as him' to take the test for him. It was hard to tell if my dad was more appalled at my uncle's corrupt behaviour or at the DVLA test centre in Chingford for passing him.

'Listen, I've got to go . . .' I said, 'I gotta get to work.' I ran my fingers through my hair, while wondering how to get to the BBC side entrance without getting spotted by Giles. I put my hood over my head and ran across the pedestrian crossing, then it was only a hop, skip and a jump (quite literally due to my pants predicament) to get onto Blackboy Road where the BBC had its more discreet entrance. I felt the crisp morning air on my face; it both awakened and relaxed me in equal measure.

'OK, love. I'll forward you the wedding invite,' Pam said.

'OK, bye, bye, bye.'

I was almost at Edits at 59 when I felt a presence, breathing heavily behind me. I was relieved to see it was just a pug and his owner. I looked down at the genetically modified creature's rolls of fat that hung around his neck like an oppressive piece of jewellery and his squashed-up face and droopy eyes that had been mechanically orchestrated not for health but for aesthetic cuteness. I was in dismay that science had been crudely seduced by capitalism to produce a dog that would be forever battling for breath and never fitting in with the other dogs that could run and play and convert oxygen effectively. I looked up at the owner and saw that he was in the very same health condition as his dog. It made me think about the book that Angela had given me for my birthday: a book of dogs that looked like their owners. I examined the drooping flesh on the pug's neck and looked up to compare his rolls of flesh to his owner's. As I did, I caught sight again of Giles's lime green baseball cap in the distance. It was coming closer towards me.

My body froze while my mind started to race. It was as if I was reliving the trauma of sleeping with him night after night. I remembered his pathetic pillow talk in which he showcased his array of luminous-coloured baseball caps. He had explained to me how he wore them when he 'didn't want to get spotted' by his 'female fans'. I had suggested that if he really didn't want to get spotted, perhaps he should choose a more muted colour range of hats, as they hung on his wall like a pack of highlighter pens. He disregarded my comment, muttering under his breath something about 'hiding in plain sight so as not to appear on the *Daily Mail* sidebar of shame for the umpteenth time this year'. Angela had later informed me that his 'fans' were all of a particular demographic: women who drank prosecco and posted 'Live, Love, Laugh' platitudes on Facebook. She also divulged that he had appeared in the *Daily Mail* sidebar of shame once and that was only because he happened to be behind Trevor McDonald at a Southwest News charity event.

Still in a frozen trance, my head didn't seem to compute that I needed to hide again. Instead, I delicately touched myself down below, trying to find out whether the bulges had gone down somewhat since rubbing in the medicated cream. I felt that they had. An hour or so ago my sores were of a magnitude of Mount Etna and Mount Vesuvius; now they felt more like the little knobbly hills we saw at my dad's research conference in the Inner Hebrides. My doctor had told me that once the swelling goes down, they start to form scabs and are no longer infectious. Taking my phone out of my bag, I scheduled in three alarms:

one at 11 a.m., another at 2 p.m. and another at 5 p.m. which reminded me to 'rub cream onto vag'.

The baseball cap was getting closer now. I was succumbing to my fate. I took a long breath in, taking in my surroundings. I could see the BBC security man, Eric, checking passes and taking in deliveries; he nodded at me and I waved back. I looked back again and to my utter joy, I could no longer see the baseball cap. Relieved, I began walking again. This time my pace was much faster; the pain was still there but it no longer penetrated my psyche. I felt spritely all of a sudden at the thought of spending all day serving hot beverages to Bristol's most sought-after lothario: Fitty McHotty.

A luminescent flash brought me out of my stupor. It was Giles's ruddy baseball cap again.

'Giles!' I proclaimed. I watched as the morning steam projected out of my mouth, merging with the green of his cap to create an almost witch-like materialisation of my regrettable multiple-night stands.

'Nadia!' he said, out of breath. 'Didn't you hear me calling you? Why did you take a little detour, this is not the way you usually walk. Are you trying to avoid me?'

'Of course not! I needed to drop a package off through the BBC's side entrance,' I lied.

'Nadia,' he said again with a strange mix of horrified concern and ferocious anger, placing his hand roughly on the sleeve of my Edits at 59 anorak as if hanging on for dear life, '. . . why have you not replied to my text messages?'

I looked down at his hand. It was violating me somehow. I felt the pain between my legs again.

'It's all over my cock. I've never seen anything like it before. What the fuck have you given me you . . . you . . . hussy!

Claudia has got it too. She thinks I've been having an affair! I told her don't be so ridiculous, darling, maybe it's that new washing detergent . . . but it isn't, is it, Nadia, because we got tested. You've given me and my wife fucking herpes!'

I felt a warm trickle of pus lactate out of my vagina and onto the sanitary towel. I really wanted to itch it but feared it would only confirm his suspicions.

'How do you know it was me?' I said, walking faster with each word, refusing to look him in the eye, momentarily raising a fake smile and nodding at Eric again as I walked past.

'Because you're the only person I've slept with in ten years other than my wife!' he hissed, trying to catch up with me.

A sudden lightbulb came on in my head. 'Maybe Claudia is having an affair . . .'

Giles paused for a moment as he considered this possibility before shaking his head. 'She's just had our third child and her bloody mother is round all the time and she never leaves the house . . . I mean!'

'People have online affairs all the time, never leave the house, phone sex and all that?' I said.

Giles breathed in slowly. 'Let's say hypothetically she was having one of these modern "online affairs" . . .' he overemphasised the air quotes, almost poking me in the face, before exploding, 'HOW THE FUCK DO YOU GET AN *STI* FROM ONLY HAVING BLOODY PHONE SEX?'

'OK, OK, OK . . .' I said, wiping his saliva off my face. 'It's no big deal, completely harmless, it's basically the cold sore of the genitals. Flares up when you're run down et cetera. I've had it for years, it's completely manageable. When you get one just refrain from any sexual activity and rub this all over your dick, OK?' I said, dangling the cream in front of him.

'And what exactly shall I tell Claudia?'

'Tell her you had a cold sore and touched it then touched yourself, at least then there's some truth in it – she got it from a complete wanker.'

I strutted off to Aretha Franklin singing 'R.E.S.P.E.C.T' in my head. I never turned back but in a car mirror I could see Giles removing his baseball cap and breaking down in the street. He was always such a drama queen.

Fatiha

ف

'La-ah, keda, yallah, bass, bass . . . iywa . . .' I said to my daughter, Yasminah, rubbing her back as she tried to sit up in the bed. 'Slowly, drink it slowly. Small drops, slowly. Alhamdulillah,' I added as I put the glass of warm tea down on the cabinet beside the bed. Then I put the cold flannel back on her brow and looked into my daughter's tired eyes for just a second before turning away. I hated how free of shame her eyes were. The barefaced shamelessness that only comes from still being in the last dregs of delirium. She wasn't even the slightest bit mortified. When fully conscious she would be full of it, I thought with surprising bitterness. *Had she not suffered enough?* the mother in me asked. Waking up in a bed that is not her own, her insides torn apart? *Isn't that what got her into this mess in the first place?* the cynical damning ogre inside me retaliated.

Throughout my career I had saved many a woman like my daughter lying before me. Many a woman like her; drunk, desperate, debauched, all disgusting and bleeding at the legs, and

21

I had done so with gentle, unjudging maternity. I had no prejudice towards these girls, the type of calm bias I had thought at the time that only came from the very pits of the maternal soul. But now when my own daughter was here, in a manner resembling these other girls who had called me their saviour, why did it take every muscle in my body not to thrash her with the back of my hand? I breathed in and concentrated on keeping up appearances, not just for my best friend Doria's sake, whose house we were in – not even for Yasminah's benefit – but for my own. The problem was that the more maternal I acted on the outside, the more the monster grew inside me.

I put my head in my hands and closed my eyes for just a second before hearing Doria's footsteps. The creak of her floorboards suddenly alerted my body upright again, my face forming a big smile as it did. I was like one of those silly puppets we had seen at the fair. One touch with the thumb, they are rigid, upright and grinning, one release of the thumb they are a bundled tangled morbid mess on the floor.

'Mama . . .' Yasminah spoke softly as if she were my child again. Her skin pale; an unusual bitter almond colour when it was ordinarily a sweet maple syrup.

I was back in my role, doting, nurturing, swallowing the vinegar and ignoring how it smarted my throat. I picked up the tea and held it out for her to drink.

'Drink, Yasminah, drink, habibbti,' Doria said, striding past the bed and hovering over me.

'Do as Doria says, habibbti, drink,' I said.

As Yasminah began to drink, small sips like a frightened kitten, I turned to my best friend, and mouthed a 'shukran'.

' "Do as Doria Says!" That should have been *Bint Al Nil*'s campaign slogan,' Doria uttered under her breath. I smiled as I always did whenever she mentioned our glorious *Bint Al Nil* days, Egypt's most controversial feminist magazine, then perhaps even more salacious; a fully-fledged political women's party and now . . . Ali, my ever-grounding husband, would tell me not to get too het up about things like legacy as it changed all the time. History books, he reminded me, used to praise the Egyptian monarchy until Naguib and Nasser's military coup. Your and Doria's work will be recognised one day, he assured me.

'Do as Doria says,' my best friend repeated, releasing a small chuckle as she sat down beside me. Her voice was a whisper, like it had been for many years since. I longed to hear fury and vitriol, like the fire that she had in her inspiring parliamentary speeches, but all I heard now was passivity and acceptance. It frightened me. I hated looking back at the past with nostalgia. I wanted to look back at the past with disdain, just like we used to.

'My mother had been a concubine from Sudan, she lived in a harem. The first time she left her harem was to attend one of Huda Shaarawi's lectures,' I had told Doria the day we first met at the Sorbonne. She, too, told me tales of her own mother's regrettable past and together we had an unspoken excitement for the brightness of our own future. Smoking in Parisian courtyards, sipping Sauternes wine even though we swore we would only drink red, like the great Islamic poets did. The wine pouring, one mouth pouting, poised and pointing a cigarette, while the other pontificated. We had felt like we were on the precipice of promise, the peak of something almost ethereal, and we were, almost.

'Do as Doria Says!' she said again, this time a little louder than before but still not at the decibel that I so longed to hear from her.

I tried to laugh but could only muster a tired smile at my

friend's mischief. Doria was always so calm and humorous in a crisis. It was one of the reasons I had called her when I came back from Mosque and seen the mess that Yasminah has made in the living room. I was paralysed for just a moment and then something inside me erased my emotional responses in favour of practical ones. I quickly ordered my husband to take Usman out; I did not want my youngest baby to see such horrors. Ali, seeing the expression on my face, asked no questions and took him for ice cream and dates on Palace Walk. As if an influx of sweetness into our son's bloodstream would erase the memory of his sister's sourest scene.

My husband knew what had happened without having to explain. A sixth sense that only accompanies the other five upon parenthood. Or perhaps the bloodied scene reminded him of what he had witnessed as a young boy, in 1919, during the protests. He said nothing. He just looked at me, blinking repeatedly, and I understood his Morse Code signal: Doria. Doria. Doria. But I delayed calling her initially. Instead, I showered Yasminah down like I did when she was a baby, holding onto one last moment with my child. I scrubbed her while she sang to herself. I didn't call Doria until I had cleared away the bottles of spirit and drank some myself.

Doria was well connected. Her feminist politics may have given her enemies in high places like the King and President Nasser, but her views and activism also gave her access to some of Egypt's finest minds. Pioneers in women's rights, philanthropy, philosophy, medicine. And, I thought as I turned to take in her illustrious mansion in Zamalek, she had money to pay for discretion.

'I have called my friend in London,' she told me as Yasminah fell back asleep. She took my hand, hers warm, mine cold like they always were but currently numb from shock too. Knowing me well, she began massaging my fingers, to get my blood circulating again. Her tenderness always made me melt and I began to feel human again, neither monster nor mother. Just myself. She slipped an envelope into my palm.

'Take this to the post office, the contact on here will get you Yasminah's pills.'

I closed my eyes and opened them again and tried to smile but instead the expression only made me cry. Doria wiped my eyes and I finally let myself fully collapse into her breast.

'Habibbti,' she said, 'these pills are doing wonderful things for women's rights. Women in England, married and unmarried, are able to take control of their own desire now. This has been a good thing not just for women but for men too. Habibbti, you now have what you always wanted for your daughter, for her to have as much freedom as your sons.'

I lifted my head up from her bosom; I smiled, nodded, then clasped my hands together and rejoiced in an attempt to prove that I was all for women's sexual liberation. But inside I could sense the feelings of despair begin to spread.

Yasminah

CAIRO, 1969

ي

I hated to admit it, but Aziz's Alibi Club was going from strength to strength. It was impossible to deny. I could see it all there in the ever-growing sea of white receipts on his desk. Alongside the trophies and framed reviews from the *Egyptian Gazette* and the *Cairo Times* (which riled Mama up). I could see it in the stashes of cash, bound like bricks, he stored away night after night in the safe. He always looked over his shoulder every time he thumbed in the code, making sure none of his friends or colleagues were taking note, and if he was with one of his white girls, he was even more scrupulous. Detaching them from his neck, making them sit on the other side of the room, ushering them to talk to me, interrupting me from my studies, while he keyed in the secret digits. I found it surprisingly sweet that he had chosen Mama's birthday given how much she hated him.

Since the club opened, I began to look at Aziz in new ways, through my own eyes and not Mama's. It felt as if I had grown up all my life with Mama telling me that the sky is red, and now,

I was seeing that it was actually blue. The club had brought out a side to him I hadn't seen before. At home he was my no-good brother, who everyone despaired of. At Alibi's, to the staff and gradually to me, he was almost a celebratory figure.

I admired how this new space he had created had allowed a reinvention of himself. I longed for a similar independence from our parents. But Ussy and I seemed to need their validation, their love, their approval as if it were oxygen. Aziz survived only on the polluted air of the Cairo streets; inhaling the hubbub of Heliopolis was his lifeline. The more time I spent at the club the more I saw a whole new way of living, independent of my mother's expectations.

'Yas, could you help at the bar for a bit?' Aziz ducked his head into the office, beckoning me upstairs.

I sighed. 'I'm studying,' I lied. I was not even halfway through the application form for the American University in Cairo that Mama had thrust in my face at breakfast that day.

I saw the desperation in his eyes. Perhaps he had a reviewer in.

'OK,' I relented.

'Thanks, sis,' Aziz said, stepping into the room. Thinking he was alone, I started chastising Mama.

'It's ironic how much Mama writes about women's freedom; she doesn't seem to care about my own,' I said, getting up and placing the application form in the cupboard behind me.

I heard Erica giggle. His white girls always giggled when they didn't know what was going on, which was all the time because none of them ever bothered to make any attempt at speaking Arabic.

I turned around, aghast. Suddenly my brother was my annoying brother again. I looked past his shoulder and smiled sweetly at Erica who must have followed him in before hissing at Aziz in

28

Arabic, 'You are so disgusting.' I did my best impression of Mama and slammed the door behind me as I marched past them out of the room. I held onto the rage until I was climbing the spiral staircase to the bar. Gripping onto the banister I felt my face soften. I realised I was not angry at all, but in admiration of my brother for taking every bit of pleasure for himself, embracing the small bits of ecstasy that life sometimes throws at you and not giving a damn about Mama.

I heard the click of his office door opening, as he stuck his head out to yell up at me, 'Yasminah! Ommy is at the bar, he needs a drink!' I could hear him laughing to himself as I bit my lip and grinned.

Ommy played snooker not pool. He was the only guy at the club who knew the rules. When I was playing with Ommy, I forgot not only myself but the whole of Cairo. There was something about the clicking of the cue, the heavy drop of the ball as it fell into the slot so perfectly. The cool crisp taste of the beer and the burn of the arak in my chest warming my constantly cold hands.

The other guys who I played with always found a way to come up behind me while taking a shot. Breathing heavily on my neck, feeling the hardness of their cue against my back. Tickling me with their lips on my ears. I liked it a lot, but I liked it even more that Ommy never did this.

And even though I felt the entire club's eyes on us when we were together, I was only focused on his.

'Who's winning?' Sharif asked, approaching the table and collecting our empty bottles and shot glasses.

'I am!' Ommy's eyes twinkled.

I laughed. 'I am letting him win.' My face had relaxed the

way it did when I was around him or alcohol. Myself wasn't really me anyway, it was just a version of me that I put out to the world. Much of my life felt like a performance; being the person others wanted me to be. When I was with Ommy, it felt like I was no longer acting. I wasn't reading somebody else's words from a script. I was improvising in the moment.

Sharif inhaled theatrically before walking away. 'Like a child playing with his mother!'

My face dropped and Ommy looked away.

'I'm seventeen tomorrow,' he said, almost to himself.

'I know,' I said, touching his hand for the first time. It was like touching the electric fence at Uncle Jeddy's farm in Alexandria. I quickly removed it, but I clasped both my hands together, as if to capture the tingly aftermath for a moment longer.

'Yes!' Sharif shouted from the bar. 'And after you are done celebrating with your family, getting your cheeks kissed by all your aunties, you must come here for the proper celebrations!' Sharif erupted in laughter, hardly able to contain himself, as if his wit was too much for his body. He straightened his face and gave the customer their change. Once they were out of earshot, he yelled to us, '. . . where you'll get your butt cheeks kissed by all of Erica's *English* girlfriends!'

The hilarity was too much for Sharif, who now looked as though he was having some sort of seizure. He leaned on the corner of the bar and tried to compose himself, but his body continued to shake. Still quivering he bent himself over the bar and mouthed that he couldn't breathe. He eventually excused himself to go to the toilet.

All the while, Ommy and I stood not knowing what to do with not only our bodies but our faces too. The oddness hung over us as we continued with the game. We played for several minutes in silence, I slowly became entranced again by the clicks of the cue and the methodical swigs of the beer as I waited my turn.

I started to wonder if Ommy was going to lose his virginity to one of the English girls. Or had he already lost it? It was always assumed that seventeen-year-old girls were virgins, but one could never be sure with seventeen-year-old boys.

It was as if he was reading my mind. 'I know nothing about any of Erica's friends by the way, I think Sharif is just teasing me, 'Minah.'

I felt a prickle every time he called me 'Minah.

I knew I should laugh but instead I found myself having to bite my lip to stop it from quivering. I could feel Ommy's eyes on me, looking up at me as he leaned on the snooker table. He was aiming for the wrong ball, he had gone out of sequence, but I didn't say anything. I had stopped letting him win.

The green ball had gone in before the yellow. 'You've potted the wrong ball,' I told him before abandoning the game and getting another drink.

Alibi's had become my third space. It wasn't home, it wasn't school, it was somewhere in between. When I was there, I wasn't Yasminah, I was 'Minah. Aziz wasn't my annoying brother, he was someone I had fun with, even respected. Ommy wasn't the young kid from Iran, three years younger than me, he was the only man I knew other than my father who treated me like his equal.

It had come to the part of the night when the club starts to dim its lights and the music gets louder as everyone gets drunker. We had played for hours and I needed to sit down. I told him it was because I was tired, but it was because I couldn't stand up. I ushered Ommy over to the small table in the corner, where we sat and continued to drink.

'Happy birthday for tomorrow,' I said, touching his knee. His knee was different to his hand. I could touch it for longer under the table.

'Shukran.'

'What are you doing? I mean other than Erica's friends?' I said sloppily, laughing perhaps a little too hard.

''Minah!' he hissed.

'What?' I said, suddenly angry that he was angry.

''Minah, I am not interested in anyone but you.'

I was stunned but at the same time I had known this for so long.

'You're too young . . .'

'Only three years . . .'

'You are a child! What will people say?'

'Who cares?'

'They will call me a hussy . . . a pervert!'

Ommy put his head in his hands.

'What?' I said.

He sat there saying nothing and proceeded to play with the label of the beer bottle before rubbing his hands through his thick hair that was the colour of sumac. The silence speaking to me, *people already call me a hussy*.

Everyone around us was dancing now. We spoke in between the music while clapping.

'Let them talk about you. Who cares? Do you know what they say about me?' he said, swallowing another arak. This time putting his hand on my knee under the table.

He leaned into my neck and said, 'I think I love you, 'Minah.'

32

Whenever men used this word, love, it always hit me like a debt that I would have to pay back. But with Ommy it felt like a gift.

I could no longer tell him he was too young, for he was more mature than any other man that came to Alibi's. I knew I wasn't thinking like myself, which made my thoughts all the clearer. I excused myself to go to the toilet.

There I looked at myself in the mirror and asked myself what did I want? Not anyone else, not what Mama wanted, not what Aziz wanted, not what society wanted. What did I want? In that moment I knew. I had to take every bit of pleasure for myself, embracing the small bits of ecstasy that life sometimes throws at you and not give a damn about Mama.

The arak, the spirit, it had completely shredded my inhibitions and it led me down the spiral staircase towards Aziz's office. I opened the door and without hesitation approached the safe and typed in Mama's birthday. I did not steal from my brother; I didn't even take what I was entitled to if Mama and Doria's law had been approved. I took only enough for one night, for a room at the Grand Heliopolis Hotel on Al-Orouba Street.

Nadia

BRISTOL, 2011

ن

'Peppermint, chamomile, spearmint, red bush, Earl Grey, English breakfast, green, jasmine, matcha, oolong tea, pu-erh tea, white, gunpowder, lemon and ginger, artichoke, barley, brown rice, chaga, chai . . .' I rolled off the list of teas that we offered at Edits at 59. I prided myself on reciting these lines in iambic pentameter. The Shakespearean beat made me feel like I was at least using my degree in performing arts in some capacity, albeit small. Other runners at the edit house who perhaps had done more academic subjects didn't have the same theatrical abilities as me and they knew it. They neither had the performance skills nor the memory to learn their lines properly, confusing matcha green tea with gunpowder green tea and whatnot. I could recite with cadence, tone and humour coupled with a sense of dramatic irony as well as remembering every sachet of tea that we offered faultlessly. I told myself it was the reason I was the longest-serving runner there. And not because I could not take the next step in my career in TV and get a job on an actual set. For some reason my application to work along-side Giles at Southwest News had been abruptly 'terminated'.

'Got any builder's?' Fitty McHotty asked after I had finished my tea monologue. He had just got into his edit suite and was grabbing papers out of his rucksack. With his back to me and the door, he sat down at his desk and looked up at his three large edit screens. Each screen had a different primate: on one a lemur, on the other some sort of simian monkey and on the third, the most coveted primate of all: Bear Grylls. Fitty McHotty was fixated; I hovered over him, trying to get his attention.

'Let me see, do we have builder's tea?' I theatrically put my hand to my chin and started reciting the teas again, this time imitating Judi Dench's 1979 performance of Lady Macbeth. He finally turned his head to me and laughed – his signature cheeky grin, revealing his perfectly formed dimples – before returning his gaze to the screens. Staring into these beautiful craters, if only for a second, turned the pain receivers off in my pants and the pleasure receivers very much on. I hadn't checked the con-tents of my underwear since I had left the flat this morning or since bumping into Giles, but I could feel the cream was doing its thing. It was dissolving the particles of my past and preparing it for its future. Fitty McHotty moving in.

'Builder's tea? Strong, knock your socks off, put a few hairs on your chest kind of tea, you mean?' I flirted. I was really very good at it. Flirting to me was simply the ability to make the object of my desire subliminally think about sex.

'I'm surprised – I had you down for a red bush man.' Or bla-tantly think of sex, I thought.

He laughed again, this time raising an eyebrow at me. He really was the most beautiful man I had ever seen. His face was completely symmetrical. Not only that, it had the perfect mix of feminine and masculine. He had a rugged Roman nose that made you feel like he could build you an aqueduct as well as fix the plumbing in your bathtub and a strong jawline that was like a moat to the castle of his face. It chivalrously promised to protect and defend your honour. Yet his eyelashes were so very feminine; thicker and longer than mine, and his cheekbones higher too. He was in many ways as beautiful as a woman. If we went out together, people would think we were a lesbian couple and that I was the butch one, I thought to myself. I admired his large, calloused hands dancing over the keyboard; his long thick fingers editing Bear Grylls who was now urinating on a dead aardvark. It was like watching Picasso at work.

'You're very good with your hands,' I cooed.

Suddenly he swung his entire chair around so that his whole body was facing away from the edit screens and towards me. His legs were splayed apart to receive me. I wanted to fall into his lap and disappear into his crotch for days. I moved over to the side table by his rucksack to discreetly itch myself down there. Bollocks, I thought. This was one of the hardest seduction tricks going. Not only did I have to pull the most eligible bachelor in Bristol, but I had to do it with a severe case of herpes in my knickers.

When I got back to the kitchen to make his tea, I found Angela and Lydia stocking up the Digestive biscuits and Lily cleaning out one of the fridges. They were laughing together, no doubt about me being such a pulling legend and outrageous flirt, but quickly stopped as soon as I walked in.

'Uergh, he is so fit and so hot!' I said, grabbing the kettle.

'We know!' Lydia said. 'That's why he's called Fitty McHotty! Heard about your herpes flare-up by the way,' she said with a smirk.

I glared at Angela. She mouthed a 'sorry'.

'You know, Nadia, I've heard rumours Fitty McHotty is a bit of a goer. I think he has shagged half of Bristol. I reckon you have actually got a chance with him,' Lily said, sticking her head out of the fridge. Lily always had her head in one of the four fridges of the four floors of Edits at 59. It was her favourite job to clean out a fridge. She said it calmed her. Lydia, Angela and I pretended it wasn't because we were paid so poorly that she was nicking all the out-of-date food to take home.

'Really?' I asked.

'Apparently his nickname is Genghis Khan,' she said, sneaking some out-of-date Muller Fruit Corners into her satchel.

'It sounds like you've met your match, Nadia,' Angela quipped, nodding.

∾

Fitty McHotty's bedroom was not as I imagined. It smelt of a mixture of mud, rising damp, cigarettes, Lynx deodorant, skunk and the undeniable pong of overheated plastic from playing far too much PlayStation. To say I was disappointed would have been a lie, for I was far too drunk to compute any of my sensual realisations. I was just grateful that the fittest and hottest man in Bristol was showing an interest in me. Even though Lydia had essentially said he was an easy lay, I still doubted someone as fit and hot as him would go for the likes of me.

In truth I didn't just want to shag him. I wanted a relationship, so my decision was to just kiss him (and perhaps give him a light hand job). Just a light one, just like it says in the Quran, in verse 4:34 (which Teta, Doria and other Muslim feminists continue to debunk), that men can beat their wives, but only 'lightly'. I planned on only beating Fitty McHotty lightly. And that's only if he particularly misbehaved.

I could hardly believe I had made it this far given the fact that I had not only been competing for his attention all day with Bear Grylls but also dealing with my infestation of herpes. Somehow, I had convinced him to go for a drink with me after work at The Nag's Head. He hadn't been sure at first but then I found myself making a terrible joke about giving head at The Nag's Head and he was quite literally putty in my hands after that. We drank a couple of bottles of wine and he was gentlemanly enough to buy me dinner, which consisted of half a packet of Space Raiders and a couple of bags of Frazzles. We got so drunk that space and time began to blur together. One moment he was nibbling on my ear in the urinals, the smell of piss, crispy bacon and lust wafting between us, the next we were here in his flat, biting each other's lips, stopping only briefly to perform niceties to his stoned housemate, Jarad. And now finally, we were just metres away from his bed. This was possibly the most productive and physically rewarding day at work I'd ever had.

He pulled me into his bedroom as if our faces could not possibly separate for one second. The rhythm by which he moved his tongue in and out of my mouth was music, it made me sing. As we sucked on each other's tongues I opened my eyes for a second and saw that his walls were covered in posters of Hollywood actresses with their mouths open. This made a change to my usual type who had posters of *Hollyoaks* actresses with their mouths open. The women all had the same expression; they looked as though they were trying to understand the theory of relativity.

'Oh, so you like Elizabeth Taylor?' I asked, though pulling my lips away from his was like pulling a magnet away from its force.

'Whatever, man, she's hot,' he said, sticking his lips back on mine. I could feel his hands trying to understand the physics of my tights under my skirt.

I recoiled. I couldn't have sex with him. Even though my sores had subsided somewhat, they were still infectious. I realised my herpes had become a form of contraception. Perhaps contracting the disease had been a blessing in disguise.

I pulled his hands out of my skirt like I was pulling out a tampon.

'I like kissing you,' I said. 'Let's just kiss for now.'

I looked into his peacock blue eyes and saw that they had morphed into a blue fire. Burning all his regular human thoughts with animalistic ones. His brain had migrated down to his pants, he tickled me with his hardness. I liked it. I couldn't deny it. I writhed forward into him. 'Yes,' I said, biting into his ear while we moved to his rhythm. I felt the beginning of a volcano down inside me. Unsure whether it was pleasure or pain. Either way I liked it. I just wanted to do this for hours and then go home and deal with whatever had exploded into my knickers later. The very thought of the mixture of pus and come I had created was not disgusting but dirty. Like having an orgasm when you're on your period.

I writhed into him more. I could feel his hands ripping into my tights.

'No . . .' I whispered again. 'Let's just keep things PG,' I said with a husky cadence, trying to sound as seductive as the woman on the M&S advert.

'No,' I said again. This time I sounded more like a sexy schoolteacher.

The lampshade on his bedside table fell off the stand. The crash distracted me for several seconds and my reactions started to slow. I jolted forward with a gripping violent thrust and realised with complete ambivalence that we had reached the point of no return. He was now inside my puss-filled vagina with nothing to protect him from my putridness. I felt for him, as his damp head buried itself into my neck. I held the back of his greasy mane as if he were my sick child. With each thrust I imagined his penis hoovering up more and more particles of the infection. His dick was now effectively as clean as a used toilet brush; for the rest of time he would have a build-up of shit which would eventually escalate so much that he would have to burn it all off with thick bleach. A prescription that would cost him £7.40 for 25 ml that you could not pick up Boots Advantage Card points on. I felt so profoundly sorry for him. He had not asked for this at all. But what could I do now?

As his rhythm continued, I found myself thinking about my own Boots Advantage Card. Feeling his sweat dripping onto me, I began mentally writing a shopping list of all the toiletries I could get for free using the points I had accrued. Meanwhile, he throttled about inside of me, completely unaware of his diseased destiny. As he penetrated me faster and more ferociously, feeling him about to come to his crescendo, I realised to my absolute horror that I had already spent my Advantage Card points. (Just the other week I had purchased a Barry M kohl eyeliner, a big tub of Vaseline and a meal deal.) Damn it, I thought, as he released his final thrust.

I sobbed for us both as he came, for my lost Advantage Card points and his soon to be pus-ridden penis.

Yasminah

ي

I slipped all of Aziz's money into Ommy's pocket. I felt one side of the coat droop under the weight of it and tried to straighten it up unsuccessfully.

'Book one night in the grand suite,' I told him between kisses. 'Say you're on business if they ask and you had a very late flight.' I kissed him again; I could still smell the arak on him. I couldn't stop. Now that we were finally away from the club, even though we were practically out on the streets, it felt as though we were completely alone. 'My friend, she works as a receptionist here, she's going to let me in the back way,' I said, fighting for breath before going back for more. Ommy's lips were so plump and pink, every time I kissed them my own sore, cracked ones began to heal. He was medicine. He tasted like alcohol, peppermint and sahlab; the thick milk with nuts we would have in winter; my favourite season. I slapped Ommy's behind drunkenly and he returned it with a pinch of my own. We both giggled as if we are at school. It felt like

I was going to bed with a friend I had known for years. It was unfamiliar to feel so safe.

After we stopped giggling, we became serious again. We looked deep into each other's eyes, and I never once looked away. It was like staring into the television, why would I look back into reality when I could remain in a dream? I had never looked into someone's eyes for so long; ordinarily if I caught a man's eyes, even just for a second, I would quickly look away, distracting myself with the zip on his trousers or biting his ear. But with Ommy, I was not embarrassed by such intimacy. I kissed him again and again. And he kissed me in equal measure. We felt flashes of people walking past us, tuts and hisses; some walked away quoting a hadith, but others stayed for several moments cheering us on and squawking like chickens.

Nothing or no one could stop us kissing in the alleyway by the side entrance to the Grand Heliopolis Hotel. Time as well as people dissolved into an alternative reality. My only understanding of both concepts was that I knew Mona would be coming out for her break soon.

Working at the hotel was the only way her father would let her out after sunset. Her breaks were the only time I could see her without her mother, who hated me, finding out. I knew her rota off by heart. For as long as I had known Mona, her schedule was always as predictable to me as clockwork, and now that we could only conduct our friendship through her shifts it seemed to me that nothing much had changed, other than the location where we met.

She would stand here, on the very spot that Ommy and I were kissing, in a paprika red suit that was far too big for her, trying desperately to fit in with the chain-smoking maids, even though she couldn't smoke and wasn't a maid. She would never fit in with them. They were from different worlds; they were all bussed in from Manshiyat Naser and she was taxied in from Maadi. Despite this she tried each time to smoke a whole cigarette with them. No matter how much I had tried to teach her, her lungs just didn't have the capacity for it. She would cough and cough and cough and the maids and I would laugh and laugh and laugh until our eyes were streaming with tears; Mona's and ours. A small part of me enjoyed making her the butt of every joke. As if mocking her innocence made me feel better about my own shame.

I had lost both my central and peripheral vision to Ommy's lips, but I could hear the girls starting to trickle out one by one. I opened one eye and spotted Mona: the brightness of her suit sticking out amongst the muddy brown of the maids. I pulled Ommy away with some force. Not from battling his strength but my own. My will finally overcame my own desire.

By the time I had done so, Mona was standing right next to us, bored and forlorn from a long night shift.

'Mona!' I squealed, hugging her. 'This is Ommy.'

Mona nodded, her eyes looking Ommy up and down before sighing like she always did. 'Yallah, come on,' she said to me.

I was embarrassed by my friend's rudeness. Could she not even say a 'salaam' to Ommy? She was acting as though he was nothing. Just another man I had for the night. Did she not see how special he was, how much he meant to me? This wasn't just a man for one night, I wanted Ommy to be mine, forever. I just knew it. I could feel it; he had lifted my heart instead of smashing it. He had opened it, instead of numbing it. He would remain in it always; I just knew it.

'OK, you go to reception and pay for the room, yallah,

Yasminah, I'll take you through,' she said, sighing again before adding, 'as usual,' under her breath.

'Shukran, Mona Ebaadi, is it?' Ommy said.

Mona nodded.

'Your father is Nebal Ebaadi, owner of Zamalek football stadium—'

'I can't give out any more tickets this year,' she said, cutting him off.

'Er, no, I am not wanting any more tickets, I have a pass of my own. I am Iranian. My father works for the Shah, and he helped design Amjadieh Stadium, the stadium that Zamalek was modelled on.'

'Oh,' Mona said.

Ommy stumbled on. ''Minah, er, well, 'Minah says you are her very good friend.'

Mona breathed in and sighed once more.

'And, er, inshallah we will meet again soon.'

This time Mona laughed, and lunged into her pockets, bringing out a pack of cigarettes. She plucked one out nonchalantly, before lighting it and smoking it effortlessly.

I stood there, stunned.

Ommy looked at me, our eyebrows both raised for different reasons. I didn't know what else to do so I just mimed to him that Mona had probably smoked something she shouldn't have. He briefly laughed and walked away, blowing me a kiss as he did.

'What the hell was that?' I yelled at Mona when he was out of earshot. 'You were just very rude to the love of my life.'

'Don't worry,' she said between puffs. 'I promise to be nicer to another love of your life, next week.'

∽

Leaving the hotel in the morning was a much easier mission than entering. An unmarried woman had two options: hiding in plain sight and pretending that she was indeed married to the man she was with from the night before while hoping not to run into anyone who knew them, or going down the service lift with the maids. I always chose plan B, as not only was it more discreet, it meant I could lose the man I was with, without us having to pretend we meant anything to each other.

'Is this the only time you wear the veil?' Ommy laughed as he watched me get dressed from the bed.

'Now we can go down together as man and wife,' I said as I covered the scruff of my hair with my hijab and then used the extra material to cover my face. I noted how my skin, although paler, had a plumpness to it I hadn't seen before, and my eyes were much brighter too. They had a sharpness to them. I looked like Mona's sister before she revealed to everyone that she was pregnant even though everyone already knew that she was pregnant because she was fat. I could always sense when women had a happy secret kept inside of them, giddy to tell but also content for the time being knowing it was just for them.

I wondered if I was. For the first time, feeling the happiness of the possibility not the horror. I knew it wasn't likely. My mother had never asked me for the details the morning I woke up in Doria's house. Several days later she handed me 'vitamins' that Doria's friend had sent from London. She had kissed my forehead and whispered into my ear, 'Now what happened at Doria's will never happen again.' I had wondered, in my naïve, delirious state how these small little pills could stop a man entitling himself to my body. It was only later that I realised. The medicine that Doria was supplying me with didn't stop a man's desire for me but allowed me to explore my own.

47

∾

'You look like my grandmother.' Ommy laughed again. 'No one wears the veil any more, it's 1969!'

I giggled. 'I do because I am very pious,' I said in a mock serious tone, scrunching my head into my neck and imitating my old Quran school teacher.

'Oh yes, Yasminah Bin-Khalid, very good Muslim girl,' Ommy teased.

'I mean I'm basically a white girl at heart. Come on, yallah, let's go, we need to be out of this room by eleven otherwise Mona will freak,' I said, throwing a pillow at Ommy's head.

∾

We were on the eleventh floor. Mona told me it was the floor where they put all the affairs and people wanting to be discreet. Everyone kept their head down in the lift because of it. Ommy and I stepped into the gold-rimmed elevator and I pressed the ground level button that was going to bring us back down to reality. I sighed. As it descended, I felt less and less drunk and more and more hungover. The butterflies in my tummy were turning into knots as we passed each floor. I was thankful Ommy could no longer see my face, I could feel my bottom lip beginning to quiver. I turned away from Ommy, so that he couldn't see the sadness in my eyes. I tried to control my shaking bottom lip with force from my top lip, but it was too heavy for it. I had inherited my mother's 'loose' lips as my father said. The bottom one overpowered the top.

I wanted to stay on the eleventh floor with Ommy forever. Instead, I had to somehow explain yet another night away from home to my parents. I would go back to the club and hope that Aziz was still there. I would ask him to vouch for me. That we had both been there all night because he had another reviewer in. And that by the time they had left it was too late to come home, only to go back in the morning and work on the accounts. In truth I hadn't worked on the accounts for months. And I doubt I ever would again if Aziz found out I had stolen from him.

I was thankful when the lift bell dinged to pick up guests on the ninth floor, for I wasn't quite ready to leave Ommy. As we did, two men stepped in. They both appeared as light and as carefree as Ommy, their physicality unlike most Egyptian men. They possessed a weightless quality I was drawn to. One was very tall, and one was very short, but they were both thin and dressed impeccably. The shorter one was in a navy-blue suit and the taller in mauve, the colour of the mallow flower. The flower of consumed love, persuasion and weakness.

'Ommy!' the mauve flower squealed. I had never heard a man squeal before. It roused me yet disconcerted me at the same time.

'Oh my god, Zaki! Kaif, Halak?' Ommy squealed back.

Navy-blue suit looked me up and down and smiled at me politely. I smiled back with my eyes.

'Alhamdulillah!' Zaki's voice began to deepen as the level of floors did.

'I cannot believe you are in Egypt, I thought you were staying in Iran after . . .' Ommy's voice was getting quieter as we descended. His body was becoming rigid.

'Well, ummm . . .' Zaki looked at me and then looked at Ommy.

Navy-blue suit cleared his throat. I copied him to fill the silence. I tried to make my eyes appear less panicked by closing them. I became possessed by an odd feeling in my stomach.

I didn't know whether I was going to throw up or faint. I was grateful when the door finally released us to the ground floor. It opened like theatre curtains onto our stage.

I watched as Ommy, Zaki, even navy-blue suit's physicality changed. They became more upright and their intimate proximity relented as they returned to formality.

'Here's my card,' Zaki said as if Ommy was now a colleague not a friend.

I stepped out of the lift and heard Ommy behind me. 'Here's mine, call me,' he said under his breath. My head suddenly raised itself, as if sniffing a foul smell in the distance. It wasn't until later that day that I realised he had whispered the words 'call me' in the same tone he had whispered into my ears the night before.

I said I'd no doubt see Ommy at the club again that night. I wanted to kiss him or at least linger with him longer, but my stomach felt blocked. I prayed that Ommy could not hear it rumbling. I rushed to the toilets in the lobby and wondered what needed undoing, my skirt or my niqab. I heaved, so I began unravelling the material around my face like an archaeologist does an ancient pharaoh. I knelt down and heaved again. But nothing came out. I had never wanted to throw up so much after a night with a man. Frustrated, I stuck my fingers down my throat and jiggled them around, tickling my tonsils until it hurt. Nothing but tears came.

Nadia

ن

There is a reason why so many British Muslim memoirs feature a scene where Ramadan aligns with Christmas. It serves as an emblem of the plight of every immigrant; the clash of cultures between what *was* home and what is *now* home. A relentless tug of war, an often-belittling battle of liminality. Immigrants are fine actors. They have quite a range too and are able to play a number of roles. My father, for example: I always marvelled at his ability to play the 'integrated brown guy up for a laugh at the local pub' and the 'good Muslim father' the next day. How he hid his Christmas Eve hangover from Aunt Yasminah before breaking iftar deserved an Oscar.

As I stood in the hallway between the kitchen and the living room, mixing the hair bleaching cream into the fizzy salt-like powder, enjoying the corrosive smell that it emitted, I watched my dad stumble down the stairs, almost tripping on his gallabiyah. The long, loose white material radiated an innocent piety, contrasting with his guttural reverberations which sounded as if he was possessed with an evil spirit. In many ways he was, and the spirit had a name: Johnnie Walker. By the time he had got to the kitchen, where the sun shone strongly through the front window, he was like a delirious Arab in the desert, confusing a mirage for his hangover cure – a full-fat Fanta as we called it. Even though we all knew Fanta didn't have any fat in it whatsoever, only sugar (which makes you fat). Alas the rusty orange bottle of glucose was out of his grasp until sunset.

My dad never admitted to being hungover. Admitting to such a state would mean admitting that he had turned his back on the Quran.

'For it says in the Quran – in verse 47:15 – that paradise has "rivers of red wine" and in verse 2:219 that alcohol contains "some good". It just says to not get intoxicated.' Then he'd launch into emphatically reciting his favourite quote whenever he sensed any sort of judgement from Kadijah and me. 'Verse 4:43, "Oh you who have believed, do not approach prayer while you are intoxicated."'

'Oh yeah, Dad, you don't get intoxicated, do you?' Kadijah said as she strolled into the kitchen wearing one of her feminist t-shirts. The one she had chosen today read, 'Brains are the new Tits'. Feminist t-shirts were her latest entrepreneurial enterprise. Female empowering slogans on t-shirts, tote bags, pyjamas, mugs, fridge magnets. She was convinced this was the future. We weren't so sure. But we were glad she had stopped trying to sell her 'disintegrating' paper straws to pubs and restaurants, finally admitting defeat after being told numerous times by several pub landlords that climate change isn't real, and nobody really cares about the turtles.

'No! Dad doesn't get intoxicated at all!' I said, spreading the bleaching cream as dextrously onto my upper lip as a bricklayer spreads cement.

'No, I don't,' he said solemnly, looking out into the front garden we shared with our neighbours. Their side was perfectly arranged, tulips and gardenias standing to attention like soldiers, grass cut with as much precision as my hairdresser cuts my fringe. Whereas our side was rather like my bikini line before a wax. Scruffy, overgrown but with a kind of Middle Eastern wild charm. The only sign of any sort of attempt at landscaping was a two-foot palm tree my dad got from Notcutts three years previously.

'No, not at all, you don't get intoxicated at all! No, you just . . .'

'Piss in Alan and Mary's garden!' Kadijah and I broke out laughing. My sister's a long cackle. My own laugh somewhat more repressed for fear of the bleaching cream dropping off my upper lip.

'That was one time, and your mother was on the toilet!' he shouted. 'Anyway . . .' he went on reciting his favourite verse in greater detail, ' "O you who have believed, do not approach prayer while you are intoxicated until you know what you are saying or in a state of janabah, except those passing through until you have washed your whole body". Quran 4:43, Kadijah! It doesn't say that you can't drink in the Quran, it just says don't drink and pray, just like don't drink and drive, don't drink and pray.'

'No, you drink and drink!' Kadijah laughed.

'Don't drink and pray!' he repeated again.

'That's what Nancy Reagan should have said to get more Muslims votes,' I said, trying not to move my mouth too much, as I scraped a tiny bit of the cream off to check it was working. I was relieved to see the black hairs had now turned yellow – a sort of luminous dirty blonde. I enjoyed the tingling sensation it brought. As if my hairs were now dizzy with excitement; now that they were blonde, they could have more fun.

It had taken years, but I finally had my moustache under control now. I went to get it waxed every four weeks and home bleached it every two. The last week before the wax, when the regrowth was at its most coarse, was the toughest. I only allowed myself to go out at night to dimly lit bars and restaurants. Shopping malls were strictly off limits and the corrosively harsh lights of Heathrow Terminal 4 were to be avoided at all costs. I was still very traumatised from getting bullied at school about my hairiness. If my puberty story was an episode in *The Wonder Years*, it would be called 'The hirsute of unhappiness'.

'Yeah, but Dad, we are supposed to pray five times a day, so it implies that there is never a time to have a drink.'

'Kadijah . . . shhh,' Dad said, holding his head as he basted the turkey. 'Shhh . . .'

'Kadijah, you're hardly one to talk. According to Teta, your boyfriend is an alcoholic!' I chuckled.

Kadijah rolled her eyes. 'How many times do I have to tell her, he's not an alcoholic, he's a DJ!'

Dad shook his head as he self-soothed by stirring the gravy. 'Ah, bollocks!' he said as the doorbell rang signifying the arrival of our Christmas guests.

Aunt Yasminah always came over on Christmas Day. As well as her son Hany, his three kids – Rania, Rasha and Rahima – and his estranged wife or, depending on the month, un-estranged wife, Rabia.

One was never quite sure if they were together or not. They announced their separation a year ago. Hany consequently moved in with his mum, Yasminah, in her flat in Shepherd's Bush. But then, according to certain sources (my dad piecing evidence together while smoking shisha, as if he was Cairo's answer to Columbo), a few months later, it was believed that Hany had moved back *in* with Rabia. Dad had his suspicions that they weren't really separating, only saying that they were to get the extra benefit money. I was sceptical. I couldn't imagine anyone ever going to that level of performativity just to get an extra twenty-five pounds a week for being classified as a single-parent family. A free flat, yes. But twenty-five pounds a week would barely cover the therapy Rania, Rasha and Rahima would need to understand their parents' complicated relationship.

Then again, we always joked that Hany's similarities with Uncle Aziz were uncanny. At one family gathering, I thought I had spotted Hany and Rabia with their feet all over each other under the table when I had leaned down to pick up a spoon. But their legs had separated so fast, one could never truly be sure.

'Salamwaylaykum! Merry Christmas!' I said, opening the front door and beginning the long line of kissing admin. Everyone had to kiss everyone twice on each cheek. It was like a game: every time you had thought you were done, you realised you had to kiss another relative. Fortunately, my other six cousins were in Egypt with Uncle Aziz, otherwise I would be in danger of getting a repetitive head injury.

I took in the scent of Aunt Yasminah. A mixture of parsley and Chanel No. 5 as she handed me a tub of tabouleh. Chanel No. 5. Simple and understated. Despite them being the same age, my aunt was a world away from my mother. Pamela's chosen scent was more indicative of a fourteen-year-old girl rather than a fifty-year-old woman. She doused herself in Impulse Vanilla Musk body spray by day and the latest J-Lo by night.

As I kissed Hany, I noted that he smelt of cigarettes, and Rabia, specifically, of Wrigley's spearmint chewing gum.

'I am on my period,' Rabia announced, explaining her mastication during the holy month. She tied her thick curls off her face, as she always did when she was getting ready to eat a big meal.

'I am also on my period,' I could hear Pamela joking as she walked down the stairs, through the living room and into the hallway to greet our guests. She smiled, nodded at them before ducking into the kitchen, no doubt to pour herself a large glass of red wine.

'You wish you were on your period!' I yelled.

Pamela groaned from the kitchen, as Kadijah and I cooed over the two youngest girls who both had what we hoped was chocolate all over their hands.

'By the looks of things, these girls are also on their periods!'

This time the laughter was harder than before. Hany started making jokes about living in a house of women with them all menstruating. Everyone pretended that we hadn't noticed his verbal slip, that he said he was still living with his supposed soon to be ex-wife.

'Wait, who is actually fasting?' I asked.

'I am!' my dad said, holding his hand to his hangovered head.

'Me too!' Kadijah said, although I knew she was really just on the five-two diet.

'I'm not eating carbs, does that count?' Pamela said.

'You know there's like a thousand calories in a bottle of wine, Mum,' said Kadijah.

'Pamela has an eating disorder, she doesn't have cake, she has a bottle of wine, she doesn't have pizza, she has a bottle of wine, she doesn't have feelings, she has a bottle of wine,' my dad said.

We all looked at him for a moment, Kadijah and I rueing the day we had bought him that stand-up comedy course on Groupon for his birthday.

∾

The few hours before we broke fast consisted of us mostly laughing at the children. We laughed at everything they did. Even when they weren't doing anything funny. It was rather like the open mic comedy night that my dad had dragged me and Kadijah to after completing the course.

'Just laugh,' she had said to me through gritted teeth, 'the silence is killing me.'

So, I laughed and cheered at everything those girls did and said. As a result of all the laughing, cooing and cheering, conversations were stunted, interrupted and at times non-existent. I retreated upstairs to the toilet to escape the inane tedium. As I did so I noted Aunt Yasminah had also withdrawn from social engagement under the guise of needing to pray before breaking fast. I smiled to myself as I remembered what Kadijah and I used to do as kids whenever she prayed.

Oh, how we loved to distract her with funny faces as she performed the stoic ritual. As she prayed, we would climb onto her back, hanging from her like a jungle gym. Squishing her face as she uttered the Quranic verses, she would crack just the faint hint of a smirk as she went from sitting down to standing up to crouching on the floor, all with us still on her back. Kadijah and I would be dying laughing, gasping for breath, in absolute glee, knowing that when she eventually finished praying, she would throw us on her bed and tickle us until we cried.

I wished we still had that closeness with Aunt Yasminah. But after everything that happened to me in Saudi Arabia, my relationship with her had changed.

∾

Later, when we were sitting down at the table, Aunt Yasminah broke her fast and popped a date, glazed in honey, into her mouth. Chewing while uttering words to Allah under her breath, she suddenly turned to Kadijah and me.

'So, how are you girls getting on in Bristol, working for television?' she said, unsure if she had used the right vernacular.

'In television,' I corrected, nodding my head sincerely.

'Are you actually in the television?' Hany interjected and Rabia laughed flirtatiously at the husband she was supposedly recently separated from.

'How did you fit *into* the TV with all the wires?' my dad added, making a silly face at the girls, before going back to assessing how he was going to carve the turkey. Hany had got up now, approaching my dad with the butter knife, and they both gawped at the gigantic bird as if they were solving a scientific equation.

Kadijah rolled her eyes at my dad, before smiling and turning to our aunt. 'It's great, Auntie. I'm assistant wildlife researcher on the Bear Grylls show – he was on *Loose Women* last Tuesday, did you see it?' Of course, she had seen it. Kadijah knew full well she had. She recorded every episode.

Aunt Yasminah's eyes lit up from a combination of the influx of sugar from the dates and the mention of her favourite TV show. 'Oh yes, I did! They showed a clip of him urinating into his sock and then drinking it!' she laughed. The rare occasions that my aunt showed any level of animation was usually because she was talking about *Loose Women*. We had no idea why she liked the programme so much, given that the panel consisted of mostly drunk white women. Maybe it was akin to why Angela watched programmes on serial killers. It seemed that my aunt had a morbid fascination with hedonistic women.

'Yeah, Bear pisses on everything. I go through the rushes every day . . .'

'Rushes are basically all the footage,' I explained to the non-TV-savvy table.

Kadijah nodded, '. . . and it's like, what doesn't he piss on? I'm kinda tired of it if I'm honest, being exposed so much to a man's, you know, it's actually quite violating, as a woman, you know. But anyway, I've got a bit of a side hustle business, selling female empowering t-shirts which is really taking off, like this one!' she said, unzipping her hoodie to reveal the t-shirt with the 'Brains are the new Tits' slogan.

'Yeah, it feels more in line with my degree too. You know, after studying politics, and, well, feminism is political and all that, isn't it?'

My aunt read Kadijah's t-shirt, somewhat stunned, before refilling her wine glass with Five Alive.

'Isn't that what you were studying, Auntie, politics?' my sister asked trying to get the conversation back.

'Yes . . . Well . . . Islamic politics . . . But I got married instead,' Aunt Yasminah said.

'What was your thesis on?' Kadijah asked.

She took another date stone from her mouth and swallowed. 'My thesis, ummm, well, I, well, er, it was looking into fundamentalist interpretations of the Quran.'

My sister and I both squeezed each other's legs under the table. We knew our aunt was pious and devout, but did this mean that she was an Islamic extremist? Surely not. She wasn't dressed for it. Her woollen fuchsia jumper was a little too hugging around the bosom, her 501 jeans a little too tight around the derriere and she covered her hair, yes, but with a hat not a hijab. Her attire, I concluded, was far too western to be considered Wahhabist.

'Oh, that's, er, interesting. Yes,' my sister said, still squeezing my leg.

'But I never finished it and I'm glad I didn't because then I wouldn't have Hany!' she added.

I looked over at Hany, as he inspected a vegetarian pig in blanket. Suspicious and unsure, like a child with a new vegetable.

'Are these halal?' he asked.

'They're Linda McCartney,' Pamela informed him from across the table.

'Is Linda McCartney halal bacon?'

'Isn't halal bacon an oxymoron?' I joked but nobody laughed.

'Yes,' my dad nodded sincerely, replying to Hany, 'Linda's halal.'

'OK. Hey, Kadijah!' Hany yelled across the table, raising his hand in the air. We all held our breath. We knew he was about to goad Kadijah's feminism. He loved winding her up. 'So, you studied politics, hey. The Quran says that politics is not a woman's business.'

I looked at my aunt and gave her a look as if to say, it was completely worth giving up your degree in Islamic politics to have a child who told women that they shouldn't get into politics.

'Ya, mama, la-ah, bardo keda!' Rabia started emphatically talking in Arabic to her husband/ex-husband, while sprinkling a worrying amount of salt onto the already heavily salted Linda McCartney pigs in blankets.

'That's not true!' Rabia yelled again, hitting Hany over the head half affectionately, half aggressively, 'Aisha! Mohammed's wife led men to war . . .' she pointed out in her broken English, now sprinkling an equally offensive amount of salt onto each of her small children's plates.

I felt a mixture of admiration at her Islamic facts and despair at her nutritional naivety.

'Yes, but Aisha she was defeated,' my dad said matter of factly. 'So, for this reason it says in the Quran, rightly or wrongly,' he continued, putting his hands up to the women of the group, 'that women should henceforth not involve themselves in politics.'

'Well, according to that basis, it should also say that Blair and Bush shouldn't involve themselves in Islamic politics!' Kadijah roared.

'Here! Here!' we all roared back, Aunt Yasminah perhaps a little too vehemently for my liking.

When we had all settled again from our collective and passionate hatred towards the disastrous western politicians, Aunt Yasminah asked what I had studied at university. My family were always 'forgetting'.

'Performing arts,' I sighed.

Every time I said the words 'performing arts' it reduced my entire family to silence. I knew my dad was furious, but after the fracas I had caused at the Muslim Menorah school in Saudi, he was just thankful I had got a degree at all.

'What is berforming arts?' my aunt enquired, struggling with the words as if they were Latin. I had explained it to her numerous times over the years.

'It's acting in plays, Auntie,' I said.

'What sort of plays?'

'Well, her final performance was *Dangerous Liaisons* where she played a naked courtesan,' Kadijah said under her breath. She kicked me under the chair.

'What was that?' Aunt Yasminah asked.

'It's just lots of rolling around in leggings, Auntie,' I said as I remembered the very many Wednesday mornings with my best mate Maz, spent in the dance studio getting taught physical theatre by Kuba, a Polish drama practitioner with an extremely shiny bald head, who had left our course halfway through because he had got a part in the Blue Man Group. Kadijah gave me a look across the table, stroking her hijab. She thought she was untouchable as the good Muslim because she covered her hair. Aunt Yasminah didn't know she only wore it because she had alopecia.

'So, when was the last time you went to Mosque, Kadijah?' I said wiping the smirk off her face.

'We used to all go to Friday prayers as a family, with Aziz, Mama and Baba – do you remember Yasminah?' my dad said.

'Yes, yes, I do,' she nodded.

'So yes, when did you last go to Mosque, Kadijah? Do you take Christian?'

Kadijah and I both manically slammed each other's hands under the table in an effort to refrain from laughing. I breathed in, trying to think of sad things. Whenever I got the giggles in front of people I couldn't get the giggles with, I always tried to concentrate on something sad that would distract me. So, I thought of Princess Diana and her poor sons, and fellow Egyptians, dear Dodi and Mohamed Al-Fayed and the fact we came so very close to having a person of colour and someone of Muslim descent as a member of the British royal family. I looked at Kadijah and knew she was doing the same. She nodded at me, and I remembered what she always said when we talked about Princess Diana's fatal car crash: 'The royal family cannot stay all white forever, it's only a matter of time . . .'

'Dad hasn't been to Mosque since Saudi.' Kadijah often mentioned Dad's slipshod Muslim ways to deflect from her own when Aunt Yasminah started probing.

'Usman?' Aunt Yasminah asked.

Dad looked up from his turkey carving, breaking his concentration, and appeared somewhat confused for a second at the sudden interrogation from his sister.

'I work on Fridays, habibbti, I'd go if I could; it's just I need to make money for this bloody divorce,' he said, glaring at Pamela.

'Oh, come on, Ussy, you got the house, I just need a little compensation for leaving the travel business and raising *your* kids for the last twenty years.'

'Our kids!'

'Yes, that's what I said, and now that I'm possibly moving to Manchester to be with Tony . . .'

Kadijah and I groaned and mimed being sick. We thought it was totally gross that our mother had met a man online. We knew that only weirdos looked for love online. We had told her that she'd probably end up dating a serial killer. As it turned out it was far worse than that. She had met someone from Manchester.

'How the heck did you meet someone from Manchester?' I had said when she had first told us, while examining the webpage, 2Becum1.

'Mum, this is well dodge, look how they've spelt "become"!' I said, almost barfing.

'Well actually,' Kadijah had said, chipping in, 'this is how we are all going to write in the future. I read an article about

63

how we'll all start writing phonetically, spelling in schools will become irrelevant,' before adding, 'but this site is proper manky, Mum.'

'Well, she has met a Manc!' I laughed, rolling around on my mum's bed.

'How the hell did you meet someone two hundred miles away?'

'Well, I forgot to set my radius,' my mum had said, biting her lip. 'But honestly, he is worth the drive!' she said, with a disgusting twinkle in her eye.

'Well, inshallah hopefully you will find a better job soon,' Aunt Yasminah said to my dad.

I could see that she felt sad for him that, upon returning from Saudi, he had been unable to find a job as a university chemistry professor. I often heard my dad fretting to Pamela, wondering if the Saudi authorities had somehow blacklisted us as a family.

'Cor blimey, what have you put in this gravy, Dad?' Kadijah asked, her face red and her eyes streaming.

'Oh yes, secret ingredient, extra hot curry powder!' he grinned.

'I like it, English food is so bland!' Rabia said with her mouth full. 'Bland potatoes, bland meat, no herbs, no spices, just boring and bland, that's why I use salt,' she said, holding up the condiment like it was a mineral that was as precious as gold.

Everyone politely agreed, while Kadijah, Pamela and I looked at each other, the three of us thinking the same thing: *Dad's ruined the Christmas dinner again.*

My dad, taking the silence as an appreciation of the meal, smiled proudly. Just then I heard my mobile ringing.

I had left it on the coffee table, which was closest to Aunt

Yasminah who turned around and, to my absolute horror, answered it.

'Aiywa, hello?' she said. 'You're calling from where?' She poked a finger into her exposed ear and put her head down in order to concentrate. I gestured with my hand for her to pass my phone to me. It was probably my best mate ringing to wish me a Happy Christmas.

'Is it Maz?' I asked.

Aunt Yasminah ushered for me to stop talking with her hand. She waited a few moments before repeating, 'You're calling from the STI clinic?'

I froze. I felt Kadijah's hand suddenly grip mine under the table, tightening around my flesh with every silent second that passed.

'STI?' Rabia asked.

'A stye is a small painful lump inside or outside of the eye . . .' I heard my dad explain as he examined my face for signs of the illness.

'Exactly!' I said, grabbing the phone off my aunt and running upstairs. In my bedroom, I closed the door and felt suddenly hot, like I couldn't breathe. My woollen Christmas jumper was suffocating me.

'Yes?' I said into the phone.

'Hello there. My name is Dexter,' a man with a thick Glaswegian accent said, 'and I am calling from your local STI clinic. I'm afraid to tell you that a sexual partner recently tested positive for an STI and is notifying you via our anonymous notification system that you should also get tested.'

'It's Zain, isn't it?' I said, not waiting a beat. I had seen on Facebook that he had left Saudi and was now living with his grandma in Liverpool.

'Well, I am afraid I cannot divulge such information . . .'

'It's Zain, I know it, the bastard's given me herpes, hasn't he? I've had it on and off for years ever since . . .' I said, beginning to cry. I had known this for years but having it confirmed by a medical professional after everything . . . I looked out the window and yelped with emotion. I spotted my neighbour Alan, mowing his part of the lawn. He must have felt me gazing at him, because he looked up and smiled as he often did when he saw me changing in my bedroom. *Who mows the lawn on Christmas Day?* I thought for a second. *Hang on, who works at an STI centre on Christmas Day?*

'Maz, is that you?'

There was a moment of quiet before I heard his infamous cackle.

'Ha ha, Zain! Oh babe, I am crying! I am dying!'

I rolled my eyes. I was getting a little tired of his practical jokes, which had increased dramatically since his dad had been diagnosed with cancer.

'Very funny,' I said. 'You know who picked up your hilarious prank? My Aunt Yasminah. I don't think I'll ever be able to look her in the eye again.'

This only made Maz laugh even harder.

'Oh babes, what happened with Giles? How's his cock doing?'

'How should I know! The last time I spoke to him was when he had a go at me in the street for giving him herpes. It's unlikely I'm going to get a booty call from him anytime soon,' I said grumpily. It was very annoying.

'Funny that!' Maz said in between breaths. He was still in hysterics. I couldn't help but laugh too. It was better than crying, after all.

I let myself chuckle.

'Merry Christmas, you massive ho!' Maz shouted down the phone. I smiled. He really was a big idiot, with an excellent range of accents.

'It's just as well you're going off to study the art of clowning at Le Coq next year, isn't it? Now, I've got to go back downstairs and explain to my Muslim family that I do not have an STI, although fortunately it got lost in translation – my cousin's wife thinks I have a stye.'

'Well, that will explain not looking any of them in the eye then! Oh. My. God. This is too much, stop, please, Nads, I actually can't breathe!' he howled. After taking a deep breath, he continued, 'Now I actually rang because I wanted to check if we are still on for New Year's Eve in London, at G-A-Y, babes? And the, ya know, the . . .' His voice trailed off.

'The breaking into my aunt's flat while she's in Mecca?' I finished. 'Yes, babe, but are you sure you want to, though, I mean with everything that's happening with your dad?' I asked gently.

'Yes, it's fine!' he said quickly. 'We are going to get so CRUNK, Nads!'

'Crunk?'

'Crazy drunk! Oh Nads, you are a total legend! Free place to crash in London, get in! Just make sure you don't get another bout of herpes before then, all right?'

'Yeah, yeah. I'll do my best,' I said before hanging up.

When I returned downstairs, I explained the prank to my family. Every one of them laughed, except Aunt Yasminah.

Fatiha

ف

D yab and Ali were still smoking and deep in conversation about the football match that was playing on the small television above their heads, when I gave my husband our signal. Looking at him from the other side of the late-night bakery, with Naila beside me, I did a big grin and raised my eyebrows before breathing in and sighing. My husband nodded, stuffing the last bits of his kunafa into his mouth, his lips glazed and shiny from the cheese and sticky from the syrup. I saw him making his excuses to Dyab and started to do the same with Naila.

I was tired and Naila had been rattling on about her design plans for her son's up and coming wedding for what felt like hours. I had a stack of papers still to mark and a lecture to prepare on Sufi Narratives of Intimacy (with particular reference to Ibn Arabi's views on gender and sexuality). I was in no mood for her wedding scrapbook that she had been adding to since their engagement two months ago. Today she was showing me a collage she had made of possible shoe choices for the bride.

'I'd go with that one,' I said, picking the first pair that came into my eyeline, a cream Mary Jane with a slightly raised heel. 'Anyway, we must go. Ali is very tired and he has to open the shop very early tomorrow.'

'This one?' she said aghast. 'Hmmm, I'm not sure, Dina is very tall, and I'm worried a heel will further emasculate Ramy. He's quite short as you know and very sensitive about it.' She bit her lip and asked, 'What about this one? It's rather flat and sensible, but you have to remember, Dina's long dress, the one I am making, will cover the shoe anyway, and this way she won't be so much taller than Ramy. I really don't want my son to feel, you know, that he isn't a big, strong boy, especially when he's already marrying a woman that,' she leaned in to whisper, 'earns more money than him.'

I sighed. Perish the thought. Sometimes it was hard to believe that Naila used to campaign for Egyptian women to have the vote. Was this what happened when you got old, I wondered. One's rebellion, anarchy and desire for a revolution faded into passivity, domesticity, and a morbid fascination for shoes.

'Sure, those shoes are very nice too,' I said, getting up, shaking my head, and gesturing for Ali to do the same. 'Anyway, we must get back, masalam,' I said, kissing Naila and nodding from afar at Dyab, who was now chewing on a piece of tobacco while glued to the café's television. I caught his eye after several moments and he nodded.

∾

I held my husband's arm as we walked the short distance from the side street of the Alexandria Bakery on Harun Al-Rashied Street, past the Grand Heliopolis Hotel on Al-Rouba Street and onto Osman Ibn Affan Street, the road where our fifth-floor apartment was in the heart of Heliopolis. Naila and Dyab lived in the much quieter suburb of Maadi. They had moved there shortly after they had got married. Age had never caused me to tire of the vibrancy and energy of Heliopolis. There was something about the tightness of the air there; it always felt like something was about to happen. The green suburbs of Maadi with its perfect gardens, pristine and precise and predictable, left me feeling flat and passive. 'It's peaceful', people said of Maadi. Whereas Osman Ibn Affan Street was exciting. It had an erratic energy which kept me on my toes. I loved the traffic and the congestion, the people from all walks of life, the flashing neon lights at night and the bold bright markets by day. Heliopolis knew that time was finite and so it was perpetually in a rush. I felt the same – I still had so much to accomplish, I couldn't stop. I never lost the pace of my younger self, unlike Naila and Doria.

A loud beep screeched in our ears as a motorbike almost crashed into a bus. I felt my heart race and Ali squeezed my hand. I smiled. This is my home, I thought. We passed Ali's shop, I could see the boxes of fruit and vegetables stacked at the front which, aided by Usman, my husband would bring outside first thing tomorrow. I would walk past here on my way to the American University in Cairo and take a bottle of sugarcane juice and halowa sandwich for my lunch that day. Ali whistled as we passed my father's shop, now his, both of us breathing in its air, humbled by the building that presented our ancestral history. He continued to whistle, as we approached the apartment block. Slightly in front of me now, he stopped short, in front of the main door.

'Wallahi!' he said, bringing his hands to his mouth and collapsing on the bench in front of it.

'Ali!' I rushed towards him. 'Ali, what's wrong?' I touched his face, rough as sandpaper, short, coarse, thick silver hairs twinkling in the moonlight. I kissed his bald head. I felt his heart, much faster than mine. He pointed at the main door, as I helped him back up again. I turned to look and saw that the glass had been smashed. Someone had broken in. I helped him to walk towards the door, 'Yallah, we must see what is going on,' I said.

We carefully stepped over the smashed glass and started to climb the flights of stairs to our apartment. As we came to the fourth floor, the Yaghoubis, our neighbours below us, were outside their flat with their three daughters. Mr Yaghoubi had brought their telephone into the hall and appeared to be talking to the police. Mrs Yaghoubi saw us approaching and yelped out, crying, 'Fatiha! Fatiha! They came, with their faces covered, I'm so sorry!'

I smiled a polite smile. A smile that said, thank you, we can take over from here. I went up the next flight of stairs and walked into our apartment ready to have lost everything, our furniture, our television, our savings under the bed; I was ready to accept these material losses. But I was unable to deal with what they had written on the walls. As I saw the words daubed above our sofa, beside the big family picture of us holidaying in Alexandria with Doria's family, I knew instantly what I had to do. I stepped out of the apartment and onto the landing. I could see my husband, who had collapsed again on the stairway, breathing heavily, crouching over with his head in his hands. I closed our front door so that the neighbours could not see what had been written and walked over to Mr Yaghoubi and took the phone out of his hands.

''Allo?' I said into the receiver.

'Cairo Police?' the voice said.

'La, yanni, there's been a mistake, sorry to waste your time.'

'Everything OK?' he asked.

'Aiywa, shukran,' I said, hanging up and smiling sweetly at the Yaghoubis. 'Thank you but I can take over from here.'

I looked at my husband, who was wiping his brow with his handkerchief.

'What did they take?' his eyes seemed to ask. I gestured for him to come inside.

'They haven't taken anything, only our dignity,' I said, as he read the wall in front of him.

He started to breathe heavily again; this time he was clutching his heart.

'Ali!' I screamed, making him sit down and rushing to get him a glass of water.

'Breathe,' I told him. 'Just breathe . . .'

When he had calmed down, he said, 'Shaz gensi, shaz gensi? What have we done to deserve this?'

I held my husband's hand and kissed the flecks of syrup and the labneh off his lips. I found the contrast between the sweetness of the sugar and the salty tang of the cheese strangely calming. The intense flavours grounding me in the moment.

'What is this about, wallahi?' my husband croaked. I led him to his armchair to settle him. Then I walked to the drinks cabinet, swishing my lips from side to side trying to add everything up. I poured myself some arak and made a strong and short coffee for Ali. My husband was still in shock as he sipped the black medicine slowly, his hands lightly quivering as he looked up to the ceiling, shaking his head. I knocked back my clear liquid quickly, feeling the spirit entering my veins as swiftly as the aniseed neat on my tongue. My mind raced as I tried to make sense of it all. It slowly dawned on me that these words were not the result of our son's promiscuity. This wasn't about Aziz. These words were about Yasminah.

Yasminah

CAIRO, 1969

ي

I held my head as if it were about to fall off, shielding my eyes from the brightness of my father's white gallabiyah. He sat at the head of the table, flicking through the *Egyptian Gazette* while slurping his glass of hot tea. He appeared to have a halo over him as the light behind him from our back balcony reflected off his baldness. Combined with his long white robe he looked almost godly. I tried not to catch his eye as I, somewhat sheepishly, took my place next to him at the dining room table. It came to my knowledge that my head did *not* feel better upon sitting down as I had originally thought. Nor was it relieved when I shakily took a few gulps of water. My head felt like Ussy's football when it thumped on the wall outside. It was reverberating. As if my heart had replaced my brain and it was now beating inside my head.

I tried to focus. Usman sat opposite me, mechanically shoving large chunks of halowa into his mouth while furiously studying. He was reading his stupid science book, entitled *Synthetic*

Molecular Replication in Chemical Warfare. His face was so close to the book his nose was practically touching the pages, and the way he turned them was as if he was reading the last few pages of a great crime novel, so eager he was to find out which chemical was the deadliest. Every so often he'd gasp to himself and write something in his notepad. What a dork, I thought, always trying to be as studious as Mama. I could hear the punching and dinging of Mama in her study on her typewriter. I knew she was about to stop to come in and eat with us, because her usual sighing and tutting was replaced with singing and humming.

'Sabah al kheir,' Baba said to me after several moments, never taking his eyes off the paper, not even to sip his tea.

'Sabah al kheir,' I croaked.

I was grateful my mother was still singing so that we didn't feel the need to converse. Baba breathed in as the singing grew louder and more impassioned. It seemed that Mama was always in a good mood when nobody else was. She bounded in, her humming suddenly stopping at the sight of me. 'Yasminah, gosh, you look terrible! What have you done to your eyes?' she exclaimed.

Baba turned over another page of the newspaper so theatrically it practically ripped. His eyes were now aghast at the new headline he was reading, no doubt about the state of the Suez Canal.

'Wallahi!' he shouted, banging his fist on the table.

Definitely about the Suez Canal, I thought, it always riled him so.

'Baba?' Ussy put his book down and looked at him, before shrugging and returning to his studies. Meanwhile, my mother, ignoring Baba's outburst, was still enthralled by my face.

'Your eyes? Is this the new fashion?' she laughed.

I touched my face and got up to take a look at myself in the mirror by Mama's drinks cabinet. 'Oh, it's just my makeup from yesterday, I forgot to take it off last night.'

'I hope that wasn't the only thing you kept on last night, wallahi!' Baba clenched his teeth; he was sitting back in his chair now. He had crumpled up the newspaper and was tapping his fingers on the table.

'Baba!' I said, my mouth agape. A European man in a grey suit, with fierce blue eyes, suddenly came into my head. I swallowed more water. My hand was still visibly shaking. I placed it under the table, squeezing my leg in a bid to somehow heal it.

'Ali . . .' my mother said in her warning tone, before changing the subject. 'Where is Aziz?' she said, as she took her paper, *Le Progrès Egyptien*, and began to read.

'Aziz!' Usman yelled. 'He is still in bed,' he said, turning back towards Mama, always trying to get extra points as the prodigal son. I stuck my tongue out at him and he stuck his back.

We continued to sit with the sound of my mother now turning her newspaper and Usman chewing and swallowing as he studied. Baba had stopped tapping and was staring vacantly into the fruit bowl, I imagined deep in thought about Green Island and the northern Gulf of Suez. We could hear the faint sounds of the weekend markets on the streets below. I drank more water and did my best attempt at consuming a slice of bread and a boiled egg with honey as normally as possible without my hands shaking. Suddenly I felt my father's eyes on me and I tried to smile at him like everything was normal but he did not smile back. Instead, his eyes went immediately back to the fruit bowl. After several minutes we heard giggling from Aziz's room, followed by muffled talking in English, before his door slowly creaked open. I closed my eyes. I didn't know whether to rejoice or to cringe at the distraction from my own debauched presence. Aziz strutted in, white girl on his arm.

'Sabah al kheir! Meet Melinda.' He stood over my father now, holding Melinda as if she were a fish he had won at a fairground.

The white girl got on her tiptoes and whispered something into my brother's ear.

'Belinda,' he corrected himself, his teeth shining.

Usman blushed, his dark skin now flushed and florid. He looked back down at his book. My stunned father mumbled a 'sabah al kheir', uncrumpled his paper and brought it over his face as if trying to bury himself in it. Mama's face was as roseate as Ussy's, but where my little brother, like Baba, made himself smaller, my mother made herself bigger.

With dramatic flair, she loudly cracked her glass of tea onto her plate and stomped into the kitchen where she began to have a fight with the pots and pans. Both bashing and verbally threatening them. I smiled meekly at Belinda and sipped on my tea. She smiled back before looking at the front door. She tugged on Aziz's jacket.

'Well, we gotta go!' Aziz said, taking Belinda's hand and walking towards the door. She turned to us all as they left. 'It was nice to meet you all,' she said in English, before looking at Aziz for reassurance. 'Shukran?' she said. 'Masalam,' I said to fill the silence.

Aziz slammed the door shut, and with that, my mother walked back into the dining room.

'Can you believe the insolence of this boy?!' She stood over my father now, wooden spatula in one hand, the other hand on her hip.

Baba calmly brought down his paper in front of him. His face was now pale and he looked grave. 'Can I believe this boy?' he asked slowly, 'Yes, I can believe it,' he said decisively before banging his fists on the table again. 'But what I cannot believe is this girl!' he said, standing up and pointing at me.

I looked up from my bread in shock. Usman put his book down, as if suddenly realising that life was much more interesting. I watched as my parents discussed my lifestyle as if I wasn't in the room.

'She is getting drunk! A Muslim girl! Every night!' he exclaimed.

'So is Aziz!' my mother spat.

I closed my eyes. My mother and father had very different interpretations of the Quran. While my mother drank, my father did not. He somewhat tolerated Muslims drinking alcohol in moderation but had always stressed that intoxication was immoral in Islam.

'And anyway, you know what it says in the Quran!' Baba said, his teeth clenched and his eyes wide.

I pretended not to hear them both as they argued and waited for him to bring up the fact that he had seen my hands shaking this morning.

I thought of Mama's nuanced interpretations of the Quran. I looked down somewhat mesmerised at the whiteness of the plate contrasted with the darkness of the specks of bread with splatters of the yellow yolk like a Jackson Pollock painting.

'The Quran says that alcohol contains both *good* and evil . . .' Mama began.

'. . . but the evil is greater!' my father finished off the quote.

'The great Islamic poets, mystics and philosophers drank wine! Ibn Arabi . . .'

'Oh, shut up about Ibn Arabi!' Baba fumed.

79

My mother gasped, unsure how to retaliate.

'Mama?' Ussy said after several moments, his voice high, before saying, as solemn as an Imam, 'The hadiths say that whoever drinks wine in this world and does not repent from that, he will be deprived of it in the Hereafter.'

'Shut up, Ussy!' I yelled, throwing a nut at his head.

Usman ducked and continued his sermon. 'Some interpretations allow wine but prohibit intoxication . . .'

'Wallahi!' Mama shouted, throwing the wooden spatula at the floor.

Usman and I both flinched.

Baba peered down at the table and started folding his newspaper in half over and over again until it couldn't be folded any further.

'I've had enough of this. I have supported your untraditional views enough throughout this marriage! But this! This!' he yelled, getting up and pointing at me. 'This has got to stop!'

'But Aziz does the same!' my mother stressed.

'I don't give a damn what that boy does!' Baba's voice boomed. I don't think I'd ever heard his voice louder than Mama's before.

'What he does is not going to get him in trouble or in danger or . . . pregnant!' he said.

Mama and Usman both gasped. I continued to look down at my plate.

'I mean, what if she got pregnant?' Baba asked, his voice slightly softer now, as if in some sort of bid to protect Usman from the truth.

I let the tears fall quietly at first.

'And what about the graffiti, the vile words they invaded our home to write?' Baba was whispering to himself now. Mama breathed in deeply. She was unsure what was worse in the double meaning of the derogatory words 'shaz gensi'; being called a homosexual by association with Ommy, or a pervert for the age gap between us. She shook her head so fast it was as if she was trying to physically remove the memory from her brain.

'Usman, please, give me and your father and your sister some privacy.' She touched my brother's arm, and he collected his book and his notepad, nodded and walked out of the room, closing the door behind him. I didn't hear any footsteps walking away so I knew he was still there, listening. But I didn't care. I wiped my tears away.

There was silence for quite a while. Mama was sitting down now with her head in her hands. After some time had passed, I got up to leave.

'Yasminah?' Baba stopped me. I turned towards him. 'If this doesn't make you stop, I don't know what will,' he said, ripping out a page of his newspaper. In a small section next to an article about a new school opening in Dokki, there was Zafarullah Zerdak's gossip column. My mother joined me, reading over my shoulder.

'Oh, what's this cretin written about me now?' she said before releasing a groan after catching sight of the article's title: 'No Daughter of our Nile'.

'Oh, how original. I've not heard that one before,' my mother said, gritting her teeth, before grabbing the paper and reading the rest of the first paragraph aloud: ' "The scarlet daughter of the outspoken women's rights agitator, Fatiha Bin-Khalid, was seen fraternising with a perverted Iranian boy, outside the Grand Heliopolis Hotel. The boy, just turned seventeen to her twenty years, is rumoured to have connections with the Shah of Iran, perhaps protecting him from his flamboyant and despicable activities, fleeting between both female and male liaisons. Yasminah Bin-Khalid, however, seems to be proving her mother wrong, that so-called equality amongst the sexes is nothing short of unnatural!"' My mother's voice tailed off at the end. She screwed the newspaper up and stared vacantly between the brown crumbs on Ussy's white plate and his grubby finger marks in the halowa. She looked down at her nails before putting them in her mouth and biting them.

'She needs to get married; she needs to get married, soon,' Baba begged. 'Soon, to stop these wicked rumours.'

'OK,' Mama said.

I gasped through my hand which had been poised over my mouth in an attempt to conceal my quivering lips.

'Mama!' I tried to yell but it came out as barely a whisper. I felt the heat of my disbelief, my breath hot on my hand. Then a panic so penetrating it pierced through my eyes, preventing me from blinking. My mother's words which had sealed my fate had frozen me in time. I tried desperately to speak, to scream 'Never!' or simply say 'No'. Instead, tears rolled down my cheeks like rain on a statue as I let out a tiny wail.

Fatiha

ف

I had never truly appreciated the simplicity of my way of life in Cairo. Back in Heliopolis there was a rigid routine and I came to realise that, although this predictability was sometimes banal and monotonous, the inevitability of it was comforting. Each morning I would wake up, have breakfast with Mama and Jeddy while Baba slept till noon. Each day I would go, books proudly in hand, to my school, al-Madrassa al-Saniyya on El Khoumi Street, which boasted Nabawiyya Musa as an alumna. Each night I would help Mama with the cooking while Baba would yell and slap Jeddy over the head for some silly reason.

Here in Paris everything was unpredictable, and the precarity of it all caused a rapid descent in my confidence. After I had received the news about my scholarship to the Sorbonne, I had dreamed gleefully about living in an apartment building with decadent eighteenth-century Parisienne architecture. While I rolled vine leaves with Mama and kneaded bread and prepared the ful for Baba's breakfast (which he had at precisely one o'clock each afternoon), I had imagined myself as regal as Marie Antoinette herself. In this fantasy, I saw myself sitting on one of those funny French couches, stuffing my face with canelés, mille-feuilles and macaroons and gorging on pains au chocolat and beignets, while coolly smoking cigarettes like Mireille Balin. All the while being stimulated by some of the most profound intelligentsia that the university was famed for.

Upon arriving in Paris, however, I quickly saw the reality of my situation. My apartment was indeed indicative of many other buildings in Paris. With each crack, flaw, imperfection shockingly evident alongside the brutal scars and devastation caused by the ongoing German invasion, my assuredness, my assertiveness descended to its lowest ebb. Meanwhile, my heart sank even lower.

Mama had been uncertain that Paris was the best place for me to study, but I told her it would be no different to the British occupation in Egypt. She had despaired at my naïvety but, sensing my determination, she eventually relented. (My father had been dumbstruck as to why I thought I needed a university education at all.) Now the confident, defiant voice I exhibited around Cairo and to my parents, the very one that had afforded me this scholarship, had been replaced by a sudden and inexplicable meekness. I had initially been aroused by the promise of palatial Parisian beauty but had found myself on arrival immediately sunken by the wreckage.

Now, as I sat on my bed, against my grubby, crumbling wall and gazed out the small window, I felt equal parts disillusioned, disheartened and disenchanted. The room was indeed 'poky', as the English girl who gave me a tour had said. At least the view was magnificent. My room overlooked a communal courtyard and shared a balcony with the neighbouring room (whose occupant I hadn't seen, only heard). Out in the distance was Paris's famous main square, Place de la Concorde, which I found to be rather like Tahrir Square's glamorous older sister, while Cleopatra's Needle, the gift Egypt gave to France, offered me much comfort. I smiled. Finally, a drop of beauty, I thought, seeing how the small black-rimmed window framed it all so artistically.

I lay on my bed looking out, clutching my satchel to my chest. I clicked it open and eagerly delved into the two books I had borrowed from the library after my lecture on the philosophic interpretation of the Islamic poets that day: Ibn Sirin's *Islamic Dream Interpretation* and a biography of Ibn Arabi entitled *Small Death*. For some reason *Small Death* had caused a fit of giggles from Marielle, the university librarian. 'Petite mort!' she had screeched, sniggering like a schoolgirl. My hopes of mixing with the world's finest minds at such an elite establishment were once again thwarted by this reality. I sighed and opened the book to study; Ibn Arabi always soothed me. I felt a tingling sensation in my stomach whenever I read his words. It was as if he was speaking directly to me, like a spiritual message from the divine. Something inside me told me to carry on his work, dissecting the realms and concepts of gender within the Holy Quran and hadiths. I hadn't yet chosen a title for my thesis but when I read Ibn Arabi I felt closer to the inspiration that would make it happen. I took out the lunch I had not had time to eat from my bag and began my nightly routine. It wasn't what I envisioned but it was all I had to reassure me. And so, with the soundtrack of Parisian nightlife playing as my lullaby, I slowly drifted off to sleep with Ibn Arabi in one hand and a baton of French bread with cheese in the other.

I awoke just shy of dawn when I heard a woman's heels

clicking on the cobbled streets outside my apartment, followed by a cacophony of cackles and snorts as she climbed up the steps to the building. The metallic tinkle of keys followed by a loud bang indicated that she was the type of woman who let a door slam instead of letting it shut carefully. Drunken white girls, I thought, rolling my eyes while rolling over. Why do they always drink to excess? Have they not encountered the great Ibn Arabi, who said that from moderation a great happiness springs?

More laughter came from next door. Perhaps the reason I had not yet met this woman was because she spent the day in bed, in order to be out all night. I tried to go back to sleep, imagining her passing out on her mattress, makeup still on, one shoe on, one shoe off. Or perhaps she was entangled between the legs of a French lover, judging from the sounds I had heard over the last few nights. I sighed. I would have my revenge in the morning. I closed my eyes again, imagining all the ways I could make noise eating my egg and croissant at breakfast, orchestrating the pots and pans and forks and spoons in my head, as if arranging the beat for a tarabuka drummer. I began drifting off again only to be disturbed once more by hysterical laughter. I opened the door with angry gusto,

'What is so funny?' I fumed. As soon as I saw who stood in front of me I instantly regretted my outburst. I put my hand over my mouth in an effort to stop the words coming out, but it was too late.

Her face alone should have won Miss Egypt. Even in my sleepy delirium I felt such certainty that it was her. Years before I had seen her in the *Egyptian Gazette*, the first Muslim woman to enter Miss Egypt. Now, on my fourth night in Paris, Doria Shafik was

standing before me. Not only this, but she was the mysterious woman next door. We were neighbours! And now she was standing outside in our joint courtyard, her legs wobbling as much as her eyes were rolling, smoking a cigarette as majestically as Mireille. I could see Cleopatra's Needle behind her as erect and alert as her eyebrows. Oh, such eyebrows! So thick and straight and as striking as exclamation marks. Just like the grammatical punctuation, her face woke me up. How did this face possibly come second, I wondered. I reminded myself that it is never the most beautiful woman that wins the Miss Egypt beauty competition each year but the most average. A face too striking threatens the status quo. Men want ordinary, traditional beauty, a bowl of fruit rather than a futuristic work of art.

Grabbing a shawl from the coat stand in a bid to maintain some modesty while meeting my idol, I continued to examine her face. I'd only ever seen her in a black and white newspaper. Letting the door close behind me, I earnestly stepped towards her, offering my sincerest apologies for my uncharacteristic audacity. As I did so, I noted that her skin was a shade or two lighter than mine and her hair a shade darker. The contrast accentuated her large eyes, which were both sharp, emitting a fondness for life, and soft, portraying a vulnerability to it.

She turned to me, taking a drag of her cigarette. 'Bonjour! Je pense que nous sommes voisines,' she said, coming in to kiss my cheeks. Although she was twelve years my senior, her cheeks felt like the soft dough of kneaded bread. So much so that as I pulled away, I touched my own cheek and inspected my finger for the residue of flour. I wondered if her youthfulness was the result of applying lotion each night like my mother always told me to do. But the way she leaned tipsily over the balcony, looking out into the distance with not a single care about being out at such an ungodly hour, I ascertained that Doria didn't seem the sort to bother with such banalities as a moisturisation routine nor concern herself with the concept of beauty sleep. Her attractiveness was down to the fact that her beauty didn't require any upkeep. Her skin was good because she was living a good life, fearlessly and ferociously.

'Je pense que nous sommes voisines!' she giggled again, as I joined her on the balustrade.

'Salamwaylaykum, we are neighbours indeed!' I said replying in Arabic. I was thankful my tone was akin to my old Egyptian persona and sounded self-assured. Yet I still felt self-conscious, unable to return her greeting in French.

'Ah Arabi! Where from?' Doria squealed, offering me a cigarette, which I took and lit awkwardly while admiring her polished red nails.

'Heliopolis,' I said, taking in the smoke and instantly coughing.

Doria laughed. 'Are you OK? You don't smoke, do you?' I nodded. She laughed again, removing the cigarette from my mouth and stubbing it out on the stone wall. 'I am from Cairo too. Well, I grew up in Tanta but then I moved to Zamalek.'

I know, I thought.

'You are studying here at the Sorbonne or have you chosen this drabby apartment on purpose?' she asked.

I nodded. I missed the cigarette and wondered what to do with my arms instead, only just then noticing how long they were. I held them by my side, the weight of them drooping my shoulders down, my posture nowhere near as poised as Doria's. Even in her dishevelled state, she had more class than me. I was relieved when I found a place to rest them on the wall of the balcony.

'We must have coffee tomorrow and talk about the mad professors at the Sorbonne,' she said between drags.

'Yes,' I said, even though I had tried coffee two days ago and it had made me jittery with a very bad stomach. I was homesick for my mother's hot sweet tea. 'Coffee would be great. I've only been here a few days and my French isn't so good . . .' I laughed.

She smiled and nodded before taking another long puff of her cigarette. In the silence I stood feeling somewhat foolish, childish and unsure of my body. She was a little taller than me in fashionable heels, like a movie star. I looked down at my egg-stained slippers and closed my eyes for just a second with mild mortification.

She took another drag of her cigarette, smiled and gazed out at the square in the distance.

I did the same and tried my best to look as contemplative as she did. I breathed in loudly, hoping my inhalation showed an acknowledgement and an appreciation of French culture. That I, like Doria, was a woman of the world.

'I know who you are,' I then admitted a little sheepishly, 'you won the scholarship from the Egyptian Ministry of Education a few years ago, I won it this year.' I blushed and then chastised myself for failing to keep my cool. I was a little star struck. I had been following her career avidly since I was eleven years old.

She chuckled. 'So many years ago, and I still feel that my thesis is not yet complete.' She continued laughing for several moments before bringing her hands to her mouth and biting her lip.

'I'm sure it is wonderful.' Everything she does is wonderful, I thought. I had read the essay she wrote on Qasim Amin, a man whom my father had always objected to.

I recalled how Baba once yelled to his friends, 'He thinks all of Egyptian's problems can be solved by giving women the same rights as men. I think he is a secret woman under cover!' before making a lewd gesture while grabbing his crotch. I remember silently wishing my father was drunk to explain his behaviour.

Qasim Amin was the only Egyptian man I respected. And he was dead. No wonder I only developed infatuations for women, like Huda Shaarawi, Malak Hifni Nawas and Nabawiyya Musa whose educational lectures I attended as a young girl.

Just then Doria's door creaked open.

'Ah, there he is!' Doria said, as a man came out of her apartment. He was wearing only a dressing gown and I could see his chest hair, which was wet and tangled like bundles of seaweed. I blushed, tying the shawl tighter around my shoulders and focusing on his face. He had perfectly round glasses and, bleary from interrupted sleep, he took them off to rub his eyes. He was handsome, despite his odd glasses, and as he came towards us catching the first glimpse of morning sun, I could see on his left cheek he had a long deep scar the shape of a tick, like the ones I got in my old school workbooks. It was as if Allah Himself had approved of what he had made.

'This is my husband, Nureldin, Nureldin, this is our neighbour! The girl next door!'

'Arabi?' Nureldin asked with an enthusiastic smile. I noticed that one of his front teeth was chipped, an imperfection that made him all the more charming.

I nodded and started to shake his hand.

'Al hum'dullah!' he exclaimed, bringing me in to kiss me on both of my cheeks. I blushed again, being so close to a man with so few clothes on.

We laughed.

'Nur misses Egypt a great deal,' Doria said, rolling her eyes before stroking her husband's arm.

'We will be back soon, I hope! My wife is telling me she is soaking up the revolutionary spirit of the French in order to bring the anarchy back to Egypt!'

Doria rolled her eyes again and primped her hair.

'I have big plans,' she said coyly.

'And does our neighbour have a name?' Nur made a bemused face and looked to Doria for a proper introduction.

'Name?' Doria laughed, shaking her head, her pale skin flushing slightly.

'Fatiha,' I said, 'Fatiha Bin-Khalid.'

I went to bed feeling giddy with excitement after the encounter. The feeling buzzed around inside me, the same way it had when I had won the scholarship and my dear brother Jeddy had told me, his eyes sparkling, 'This is a very big day in Fatiha Bin-Khalid's life.' I looked out of my window towards Cleopatra's Needle, before drifting off to sleep with the vision of Doria standing in the doorway etched in my mind. I had found the beauty I had dreamed about, I was certain of it.

Yasminah

CAIRO, 1970

ي

'**A**hmed isn't bad-looking, it's just he's not . . .' Mona said.
'Good-looking?' I offered.

Mona threw her head back and giggled. 'And he has the added benefit of only being your second cousin not your first.'

'That's true,' I deliberated. We were both sitting on her bed, flicking through her mother's old magazines. We had found them in the back of her wardrobe after she had left that afternoon.

Mona turned up the volume on Radio Sawt-al-Arab; another of Mohammed Abdel Wahab's nationalist songs was playing.

'I love this song,' Mona cooed, bopping her head back and forth with as much swagger as someone with two left feet could. I knew she was lost in the music because she had her mouth wide open, revealing the buck teeth she was ordinarily self-conscious about. Mona's protruding tea-stained teeth flashed in and out of my periphery unsyncopated and for the first time I noticed that both my best friend and my potential husband were cursed with not only the same lack of co-ordination but the same dental afflictions. I wondered if this was a good or a bad omen.

I loved Mona but I didn't want to marry her.

I rolled my eyes. 'Wahab's always singing about Egypt, it's pathetic, pandering to Nasser. I mean, name one song that doesn't have the word Egypt in it.'

Mona stopped to think for a beat. ' "Hay Ala El Falah", "El Watan El Akbar", "Hob El Watan Fard Alyi", "Ya Nessmet El Horria" – "Oh What Freedom!" '

I had forgotten that she was Wahab's biggest fan. 'Freedom! Freedom under Nasser is an oxymoron, my mother says.'

'Whatever, he could be singing about his grandma for all I care, his voice makes me melt.'

'I just don't like this station, they reported the Six-Day War inaccurately, making out Egypt was winning when it was getting obliterated by the Israelis. You can't trust it.' I switched the radio off, interrupting Ahmed Said's famous tagline: 'Calling on the Arab nation from the heart of Cairo.' So that it stopped right before 'the heart of Cairo'.

'The arse of Nasser . . .' I finished it off.

Mona giggled before quickly biting her lip to stop. She could see I was annoyed. She always got nervous when I was rattled. As if my political rants were personal insults to her.

'Your mother is so cool,' she said. 'Look at the article she wrote, "The Naserian regime is more gruelling than a woman's beauty regime",' she said, suddenly showing me the cover of the magazine she was reading. I felt my eyes widen as I saw the familiar cover from my childhood. 'No wonder the government shut them down!' Mona screeched.

I grabbed the magazine from her hands, 'Your mother used to read *Bint Al Nil*?'

'I guess so! My father would freak.'

I glanced at the year. 1957. 'That was when Doria was on hunger strike,' I muttered to myself.

'I can't believe your mother knew her,' Mona cooed.

'Knows,' I corrected.

'Wait, what? Are you telling me she still sees her? I thought she was under house arrest, mish keda?'

I shrugged, pretending to be staring at the poster of Omar Sharif on her wall. Another predictable heartthrob. Doria was no longer under house arrest, but she rarely left the house these days because of her hem, Mama said. According to my mother, hem was a type of confusing sadness where you don't know why you are sad, which is the most frustrating type of sadness there is. She said that the hem causes women to stay in the house and that English women call it the problem with no name. I was just glad I didn't have it. I did everything I could these days to stay away from home.

Mona had stopped looking at me for an answer, I wasn't in any mood to discuss Doria and my mother's heyday. Instead, like I always did when I was procrastinating, I chewed on the fat on my cheeks greedily, contemplating an eternity with Ahmed.

The problem with Ahmed was I neither loved nor hated him enough to marry him. Instead, I was indifferent, unaffected, and unaroused by his presence. Perhaps I was still in love with Ommy? No, I thought, digging into the inside of my cheek again, this time breaking off a piece and swallowing it. Knowing an ulcer would form, I continued chewing. Ommy had told me that the greatest tragedy of his life was that he didn't love me like that. Perhaps if Zaki were a woman I would have been consumed with jealousy. But I loved Ommy, so I let him go, back to Iran with Zaki. They had both asked me to come and visit but I did not take it seriously.

I let my head fall back onto Mona's bedroom wall as if trying to knock the proverbial sense into myself. I wondered, would the greatest tragedy of my life be not going with Ommy to Iran and marrying Ahmed instead? Ahmed was the more stable choice. Ahmed was offering me love. Ommy could only offer me friendship. What would that get me? It made sense. Ahmed made sense. Baba had even said it himself, when explaining to me the benefits of marrying my second cousin.

'See, habibbti, economically it makes sense: marry into the family, all the money stays in the family! Mama might have had a loose mouth, but she had a tight wallet!' he half joked.

'Yes, I'm just not sure it makes sense evolutionarily,' I had said under my breath.

Genetics aside, I knew that marrying Ahmed was a sensible option. He had a highly successful pigeon-selling business which was largely only thriving because the pigeons he sold were all homing birds. Every few days, he had said to me, new stock would show up without warning for him to resell.

I had smiled politely as he talked about his pigeons. He blithered away, while I took in his musty smell, a mixture of straw and dust and feathers. In this moment I realised even his pheromones bored me. He was the very embodiment of bland. Invoking only passivity when I longed for passion.

Emotionally, marrying Ahmed was the equivalent of promising that every time you step into Groppi's Ice Cream Parlour you would order two scoops of vanilla, no sprinkles, for the rest of time. If only I hated him or was repulsed by him, at least then I would know. I would feel real human emotion instead of ambivalence. I had neither time nor reputation to be fussy. I hadn't done too badly, I told myself. Second cousins didn't even really feel like a relative. I never played with him as a child. So, at least he didn't feel like family. I still had so much to get to know. Although this allure failed to excite even the smallest part of me.

Instead, I focused on the positive sides to him. In certain lights (on the balcony at night, overlooking the golden lights of the city, with the shisha covering his lack of a jawline) he was almost handsome, kind of. Definitely so when we both took our glasses off.

Now in Mona's bedroom, I made a decision. When I got home, I would tell Baba to accept Ahmed's family's proposal to marry. I felt relieved. Ahmed was a good man. I was now trying to surround myself with people who were good instead of people who were exciting. The men I had been with so far had always swept me away from myself, away from mediocrity, away from the life I was supposed to be living. The path that was set out for me. But with the exception of Ommy, they were not good men. As boring as it was, it was time to choose someone dependable, sensible, kind, who would treat me with respect. Rather than someone wild, fun and rebellious who would treat me like I was nothing.

I watched as Mona switched the radio back on; this time I let her keep it on as Ahmed Said blared out his infamous catchphrase. Ahmed. I thought. I was unsure if this was a good or a bad omen.

The jingle of the mazhar and the riq indicating the start of an Umm Kulthum song tinkled, the brass zills shaking through the radio waves. Mona adjusted the antennae sharpening out any fuzziness. A clarity and crispness came through. I wished I could do the same thing with my own mind. The volume increased as the transmission got clearer. We got up to dance – it was impossible not to.

Mona reached out and I took her hand; it was clammy and warm unlike my own. I used it like a slippery lever, pushing it up and down, trying to get her body to move in time to the music, until finally we were in sync, and she followed my lead as we sang.

We moved our bodies to the music, circling round to see out of her bedroom window, provocatively dancing now to an audience on the street who were too concerned with the hubbub on the roads to notice us. We overlooked Al-Orouba Street and with it the giant fortress, the Baron Palace and the Grand Heliopolis Hotel where Ommy and I stayed that night. I was dancing between the old fortress and the new hotel. It felt like I was torn between tradition and modernity, conservativism and rebellion.

Mona suddenly slammed the radio off and pushed me onto the bed.

'Mama!' she yelped.

I turned around to see Umm Rhami standing in the middle of the room. She smiled at me sweetly, revealing her teeth, which were stained yellow, the colour of turmeric. She had a large gap between her two front teeth, which meant I could see that her tongue was tightly pressed onto the roof of her mouth. I imagined she was on the verge of releasing it like a snake. A long, thin, venom-filled tongue the colour of fury would hurl right at me. Right now, the snake was in placation mode. It was winding around us both like a boa constrictor.

'Mona, I would like to talk to you about something,' she said, ushering her daughter out of the room using only her eyes.

I slowly slid the *Bint Al Nil* and the pile of other magazines under Mona's bed with my foot as Mona walked out with her mother. I could hear their hushed voices in the hall.

'Mona, I thought I had specifically told you not to hang

around any more with this girl, do you know what people are saying about her with that disgusting younger Iranian boy?' Umm Rhami's whispered taunts crept through the gap under the door.

I started humming the song again in my head to try to block out their voices as I gathered my coat and bag, ready to leave as soon as they came back. I had not a single ounce of sadness or embarrassment in my heart. Instead, I felt only gratitude and clarity as I pushed an irritating tear away. I crouched down under the bed and pulled the *Bint Al Nil* magazine back out. I picked it up and walked out.

'Masalam, Umm Rhami,' I said, placing the magazine in Mona's mother's hands as she raised an eyebrow. 'Masalam, Mona.'

Fatiha

CAIRO, 1951

ف

Ceza Nabaraoui is a witch. I was unsure, along with the Egyptian press, as to why Doria had invited her and the rest of the Egyptian Feminist Union to this meeting at *Bint Al Nil* headquarters. Had she not forgotten how Ceza had sabotaged our involvement with the EFU by spreading vicious rumours about Doria to its founder, Huda Shaarawi, all those years ago? Such rumours had involved Ceza maliciously scrutinising why Doria was not accepted to teach her course on Women and Islam at the national university. The witch had the audacity to suggest to Huda that the nature of Doria's relationship with the university dean, Dr Amin, was less than savoury! When the truth of the matter was that Dr Amin fretted that Doria's feminist politics at such a conservative establishment would cause a 'violent storm' for which he would be responsible.

Ceza had always been jealous of the bond that Huda and Doria shared. Ever since Huda invited her to speak at the

Ezbakiya Gardens Theatre, after she was awarded the Sorbonne scholarship, she had always been catty to her. I'll never forgive her for using Doria's rejection at such a prestigious university to break that bond. And now she was bringing this despicable woman into her home, along with the very establishment, the Egyptian Feminist Union, that refused her entry and mine by association!

I did not dare to show it, but I was furious at my best friend. We had both agreed long ago, after we were snubbed, that the Egyptian Feminist Union represented the past. It was brought about thirty years ago when nationalism infused the land. Now we were brewing with so much more for Egypt.

Our *Bint Al Nil*, once merely a magazine, was now practically a fully-fledged political party. We were the future. *Bint Al Nil* is youthful, modern, cutting edge. The EFU was tiresome. I didn't want to be in a room with such outdated women. 'It's a shame they removed their veils for their faces are wrinkly old prunes!' the venomous journalist Zafarullah Zerdak had once written about Ceza and her precious EFU. Doria and I of course had tutted, outraged at how a man with a large bulbous nose and ears that protruded so haphazardly could possibly possess the audacity to scrutinise women's looks so publicly. As we did, we both bit our bottom lips and clenched our fists under the table, and tried not to look each other in the eye, which we always did when we were trying not to laugh. Zafarullah Zerdak did have a point. They *were* old, what did they know? And Ceza might have been there alongside Huda Shaarawi, contributing to *L'Egyptienne*, which might have *technically* been the first Egyptian feminist magazine, but it only reached French speakers. Our magazine, *Bint Al Nil*, reached the masses, not just the elite cosmopolitan and French-speaking Egyptian women, but poor women in urban areas who could only speak Arabic. This was what Doria and I believed to be the future of women's rights, supporting all women regardless of demographic. It was what we had planned all those years ago during our studies at the Sorbonne. On returning from Paris, Doria used her connections to secure us sufficient magazine experience working for King Fuad's first wife's new magazine. Princess Chevikar's *La Femme Nouvelle* was a thriving literary and culture magazine and Doria's talents and charms eventually secured her the position of editor-in-chief. Although we were afforded the freedom to write the articles we wanted to write, like political commentary on Egypt's history and cultural heritage, we were specifically asked to write in French as the magazine only targeted the upper classes, much to our frustration. *Femme Nouvelle* was no different to Ceza's *L'Egyptienne*, so we left and set up *Bint Al Nil*. I looked at Doria, my eyes wide, as she brazenly brought this witch – this vulture – into our precious realm, alongside her two other side-kicks: Hiba and Samia.

'Trust me,' Doria said, as she went towards the door of her office, 'this collaboration is an excellent step for the future of Egyptian women.'

I forced a smile. We all did. Rashida, Shula and Naila were sitting rigidly around the coffee table. Rashida fiddled with her ivory misbahah beads, a recent gift from her beloved mother-in-law after completing Haj. I touched her shoulder, and she looked up at me. We both exchanged a look using only our eyes; wide and unblinking. Shula was trying to actively dispel her discomfort by fiddling with the cups and saucers, moving them from the centre of the coffee table to the side and back to the centre again, as if performing some sort of magic trick. While Naila, vacant as always, no doubt thinking about whether she would make it home in time for her favourite soap opera, stared out of Doria's large window at the island of Zamalek, a city that was both a part of Cairo but also independent.

The Asr el Nil separated Zamalek from the rest of the city but stayed connected via the Khedive Ismail Bridge. The island was man-made and had an entirely modern feel. It suited Doria and Nur and their two little girls. It was quieter than inner Cairo so Doria could work without being in the constant limelight of the press, and much of Nur's work as a lawyer involved defending wealthy businessmen who resided there. Their work supported each other; the more infamous Doria got, the more work Nur got, and the more work he got the more influential people he could get behind Doria's cause.

'What's that?' Naila asked, breaking the nervous silence. She was always a little slower than Rashida and Shula, never fully understanding the gravity of our work. Rashida had told me that Naila had once confessed to her that her husband hadn't anticipated the magazine to be quite so provocative. Naila had thought we'd be working on articles on how to please your husband or how to make a sweet dress out of an old tablecloth. Not on how to solve women's primary social problems and to ensure their inclusion in Egypt's policies or the importance of education for girls and eradicating illiteracy. As a result, Naila always looked a bit like a rabbit caught in the headlights.

'I think she just wants us all to have a pyjama party and paint our nails,' I heard Rashida say to Shula, giggling together in Doria's kitchen one night.

I heard the creak of Doria's front door open out into the street and I tried my best to swallow my despair. But my angst could not be shut up long; I heard the groan from my stomach. I had skipped breakfast and had been quelling the empty feeling in the pit of myself with coffee all morning. Coffee never agreed with me, but I drank it anyway to seem continental and believing that one day it would agree that I was. My stomach groaned again as Hiba and Samia came into the room. I grabbed some dates and nuts from Doria's fruit bowl in the middle of the coffee table and beckoned for them to sit down around it next to Naila, Rashida and Shula.

'Ahlan wa sahlan!' Rashida said, suddenly seeming positively brimming with ecstasy at the prospect of sitting next to our enemy. She was always such a great actress.

'Shukran,' Hiba said somewhat meekly.

'It is lovely to reunite with you!' Samia gestured to Shula who had contributed several articles to *L'Egyptienne* back in the day. We couldn't use it against her because, well, so had Doria, before Ceza sabotaged her friendship with our beloved Huda Shaarawi (rest in peace).

We waited awkwardly for Doria and Ceza to come into the room, but I could hear that they were still at the front door. We heard the clicks of photographers, no doubt in shock at the reunion between the two. Doria's former fiancé and outspoken critic, Ahmad Al-Sawi, had been quoted in *Al-Ahram* newspaper saying that it was 'inconceivable that we would see Doria Shafik and Ceza Nabaraoui exchanging kisses in the street but that is exactly what is happening now that they have announced they are joining forces'.

I still didn't really understand why we were, as Doria put it to me privately, 'temporarily merging'. I latched onto the word 'temporarily' even though she had declared to the press that we were 'all in favour of prolonged unified action'. She told me that at this meeting all would be revealed.

My stomach groaned again as we all waited for Doria and

Ceza to step into the room and start the meeting. I clutched it, embarrassed by its volume. It seemed to be groaning for me. No matter how much I tried to stay silent and pretend, my body always told the truth. I stuffed another few dates in my mouth, my tongue removing the stones into the sides of my mouth while the other side of my mouth swallowed the sweet flesh, as if it were a factory. I spat out the pits into a tissue and placed it scrunched up onto the table.

'Coffee?' Rashida asked the group.

'Aiywa,' Hiba said.

'Please . . .' Samia whispered.

'Oooh, yes please . . .' I said, taking another cup of the black poison. If Doria was choosing to self-sabotage, I might as well go down with the ship too, I thought. I gulped the coffee back as if it were a shot of arak and gazed at Samia's tired face. Her chin sagged around her neck like an empty sack and her forehead was so creased that for the first time in my life I wanted to get the iron out. The skin above her lips was as yellow and as crinkled as papyrus and was spotted with about a dozen thick short coarse black hairs. I never wanted to get so old that I couldn't be bothered to sugar wax my lip hair, I thought. Samia had a walking stick which she had perched on the edge of the sofa. I looked at it as if it was a physical manifestation of everything I feared in life. Being old and irrelevant and unable to stand on my own two feet.

'Salamwaylaykum!' Ceza boomed into the room, kissing us all twice on each cheek. She was just as sickly sweet as I had remembered. Only she had grown more so with age.

Doria delicately walked in behind her and let everyone exchange niceties. She waited until we were all silent, even Ceza. Until you could hear nothing but the faint sounds of the journalists waiting outside, to get their 'exit shot' no doubt. I worried my stomach would rumble again. I sat in the silence uncomfortably praying for someone to speak.

'Shukran for coming today, Ceza, Hiba, Samia . . .' She nodded at each of them. She was a true politician, charming, erudite, looking each of them in the eye. She had once told me, 'A great revolutionary makes politics personable.' It sent shivers down my spine. It still did.

'What I am about to tell you today must stay within this group. I have called the EFU and the *Bint Al Nil* Union together to . . .' She paused and cupped her head in her hands. We all leaned forward, our eyes big, sitting on the edge of the slippery leather sofa, waiting to hear more from our leader.

'First, we must . . .' Doria said.

'Yes, first we must . . .' Ceza joined in and I felt a pang of jealousy smack through my spine, making me sit up and grip the screwed-up napkin of date stones on the coffee table.

'. . . swear on the Quran,' they both said in unison, laughing.

I felt myself become as green as the book. The way they laughed together was the way Doria and I laughed together. As if we held a secret that no one else knew. I bit my lip and tried my best not to cry even though it felt as though Doria had taken my heart and given it to Ceza to stamp on.

I tried to concentrate on the Quran; it always grounded me. They both held it out towards the middle of the table for us all to touch and swear on Allah.

'You must swear a solemn oath on the blessed Quran not to divulge any of these plans to anyone, not even to our husbands!'

Naila breathed in, shocked. We all looked at her and shook our heads. She was a newlywed and a chatterbox, and we were well aware she was telling her husband Dyab everything; our only relief was that we knew he wasn't listening.

'Not even to our husbands,' Doria stressed again. This was fine with me. Ali was proud of my feminist achievements, but he did often stipulate that he preferred it if I didn't bring my work home. He once joked to me that he wanted me to be 'a wife and mother in the home, a feminist on the streets'. At least, I thought he was joking. Besides, we had got to the point in our marriage where we only talked about the children. Aziz and Yasminah took up all our emotional energy when we were together.

'We swear,' I said, feeling like a teacher's pet, and the others followed.

'OK,' Naila said finally.

'We are only playing, what we are doing is no longer enough!' Doria said suddenly, shooting up from her chair and banging her fists on the coffee table so that the nuts rattled, and the dates bounced, and my stomach rumbled in trepidation once again. 'We must get onto the streets!' She sat down again and in a low voice added, 'Why don't we organise a demonstration?' A silence hung over the room that not even my stomach could break.

'Why don't we storm parliament and demand our rights?'

I thought of Ali. A feminist on the streets. Well, he did ask for it.

'There's only so far the written word can get us,' Ceza added.

I smiled at Doria and then I surprised myself by smiling at Ceza. I saw them hold hands under the table. Even though it pained me to see my best friend with another woman, I leaned over to them and placed my hand onto both of their own. Then Shula, Hiba, Samia, Rashida and finally little Naila did the same until all our hands were on top of each other and you couldn't determine which hand was our own and which hands were those of our comrades.

Yasminah

CAIRO, 1970

ي

I wondered if it would feel different with Ahmed. I suppose it felt different with every guy but perhaps now we were married, now that Allah was involved, it would feel new again. I much preferred to think of Allah than think of Ahmed when I thought about being intimate with him. Ommy had told me that attraction wasn't about looks, it was about the person. So, I focused on Ahmed's kindness, and I fixated on his consistency. There was something very reassuring about his predictability. Even though I relished Ommy's rebelliousness, Ahmed's stability I knew was what made a marriage. Ommy and I were too similar, we couldn't ground each other. Ommy wasn't safe. Ahmed was. This was what marriage was all about. A cocoon not a circus. Dependence not danger. Predictability not precariousness. Tradition not revolution. As much as I enjoyed the butterflies that Ommy gave me, I no longer wanted the excitement. I wanted peace now.

I guess this was what Mama meant when she said that in marriage, butterflies turn into moths. An irritating, yet incredibly loveable moth, she'd say, smiling at Baba crunching his pistachios while watching the news.

Ahmed was always a moth to me. What did it matter if I skipped the butterfly bit?

∾

Like most brides I didn't want my wedding day to be over. The elated joy, the dancing, the celebration was all a saccharine soundtrack in a horror movie. I finally had to let Ahmed do it. I hoped he really was a virgin like he told me he was, for it would mean it would be brief. I looked forward to going to sleep; in my sleep I could pretend that it was all a dream.

'Oh, my beautiful Princess Yasminah,' Ahmed slobbered into my ear as the door clicked closed on our hotel suite. 'Finally, we are alone,' he said into my neck. At least he wasn't staring into my eyes. When he was on my neck, I didn't have to look at his face. All I had to worry about was just making the right sounds. Like an actor in a radio play.

'Yallah. Let's get this off,' I said, undoing his trousers. I wanted to get it over with.

'Wait! Habibbti, let's take our time, I want to embrace every part of you, I want to hold you in my arms, I want our bodies to slowly melt into each other, I want us to become one.'

I buried my head into the pillow, desperately searching for a portal to another dimension where I could be free, but all it did was make me feel more suffocated. I ducked my head up and took a deep breath in.

'Just take me, take me now, Ahmed, I can't wait any longer, I want you!' I roared, half fantasising about covering his head with the same pillow.

'And I want you, but first, habibbti, let us pray.'

∾

After we prayed together, he took the Quran and a book of hadiths from his bag and motioned for me to sit with him on the balcony of our hotel room. Maybe he didn't want to be intimate with me at all, I thought. Maybe he was like Ommy's friend Rahim who married a woman he didn't love and would never love just to please his parents. I prayed, I prayed he was like Rahim. After all, he'd heard the rumours about Ommy and still wanted to marry me.

'Come, come,' he said, gesturing for me to sit with him on his lap. He thumbed through his book of hadiths until he came to the verse he wanted. I stared down at his Quran, the emerald-coloured book with pages as thin as feathers. He followed my gaze, picked it up and kissed it three times before lunging onto my lips, inserting his tongue into my mouth for the first time. He wasn't like Rahim. My heart sank. He swirled his tongue around my mouth three times anti-clockwise.

He pulled back and touched my face, pushing back loose hairs behind my ears. He had set the Quran aside and yet it felt odd being so sexual around such a sacred book. But we were married now, Allah was involved. He opened the book of hadiths again and read, '. . . a woman should never lie with another woman and a man should never lie with another man.' He leaned in again, this time stronger than before, grabbing my face and terrorising me again with his tongue as fat and slimy as a slug and with as much suction as a leech.

I struggled, trying to pull back. When I was finally released, I touched my lips as if to check they were still there. I saw that his eyes had now changed. They were no longer kind and grey, the colour of his pigeons; instead it looked as though black ink had been poured into them. His pupils were exploding.

'Now that we are married, habibbti, I don't think it is a good idea for you to see Ommy again.' He pulled me back into his embrace and again I felt the half-slug half-leech creature sucking everything I had out of me and replacing it with his thick slime. He was imposing his words with his tongue. His speech was tender and soft, tickling my ears; his tongue was a beast, forcing himself onto me. I tried fighting back with my own.

'He lives in Iran now, I don't think he is going to come back.'

Ahmed laughed. 'You think I don't know about the letters you write to him, habibbti?' He started biting my ear. 'And the phone calls?'

'Ow!' I recoiled, holding my ear with my hand.

'Yasminah . . . I didn't mean to . . . I'm so sorry,' he said genuinely, his eyes beginning to fade back to grey. He came in to kiss my forehead before his lips started pecking on my neck like one of his pathetic pigeons. 'I've heard you like it a bit rough,' he said, carrying me back into the bedroom and dropping me on the bed.

I was shocked. His words were matching his tongue now. I was scared. I was excited.

I caught sight of my own eyes in the mirror by the bed. I was enjoying myself.

'Now that you are my wife, no phone calls, no letters to other men, especially Ommy. Ommy is sick in the head. Just because he has lain with you does not cancel out the fact that he has lain with men.' He held my arms tightly, too tightly, just the way that I liked it so that I hissed like a snake. He released one of his hands from my wrist and slapped my face. It felt like heaven and hell at the same time. The sting made my whole body go into default mode, I could feel my brain starting to shut down, as he invaded me. My last thought before my brain completely disassociated itself from my body was that it was absolutely no different when Allah was involved.

Nadia

M az put his phone away and we linked arms. We trudged up the steep grey steps that led to Aunt Yasminah's building, a three-storey converted townhouse, now separated into three flats, just off Shepherd's Bush Road. The entrance to the three flats was governed by a wide red door with a large golden doorknob, so quintessentially English, it felt like we were in a Richard Curtis film. Maz and I snuggled into each other, both feeling more 'Christmassy' than ever. I effortlessly unlocked the main door as if it were my own and Maz followed me, the cheap linoleum floor squeaking as we walked through the hallway to my aunt's door. Turning the key that I had stolen from my dad's briefcase, I looked up at the Arabic calligraphy above her door. The opening surah of the Quran, the Al Fatiha written in gold:

' "Bismil laahir rahmaanir raheemal hamduallilahi rabiil aalameen, arahmanir Raheem," ' I recited at full speed before theatrically curtseying to Maz.

'Maybe you should have done that at our drama school

audition, instead of that monologue you wrote about the masturbating Irish nun!' Maz laughed. 'Oh babes, you are such a good writer. You had the whole room in hysterics.'

'Didn't get in though, did I?' I said as I opened the door, pretending to still hold a grudge about my many failed attempts at getting into RADA.

Maz gave me a consolatory pat on the shoulder before strutting past into the flat. 'Ooooh, look at Auntie Yasminah's bachelorette pad! God! I'm gagging for a drink.'

I let him boom ahead, as I carefully wiped my feet, smelling the familiar rose and cinnamon of my aunt's incense sticks that she was forever burning. The scents permanently lived in the walls alongside the smell of tobacco and charcoal from her shisha. I thought of her now in Mecca, embarking on the pilgrimage of Haj and I with my best friend, about to get twatted on New Year's Eve. I registered a feeling of unease rise within my chest at the thought of being in my aunt's space without her consent.

'Didn't your aunt go to Mecca last year?' Maz called out from the kitchen.

'Yeah,' I called back. Even though it says in the Quran that you only have to go once in a lifetime, my aunt had been going every year for the past five years. She told us she was going for all the people she knew who would never go, which I can only assume was a passive aggressive way of telling us that she was going once for me, once for my dad and three times for Kadijah for going out with a DJ called Christian.

Maz laughed. 'We are going to get shit-faced tonight!' His voice invaded the flat. Filling it with a foreignness I was uneasy with. My memories of Aunt Yasminah's flat were always so peaceful. There was a simplicity to the way she lived. Despite the hustle and bustle of nearby Shepherd's Bush Road, her flat was a sanctuary. Maz, on the other hand, was complicated and manic. I ordinarily loved his dramatics but in Aunt Yasminah's flat it started to feel like noise. Now here, a small part of me began to regret bringing Maz to this third space that was neither my home nor his. But what could I do? I couldn't turn back now; I couldn't let Maz down on New Year's Eve. He never spoke to me about his dad and what was going on at home as his family prepared for the inevitable result of a terminal illness. But, having been his best friend since we were fourteen, I knew that his behaviour wasn't normal. Maz was always the life and soul of the party but now it felt like he was artificially amplifying his personality. It seemed to me he was trying to overcompensate for his loss by making everything else in his life bigger. Now he was camper, louder, goofier, drunker. And so, despite feeling somewhat guilty about invading my aunt's space without her consent, I was conscious of giving Maz the New Year's Eve that he wanted. It was all agreed months ago. We had got tickets to G-A-Y, a club where his favourite band were playing, and needed a place to crash in London. With Aunt Yasminah in Mecca, it would have been silly not to make the most of her empty flat.

'Wine. I need wine,' I said to him. Maz laughed again but I wasn't joking. I needed alcohol to kill the looming sense of panic. I watched Maz as he raided the kitchen cabinets like a soldier pillaging.

I turned my back to him and peered out the window. It was late afternoon but practically dark except the light from a neighbour getting shopping out of his car. I could see the entrance to the Queens Park Rangers' stadium, behind him, reminding me of the Irish side of my identity. My always-drunk Uncle Christopher frequented the football grounds often to participate in his favourite sport: hooliganism. Christopher was Pamela's brother. We called him Christopher and not Chris because he had been to prison. Anyone called Christopher and not Chris tended to have been to prison.

A strange realisation suddenly flushed over me. I looked down and touched the goosebumps on my newly waxed arms as if they were braille. Queens Park Rangers football stadium and my aunt's flat were, I began to see, in a rather symbolic positioning. The very topography seemed to me to be the co-ordinates of my cultural purgatory and liminality. The equator of my cultures, if you will.

'Here ya go, babes.' Maz suddenly appeared beside me by the window and handed me my glass of wine. I gulped it back, trying to grasp the differences between my drunken Uncle Christopher and my pious aunt. Why was my family so full of extremes? I enjoyed the acidity of the wine trickling down my throat where it dropped into the pit of my stomach, dissolving all the dread. I enjoyed the dry tartness it left in my mouth. It made me thirsty for more. With each guzzle, the more parched my mouth got and the harder it was to speak. Alcohol, I had started to notice, muted and minimised me. It began to occur to me that perhaps like Pamela had said about Uncle Christopher, alcohol was not my friend. Or rather it was masquerading as one, like a toxic girl I once knew. A friend who was sweetness and light one minute and then stabbing me in the back the next. But alcohol had been a part of my life for so long, I realised I rarely tasted its sweetness any more. Now all that alcohol left me with was a stabbing pain. I looked at Maz and wondered why his body was not reacting in the same way as mine.

Whenever Maz was drunk his lips got bigger and wetter on account of him talking faster and laughing harder. I touched my own chapped lips and delved into my handbag for my big tub of Vaseline that I had bought roughly twelve years ago for 79p and had used barely a third of. As I dabbed my lips with the emollient, I became fixated on Maz's mouth as he spoke. Like most people I was usually transfixed by his eyes which were 'boyband dreamy' but in my stupor it was his mouth that I was now gazing at. I felt as though it was independent from his body, just a set of lips and chin talking to me like on a trippy children's TV show.

'When I'm in my swanky Parisian Le Coq digs, Nads, we can party all the time. You know Le Coq . . .' Maz rattled on but all I could focus on was a stream of saliva which was flowing from his lip as he fantasised about his new life in Paris.

'Ferme la bouche,' I said, necking back my wine as if it was a tequila shot, 'I get it you love the cock.'

'Le coq!' he laughed. 'Yes, I love L'École Internationale de Théâtre Jacques Lecoq,' he said in a perfect French accent before launching into his Geordie twang. 'Clown school to the likes of you and me, man.'

'Careful!' I screamed again as Maz poured me more wine.

Maz breathed in before shouting, 'Yes, babe!' I could tell he was annoyed. He wanted me to lighten up. He had not accounted for this feeling of unease. Neither of us had. What if we caused some damage? I told myself that we were going out soon, how much damage could we really make to the flat when we were only really using it as a place to crash?

Maz tried his best to relax me by putting on some music. But it only made me silently freak out about the neighbours. I drank more while I watched him dance.

'Why don't you come to get some coq with me, babes? I mean now that you've infected half of Bristol with herpes!'

he shouted over the music. 'We could be a great clowning double act!'

I laughed as I felt the dread twirling in the pit of my stomach again. I drank more in a bid to quell it. Although galivanting off to Paris to become clowns with my best friend was tempting, there was something telling me that I had to stop performing. I didn't know what I wanted to do, really. I thought I was happy working in television, but in reality, it didn't offer much career satisfaction. It just meant fetching teas, coffees and sometimes condoms for editors, producers and directors, or in my case occasionally sleeping with them and then accidentally giving them herpes.

The truth was I didn't know what sort of job I wanted. Other than the fact that I wanted one that meant I could sit down at a desk all day, where my boss couldn't see my screen. Away from the prying eyes of a boss meant that I could mess about on the internet all day. Perhaps I could even while away the office hours and write a script or a play or even become one of those bloggers on MySpace who writes about everything they had eaten for lunch. I shook my head. Who'd be interested in what I put in my mouth anyway? So far I'd eaten a Boots meal deal which consisted of a sweet chilli chicken fajita wrap, a packet of Quavers and a strawberry Ribena with Maz on the train over here. Hardly newsworthy! Even despite the fact that the purchase had awarded me a double points voucher should I choose to spend over £25 on Rimmel's new range of 'age-defying' makeup. I sighed and again I drank, not because I wanted to but because I didn't know what else to do.

Maz was still dancing as he sauntered around the room, sipping wine and checking out my aunt's stuff. He found her Holy Quran alongside a collection of hadiths by her bed and flipped through it like he was perusing a magazine. I took a large gulp and tried to distract him from the Quran by ushering him into the middle of Aunt Yasminah's bedroom. I hoped dancing would loosen me up, but I couldn't let go of this nagging feeling in my mind. If QPR on Ellerslie Road was the equator of my cultures, then this point where I was dancing in my aunt's bedroom was the world breaking in two. I was falling through the crack into my cultural purgatory.

I fell onto my aunt's bed where the Quran and hadiths lay. I, like Maz, also began to flip through them like they were magazines. Half-heartedly reading the scripture while I drank. It should have felt odd drinking alcohol while reading the holy scripture, but it felt completely natural. The dog-eared pages she had marked made me feel like I was reading her diary. I smiled, seeing that she had studiously outlined a hadith in thick red felt tip pen. I read it to try to understand her:

Narrated Ibn Abbas: The Prophet (peace be upon him) cursed effeminate men (who assume the manners of women) and those women who assume the manners of men, and he said, 'Turn them out of your houses.' The Prophet (peace be upon him) turned out such-and-such man, and Umar turned out such-and-such woman.
Sahih Al-Bukhari – Book 72, Hadith 774

I closed the hadith in horror and threw all the scriptures on her bed. Then I looked up at Maz who was shaking his arse at me while mouthing the words to Queen's 'I Want to Break Free'. Downing my wine, I beckoned with my head to the door.

'Come on, let's go out and get drunk! It's New Year's Eve!'

Fatiha

CAIRO, 1951

ف

'Our meeting today is not a congress, but a parliament. A true one! That of women! We are half the nation! We represent here the hope and despair of the most important half of our nation. Luckily, we are meeting at the same hour and the same part of town as the parliament of the other half of the nation. They are assembled a few steps away from us. I propose we go there, strong in the knowledge of our rights, and tell the deputies and senators that their assemblies are illegal so long as our representatives are excluded, that their Egyptian parliament cannot be a true reflection of the entire nation until women are admitted. Let's go and give it to them straight. Let's go and demand our rights. Forward to the parliament!'

Ceza and I were pinching each other's hands throughout the entirety of Doria's speech. I felt her palms dripping with sweat, which she had confessed to me in recent weeks always happened when she was particularly nervous or excited. The heat from them warmed up my own which were always cold. A circulatory problem I had had since I was a child. I looked down at our fingers speaking to each other in ways we would never do vocally. Her own, red and swollen, and mine practically blue. With the exception of my three-year-old son, Aziz, never had I loved and despaired of someone at the same time. I was right about Ceza Nabaraoui. She *was* devious, and I suspected she wanted all the glory for herself, but she had good ideas, and she was funny. She made me laugh until I couldn't breathe and I was snorting coffee out of my nose. I might not like her, I might not trust her, but I couldn't deny being around her was joyous. This complicated relationship that I had developed with Ceza made me think that perhaps there really was some truth in keeping the proverbial enemy close. In a way, didn't many women practise this by marrying men who oppress them, who made them lesser than their potential, which minimises their sense of self? I looked up at the woman on the podium as my heart sang from the crowds. What sort of woman would I have been had I not met Doria, I wondered. A lesser woman than I was now, I suspected. And yet had I not met my husband, dear Ali, would I be more whole? It struck me that it was Doria who filled the side of me that Ali unwillingly extracted from me. It was she and my husband who made me who I am today. A mother, a wife and a woman in my own right. I gazed up in awe at this woman with the fringe that was always so accurately coiffed and with the eyebrows so perfectly plucked, speaking her manifesto, her truth as fearlessly and ferociously as she spoke to me in Paris, the first day we met and went for coffee. Now she was standing at Ewart Hall at the American University in Cairo, the campus not only a symbol for the young women of Egypt, but a symbol of the merging of the Middle East with the west. Perhaps it was a reminder of the fact that we are stronger together than apart; the EFU and the *Bint Al Nil* Union, the old and the new, tradition and modernity.

The microphone squeaked and I noticed that the skin on Doria's creamy cheeks was flushing a tantalising pink as she was leading us women to war. I was reminded of the popular hadith of Aisha who asked, 'O Messenger of Allah, can women engage in jihad? Allah said: "Jihad in which there is no fighting: Hajj and Umrah . . . and because women are not able to fight because they are (physically) weak." ' How can this be true? Doria was one of the strongest people I had ever met. My studies at the Sorbonne had shown that Aisha's so-called hadith was not written by Aisha herself but narrated by Ahmad and Ibn Maajah. Now we were about to prove these men wrong. We were getting ready for battle.

'I said let's go and demand our rights! Forward to the parliament!' Doria said, then she stepped off the podium and Ceza rushed towards her and the photographers to ensure that it was her face as well as Doria's in the papers the next day. I stayed in the background and did what Doria had requested; summon the fifteen hundred or so women who were now on the streets to follow us towards parliament, to keep chanting. I stepped aside, breathed in and took in the crowds. Their placards revealed their social status. Some women were intent on getting the vote – these were the married, affluent and educated women, as it would only be their demographic that would have any chance of getting it. 'The privilege of the rich is that their concerns become less personal, more political,' I had recalled Doria once saying. I wondered if she was talking about herself. It was true, the women from less well-off households were more concerned about issues affecting their personal lives rather than empowering their political selves. The

women who held signs concerning divorce and polygamy laws –
these were the middle-income families, their concerns focused on
improving their personal relationships. And then you had the
poor women, who did not have the privilege of entertaining politically charged demands or personal desires. Their demands were
practical. These poor women who were forced to work for sur-
vival, unlike my mother who did it for self-worth, were yearning
to be paid the same as their male counterparts at last. We had
included all types of women, just like our magazine had.

With sudden passion I hoisted myself up onto the podium
and took the microphone. I felt the flash of photographers on
my face and with it the manic sneer of Ceza.

'Your demands will all be met, just follow us into parliament!' I roared. 'They cannot refuse us any more!' I wanted to
invigorate them and assure them that the bravery it took to leave
their houses, their husbands, their children, their jobs to fight
today was not going to be in vain. Doria clapped and cheered
with approval and delight. I closed my eyes for a second and
smiled. I jumped back down, took Ceza's hand, and with Doria
in front of us and the women behind, we nodded at each other
and began to walk.

A thunderous voice from the crowd suddenly boomed,
'Naguib! Nasser! Listen to our demands! Naguib! Nasser! Represent women!' and with that we were all chanting. I turned
for a second to see Shula, Naila and Rashida marching behind
me. Shula and Rashida's cheeks appeared to be inflamed, their
eyes alight with a look of determination, while Naila was
flushed with fright. Her eyes were wide and unsure like a baby
deer's. She was between Shula and Rashida who were holding
her hand as if she were a little girl. I winked at her and she
finally smiled, taking her hand away from Rashida's for just a

second to shake her arm up towards me, as she too joined in the chanting.

We had already walked from Sheri-Al-Nil Street to Tahrir Square and now we were putting our money where our mouths were, making our way to the House of Representatives, shepherding the crowds via Al-Kasr Al-Aini. I felt electric, like my body was on fire. I felt certain that today was the best day of my life. Having children, marrying Ali – neither could match this feeling; that I was not only making history but saving it. It felt as though we were all collectively giving birth to a new and improved version of Egypt.

Walking through the streets where I had grown up, past the shop which my father once owned and now had been given to Ali elevated me so much I could practically taste the sweet nectar of the sugarcane juice that he sold. My father never understood me in life, but now that he was dead, I felt he was somehow spurring me on. As if Allah had had a word with him, helped him to understand. As we veered into Meret Bashr Street by the Cleopatra Hotel, we passed the laundrette where my mother worked, a job she refused to give up when she married my father. 'For the money!' she would insist. My father tutted, 'Bismillah!', but my brother Jeddy and I knew it wasn't anything to do with economics but everything to do with her self-worth.

The thought of my parents brought a sense of powerless vulnerability I could not control. The tears I hid with my sunglasses. I never thought crying was weak, but men did, and I didn't want some sad journalist claiming that we were hysterical or that it was down to us being on our periods or some other ridiculousness.

As we got to the gate of the House of Representatives, I was relieved to see that the big illustrious black gates, fringed in tacky yellow gold paint, were unlocked and the two security guards could not hold us all back. Several of us rushed the gates like martyrs, clawing onto them, climbing them like trees, letting the rest of us free. However, as soon as we found ourselves inside the great hall, the roar of the battle was reduced to a hum of excitement as fifteen hundred women took in their surroundings, waiting with bated breath to see what would happen next. All that could be heard was the click of our footsteps on the beige ceramic floor. We walked the length of the hall's corridor for what seemed like minutes but could only really have been moments. We saw the door at the end, that led to the chamber of deputies and as we edged closer to it, a man appeared in front of it, finger pointing in the air, about to begin a profound monologue, like the start of a Shakespearean play. Only it wasn't King Lear it was Bottom, for he wasn't the president of the chamber, but merely its vice. Such a prestigious position was awarded to him not by merit but by nepotism – his cousin was Fouad Serageddin, leader of the Wafd party and Interior Minister. Unlike his admirable blood relative, Gamal was a bumbling fool of a man with a shaky voice and an even shakier disposition. I no longer felt nervous. This was child's play. He was the clown and this was a comedy, not a tragedy.

'Ah, ah, ah . . . What do you think you are doing, Madame Shafik?' he asked, mopping his brow with a handkerchief. 'I fear for the legality of your actions.' His voice inflected on the word 'legality' like he had just learned the word.

Doria didn't miss a beat. 'We are here by force of our right.' We all cheered. The sound tickled my spine; I felt warmth rushing down it, despite my cold hands and arms which were sprinkled with tiny goosebumps.

'My husband thinks I'm at the laundrette,' I heard one woman

say loudly. Laughter. 'Mine thinks I'm visiting his mother.'
More laughter.

'Tell your girls to hold their tongues!' Gamal said to Doria.
He tried to look angry and strong, but his trembling hands and
cold sweat were conveying an entirely different narrative.

'For over two years we tried to make ourselves heard in a correct manner. It is time that you listened to us. They will not keep
quiet before I have a promise on your part.' Doria was doing her
threatening voice; it made even Ceza back down and come
towards me. She squeezed my hand again and I squeezed it back.

'Seeing that the president of the chamber refuses to meet our
delegation, we demand to meet the president of the senate and
put forward our grievances.'

'Ah, ah,' Gamal stumbled, 'the president of the senate, I'm
afraid, is ill today, he hasn't come into the office.'

We all groaned. The noise of one and a half thousand women
groaning sounded like a whale. We were beached. We had come
all this way, got this far and the president had pulled a sickie?

'If he is ill, we will call him on the telephone and put forward
our demands then!'

We cheered. She was our Evita. Gamal hung his head before
stepping aside. And then we truly stormed into parliament. Oh,
how glorious it was, to tread on the floors of parliament, to
stamp on the ground of history, to march to the tune of a new
Egypt, to sing our song of protest to recite our political, personal poetry. We were euphoric. An energy that could never be
broken only transferred from woman to woman, from generation to generation, the baton passed, the race won.

We laughed, we cried, we banged our fists on the tables and
howled like animals. All the while, Doria without any hesitation, understanding that the president was ill, went straight for

His Excellency Zaki Al-Urabi Pasha and spoke to him about what we wanted and what we needed and that we would not stop until we got it. Then the room went suddenly quiet, until all that could be heard were shushes and inhalations of breath, as everyone went quiet while Doria telephoned the president of the senate.

'Excellency, we have forced open the door of parliament. I am calling you from your own office. Over a thousand women are with me demanding their political rights, based on your interpretation of Article Three of the constitution, which states that all Egyptians have equal civil and political rights. You yourself have declared that the term "Egyptian" designates women as well as men. Nothing in the constitution stands in the way. Only the electoral law discriminates against women. We are convinced you will not go against your own words.'

We waited in the silence, as he replied.

'Aiywa?' Doria said. We all gasped. 'La, la . . .' We all groaned. 'Aiywa? Shukran, shukran . . .' We let out a collective breath. I embraced Naila, Shula and Rashida who had come from the depths of the crowd to join Ceza and me at the front.

'Aiywa,' Doria said again. I could not yet read her face. She hung up and turned to the crowd and smiled her dazzling smile, the smile that was both wicked and sweet.

'He said he would take our demands personally in hand!'

The crowds cheered as my heart sank. It was something about the word 'personally' that I did not trust. But I told myself I was being cynical, that what we had achieved today was worth celebrating. So, I put my concerns aside and concentrated on the joy of the moment and not the doom that was knotting itself over in my stomach. But for the rest of the day, I couldn't shake the feeling that it all seemed too good to be true.

Yasminah

CAIRO, 1970

ي

I always thought it would be Baba's conservatism that would distil my mother's liberalism. In truth it was her own shame. No matter how much I resented the Egyptian press for their scrutiny towards me, I hated the judgement I felt from my own mother even more. She refused to call Ommy by his name, referring to him now, as my 'strange friend'. She had spent her life's work campaigning for women to have the same rights as men, but now I realised it was all for show. She didn't believe in equality of the sexes. How could she when she spoke so unkindly about Ommy and his equal love for men and women? The truth was that my mother was a fraud. At work with Doria, she was an accomplice to the heroine of Egyptian women's rights while at home she revealed her true self; that she lived in fear of change and did not wholly support it. Gone were the days where I could be as liberated as Aziz at his nightclub or as carefree and playful on the streets as Usman. The thing with Mama was that she never said I couldn't do something, she had just been complicit in men orchestrating restrictions on my life. Of course, she never would admit to her own hypocrisies, pretending that she was on my side and that it was Egypt that was the problem.

She said the local newspapers were sycophants to the president and, given her history, I was low-hanging fruit. Mocking my circumstances gave them the narrative they wanted. That 'emancipation wasn't all it's cracked up to be', and that 'this is what happens when we let our daughters do as our sons do'. She said they preached 'equity not equality' when their only real agenda was humiliation not humility. All the while, she spent her life publicly campaigning for a revolution amongst the sexes, but when Ommy came along who embodied just that, she closed the door in his face, quite literally. As much as she had spent her career standing up to the Egyptian press when it came to their terrible treatment of her best friend, she couldn't do it for her daughter's best friend; or even for her own daughter. At least Baba was upfront about it all. He held his politics and wore his heart on his sleeve, telling me it wasn't right to be fraternising with Ommy with his 'weird sexual behaviour'. Instead, Mama simply told me it was best to disassociate myself from him for fear of Hany's paternity being questioned. The journalist Zafarullah Zerdak had started alluding to such in his column and Mama had used it to her own advantage; a means to rid Ommy from my life completely while maintaining her so-called liberal stance.

I never had any doubt that Hany was Ahmed's despite the gossip. His lack of jawline meant he came out too easily for Hany not to be Ahmed's son, I had joked with Mona as we read Zafarullah's insinuations in the paper that day. She gasped when I wanted her to laugh. I held Hany to my breast, lifted my head back and cackled without her. I had started to find it all quite funny now. How little people thought of me; even my own father's eyes darted between Hany and Ahmed, looking for clues of who his father was. What I once found shameful had melted into embarrassment, which had eventually dispersed into humour. I had become like those mad people who snigger to themselves at the absurdity of life. I knew what I knew. Hany was Ahmed's. Not Ommy's.

Although at times I wished it were true. It would be so much easier to love Hany if he was.

I took him off my breast as soon as Mona left and fed him by the bottle. I increased the volume of the television and found myself falling into a trance. Since he had been born, I had been falling into these long trances where I wouldn't blink much but I could hear people around me.

'. . . it's because she is not sleeping, do not worry. This is very normal,' I had heard Baba say to Ahmed when he had first complained about my sudden trances.

Ahmed didn't tell Baba the truth. That I *was* sleeping. Lots. Ahmed did everything. I had the unusual capability of being able to hear my baby cry and not feel compelled to soothe him. I told Ahmed it would make Hany strong, able to sleep on his own. But Ahmed was as weak as Hany – he couldn't bear him wailing through the night and he didn't understand how I could sleep through it. My body had acquired a strange new faculty since giving birth to block out sound. I could go a whole day barely hearing anything.

I looked at the phone and saw that it was tremoring. I stared at the singer on the television. I was enrapt by her changing facial expression. Her lips soft and quivering then open and trembling. She laughed at the end, as the audience applauded and then cried as they gave her a standing ovation.

The phone eventually stopped tremoring and, with it, Hany's cries. Breathing in, I allowed myself to blink. I then forced myself to look at my child. Hany's big round eyes looked up at me as he came to the end of the bottle. I hated the way he always looked at me as if I were a god. The sheer size of my duty to him overwhelmed me and his neediness repelled me. Like his father, I only touched him out of necessity, never out of affection.

The phone rang again; this time I could hear it and felt an urge to answer it.

'Aiywa?'

''Minah?'

I started to blink excessively. It was Ommy. He had called me almost every day since returning to Iran with Zaki. Despite his contact, I could feel him slipping through my fingers with each phone call. His voice that used to tickle my ears with the besotted ecstasy of lust now felt like a ringing tinnitus; paternal, protective, platonic. I carefully placed Hany into his cot beside me on the sofa.

'Ommy.' My voice was once again clear and loud. I touched my mouth, as if surprised by it.

'Please come to me, everything is wonderful here, you can give Hany a good life here. You live in squalor and shame in Cairo compared to Tehran. No one cares about your past here. No one knows about your past here. Please, 'Minah, please.'

'You are the only one who calls me 'Minah,' I said.

''Minah . . .' I could hear his tears fall. 'Please come to Tehran, please, I miss my silly friend. Zaki too.'

I'd heard him say this a million times. When he left six months ago, he had tentatively suggested that I join him at his father's place, where he worked for the Shah. However, these days he was practically begging me. 'It is a palace!' he'd say. 'You can be treated like a princess in Tehran; in Cairo you are treated like a prostitute.'

But Ahmed had been so excited that I was pregnant. He was even with me in the delivery room. He saw everything. When I couldn't push any longer, Ahmed had pulled Hany out. Removed him from my body.

'Look, look, habibbti,' Ahmed kept saying but I could only look up at the hospital ceiling. I had thought then, that this was the hanan that Baba talked about that would cure my hem. This was what was going to make me OK. But if anything, it made the hem reach deeper into my body, to places I didn't even know existed.

'I can't leave Ahmed. I can't do that to him. He is a wonderful father. I just can't.' Ahmed *was* a wonderful father. He was. Perhaps staying with Ahmed was proof that I *did* love my son. He would have slapped me if he knew about this phone call, just like he did all the other times he caught me with Ommy after I had promised on the Quran never to see him again the night of our wedding. Perhaps Ahmed was right, perhaps I was a disgusting woman who enjoyed bringing shame on our family. I deserved to be slapped. I was a terrible mother, but at least Hany had a good father.

'I would be a wonderful father,' Ommy said, reading my mind. 'Don't you think I will be a better father, with my father working for the Shah of Iran? What sort of father will Ahmed be with his pigeons?!' Ommy laughed.

We always laughed when we talked about Ahmed and his pigeons but this time I didn't. I hadn't developed any love towards my husband but at least I had developed some loyalty.

'You are young, you're barely even eighteen. Go live your life with Zaki – how can we be a proper mother and father to Hany when you are with him?' I could feel myself beginning to crumble all over again.

'They say it takes a village to raise a child. Hany will have you, me and Zaki as well as the love of all my friends, our friends in Iran. What friends have you got left in Cairo, 'Minah? Mona has to meet with you in secret! There are no secrets in Tehran, we all live our truth and there is no shame here. Cairo is stuck in the past, Tehran is the future, habibbti, please . . .'

I clicked the two white buttons to end the call but didn't put the phone down. I needed to hear the long persistent beep, it felt good to hear again. I felt like I could listen to it forever but knew at some moment I would have to hang up. I resisted for several more minutes. The singer was being interviewed by the host, who had just announced they were going into a commercial break. I told myself I would wait until the programme was back and then I would hang up.

The long beep stopped before I could and the line went silent.

I couldn't remember putting Hany down, but he was now gazing up from his cot and no matter how much I tried to engage him he never took his eyes off the ceiling.

Nadia

Aunt Yasminah was at my bedside, sitting on one of those awkward clinical chairs that was the same shade of cerulean as the bed sheets and my hospital gown. The room was so bright I could see the downy hairs on her face and each pore they came out of. She had a slug-like trail of saliva slowly trickling down from the corner of her lip towards her chin. She dozed in and out of sleep, her head drooping, waking herself up each time as the weight of her head bobbed back and forth like a metronome on a piano. Occasionally, she glanced over at my body on the bed in mild panic, checking to see if I was still sleeping, still breathing, still alive. She held a polystyrene coffee cup indented with teeth marks on the rim. Underneath her dental indentations was the provocative plum stain of her lipstick. The very shade of Revlon that Kadijah and I used to try on when we had grown bored of climbing all over her when she was praying. The coveted lipstick we stole from her dresser, staining our lips in the very shade of crimson that straddled the lines between embarrassment and shame.

Now she was much more dishevelled than her usual perfectly made-up face. Her long, wiry hair, which was always off her face in a tight French plait and covered mostly with a hat, was in disarray. She had removed her hat and now stray and frizzy aniseed-coloured threads orbited her head. A whole solar system above her; an astrological realm.

I lay in the hospital bed, completely still, sneaking glimpses of my aunt beside me. A calmness overrode the tirade I felt was imminent. I could feel my injuries but there was no pain, only relief. Like when a baby is crying all night and hears his mother's footsteps at the door.

Making sure my aunt was still dozing, I touched the side of my face that was dry and cracked. It felt like the back of a nail file. I touched the other side. It was hot to touch, inflamed with large bumps. My lips, swollen with multiple cold sores on the verge of exploding like a water balloon.

Minutes later, pain gushed through every crevice. So excruciating it paralysed me. My headache so debilitating I could not wail. My dry mouth so dehydrated I could not groan. My eyes so sore I could not cry. All I could do was lie there. Feeling my own pulse. Absorbing my own heartbeat. Then my ears began to prickle, as if finding a radio wave; they rang like a fire alarm. I began to move, to writhe around and with the movement came the panic. I watched my aunt's faded crimson lips forming a mixture of comforting Arabic words followed by cautious English ones. She wrapped the sheets tighter around my body; they felt stiff and sterile and smelt faintly of bleach.

'Nadia, habibbti . . .' The ringing stopped. The sound was so clear now I could hear the misophonic sound of her tongue hitting her gums. She came towards me and touched my forehead. I flinched. Her thick pillared brows furrowed. It was the same face she made when she collected us from Heathrow Terminal 4, returning from Saudi Arabia, and the same expression when she failed to see the funny side after Maz's STI prank on Christmas Day. I remembered the hadith of Sahih Al-Bukhari she had highlighted in thick red felt tip pen. I threw up onto my blue bedsheets, a dirty weed colour.

'Auntie!' I heaved again but this time nothing came out. I wanted to ask why was she here, but instead I asked where my parents were.

'It's OK, you had an epileptic seizure at my flat, habibbti, it's OK,' she said. 'Maz and your parents are outside getting drinks.'

'Oi! Oi! What a way to start the new year, Nads! I would have bet money it would have been a police station, but hospital, touché!' Maz cackled for several uncomfortable moments while my eyes tried to get him to stop. I saw my aunt flinch and look down at the floor. She hates him, I thought. She hates him because he is gay. My parents followed sheepishly behind him. Maz held a stack of polystyrene cups and handed them out as if they were shots.

'Get that down yoursen'!' he said, his Geordie accent always thicker when he had a larger audience. He reached for his satchel underneath my bed, fingering around for his Kylie Minogue fluorescent pink hip flask, the one he had purchased when we had been shopping in Urban Outfitters, the same day he found out his father's cancer was terminal. Ever since he had carried it everywhere with him, always full of gin. He poured it into his coffee while my parents pretended not to notice. They both handed me a stack of leaflets. 'Here you go,' Pamela said, leaning in and kissing me on the cheek, the way she used to do when she was tucking me in as a child. I looked down at my lap. 'Controlling your Epilepsy', one of them read.

My parents told me that if it weren't for Aunt Yasminah coming back from her Haj early, things might have got worse. I was told that Maz was too drunk to think straight. 'No pun intended,' he had added. To which you could see the thoughts running through my dad's head like rats scurrying across a train-line. He always thought Maz was my boyfriend so references to Maz's homosexuality only confused him. My dad was the sort of guy who couldn't fathom having friends of the opposite sex.

'You fell on Auntie's radiator in her bathroom and started going into a seizure. The radiator was really hot, and you were flailing around it, burning and bruising your face.' Pamela could barely finish the sentence before weeping dramatically and turning away. She was worried I had ruined my face. I closed my eyes to stop them rolling. I was trying to process it all and didn't want to get distracted by her theatrics.

She eventually stopped crying when the doctor came in. She looked like both a young student and a pencil. Everything about her was elongated, like she had been physically stretched. Her long lanky body towered over us like an air puppet at a car showroom. I couldn't take my eyes off the tip of her nose, which was so sharp that every time she propped her glasses up I thought she was going to draw blood. She told me that I was to go on medication and that I wasn't allowed to drink alcohol ever again.

'Like you shouldn't drink on antibiotics?' Maz nudged me. My aunt looked down at her nails. I attempted a smile. In my head I already had my Uncle Christopher's words in my ears, 'doctors are full of shit, I can still drink', and my fingers were practically already googling 'ways to still drink on epilepsy medication'. I got this, I thought. I don't look for problems, I look for solutions. If someone tells me I can't do something, it just makes me want to do it even more. Anarchy and rebellion were in my blood.

The doctor looked at me as if she was reading my mind. She took her glasses off and I realised her nose was a perfect isosceles pyramid. I wanted to measure the angles with a protractor. I wanted to make sure each angle at the base was precisely sixty degrees. It was as if calculating the sum of her parts distracted me from the seriousness of what she was saying. 'Nadia, this is not like drinking a few glasses of wine on antibiotics; this is affecting your brain. If you combine this drug with large amounts of alcohol, you could risk going into a seizure and severely disabling yourself, or worse, dying. I say to patients if you absolutely have to have a drink, then drink like you are pregnant – 125 millilitres of wine a day tops.'

'Nads has 125 millilitres of wine for breakfast,' Maz joked.

Still no one laughed. Suddenly my aunt ran out of the room, trying to hide her watery eyes, mumbling something about the vending machines and getting a 'Dr Bepper' as she called it.

When she was gone, I sat there stunned. I don't think I'd drunk *just* 125 millilitres of wine ever.

'The only time I've measured out that much liquid in millilitres is at airports,' Maz joked again. I saw that his eyes were popping out of his head the way they did in our drama classes at university when he had forgotten his lines. The silence was hindering the efficacy of his main coping mechanism for any discomfort that he had started to implement since his dad's diagnosis. Thank goodness his clowning course at Le Coq in Paris was imminent.

'You really must be very careful with alcohol, I can't stress enough, no more than 125 millilitres of wine, and even that . . . Total abstinence is advisable.'

This was the beginning of the end, I thought. My raison d'être, the thing that punctuated my day, was being taken away from me.

I might as well die.

The doctor went on for another few minutes about MRI scans before showing me an x-ray of my brain. Of course, my dad made a joke about being surprised that I had one and everybody laughed. But as I looked round the room at Pamela, my dad and Maz, their bodies tickling and trembling, I saw that they weren't really laughing at all; their bodies were merely releasing trauma.

Fatiha

CAIRO, 1951

ف

'The feminist movement is a plot organised by the enemies of Islam and the Bolshevik-atheists, with the object of abolishing the remaining Muslim traditions in this country. They have used women, Muslim women, as a means to achieving their goal. They made the woman leave her realm, which is the home, conjugal life, maternity. They have followed these hypocrites by participating with them in acts of charity which are nothing other than evil and corrupt. Not content with their exhibitions, hospitals and dispensaries, now they have created associations and parties that strive to demand equality with men, the limitation of divorce, the abolition of polygamy and entry into parliament. Your majesty, protect the Orient and Islam!' I screwed up the newspaper reporting the scathing words from the Association of Sunnites against our cause. They had set up an anti-feminist petition, two days after we had stormed parliament. 'Can you believe these arseholes?' I said to Ali as he juggled cutting up balls of tam'eya and dropping them onto Yasminah's plate while feeding

Aziz spoonfuls of molokhia. I half thought about going into the kitchen and retrieving a knife for him to use to cut up the tam'eya instead of Yasminah's flimsy little plastic fork. I perhaps *should* have intervened, but Aziz was in the midst of using his spoon as a slingshot and as a consequence, globs of the slimy green soup were now flicking across our dining table.

Since the authorities had called us to trial, my mind had been a whirl. I was overwhelmed with a mixture of joy at the sensation we had caused and despair. All the girls were incredibly anguished that our leaders had gone back on their verbal promise. And now to add insult to injury we were being charged with illegally entering parliament.

'Bismillah. What an arsehole,' Ali said unconvincingly. I wondered if he had even been listening to me recite Muhammad Hamid al-Fiqi's petition calling for Egypt to 'Keep the Women in Check' reported in this morning's *La Bourse Egyptienne*.

'I hate how he has brought Islam into it, as if it is Allah's wish that women be second-class citizens,' I spat. 'And comparing us to communists and atheists? It's scaremongering, propaganda, false interpretation of the facts . . .'

'Mama.' Yasminah put her arms up. I resisted her for a second. I had on my best suit for our meeting with our defence lawyer, Mufidah Abdul Rahman, and I did not want Yasminah's slobber all over it. I sighed before taking her into my arms, bobbing her up and down on my lap. Mufidah would understand, she had nine children herself – four of which Doria had told me she had given birth to while studying for her degree at Cairo University – but still, I wanted to look sharp. Sharp. I was about as sharp as the plastic fork Ali was using.

I leaned my face into Yasminah's soft curls and took in her smell, enjoying a few moments of tenderness.

'Well, you have been getting mostly positive press. What about that one in the *New York Times*, what was the headline again? Oh yes, "Nahas Pasha's Snub to Suffragettes"!'

I smiled at my husband's attempt to placate me. 'That was the London *Times*, habibbi. The *New York Times* went with "Rising Feminism Bewilders Egypt".'

The way the western press was reporting us was both supportive and exasperating. The articles were indeed in commendation of our feminist exploits but at the same time scathing of our country, our culture, our religion.

' "Bewilders Egypt",' I muttered mostly to myself, as Yasminah fiddled with the buttons on my suit. 'I don't like the word "bewilders". It's implying that Egypt is in some way not intelligent enough to even grasp the concept of a woman wanting her rights.'

'Well . . .'

'It's not that the men of Egypt do not understand what we want, it's that they do not *support* what we want . . .'

Ali sighed.

'Sorry,' I said, realising I had cut him off again. No wonder he didn't listen to me, I thought. I didn't let him get a word in. In recent weeks I had helped Doria to write so many speeches I had forgotten the art of conversation. It involved listening and being silent. Two things that were no longer in my wheelhouse.

I leaned across to him, dodging Aziz's aim, and touched his hand. He responded by closing his eyes for a second and bowing his head. He understood. I was appreciative that he had got his brother Fadi to run the shop for a while so he could do the majority of the childcare while I worked. Ali might not have the words to support me, but he had the actions, unlike our prime minister. There I go again, I thought. Even my inner monologue is politically charged.

I looked down at Yasminah's angel-like face, reminding myself that I was a mother outside of all this. Her big eyes glowed up at me. I was doing this for her, I reminded myself. Then I looked at Aziz and his long, thick eyelashes and thought the same – I'm doing it for him. I wanted my son to grow up with respect for women, knowing that they are his equal.

I gazed at Yasminah again, her face practically immaculate for a two-year-old; then I looked back at Aziz, whose face looked as though he was in a war zone. It was stained a camouflage green from the slimy spinach dish. I wondered how my two children could be so different. I touched my belly and prayed that Aziz was a fluke and the new one on the way would be more like their sister than their brother.

'Yallah, I must go, masalam,' I said, gulping down the last dregs of my tea, grabbing my handbag and kissing Yasminah before dropping her into her father's lap.

I walked down the stairs from our apartment to the street and before leaving I covered my face. I was in no mood to be recognised. What wasn't mentioned at dinner was the amount of press we were getting that wasn't anything to do with the cause at all. Some of the lower-grade publications had been choosing to report not on our political demands but on our personal appearance.

They were saying smutty things about our bodies, denigrating our looks, commenting on our clothes and rating us. Putting us in some sort of beauty contest that none of us had chosen to enter! Doria was of course deemed the most beautiful, but I had been a little saddened to find that Ceza, despite being over seventeen years older than me, had been ranked before me. Ali had tried to console me, saying it was because the man who wrote the article entitled 'The Prettiest Feminist: Who is the lesser of the uglies?', was Ceza's husband's second cousin twice removed or some ridiculousness. I despaired of these lesser-known, smuttier publications. There was a whole article in *The Cairo Quarterly*, for example, all about the shoes worn by the women at *Bint Al Nil*! Shoes! We were not storming the parliament for a woman's right for shoes! It was embarrassing and belittling of the work we were doing. Covering my face was the best option so as not to fuel any more distracting nonsense. If only I could cover my shoes, I thought, as I looked down to see that my boots had been a casualty in the Great Molokhia War at dinnertime. I flagged down the bus, despairing of my grubby son.

The hour-long bus journey to Doria's was the one part of my day where I allowed myself to be silent. We mostly met at night for our meetings. And so when I got on the bus it was that perfect mix of day and night. The mellow orange dusk calmed Cairo's hyperactivity. The roads were still as jammed and claustrophobic as during the day, but at this time, the morning buzz was replaced with a quiet acceptance of the city's lack of capaciousness. That there wasn't room for us all, but we'd all at least try to get to our destination in as peaceful a manner as possible.

I listened to the hum of the bus as it went from Heliopolis to Zamalek. From the urban east of Cairo to its affluent west. Before getting to its halfway point at the Mansheyet El Bakry Hospital it was awash with largely late-night factory workers beginning their commute and beggars with babies often at their breast.

Today was no exception. A child no older than fourteen came

to stand by my side. She told me she needed some money to feed her two children. I listened to her story and gave her five piastres and the bread and halowa from my bag. She thanked me, her eyes slightly softening in relief, before demolishing half the bread in one bite and rushing to the two small children she had left at the front of the bus. Another beggar came to me, encouraged by my public generosity, and tried to sell me five almonds. I pretended to think about it for a moment, inspecting the almonds before nodding and paying her.

'Shukran,' she whispered, counting out the almonds to place in my hand. I stopped her and told her I no longer wanted them. She groaned and began to return my money. I stopped her. 'La, la . . .' I told her softly.

She was confused for a moment before realising I never wanted the almonds in the first place. 'Yerhmek Allah,' she said, blessing me.

I wished I could give her more, but we weren't making as much money this month because we were paying Fadi to work in the shop and on top of that we had another baby on the way. Passing the Bab Al-Louq neighbourhood, the roads began to widen and with it my mind became less cluttered. I could almost see the bridge to Zamalek on the horizon. We passed the Ramses Railway Station and, as always, I thought of my mother who told me the story of Huda Shaarawi. How in 1922 coming back from a conference in Rome, she removed her veil and caused a sensation across the land, with many other Egyptian women, including my mother, following suit. I touched my own veil, draped across my face, the material tickling my cheeks. Now I was wearing the veil as an act of empowerment.

'Yerhmek Allah,' the beggar said again, and I reached out to touch her hand.

I wanted to tell her that I was on my way to a meeting that would ensure that her children would not lead the life that she led. That I was already working to help better these poor women's situation by going to this very meeting. A meeting that would help overturn our prime minister's decision to overlook our demands. That we would help to eradicate such poverty by educating women and thus fuelling the Egyptian workforce. Just like Qasim Amin's manifesto *The Liberation of Women* in 1899 asserted. The answer to all of Egyptian's socio-economic problems could be solved by liberating Muslim women, through education and self-employment. Imagine if half the population had an equal participation in Egypt's economy? I felt a spriteliness return to my veins, which was promptly flattened when we passed the Ministry of Interior that separated the Bab Al-Louq neighbourhood from Tahrir Square. The sight of the illustrious, overly decadent building in contrast to the modest residential buildings on the same street only highlighted the disparity between the humble citizens of Egypt and its law enforcement.

The Ministry of Interior, the centre of Cairo's tyrannical policing government, riled me. This was the very institution that was charging *Bint Al Nil* and the EFU with going against the laws of the land and daring to want something more than the status quo. Doria called our cause 'pursuing the absolute'. It was a calling from Allah, it transcended our sense of self-importance or self-worth or political agenda or even the very thing that men thought we were doing it for: power. This wasn't an exercise to expand our egos; it was a mission from God. So sure, Doria was right about our work – it *was* absolute.

∿

Mufidah Abdul Rahman's feminine heart-shaped face and delicate features offset her brashness. I walked into the meeting a little later than I had intended, blaming the Cairo traffic when, really, I should have been blaming Aziz. I had got off the bus two stops early to find a shop to buy some tissues and to ask for some water to scrub the green stain off my boots.

'It appears to me there is no crime in going to lodge the petition in parliament,' she said as I walked into Doria's office. Her housekeeper had let me in the side entrance, and I had said a quick hello to Nur before rushing up the stairs to join the meeting.

Only Naila looked towards me as I walked in. She smiled and patted the space next to her for me to join. The others remained silent and still, transfixed by Mufidah.

'As regards to having forced the gates: we know that the public is not banned from parliament.'

'Exactly,' Doria concurred.

'Sessions may be observed for people who have an invitation but is there a law to say that one should have an invitation? Such a law does not exist!'

'Yessss . . .' Naila said, clenching her fist and tugging it into her chest in celebration.

'The women went to parliament to demand their property, to demand the right which is denied them and which they cannot obtain by other means. The door of parliament ought to be open like other doors – those of factories, of the professions and of higher education. All women, literate or not, have the same right as men to participate in the social and political life of the nation.'

The telephone rang as if in applause. Mufidah was already the first woman to practise law in Cairo. If we gave her this case, she would be the first woman to plead a case before a military court in Egypt. We had spoken to many other lawyers, mostly women who had come rushing to defend us, but none had been as convincing and as self-assured as Mufidah. She was the one.

"Allo?' Doria answered the telephone and our eyes, which had been momentarily locked on Mufidhah, suddenly darted to their usual position, fixed on our leader.

'King Farouq?' she gasped. We all took in a large inhalation of air. Naila, an audible gasp.

Moments later Doria hung up. Despite her lack of sleep, her eyes had remained permanently alert and now they were even wider than normal.

'As a symbol of solidarity, four female Egyptian university students submitted a petition written in their own blood to King Farouq, demanding . . .' Doria tailed off as she collapsed on the floor. We all rushed towards her except Mufidah who remained calm, her only sign of emotion a micro movement indicated by the squeak of the leather armchair that she sat on.

We helped Doria up. '. . . a symbol of solidarity for our demand for women's rights,' she said finally.

This time we didn't even gasp. We couldn't believe the unbounding female support from our nation.

Doria sat down again and taken over by emotion at the students' gesture, she roared, 'I assume full responsibility for what has happened, and I am ready to go to jail for the cause!'

We all reached over to embrace Doria, to touch her hand at the very least.

Meanwhile, Mufidah sat back, saying, 'It won't come to that, Doria, it won't come to that, not with me on board.'

Yasminah

ي

'I told you I was right! Oh Iran, my beautiful country, Iran, I love you!' Ommy boomed into my bedroom holding the newspaper; he stopped at the edge of my bed and brought the pages to his lips and kissed them. I scurried under the sheets, as the sunlight hit my eyes, my hangover simmering on a low heat. By the afternoon it would be stewed.

'Go away, please, I need privacy. How do you know I've not got someone under the sheets with me?' I moaned, sitting up and pulling a face before letting the creases of a smile form. Ommy knew I loved him coming into my room each day, stroking my forehead as he read the paper to me, cigarette between his teeth while I rested on his naked chest. I strummed his alignment of washboard muscles as if he was a guitar while he sang to me.

I looked up at the man I was so sure I was in love with all those years ago and blushed for my past self. It was true, I had fled Egypt to be with him in the hope that he would love me, not platonically as he always said but romantically: like he once

151

had. I flirted with the preposterous fantasies in my head that Zaki was just a phase he was going through and that he would eventually see me as his real future.

Yet something began to change in me upon arriving in Tehran. Perhaps it was a blessing leaving Hany behind, for I started to see myself in different ways. I had turned my back on my marriage and my child, and with that a new way of living devoid of societal expectations suddenly became possible. Ommy's friends, now my friends, intrigued me with alternative philosophies of what makes a life. What if my one aim in life wasn't to find a man and settle down? What if there was something more for me? Of course, my mother had always told me the perils of relying on a husband for money and encouraged me to forge my own career. But it always came under the expectation that I *would* find a man and her advice was always how to juggle a career alongside that narrative. There was never a suggestion of another way, a life without marriage, a life without that juggle, a life without a man.

Here I was in a progressively liberal country, a free individual without anyone's expectations thrust upon me. I was not 'Fatiha Bin-Khalid's daughter' or 'Ahmed's wife' or 'Hany's mother' or even, as I had so longed for, 'Ommy's girlfriend'. I was just Yasminah. Yet despite this sudden liberation, I didn't know who Yasminah was. Nor did I know what she wanted, or what she desired.

Tehran, I quickly, saw was the place to find this out. Here I could breathe. Egypt's constant and corrosive condemnation of me had made it impossible. Here I wasn't only an unknown to Tehran, I was unknown to myself. It was the place for me to be reborn; I sensed the country forging a revolution inside me. With each day here, I felt myself slowly shedding my old persona and getting closer to who I really was meant to be, deep in my heart. I never once stopped loving Ommy, I just began to love him in different ways. But perhaps the most interesting thing was that this different way of loving Ommy encouraged me to love others in ways I had never imagined doing so before.

'Mohammad Reza Pahlavi, Shah of Iran, I salute you for announcing in this very paper, the *Alik Daily*, a same-sex wedding!' Ommy giggled; his delight was captivating. I could feel his excitement begin to rub off on me, my hangover beginning to subside. I hit him with my newfound energy.

'Oh my, wallahi!!' I said, grabbing the paper off him to see it for myself. It was a tiny article, but an article no doubt. All we had ever wanted was to normalise our lifestyle. Ommy had always promised me Iran was more forward thinking than Cairo, but I had not expected this.

'This is almost as controversial as when his father did the mandatory unveiling of women, the blessed Kashf-e hijab!' Ommy played his fingers on my head like a piano. 'Get your miniskirt on, 'Minah, let's take to the streets, I'll ring Zaki, you can try Farah. Are you still . . . ?' He looked at me, eyebrow raised, before letting out another chuckle, but the mention of her name penetrated me like a papercut. 'I feel a revolution coming along!' he sang.

I smiled and bit my lip. I was trying to understand it all. It seemed a world away from Cairo, where we had been made to feel like animals. Now Ommy was even talking with some of our friends at university about setting up a gay rights group. A group where we could be proud, not ashamed, of who we were. He told me I should be president given that my thesis was asserting gay rights in Islam. Ommy said that activism was in my blood and that I should channel all my obsession for Farah into politics. I wasn't so sure. Despite my provocative thesis, after everything I now craved privacy not publicity.

The word 'gay' still left me discombobulated. I wanted to sit with the word, privately on my own, to grow accustomed to its meaning, to try it on like a t-shirt I hadn't bought yet. To rent it like a car, to view it like an apartment, to see its possibilities for me. It seemed that there was no interim with the word, no dress rehearsal; it was all or nothing. You either kept the word locked and buried in your heart, chained in privacy, the dry desert of discretion and punctuated only by a mirage, the odd illicit rendezvous which felt more like dreams than reality. Or you were out, proud, loud, practically bellowing it on the streets. The word became impersonal; it became your political party. It defined you in every which way. It was quite tiresome. Did I really want to enter into politics like my mother, when all I really wanted was a simple courtship with Farah? Oh, dear Farah. I had lost almost all hope. Her heart was locked and the key thrown overboard into the vast sea of heteronormativity. I would understand it in Egypt, but in Iran? No one cared if you were gay here. Even the *Alik Daily* article about same-sex weddings was nowhere near as salacious as the smut that Zafarullah Zerdak insisted on writing about me. I was still holding the newspaper in my hand, and as my head battled my hangover my heart was still dancing. It was a small and considered column celebrating the union on page eleven, an entire world away from the Cairene columns which crucified me day after day. I sighed, covering myself with the duvet and succumbing once again to my hangover. Each day in Tehran was a blessing, I thought, as parts of my brain felt like they were shattering into a million pieces.

In my daze, I thanked Allah for the freedom that I now had;

the lack of shame walking down the street, the absence of rumours and wagging tongues was a blessing. But the oppressive voices of my mother and Ahmed still existed in my head along with my dear baby Hany. He was my only regret. The only one I hated leaving behind. I wanted so badly to go back and get him. I didn't initially, my hem was too much for me to think straight. But now I felt clearer. I had written several letters to Mama, asking, but nothing. I tried calling but as soon as she heard my voice she would hang up.

I loved my new life in Tehran, but I still felt the shame of the past few years which stamped down my dizzy freedom like a paperweight. It brought me right back down to earth. I hated that the only way to free myself was to run away.

'We must go dancing at Rainbow tonight – let me call the guys!' Ommy said, ruffling my head as he got up to open the curtains, letting all the light in the room, exposing the grandiosity of my bedroom. Three years and it still shocked me every morning, the decadence of it all was vulgar. My bedroom was practically the size of our whole apartment in Cairo. It made me sick to my stomach that I was living this life and my son was living with Ahmed. My stomach groaned every morning with the unfairness of it all and churned with the shame of it. There is no worse shame. I could handle any other kind and lock it up in my heart and swallow the key and feel it erode in my stomach . . . but I could never escape from the shame that I was a bad mother. I was still a mother and I could never shed that part of myself. I couldn't bury it, try as I might. I could only put other things on top of it to distract me. Like my university thesis, my friends, Ommy, and being free.

'I'm not sure everyone is as pro-Shah as you, Ommy,' I said, reaching for my cigarettes. 'Even our friends are only pro-westernisation to a certain point. Abdullah, Yasmeen and Farah were saying just the other day, in fact, after our lecture, that the Shah's perceived enforced westernisation is something of an oxymoron. For the very idea of westernisation is to liberate Iranians . . . but to force sections of society who don't want to be liberated? Forcing Iranians who believe that westernisation is antithetical to Islam?' Aisha, the maid, had brought in the coffee. I thanked her with my eyes and took a sip, knowing the black medicine would add more fuel to my political pontifications.

Ommy took a gulp, preparing to retaliate.

'The Islamists are happy to accept westernisation when it comes in the form of science and technology, when it comes to making money, when it comes to new ways of extracting oil, for example . . . but they are not willing to accept westernisation when it comes to the arts, or culture or individualism.'

'I think you are perhaps confusing westernisation with commercialisation. Look, all I'm saying is, I know we have your dad's work with the Shah to thank for living the way we do but all that shines isn't gold. It's undeniable that the Shah is distributing oil wealth unfairly and the SAVAK, these secret police, are controlling the Iranians' self-expression – no one can freely say anything bad about him. He is all for freedom, but only what he constitutes as freedom. It is not Iranian liberty; it is *his* liberty!'

Ommy had his eyes closed as I was speaking. He brought his thumb and index finger to his brows and inhaled. I waited for him to release his hands and begin his attack but instead he remained silent.

I smiled to myself, having had the last word, and looked down at the street below. It had the same hectic pace as Heliopolis, but everything felt sharper. The people, the cars, the roads were cleaner and brighter. I could see from my window the Milad Tower that Ommy had told me was a symbol of Iran. A tower of communication. This is what Iran symbolised for me too. My voyage here had opened up a communication for the first time with myself. I had finally found out who I was. Not who others thought I was.

I sipped more coffee and thought about Hany. I had begun to wonder who he was. What did he look like? What was his life like? Was he happy? It was as if finding out who I was afforded me new space in my mind for Hany. *I have a son!* I would think to myself. *I left him behind!* I would think again. Then these thoughts would seep into my veins and I would feel my heart start to ache. Perhaps Usman could help. He was always Mama's favourite. I knew that Ahmed let Mama and Baba see Hany. If I could just get Usman to convince Mama to take Hany and his passport. I stopped my far-fetched fantasy. Fathers or male guardians had all the rights at airports. No one could take Hany out of the country without Ahmed's consent. I succumbed and let warm tears run down my cheek. They took some of the coldness away from me.

Fatiha

CAIRO, 1975

ف

The most painful moments in my life have always been silent. When I came home from school and couldn't hear my father's slurs, hisses or curses at my mother, I felt the numbness that silence emits. Or when I couldn't hear Shula's baby cry after she gave her final push. That was when I realised the grief that silence emits. And now I could no longer hear the ferocity in Doria's voice; the cheers from the crowds now ghosts, the clicks of photographers' cameras as she went for her long walks along the Nile, absent.

I liked my life to be loud. Noise meant something was happening, whether it was good things or bad things, as long as it was loud then it was exciting. I wanted to live a life that was kinetic not paralytic. That was active not passive.

Perhaps that's why I adored the liveness and loudness of my beloved city of Cairo, and secretly detested visiting my brother's farm on the outskirts of Alexandria. My little brother got strength from the quiet of his camels and the docility of his donkeys out on his wheat and tomato fields, equal distance between the Coptic monasteries and the El Qaed Ibrahim Mosque. His day punctuated only by the faint sounds of the ringing of the monastic bells and the distant call to prayer. For me this quiet no-man's land was torture. Whenever I got back to Cairo it felt like I could breathe again.

Now with Yasminah in Tehran, Ussy pursuing his PhD in molecular chemical warfare in London and Aziz's club affording him the ability to buy a ridiculously ostentatious mansion in Zamalek, I had what Doria's English friend called an abandoned nest. But although I missed the buzz of a busy household, it was Doria and *Bint Al Nil* that made the silence particularly palpable. *Bint Al Nil* had now been completely shut down by Nasser, who had also ordered that Doria be silenced in the press, her legacy effectively obliterated and written out of history. I had my work at Cairo University of course but marking Islamic Studies essays with titles that stated the obvious, like 'Why there is only one God', wasn't exactly as challenging as writing articles for *Bint Al Nil* magazine with titles like 'Communist Colonialism' or 'The Problems with the Egyptian Family'. Life wasn't only quieter now, it felt as though it hadn't even happened. I found myself thankful for Aziz who had begun to father children at an alarming rate. My grandchildren, these little terrors, helped to occupy my mind on the rare days he came over with them, usually unannounced.

My grandchildren were the substitute for the chaos I so missed and so craved. I lapped up Aziz's little adorable snot bags. I gave them more love than I ever gave him, for now they were the only things that gave my life its loudness. Of course, there was also little Hany, who I saw as often as Ahmed would allow. But he was such an eerily introverted little boy, sometimes he disconcerted me. I expected so much energy when he came, and instead, I often handed him back to Ahmed feeling deflated.

'Sabah al kheir, habibbti,' Ali said, walking into my office. I jumped and began busying myself, opening drawers and books and realigning the paper on my typewriter.

'Sabah al kheir,' I said, looking him in the eye for just a second before busying myself again. I cleared my throat as if to indicate that I had a great deal of work to do, and he sighed and left. I could hear him in the kitchen, and I was thankful for the aggressive sounds of the pots and pans, the sticky sound of the fridge opening and shutting and Ali's coughing which had grown more guttural with the years. He was starting to sound like Mr Yaghoubi downstairs. The thought made me almost shiver. Did this mean I was Mrs Yaghoubi? I tapped my red nails over and over again on the wood of the desk and tried desperately to compose myself. The brightness of my nails awakened me. Red was my colour. Red was loud. Red was dangerous. Perhaps that's what I missed most of all, the danger.

I touched the keys of my trusty typewriter, as if trying to absorb its past glory. The days where I always saw red. I closed my eyes and saw myself years ago, savagely typing, viscously writing, my heart palpitating, hot blood flowing through my veins, feeling as if time was running out and that my life's meaning was on those pages. The glorious black type showering the whiteness of the page like the sumac and black sesame I ground into rice. Words were spice. Words were everything. I opened my eyes again and stared at the blank sheet of paper. Its glaring whiteness antagonising me. I wanted to write. I wanted so desperately to write. I needed it. Writing filled the silence in my head. But for the first time I had nothing to say and no one to say it to. I switched the radio on as if it would also switch something else on inside me. I listened for a while, staring out the small window. I saw that Ali had gone down to the ice cream parlour and wondered why I hadn't heard him leave. He was sitting at the tables overlooking the markets on the street, talking to the owner, Walid, while they both shared a sweet tea and talked shop. Ali's heart troubles meant that Fadi had now become a necessity, opening and closing the shop most days. For this reason, I knew that Ali, like me, had a similar silent void in his life too. I felt guilty that I didn't allow him in, where we could fill each other's silences. But for me the only person who could ever do this was Doria and he knew it.

I stared again at the blank sheet of paper before gazing at the pile of books beside my typewriter.

I looked back down at Ali and Walid. I thought about joining my husband, taking his hand and going out for pastries at El Fayoumi's like we did in the very early days of our courtship. The days where we had so much to say to each other, both our hearts beat faster from speaking in such frenzy. The days where he made me laugh so much, I cried until I couldn't breathe and begged him to stop, wiping tears from my eyes. Now he had stopped but there was too much silence between us for me to ask him to start again.

I sighed and plucked a book from the pile and attempted to read. It was my favourite, *Tahrir al mara'a* (Qasim Amin's *Liberation of Women*). But the words all blurred together, and I couldn't focus. I tried another book, this time Doria's novel about the slavery of a woman to a man entitled *L'Esclave Sultane* (*The Slave Queen*). Again, the same thing happened: words that I ordinarily so readily and greedily consumed failed to satiate me.

I lit up a cigarette and gazed out at Ali again. He was laughing at Walid regaling a story, emphatically using his hands and making wide gestures with his legs and arms. Ali continued to laugh. But I knew he wasn't really laughing because his eyes were full and round and watery, not closed and squinting and scrunched up like they were when he was really laughing. I hadn't seen him laugh loud and long since Yasminah had left.

With that, a sudden energy propelled me to open the bottom drawer of my desk. It was the drawer that I never used because it was wonky and hard to open. Sometimes you had to wrestle with it and had to tug hard before it would fly out at you. Perhaps that's why I had stuffed it inside that very drawer that day, as a deterrent to stop me from reading it. But now, seeing the sadness and lack of life in Ali's eyes, I felt compelled to contend with the wonky drawer and read the thesis that Yasminah had sent me from Tehran many months ago.

I got down on my hands and knees, expecting to have a fight with the drawer, preparing to use the powers of manipulation to negotiate a smooth withdrawal. But to my surprise it opened effortlessly. Ali must've fixed it for me, I thought. I looked down and there it lay, the pages only slightly crumpled from the international post. I picked it up as if it were a baby in a drawer not a paper, my hands linked together scooping it up and then just staring, staring at the title page and seeing my daughter's name next to the word 'gay'. I couldn't do it. I couldn't read it. But this time I didn't stuff it back in the drawer. I placed it next to my typewriter and rang Doria. Doria would read it for me.

Perhaps it was all a ruse to get Doria to come to our apartment. It had been years since she had come over. Nasser had ordered the cancellation of her name in the media and the press but it felt as though she had also cancelled herself. She retreated from everything. Her life was now lived in silent solitude. The worst thing was that nothing riled her any more. I spoke to her about the unfairness of Nasser's regime, and she would just nod and shrug her shoulders. Injustice no longer rattled her. But I knew there was something about Yasminah's inequity that had always fascinated her.

I could hear her now, her shoes clicking up the flights of stairs. They were slower than years before when she would run up to me with gusto. But the anticipation of seeing her still made me giddy. It felt as though the volume in my head was amping up again.

I could hear her lingering outside our apartment now and see her iconic silhouette through the tinted glass. I opened the door and took her in. Her perfume momentarily dizzying me as it always did. Her big eyes, albeit with slightly less sparkle, still mesmerising me, her doughy skin beguiling me. I kissed her on both cheeks and heard the sounds of our city again. I was breathing longer, deeper breaths now. My hands were perspiring; I touched my thumbs with my fingers and felt the moisture, the lubrication, the blood pumping, the life we lived together!

'Salamwaylaykum, habibbti,' I said, gesturing for her to sit down.

'Waylaykum wasalam,' Doria said, hanging up her coat and then brushing past me and into my office.

'Doria, man fadluk, please, sit down first!' I yelled, following her.

'La, la, la, fin Yasminah's thesis?' she asked.

We were standing so close to each other now, in my poky little office, so close I could feel her soft breath on my face. I closed my eyes for a glorious second, as if to stop time, or to bend it and go back twenty years. Before I had a chance to open my eyes again and answer, she saw the thesis by my typewriter and grabbed it.

'Yallah basora!' she said, gesturing towards the living room. She sat down on the armchair beside the telephone and I sat on the sofa next to her.

'Tea?' I asked, getting up again.

'Shhhh!' she said as she started to read.

I sat down again, not knowing what to do with myself, feeling for a moment as awkward as when we first met that day in Paris. But slowly I became entranced by the way she was reading, so eagerly. I relaxed and sat back on the sofa, watching her, feeling like myself again. For the first time the silence in which we sat didn't scare me. For the first time I realised the peace that silence emits.

After some time, she came to the last page and began mumbling inaudible things to herself. She got up and walked around the room, continuing to talk to herself. I followed her like a pathetic dog before sitting down again. Try and stay cool, I thought. I could tell she needed to think. So, I waited and watched her process everything. She had her back to me now and leaned her hands on the television as she gathered her thoughts. I admired the thickness of her hair, tied back in a low slick bun, with just a few endearing straggles of grey, compared to my own almost completely silver scalp. She looked just as sophisticated, just as ethereal and just as alluring as she did the day we met.

'Ibn Arabi of course, and yes . . .' Doria suddenly slapped her hand to her forehead and laughed dizzily. She turned towards me, still giggling. My eyes grew bigger, I hadn't seen her laugh like this in years. *How was Yasminah's thesis funny?*

'Doria?'

'Yes, habibbti,' she said, walking towards the armchair and

sitting down. She sighed happily to herself like she had just completed the cryptic crossword in *L'Egyptienne*.

'Why are you laughing?' I asked, edging closer towards her on my seat.

'Ahhhh,' she said, rubbing her brow, 'because it is all the same, all the same! Yasminah's work is my life's work, it is your life's work!' she giggled again.

'What?' I said, confused as to how she was connecting our work with women's rights to my daughter's strange lifestyle.

'Asserting gay rights in Islam is the same methodology as asserting women's rights in Islam. It involves a contextualised dissection of the hadiths which takes into account the social, cultural and political situation of the time and readjusting them to the present day.'

'I'm sorry, I'm not following . . .'

'What do we always say, habibti, about the hadiths?'

'That they are often written by unreliable narrators with an agenda pandering to that of the female oppressive system, the Islamic patriarchy of the time?'

'Exactly!'

'Take out the word "female" and change it to the word "homosexual",' she said, flipping over her palms, as if the answers were in her hands.

'What?' I said again. She leaned closer to me, so that our noses were almost touching.

'Take out the word "female" and change it to the word "homosexual",' she whispered again.

Hearing Doria say 'homosexual' sent a thrilling chill down my spine. She said it like she said her French words, over-pronouncing each syllable, so that it flowed like music. I wanted her to say it over and over again.

'Hmmm?' I moaned, while fixated on her lips.

'Yallah, look, the hadiths are often written by unreliable narrators with an agenda pandering to the *homosexual* oppressive system of the time, or what Yasminah calls,' she read from her paper, 'heterosexist lens.'

'Oh,' I said, receiving the thrill again. 'I'm sorry.' I shook my head. It hadn't really sunk in; I was too mesmerised by the sudden life in my best friend and the way she said *that* word. That very word that had always scared me – now with Doria saying it, singing it so beautifully, the fear was fading.

'Look,' she said, taking Yasminah's thesis and turning to a page with the subtitle: *Lut and the cities of Sodom and Gomorrah*.

'So, remember,' she said, edging me closer to her so we could both see the thesis, 'as I said, reliance on exegetical works that are filtered through a heterosexist lens leads to paradoxes, aiywa?'

I nodded. I felt my pupils dilating again, as were hers. I couldn't believe I was finally hearing that glorious fire in her voice again.

'Right, so, many Islamic scholars focus particularly on the damning of Lut's people, by which they are described as doing many terrible things to destroy the cities, including robbery, the sin of inhospitableness and . . . ?'

'Men approaching other men with sexual desire and not women,' I replied.

'Yes! But think of it another way. These men were bad, they were robbing citizens, causing havoc and destruction. Now it's important to deconstruct this, for Yasminah explains we can look at it in a heterosexist lens, that the men were filthy because they were approaching other men with sexual desire, or were the men filthy because they were assaulting other men?'

'I don't quite understand, isn't this the same thing?'

Doria put her head in her hands and breathed in and shook her head manically, before getting up and standing in front of the television. 'Habibbti! La, la, la, their crime is sexual assault not the act of gay intercourse. The sex was non-consensual and *that* is the sin!' She went to sit down again and fingered through more of Yasminah's thesis.

'OK, so there is an argument that all sex is for procreation but what about couples that cannot have children, are they sinning? And that the purpose of marriage is to have sex for procreation. But it is perfectly respectable for a woman to stay with her husband when he has been injured in war, for example, and can no longer perform sexually, aiywa?'

I nodded, rapt by her conviction, unable to take my eyes off her or muster any thoughtful words to balance her own. So, I chose to remain passive and quiet.

'And as Yasminah explains, if every couple could procreate effectively, we would be in a dire state of overpopulation, wouldn't we? She suggests that perhaps homosexuals were put on this earth by Allah to prevent overpopulation, naturally, not unnaturally!' she said triumphant.

She was now reading verbatim from Yasminah's thesis: '"Uthman ibn Salih reported: Al-Hasan ibn Dhakwan, may Allah have mercy on him, said, 'Do not sit with young boy singers, for their appearance is like that of women. They are an even greater temptation than young virgin girls.' This passage only emphasises that homosexual feeling is as natural as a man being attracted to virgin girls. And tell me what man has ever felt sinful about deflowering a girl whether it be on their wedding day or otherwise?"' Doria started laughing again. 'Oh darling Yasminah, habibbti!'

Doria darted over to me and sat next to me on the sofa, she took my hand in her own. 'You must forgive her, habibbti, you must forgive her for leaving, she had no choice. Egypt trapped her. Just like Egypt trapped me. The press won't be satisfied until we are dead!' She looked deep into my eyes; I saw sadness just like I had seen in Ali's. I became so overwhelmed, for a delirious moment Doria's eyes became Ali's eyes and I felt my soul melting into them as my head leaned forward towards her. She tightened her grip on my hand pulling me out of my stupor. I touched my lips, my flesh, as if to check I was not in a dream.

'Write to her, tell her, go to her, you must, tell her that her lifestyle is not haram, tell her that you forgive her, and that you accept her lifestyle. And then you must, you must, try and get Hany to her somehow and away from that drunk! Promise me, habibbti, Fatiy, promise me you'll do this.'

I let a silence hang between us. I could not take my eyes away from her. I wanted this moment to continue forever. I would have said anything to keep her there.

'I promise,' I said.

She must have seen the doubt in my eyes. The uncertainty. Because she made me swear on the Quran.

As she put on her coat, she turned to me and said, 'You know, Ibn Arabi, in the thirteenth century, advocated for female imams because he said that spirituality transcended gender. Can you not make parallels with this assertion with Yasminah's lifestyle? She does not see gender. She sees the spirit. Just like your beloved Ibn Arabi.'

'I never thought about it like that,' I admitted.

'And the hadith that says beware of effeminate men and women that act like men? What would Ibn Arabi say to that?'

She had a point. If Ibn Arabi took gender out of the equation completely, what did it matter if people had a mixture of the feminine and the masculine in them which contradicted their sex at birth? I had written an entire thesis on Ibn Arabi not realising that my work could be used to support Yasminah's lifestyle. It was exactly like Doria had said: her work is my work, and our work is Yasminah's work. It was all the same.

I thanked Doria for helping me see things differently, from a new and nuanced angle as she had always done over the years. I kissed her on both cheeks, but given the gravity of our meeting today, it didn't feel enough. I embraced her in my arms. Touching the small of her back before gliding my hands through her hair. I breathed in her delicious scent and thanked Allah for our reunion today. I prayed for many more days like this with her. These stimulating and passionate conversations were what I lived for.

Yasminah

ي

I lay in bed all day distracting myself with my books, underlining homophobic passages in the Quran and hadiths in thick red pen to deconstruct later and called Farah, my friend who had dreams of becoming a female judge. I pretended I didn't understand things about my studies just so I could hear her voice, which sounded to me as sweet as Umm Kulthum's. I held the phone to my ear, and lay in my bed with my eyes closed, trying to capture this feeling. It was like capturing a butterfly – you never would, you could only admire it from afar.

Farah was beautiful. Seeing her face each day helped me to find my new way of living. The first time I saw her, in the university cafeteria, it was as if all the feelings I had for Ommy had transferred onto her; a celestial astral projection. But, just like Ommy, she wasn't interested in me, not like that anyway. Our friendship had grown from her fascination with my mother and Doria and their work with Mufidah Abdul Rahman, Egypt's first female lawyer. She had defended my mother and

Doria after they stormed parliament in the fifties to get the women's vote. Farah was fascinated by me and my connection. I had enjoyed the attention at first and used it as a way to get close to her but now I felt that that she didn't see me, she saw Doria, she saw my mother, she saw the excitement of a revolution in Iran and she wanted me, my mother, Doria to be part of it in some distant way. It was tiresome. Everything was political when all I wanted was something personal, something intimate, something that was real between two people, not an entire community.

'I saw the same-sex wedding in the paper today. This is great, I mean especially given your thesis and everything,' Farah cooed down the phone as I lay in bed, still hungover, her words awakening me. I knew Farah's support of the gay movement at our university was just that, support not participation, but a small part of me hoped that her desires could be changed; that I could make her fall in love with me, so any interest she showed towards gay rights and my PhD I took as a possible interest in me. I particularly loved our conversations about my thesis. She was deeply fascinated by it, she used words like 'ground-breaking' and 'revolutionary' which made me blush with modesty. Spurred on by her encouragement I felt able to tell her things I hadn't told anyone before. That I had dreams that one day it would be a published book and that it would help other gay Muslims come to terms with their sexuality.

'Yes, Ommy is simply ecstatic about the same-sex wedding article . . . He's arranging . . .'

'Yes, he already invited me,' Farah said quickly.

I was surprised. Ommy was always telling me I was wasting my time on Farah. That she might not be straight, but she was definitely straight-laced. That she wasn't the sort of girl to go against convention even if her heart said otherwise.

I smiled. Perhaps she was finally letting go and it wasn't just me who felt this electricity between us. It could no longer be denied. A magnet could only feel something that wanted to be picked up.

'I can't come, I'm afraid, I am meeting another potential husband.'

My heart dropped and with it, I heard the call waiting.

'I have to go,' I said, 'I have a call on the other end.'

'Oh,' she said, surprised that I was dropping her for another. But there was something inside me that said to give up on this girl, to hang up on this girl, disconnect. If she missed me maybe she would realise what she had lost.

'Masalam, see you in Kabbeer's lecture on Monday,' I said distantly before clicking the button to receive the new call.

'Aiywa?' I said yawning.

There was a long silence. 'Aiywa? Hello?' I said again.

Another silence. Something told me this wasn't a faulty line. This was Mama. Mama was calling me!

I got up from the bed and walked towards the window. Talking to the Milad Tower as if it were a real person 'Mama, is that you?'

I waited for an eternity before I said, 'Mama, if that's you, please, please, I need Hany here with me, I want to give him the life he deserves, we live like kings here, please . . .' This time my tears were cold and fast.

'It's not, I'm not your Mama, I'm sorry, habibbti, it's me, Mona.'

It took me several seconds for me to understand the words, so sure I was that it was Mama.

'Mona?' I asked. 'Mona, not Mama . . . Mona! How did you get this number?'

'I paid Aziz to get it for me. I went to his nightclub . . .'

This was so unlike Mona. I was bursting with delight and pride that she had finally got out of her mother's house and done something that incited such anarchy!

'You went to his nightclub?! Oh habibbti, inshallah, alhamdulillah!' I screeched.

'Your brother charged me a hundred Egyptian pounds, said it was a way to get the money you stole off him!'

I swallowed.

'I'm joking, well, he was joking. Aziz told me you were the only one in the family who ever had any balls. He said,' Mona suddenly began imitating Aziz, 'Mama thinks she's the balls of the family, but it's Yasminah who really has them!'

'He didn't!' I screamed.

'He did . . .'

We both let the silence hang between us, as we let our laughter settle. It was peaceful and warming to have Mona in my ear; her voice always calmed me. I always used to enjoy her predictability but now I was in awe of her precociousness.

She cleared her throat. 'I'm afraid I'm calling to tell you some bad news which I think you deserve to know.' I was suddenly brought back to it all. Burning in Heliopolis, the memories still tarred my psyche.

'What is it? Is it Hany? Oh my god, is Hany OK?'

'Hany is absolutely fine. I see him sometimes walking to the El Nasr school each morning with Ahmed but sometimes Fatiha too.'

I closed my eyes. Full of thanks that he was safe but crushed that his life didn't have me in it.

'I'm afraid I have some bad news about Doria. She's dead.'

∾

That night I went out with Ommy and friends and commemorated not only the death of Doria but the death of her dream for a better Egypt. An Egypt where all women, all people could be free. Now in Tehran, like Mama and Doria, Ommy and I were embarking on the very same dream. Liberation. Our debate about the Shah had proved there were very many definitions of freedom. There was religious freedom, and women's freedom and gay freedom, which all seemed to ultimately mean personal freedom. But where Mama and Doria had successfully blended religious and female freedom to stand for women's rights in Islam, I was finding ways to assert gay rights in Islam. But as I danced with my new friends in Tehran that night, I felt a pang in my chest. A pang that told me that my version of freedom was different to my mother's in some way.

I thought about how much she had fought for other women's rights, yet she could not fight for her own daughter's.

I didn't go back to Cairo for Doria's funeral. I stayed in Tehran so that I could save my life. I could not be a martyr for gay rights like Doria had been for women's rights.

Ne Nothi Tere Te
Don't let the bastards grind you down

That's what Doria used to say. But she had. She had got us the vote but at what expense of self? She had been silenced, cancelled, written out of the press; even her supposed suicide wasn't reported in the Egyptian press, as instructed by Nasser. The press preferred instead to engulf its pages in anti-feminist propaganda about all the 'sluts of *Bint Al Nil, Daughters of the Nile* magazine'. They preferred to reference the debauchery act when mentioning my name and Ommy's when they themselves were the ones drunk on power. They were the ones infiltrating the minds of Egypt without anyone's consent. Filling their brains with sewage water and drowning their souls.

I danced all night thinking of Doria and her inevitable loss. Like me, the only way she knew to have true freedom from her life was to escape it. As the music took control of my body, I reached out to a figure walking towards me in the distance. The bright lights of the disco momentarily blinding me. I squinted, holding my hand to my eyes; the figure came closer until we were just a breath away. I could see her now. It was Farah, she had made it to the club after all. She didn't say a word, she just smiled. I took her hand and we danced.

Nadia

ن

Kadijah and I tolerated our housemate Angela's boyfriend, Mr Tennis, like most people tolerate their housemate's boyfriend. We always acted happy to see him in our living room but underneath we were silently calculating the extra electricity they were consuming, the extra heating they were using, the extra time away from our friend they were taking.

After seven months of Mr Tennis living with us on an unofficial basis, we broached the issue with Angela.

'Perhaps he could contribute a little extra each month?' Kadijah asked in her sweetest voice. She opened her mouth big and wide showcasing her gleaming teeth, which she had just had chemically whitened. They looked ridiculous. I had told her she looked like Jim Carrey in *The Mask*. She had hit me over the head, I then hit her over the head. Mr Tennis had been there at the time and had got quite aroused at the sight of two girls fighting. She hit me again, I hit her again, her hijab had fallen off, exposing her perfectly bald head and then she had run out of the room ugly-crying.

'Well, to be fair I don't think he needs to contribute to the water bill, because we always have showers together!' Angela said, showing off.

I threw a cushion at her head and Kadijah mimed throwing up.

'And as for the other bills, well, I really don't feel comfortable asking him because he's going through a really rough time at the tennis club at the moment. He's thinking of leaving and setting up his *own* club, that's why he's doing so many extra hours at the moment, so he really has to be careful with money, so I can't ask him, sorry!'

I could hear Kadijah breathing in.

'OK, that's fine,' I said, not wanting any confrontation. At least we had asked, and perhaps once Mr Tennis's business was up and running, he could back-date some of his payments. Angela smiled, getting up from the sofa. Her face looked satisfied. If a little smug. I could tell Kadijah was thinking the same thing.

Kadijah banged the coffee table with her fist. 'No!'

Angela turned around. 'What?'

'I'm sorry, Angela, but it's my name on the lease and if Mr Tennis doesn't start contributing soon, I'm afraid, well . . .'

Ironically, Angela's eyes looked like they had been plugged into our entire electricity supply.

'What the fuck? Who the fuck do you think you are?' Angela's anger came out of her like fire from a dragon.

'I am the lead tenant on the contract, so what I say goes!' Kadijah screamed back.

I sat in the middle on the sofa, mouth open, eyes darting between them, watching the fracas unfold like a tennis match.

∾

Two days later I was getting the morning-after pill in Boots. The price had gone up more than the rate of inflation since I last bought it.

'For fuck's sake,' I said to the cashier, 'I'll have to put it on my credit card.' I was shaking my head, chastising myself for agreeing to go Dutch with the guy from the night before when I was paying for the contraception the next day.

'That's £38.75 please then.' I looked at the cashier's name tag. *Ricky*. Ricky looked about fifteen. He had a layer of inflamed and encrusted acne on both cheeks which was almost as loud and thick as his West Country accent.

'Can I get it on my points?' I asked, leaning on the counter and crouching down to his level.

'No,' he said. The decibel of his voice was like that of a loud-speaker, so much so that it actually blew me away momentarily. 'I'm sorry, you can't get the morning-after pill on your Boots Advantage Card, I'm afraid!' I turned around to see that he had also told half the queue about my sexual activity. I checked the faces; one was a sweet old lady with hair the colour of pearls and skin so see-through her veins looked like a bundle of purple and blue thread in a sewing box. Her expression didn't change so I knew she hadn't heard. Behind her was a middle-aged man in a construction site hard hat and with headphones on and a young couple too concerned with groping each other's arses while sucking each other's faces to care. I stared at the couple for a while; the man looked vaguely familiar even though I could only see the back of his head.

I turned back to the cashier and begrudgingly paid the full amount while silently chastising the unfairness of the fact that you didn't get Boots Advantage Card points with the morning-after pill. As I picked up the bag and walked out, I contemplated starting a Change.org petition about the inequality of it all. I knew for a fact that condoms, a more common male purchase, were redeemable for Advantage Card points, for example. I had, after all, signed several Change.org petitions on the tampon tax, and I felt pretty sure that this was of a similar gravitas. I made a mental note to start the petition on the late shift at Edits at 59 that night.

As I stood silently wording the petition in my head, the couple walked out hand in hand. This time I could see their faces. I stood with my mouth agape realising who it was: I knew that face. I saw his mop of chestnut hair which flopped around like that of a bumbling English gentleman in a rom com almost every morning and every night. It was Mr Tennis. And the girl he was with was not Angela. Instead, it was a woman with hair as dry as my mouth now was, the colour of straw, in a cropped eighties-style mullet.

I couldn't believe it. This is the sort of thing that happens in soaps. Real people didn't actually have affairs, surely not! I ducked behind a bush as they walked past me. I cradled the bag with the morning-after pill to my chest and rang Kadijah; she would know what to do.

Angela's face did not move when we told her. But that might have been because she was wearing an avocado and banana face-mask from Boots. I wondered if Mr Tennis had bought it for her that very day I caught him sucking face. I also wondered why a facemask, which was largely used before a date to make one's face attractive to the person one was seeing, accrued Boots Advantage Card points when the morning-after pill, which was largely used after a date, was not.

'I don't believe you,' Angela said between gritted teeth. The mask had cemented itself on her face now and gone from a ripe avocado green to an envious deep spinach colour.

Kadijah whacked me. We had rehearsed this. As I had witnessed the whole entire affair, the X-rated amorousness in Boots, it was me who was going to regale the whole sordid tale. Only I was not as confrontational as Kadijah. I couldn't quite find the words that would inevitably break my best friend's heart. Instead, I said as little as possible while Kadijah told it to her straight.

'He's fucking cheating on you! He's got a full-on girlfriend by the sound of things, a whole double life! You need to dump him!'

'Oh, how very convenient!' Angela's voice now had a less rigid tone. Emotion was melting through the facemask and as a result, clumps were falling onto her crimson dressing gown. The contrast of the red dressing gown and the green gloop gave an almost Christmas-like quality to the proceedings.

'What do you mean by that?' Kadijah asked.

'Well, you want him out, don't you?'

'So, you think we've made up this story? What, are you sick?'

'It's true,' I said softly. 'I'm sorry, but it's true.'

'As if I'm gonna believe some bald girl with teeth like Jim Carrey and a drunken whore with herpes!' she said, getting up and glaring at us both, before adding, 'You're going to regret this, you'll never work in TV ever again, both of you!'

'Now, Angela,' I tried, tears falling down my cheeks, in disbelief that my best friend had called me a drunken whore with herpes and was threatening to terminate our careers. Although, in fairness, I was thinking of leaving the world of television anyway. There was only so long I could go on pretending I was interested in car boot sales or antiques or even fancy wildlife documentaries about mammals or whales or exotic frogs, which are no different to normal frogs really except they are a bit nicer to look at. And I had definitely seen enough raw footage of Bear Grylls' penis urinating on some poor creature to last a lifetime.

'You both seem to be forgetting that my cousin's best friend's aunt is Director General of the BBC. You'll never work in TV again!' she yelled a second time.

'Like I care! You know my side hustle feminist tote bag business is going from strength to strength anyway!' Kadijah screamed back.

'Yeah, whatever! What about your stupid sister?' she said, looking at me. 'Your stupid drunken sister with herpes who has probably infected every TV producer, director and editor in Bristol with it too! I'm gonna tell everyone I know in TV to stay away from herpes girl and that her bald sister is a friggin' freak too!'

I stood dumbfounded; I was expecting a feeling of panic to wash over me but instead Angela's threats only calmed me. It was like I had just drunk an entire bottle of wine and followed it up with a vodka shot, I suddenly had such clarity of thought. Einstein described the moment when he visualised the theory of relativity as his 'best thought'. Was I having mine now, standing over Kadijah and Angela as they launched themselves at eachother? As they wrestled each other to the floor (somewhere Mr Tennis's head was exploding), my brain, like Einstein's, began also having its most significant thought. As if to accommodate this profundity, the fact that my sister was trying to tear Angela's hair out while Angela tried to tear my sister's hijab off did not faze me. Instead of focusing on what was in front of me, I focused on what was happening inside of me.

Why was I working in television anyway, I wondered in my

ethereal state. This wasn't my dream. I had finished my performing arts degree intent on becoming an actor. I only got into television because Kadijah was already working in it, and she had convinced me that if I worked my way up behind the screen, I could eventually get a job in front of the screen. But after three years, all I had succeeded in doing (apart from daily performances of the tea and coffee menu) was limiting my aspirations to merely wanting a simple desk job where my screen couldn't be seen by my boss.

'You don't even fancy Mr Tennis, you're only using him so you can get help with your backhand!' The sounds of Kadijah, now struggling on the floor, pulling at Angela's mop of yellow hair, failed to awake me from my trance.

'As if! My backhand is second to none!' Nor did the shrieks of Angela rile me as she straddled my sister.

Just as Angela slapped my sister with her 'second to none' backhand, I began having my most profound thought. Everything at once became slow and silent. I could see only whiteness on a screen. I could see only possibility and opportunity from the tragedy of my television career. Maybe, I thought, if I sat down all day, in front of a computer screen that couldn't be seen by my boss, maybe, just maybe, I could write? Write. A chill ran down my arm. Write. My palms began to sweat. Write. My fingers became hot. The more I said it, the more the white screen in my mind filled up with words. I am a writer. I could see the story now, right in front of me. My story. I felt a warm tingle in my stomach as I came to my best thought: I want to write. 'I want to write,' I whispered.

'You . . . you . . . witch!' Kadijah screamed at Angela as her hijab was ripped off her head for the second time that week.

Yasminah

ي

All I had was one red suitcase. It had been Mama's. Her
mother, my Teta, had bought it for her from Les Grands
Magasins Cicurel, the finest and grandest French department
store in Cairo, at No. 3 Avenue Boulac. It had been her gift to
my mother after she won the scholarship to the Sorbonne. Since
then, the suitcase had travelled all over the globe. Not just Paris,
but to various International Women's Conferences across the
world, from Italy to India and from Austria to America. It was a
royal red colour, with a gold buckle.

'Red and gold are the colours of the British!' Baba would tut.
'You look like an Anglophone,' he would tell her as she set off
on another exciting voyage alongside her Queen of Egypt. My
mother always used to tell me that Doria showed her the world
and Baba grounded her. She told me to always have two people
in my life that I love equally that do these opposite things. It was
the secret to happiness.

'As Ibn Arabi said, "Out of moderation a pure happiness

springs",' she'd repeat to me as she painted her lips, waiting for her taxi.

When she holidayed with Baba each year in Alexandria, she took a large brown satchel and dressed plainly. For there were no fancy dinners or glamorous balls to attend on my Uncle Jeddy's farm. I placed the suitcase on the bed, touching the cracks in the leather. They reminded me of the wrinkles around my mother's eyes when she smiled. I sighed and began to pack, as instructed by Ommy's father.

The revolution had begun as Ommy had predicted and with it there were rumours that the exiled Shah was about to be extradited and that the Islamic State would win the polls and take control. We were to move temporarily into Zaki and Aysegul's two-bedroom apartment until Ommy's father had secured a new job, hopefully still in government. I was rather annoyed, seeing it as a move on Zaki and Ommy's part to set me up with Aysegul rather than escape getting in the mix of civil unrest.

I opened the suitcase and began to pack. I lay the small amount of clothes that I had brought from Cairo on the bed. Each piece reminded me of a night spent hanging out with our gang at Rainbow, the not-so-closeted gay nightclub Zaki owned, just off Jomhuri Square. The newspapers referred to clubs like Rainbow as 'gharbzadegi' or 'westfication', the terms used to describe the Americanisation of Iran, and it was dependent on a newspaper's agenda as to whether this was used to scaremonger or not.

We hung out at Rainbow most nights, occasionally deviating in the summer to spend weeks on Shomal, the Caspian coast. Escaping the crowded condensed confines of our city, in favour of beaches, greenery, wooded mountains, the purifying rain.

But we would always enjoy coming back to our beloved Tehran. Like my mother, we needed both the cosmopolitan and the ordinary to feel balance. Now, everything felt completely *off* balance as suddenly, it seemed that friends were retreating to their holiday homes on the coast, with no telling when they would return.

I gazed at my miniskirts and short dresses out on the bed. It was like looking at old photos of myself. I cringed. I can't believe I used to wear this stuff. Now I was far more modest and felt more liberated for it. I wore less makeup too and not only had I stopped dying my hair but I now covered it too. It was humbling, I'd never felt more beautiful baring my naked soul.

I heard Ommy knocking. I made a face and came to the door.

'Knocking?' I asked. 'When have you ever shown me such respect for my privacy before?'

He forced a smile. I gestured for him to come in and he sat on my bed, his face theatrically glum. I knew how hard this was for him. I tried to take his mind off things, by getting him excited about finally being able to live with the love of his life, Zaki. In the same bed!

'I will be sleeping on the sofa,' I emphasised, 'I will not be sleeping in bed with Aysegul.'

'But she likes you . . .'

'I know. This is exactly why I am not going to sleep in the same bed with her, I don't want to lead the poor girl on.'

Ommy grunted. 'She's never going to leave her husband, 'Minah, Farah is never going to do that for you, and you know it.'

I slammed the suitcase closed and zipped it up. I remembered how my mother used to get Baba to sit on it, so full of clothes. When I fled Cairo, in my mad dash, I didn't have the luxury of overpacking.

'I feel quite emotional leaving this place,' I lied as tears fell, thinking of the enormity of leaving behind Hany on that fateful day.

'I know,' Ommy said, getting up to hold me. I burrowed my head into his armpit and breathed in the salt of his sweat, and then burrowed into him further. It was as if I was searching for a new portal, into the past or into the future, I didn't know which.

'Hey!' he said, holding my arms tightly and looking into my eyes. I would have done anything for those eyes. I listened and nodded.

'This is a new start, it's exciting! This revolution, perhaps it will be better! What do we say?' He shook me, more trying to convince himself than me. 'What do we say?!'

'Change is good, change is growth, everything must change . . .' I recited.

'That's right! And tonight, we're all going to embrace the change by going to Rainbow!' Ommy began dancing around my room, taking a scarf hanging by my mirror and wrapping it around his waist.

I wiped my tears and laughed.

When the evening came, I felt a thumping in my head that would not relent. I looked at my face in the bathroom mirror and gasped at my pale skin and hollow eyes. I opened the cabinet for the painkillers, barely able to see from the intense throbbing. I fumbled desperately with the packaging and finally popped out two white pills onto my shaking hands. I gulped them back instantly, swallowing them along with the lump in my throat with no water, and rubbed my head. I hoped I would be better for Rainbow tonight. Farah might be there, I thought.

I stumbled back to my bedroom, turned out the light and lay with my head in my hands, in a bid to sleep out the headache by killing it with darkness. I dozed intermittently, yelping out in agony upon waking, before falling into a thick slumber again. When I woke hours later, the headache had subsided only marginally and now I was shivering.

'Ommy,' I yelped. 'Ommy,' I said again a little louder, my voice shaking and every syllable draining me.

He strutted in, wearing his infamous flares and platform boots. He wore a shirt, the first three buttons open, the faintest shade of purple, the colour of the syringa flower.

''Minah, why aren't you dressed, what's wrong, habibbti?' he said, wiping cold sweat off my brow. 'Wow, you're burning up!'

'I can't go to Rainbow tonight . . .'

'Habibbti, of course you can't go, you must rest. Aisha is here, she can help you. Aisha!' he called out to the maid.

I opened my mouth to protest before closing it again, too weak to say anything. Instead with every fibre of my being I willed for him to stay with me that night and hold me. When I awoke in the middle of the night, to the sounds of drunken brawls in the street, I realised my fever and headache had gone. In its place I was left with a disorienting numbness in the pit of my stomach that told me it was finally time to let Ommy go.

It was the sunlight that streamed through the cracks in the curtain that woke me up that morning, not Aisha's weeping. I stretched and felt a sense of complete gratitude that comes from being so sick in the night, that you wonder will you ever feel normal again and when you do you rejoice. I smiled to myself.

With my newly restored health I was now giddy to hear the stories of the night.

I shot out of the bed, grabbed my robe and walked into the living room. It was then that I saw that Aisha was weeping in the armchair. She held a crumpled newspaper. This wasn't uncommon of late but there was something about her cries, more guttural than I'd ever heard before.

'Aisha!' I called out to her. 'Please don't cry – as soon as Ommy's father gets a new position he will re-hire you!' I said, repeating what Ommy had told her just yesterday.

Aisha cried harder, almost hysterical now. I ran over to her and took the newspaper out of her hand.

'Do not read this! Journalists they lie all the time! Do not worry, it's never as bad as it sounds.' I took the newspaper and set it down on the coffee table.

Aisha continued to cry. 'Oh Yasminah,' she said. 'Oh Yasmi-nah,' she said again, rocking back and forth. I closed my eyes and turned away from her and back to the coffee table to see what 'catastrophe' she was flailing and fretting about today.

I read the headline on the paper and the numbness from the night returned.

'Five dead in Rainbow Nightclub attack.'

Nadia

ASCOT, 1994

ن

When my dad told us that we would be moving to Saudi Arabia we all cried for different reasons. My mum, because she had just passed her driving test, and Kadijah and I because we had been watching CBBC *Newsround* and thought we were going to Sarajevo.

'I don't want to go to Sarajevo, people are dying in Sarajevo!' I wept.

'Saudi Arabia, darling,' my mum tried to soothe. 'It's very different . . . I think.'

'Oh,' I said, relieved but still confused.

'Women can't drive there or vote,' my mother uttered to herself, while staring blankly into space as my dad continued his presentation. The last time we had a family meeting like this was when Kadijah had joined the St John Ambulance and had become obsessed with health and safety regulations. She had decided we'd all better think out our strategy if the house went up in flames and had rallied us all into the living room. We weren't ordinarily the sort of family to meet up and discuss an issue collectively. It all felt very alien; very democratic.

However, at this meeting my parents seemed more polarised and frosty with each other than ever. My dad hadn't gone to quite the same efforts with his stationery as Kadijah had with her slides, although he did have a flip chart. On it he had written: *Tax haven*. And: *It's only for a year*.

My mother remained stoic.

'Saudi Arabia is tax free!' my dad roared like he was a double-glazing salesman. 'Imagine all the clothes you can buy with that, Mummy!'

Kadijah and I groaned. My mum and dad were definitely not getting on. Whenever he referred to our mum as 'Mummy!' and adopted a high-pitched voice it was always a passive aggressive tactic to get my mother to stop sulking from an argument they had no doubt already had.

The fact that my mum and dad weren't seeing eye to eye on the move to Saudi made us feel even more trepidatious about moving to this distant foreign land.

'Yeah, except we won't be able to wear any of the clothes that we can buy with all this tax-free salary of yours because we'll have to cover up in an abaya.'

My dad made a face at my mum, his eyes big and blinking. 'Shut up, woman, I thought we agreed on this!' The exchange appeared to change something in her and she too started sounding like she was reading a script from the Saudi Arabian tourist board.

'You'll be just minutes from Dhahran's idyllic beaches and your compound, King Fahad University of Petroleum and Minerals, is the biggest compound in the kingdom, second only to Aramco. KFUPM boasts five outside pools, just metres way from your luxury apartment, and in Al-Khobar it's sunny all year round.'

Kadijah suddenly perked up. 'Saudi is the Red Sea, right?'

'Yes!' my dad said, suddenly surprised by her change from low level dread to a perked-up enthusiasm.

'I've never scuba dived in the Red Sea before! Can I still scuba dive, Dad, because I really need to complete my PADI Advanced Open Water Diver certificate. Will I be able to continue with the course?'

Kadijah had been obsessed with scuba diving since she had enrolled on a PADI course our school had offered as part of the after-school programme. I hadn't been able to do it because I was asthmatic. Instead, I did Drama Club. In Drama Club they didn't mind if you had an asthma attack on stage; in fact, they somewhat encouraged it.

I rolled my eyes. I was very jealous that she left school thirty minutes earlier on a Wednesday to account for filling up her oxygen tank and getting into her wetsuit.

'Can she, Usman?' my mum asked.

'Yes!' my dad said instantly.

All three of us looked at him with suspicion.

My mum broke the silence. 'Have you told Fatiha we're going yet? I mean, what does she think?'

'She's actually very happy! Inshallah!'

'Your feminist mother is happy we're going to bring up our daughters in Saudi Arabia?'

'It's only for a year!' he roared again, banging the flip chart. 'And yes, she is . . .' he stumbled, '. . . very happy. That we are going to be closer to Egypt to visit her more often.'

We all groaned. Teta was always pressurising us to visit her more. It wasn't that she was lonely; she had lots of visits from the many grandchildren that Uncle Aziz had fathered over the years, and she was still working in the Islamic Studies department of Cairo University. However, my dad knew that she was struggling with caring for Dodo and managing his illness, and she wanted her favourite child by her side to assist.

'Your dad is Teta's favourite,' my mum would tell us. We were never sure why; we knew she despaired of Uncle Aziz, we all did, but what was possibly wrong with Aunt Yasminah? And surely if she was this great feminist, she would give preference to her only daughter?

'Seriously, this is going to be a great move for us as a family, get away from this grey English weather . . . and the KFUPM campus compound I am told is incredibly westernised. Even though women can't drive in public, they can drive if they are *in* the compound . . . And you can wear what you want there – you only have to wear the abaya and the hijab when you go out of it.'

'Compound sounds like such an oppressive word, like where you lock up dogs or something.'

My dad looked at my mum again, this time shaking his head.

'Look, I know it's a big change, but the money is too good to pass up. I've spoken to other British expats, and they say the sun, sea and swimming lifestyle outweighs the, er, questionable human rights laws.'

'What's not to like, sun, sea and Sharia Law!' my mum said.

'It's only for a year.'

'Is it, is it, Usman? Because in my experience whenever you say, "it's only for a year", it always goes on for much, much longer.'

'I don't know what you're talking about.'

'You know you can't drink in Saudi Arabia, Usman.'

'Yes, this is no issue for me. Is it an issue for you, Pamela?' he said, staring at my mum who stared back, bemused.

'Of course it isn't! You know I just have a couple of glasses of wine a week. I'm just worried about you.'

'Oh, I'll be fine!'

'Oh really?'

'Yes! Really!'

There was a long pause while they glared at each other before my father finally relented and his face softened. 'Actually, Pamela, I know a few expats who brew their own wine.'

'Oh, thank god!'

They both chuckled.

It was the first time we had seen them laughing together for a long time.

Fatiha

CAIRO, 1954

ف

' The British hate you for the English tragedies of Black
Saturday,' I said to Doria, turning the television down and
ushering Ali and the children out of the room, 'which – other
than the peaceful protest outside Barclays bank – we had nothing to do with,' I swallowed my fig roll and rubbed my large
belly, 'and, er, Islamic scholars hate you,' I put my two fingers
on my brow trying to remember the wording in the article in the
Gazette, '. . . for putting forward a modern version of the "Arab"
woman to the west. Not a woman of modesty but one character-
ised by glamour, beauty, independence whose fashion is a nod
towards western sensibilities and, er . . .' I said, transferring the
weight between each leg, while holding the small of my throbbing back. I winced, wondering whether to omit this last bit.

'Go on,' Doria said.

'Well,' I breathed in, secretly hoping the line would go dead,
'polls reveal that a large proportion of Egyptian women ha—,
er, dislike you, for wanting to be on the front pages of the

international press. They think you are more oriented to the glamours and fame of European society than towards your own Egyptian community,' I finished.

I waited several moments. I imagined her eyes madly flicking, as they did when she was sizing up a situation. Her bottom lip swishing. Her prominent eyebrows in their signature raise. I could hear glasses clinking in the background, the faint sounds of an audience applauding, microphones squeaking.

'Anyway, what's Reading like?' I asked, trying to change the subject and reaching for another fig roll. The sun was setting, and huge chunks of orange were coming through the gaps in the door to the balcony intermittently. As a result, I found myself squinting every few seconds, as my face came into the light and out of it again. I could hear little Yasminah laughing out on the balcony with Ali. I suddenly found myself turning, accidentally wrapping myself round the telephone cord in a bid to locate Aziz.

'It's pronounced "redding" not "reading".'

'Oh,' I said. I sighed, wishing I wasn't pregnant so I could have attended the International Council of Women conference alongside her. I imagined it to be like our university days in Paris, enjoying the fruits of European culture. I had never been to England, and Reading sounded most sophisticated. I saw it as a good omen; that the town's name was a reminder of our women's literacy clubs that we had set up throughout Cairo and beyond. The *Bint Al Nil* Union was singlehandedly and inexpensively 'eradicating illiteracy for both men as well as women and with it the ignorance of Egypt', Doria had told the press.

'Yes, well, the town is quite industrial, not quite as extravagant as London. But the university, is, well, quite smart. Fatiha?' she said.

'Yes?'

'It is time for me to do something dramatic.'

'Oh,' I said, wondering what she thought our protest against the British occupation was two years ago outside Barclays bank, if it wasn't 'dramatic'. It was certainly theatrical. Or the fact that Doria had cunningly devised a plan, involving a peculiar Egyptian loophole that allowed her, a woman, to put herself up for electoral candidacy in the district of Abdin. Wasn't that an ostentatious publicity stunt in itself? Or when the Grand Mufti of Egypt loudly contested, saying that in Islam votes were degrading to women, and the ridiculous consequent fatwah condemning feminist agitation in Egypt and publicly rebuking her and the work of the *Bint Al Nil* Union – wasn't that something that would go down in history as a dramatic turning point? No. These were all amateur! I thought. Now it was time for the real pièce de résistance! I sighed and allowed my head to hang for a moment.

As stressful as it was being best friends with 'women's rights agitator' Doria Shafik, I couldn't deny it was always exciting.

'Yes?' I asked. I flailed my arms at Ali through the gaps in the door. I had located Aziz. He was playing in the hallway with the radio and a kitchen knife. Ali ran towards him, picked him up, knife still in hand, and placed him on the balcony where Yasminah was having a tea party with her dolls.

'Fatiha, I want you to write down what I say now, a statement that we will issue to the press. Are you ready?' she asked.

'One moment,' I said, while flailing my arms at my husband again, getting his attention and then doing a stabbing notion with my hands to indicate that it wasn't enough that he took Aziz away from the radio, he also needed to take Aziz away from the kitchen knife. He nodded and rushed out again to the balcony. I clicked the phone down in the living room and walked past the kitchen and into my office. I could smell the lamb roasting in the oven and with it my mouth began to salivate. I quickly grabbed some more fig rolls off the kitchen table and popped one into my mouth. If Doria was going to dictate a press statement, they were usually long and laborious, and I would need more sustenance to keep me going.

My office was cooler than the living room and going into it I instantly felt more awake, but I stuck the fan on anyway, as when I wrote my ordinarily cold hands became hot.

'OK. I'm ready.'

'I have taken my decision to begin at noon on the twelfth of March 1954, in the Press Syndicate, a hunger strike until death . . .'

'Doria!' I whispered.

'. . . in protest against the coming formation of a founding committee to create the new constitution in which no woman has been included. I refuse to be governed according to a constitution in whose drafting I have not participated . . .'

I looked at the words on the page, my heart beating as fast as she was saying them, my hands dripping with sweat, the pen almost slipping out of my grip, as she continued.

'. . . I make my hunger strike at the Press Syndicate because the latter, by its very essence, is intimately connected with every movement of liberation. Signed Doria Shafik.'

'But Doria, when your ideology affects your biology, wallahi, mish keda, please, think about this for a few days. You must be tired from your travels,' I said.

'Fatiy . . . when I was in the Sorbonne writing my thesis on women's rights in Islam, I wrote freely, envisioning an Egypt of the future . . . A liberated Egypt cannot be liberated without the liberation of all its people, its women. This is my absolute. This is what I meant when I said I wanted my life to be a work of art. Egypt is hiding behind the outdated version of Islam as an excuse. How can it be true what the Grand Mufti says that women should not have the vote because the wives of the Prophet were veiled? The veil is a contentious subject as you know, but the very fact that veils, the niqab are not permitted when a woman undergoes the great pilgrimage of Haj goes to show that the veil is neither a symbol of oppression nor a symbol of progression, it is simply a matter of choice. And he is using it as a symbol to suggest that because the Prophet's wives all wore the veil, then that renders all women voiceless. Why are people listening to this bumbling old fool? Just because he is a graduate of the Al-Azhar University, the thousand-year-old, intellectual centre of Islam, does not make him . . . Allah! Islam does not require that women be deprived of their rights. Look at Syria, Turkey, Pakistan – where a woman's right to vote is both secured and practised. Send it to the press, Fatiha,' she instructed, 'send it to the press tonight.'

She hung up and I let the dial tone ring out for several minutes. I eventually found myself putting the phone down and joining my family on the balcony.

Yasminah

ي

'People think the word "revolution" is great and noble but it really comes from the word "revolting",' Hany said to me matter of factly in a mixture of Arabic and English. I was relieved to see that his chin that was pulled out of me by his father like it was his and only his had developed into a handsome jawline. A Bin-Khalid jawline, I liked to think. I stepped back from my son who was sitting at my kitchen table ravenously gnawing on a jam doughnut from the bakery we liked to frequent on the part of Shepherd's Bush Road where clientele ranged from Muslim immigrants to Australian travellers.

His mouth had matured since I'd left him; it was as if time hadn't decayed but crystalised his features. His lips, his chin, his jaw had grown beautiful and the agonising wails that I had found so petrifying had turned into words of poetry. I stared at my creation in front of me as if I was a great artist. The jam exploding onto his thick, plump lips, the redness of the strawberry sauce on his cinnamon skin making my eyes weep with joy.

I nodded in agreement while wiping his chin. I spat onto a handkerchief and rubbed rigorously, not stopping even when he protested. I hadn't touched my son in years. I had left him as a baby in his cradle; now he was a boy of eleven, soon he would be a young man. I would stand here forever and clean and rub and mother his face. I was his mother now. Mother. I was a mother again and I *had* a mother again. It felt like a dream. Perhaps it was? After Ommy, my nightmares and life had merged into one. How could I be sure that Hany was really here?

I heard the click of the bathroom door, the creak of the floorboard, the loud guttural clearing of her throat, all signifying that she was about to walk in on us. My heart dropped and with it a confirmation that this was not a lucid fantasy. For in a dream, I would not have had my mother chaperoning my time with my son. Making sure I was a capable mother, that I would not have any 'relations', as she called it, distracting me. Her lack of acceptance of who I was pained me; if it weren't for Hany, I would have closed the door on her when she turned up three days ago. I'd already metaphorically closed the door on my whole life in Egypt. I had slammed it shut and locked it with a padlock. I had made my peace with it all; I was no longer in a prison – they were. I had the padlock buried in my heart. Not them.

'You're right, some revolutions are bad, but a lot of them were effective,' I said, stroking my son's hair. He flinched. At times he was not ready for such affections. But his obsession with war and rebellion and his encyclopaedic knowledge of literature and history had blown me away. I had never felt such pride before. He was a chatterbox too, seemingly completely unfazed by his uprooting from Cairo to London. I had not been the same. I had left Tehran immediately after the unspeakable happened, deciding that England could give me the fresh start that I needed. But it had taken me a while to adjust to my new London life.

'. . . like the Industrial Revolution and the French Revolution,' he said with a look of consideration and contemplation.

I looked at my mother. She had her thick eyebrows raised; she was like a bad tribute act of Doria Shafik, I thought with sudden bitterness. The contrast between my love of my flesh and blood in a child and my disdain and hatred of it as it manifested in my mother was overwhelming. Why did everything that brought me joy in life also bring me such pain?

'I got Baba to sign everything for you, habibbti,' she said, touching my arm. I flinched like Hany had. Too much too soon. We had talked, yes, but I had not forgiven nor forgotten. And nor had she. She never understood my hem, she never understood my shame, she never understood my yearning for what she called the 'unconventional' and she still didn't.

'He is his male legal guardian now that Ahmed is . . . incapacitated. The authorities don't know about Baba's mind, I've managed to keep that private at least.'

I shivered at the word 'incapacitated'. Then I looked down at the floor, focusing on the tapestry on the rug, the way the colours criss-crossed through each other, the borders of red and gold, the diamond shape in the centre of it all.

'Inshallah he will get better, beat his demons. Stop drinking,' I lied, still staring at the floor.

'His body is ruined, his mind is . . .' she hissed and mimed a bullet to her head. I was unsure now whether she was talking about Ahmed or Baba. I didn't ask any further questions about my husband or my father, instead I focused only on my son. My mother had told me that Hany was fiercely intelligent academically but emotionally stunted.

'Like a robot,' she had muttered under her breath. 'He is very particular, very rigid, constantly counting things, he only likes vanilla ice cream, no sprinkles when all the other kids are . . . Wallahi!'

I hadn't found my son robotic at all. I had found these last three days getting to know him life affirming. He was full of it. Life. I would give up anything for him to be my life.

∾

Mama, Hany and I walked to the park by the tube station. Passing by Shepherd's Bush Market, I saw Mama clock several Muslim women buying meat from a halal butcher.

'Halal? Mish keda?' she asked, pointing.

'Aiywa,' I nodded.

'Teta,' Hany said, 'London is multicultural.'

'That's right,' I smiled.

'Wallahi,' Mama said.

'Here we are!' I said as we arrived at Shepherd's Bush Green.

Hany and Mama both put their hand to their foreheads, squinting in the late afternoon sun as they perused the extent of the park. Hany nodded in appreciation but Mama began sighing and uttering inaudible words under her breath.

'Al-Azhar, yanni . . . Cairo, la, Egypt, Al-Azhar . . . Umm al-Dunya!' she laughed before clenching her fists at me and emphatically repeating the Egyptian platitude 'Umm al-Dunya! Umm al-Dunya!'

I turned my head the other way, so she could not see me roll my eyes. Egypt is the Mother of the World? I grimaced. She spent her life prattling on about Egypt's injustices, Egypt's lack of this and lack of that, and now she was proclaiming that Egypt was the Mother of the World, insinuating that there was nowhere greater? The hypocrisies of this woman! My anger towards her treatment of Ommy and my resentment at the lack of acknowledgement of my thesis suddenly surged through my body. I knew I had to do something with this impassioned energy, while at the same time avoiding sabotaging my second chance with Hany.

I took a long breath in and chewed on the inside of my cheek. We walked for several moments in silence. Biting hard into the side of my mouth dispersed some of the anger but not all. Breaking off a piece of flesh and tasting blood helped to rid me of some of the resentment but still left a residue. I swallowed and began gnawing the other side in a bid to be completely free of aggression. So many years had passed and still she riled me as if I were eighteen again! Finally, Hany spoke.

'Is that a skatepark up there on the hill? Oh cool!' He pointed in the distance. 'Can we go see it?' His large eyes looked up at me, not Mama. I stopped biting my cheeks to smile.

'Yes, of course, let's go.'

Hany zoomed right ahead leaving us both behind. We still did not speak and I couldn't bear to look my mother in the eye. We both focused on Hany ahead. Mama, never comfortable in silence, began humming a familiar Umm Kulthum song as we trudged behind. Before long, her humming had turned into grunting and just a few metres away from the skatepark her grunts had formed into groans. She stopped to get her breath and then insisted we find a place to sit so she could rest her legs. I could see that Hany who was waiting metres ahead of us was getting frustrated.

'You go check it out on your own, Hany, you don't want us embarrassing you!' I yelled, laughing. 'I'll sit down with Teta.'

'Oh, awesome!' he said running off.

Mama and I found a nearby bench and sat watching him in the distance. It was a relief not to have to look her in the eye. After some time, in my peripheral vision, I could feel my mother's disapproving gaze on me. Examining everything, starting with the hat that I used to cover my hair right down to my shoes. She sat with her handbag perched on her lap, her posture straight, her sturdy boots and A-line skirt and lack of veil controversial in her heyday now only evoked conservatism. I heard her click open her handbag. Taking my eyes away from Hany, I looked down at my mother's hands. In them, she had the annotated Quran and hadiths that I had sent her all those years ago, from Tehran, and with it, now crumpled and curling and yellowing like papyrus, my thesis on gay rights in Islam. The very thesis that I had sent to her in vain, in an attempt for her to finally understand who I was.

'This is for you,' she said.

She placed the Quran, hadiths and thesis in my hands, and I felt my eyes begin to water. I kissed the holy book three times whilst clutching my old thesis, marvelling at its frayed, yellowed edges. Then she opened her handbag again.

'A letter from . . . Baba, he wrote it when he was in good spirits.' She smacked an envelope with 'Yasminah' scrawled in not Baba's but her own handwriting. Overwhelmed I also kissed it three times.

She held my hand for the rest of the afternoon on the bench. Afterwards we took Hany for ice cream where he deviated from his usual three scoops of vanilla, no sprinkles, to a Neapolitan trio with extra sprinkles.

∽

The next day Mama left for Cairo. I was finally a proper mother with my son. I tucked him into bed, and he let me kiss him on his forehead. I closed the creaky door that was now his bedroom. At the same time my stomach rumbled. I had been in such a state of euphoria I had barely eaten. My happiness was like being drunk. I didn't need food. But I was a mother now, I remembered, so I gave myself permission to mother myself. I microwaved a bowl of lentil soup and sat down with the letter from Baba that Mama had given me. I opened it greedily, suddenly impatient, I had waited so long to connect with Baba, I had missed him, in many ways more so than Mama. I ripped open the envelope; it smelt like Heliopolis, a mixture of white sage, lemons, oil, tobacco, sweet halowa mixed with honey and petrol, tar and smoke. Mama must've written on the envelope for him, I thought, seeing the handwriting on the front again.

However, on seeing it all on the page my energy suddenly evaporated. This was not Baba's handwriting, this was Mama's. She had been too shy to say that she had written a letter to me. Why couldn't she have said whatever it was to my face? I breathed in and started reading.

I consumed the words as if they were food nourishing my soul. Never before had words made me feel such happiness. I felt the way I always do whenever I am euphoric, I felt the presence of Ommy shining through my body like light through a window on a sunny day. My mother had read my thesis and finally accepted me.

Nadia

ن

As I walked down Shepherd's Bush Road to my new job as a junior editor of a somewhat controversial magazine, I felt a newfound affinity with Teta. We were both passionate journalists wanting to make a difference to society. I pinched myself because I couldn't believe that I had finally landed my dream job.

Writing was what I wanted to do now. After all, it was in my blood. Television and performing arts were of course exciting. But with excitement also comes drama, and after the theatrics of herpes and Angela, I now sought peace. Writing pacified and soothed me. I couldn't believe I had secured a job where I could do it all day. On reflection perhaps I always knew that I wanted to be a writer. After all, all I had ever wanted was to sit down all day, in front of a computer screen which couldn't be seen by my boss. I could see now that this desire was so that I could write all day (and piss about on Facebook). And now as I heaved open the glass doors to my new life in London, I realised I had landed it! Well, sort of.

'Hi, I'm Nadia Bin-Khalid,' I said more shyly than normal to a very attractive girl on reception. I was taken aback by her cleavage which was so brazenly on display.

'Hi, Nadia, yes, I'm to show you to your desk. Follow me.' As she came round, she looked me up and down before staring at my shoes. 'Did you bring any flats?'

'I'm sorry?'

'Your shoes, they are too high, Derrick likes women to be shorter than him. I have a spare pair if you want to borrow, what size are you?'

I was rather taken aback. My cream Mary Janes with the kitten heel weren't even that high. 'Size six,' I said.

'Perfect! I'm Clare by the way.' She handed me a pair of animal print ballet pumps. I quickly changed into them and gave her my heels. 'Can you keep these until the end of the day?'

'Sure!' she said.

She took me up a rickety old staircase, the sound of MTV music channel growing in volume as we rose to the top. The building was like an old man, creaky and rather dishevelled. Very unlike how I dreamed my first job in magazines would be. I knew it wasn't going to be as glamorous as *Vogue* or *Style*, but I was prepared to work my way up in the magazine industry. Just like I had done in television until Giles and Angela had spoilt it for me. Giles by terminating my Southwest News application and Angela for bad-mouthing me to every TV executive she knew.

Clare led me down a very low-ceilinged corridor and into a room where the music was blaring out from. She knocked on the door before quickly saying under her breath, 'Now don't take Derrick too seriously, he has a very un-PC sense of humour.'

She opened the door and with it a new world. I was expecting a team of writers, journalists, editors consumed in a hubbub of creativity, a buzz of artistic innovation. People yelling, 'Get it to me by Friday!' and 'Fifteen hundred words on the fashion movement in Paris, please!'

Instead, it was just two middle-aged men, one perched on the other one's desk.

'What do you think of this one, Craig?'

'Yeah, number 42 and 57, blow it up big, zoom in on the tits, photoshop the lips, bigger, bolder, redder, yeah . . .' Craig sounded like one of Uncle Christopher's friends.

'Hi,' I said even quieter than at reception. 'I'm Nadia, I start as junior editor today.'

Craig, the guy perched on Derrick's desk, turned, looked me up and down and sneered.

'Welcome to *Bangers* magazine.'

∾

If Teta knew I was here today, working at *Bangers*, she would have wept. *Bangers* was a world away from her Egyptian feminist magazine *Bint Al Nil*. The 'Lad's Mag' hadn't exactly been my first choice of magazine internship. Obviously, I would have preferred something a bit more highbrow like *Gracious* magazine, *The Cistern* or even *Hot!* magazine. But beggars couldn't be choosers. I had to work my way up from the bottom. Literally, it seemed.

'Yeah, get right in on her arse, Nadia, that's it . . .' Derrick was leaning over my desk, urging me to 'go deeper' and zoom into a *Hollyoaks* actress's derriere on Photoshop. His eyes would dart from her bum to my boobs methodically. They say men are either an arse or a tit man. But Derrick was more an arse *and* a tit.

'Your dad's Ussy Bin-Khalid, right?' I found Derrick suddenly looking me in the eyes for the first time that day.

'Yes,' I said shocked. He had appeared on a few very small sketches in a BBC Three comedy show, where he had been hired to play an Indian shopkeeper. He had found no shame in putting on an offensive Indian accent, which Kadijah had chastised him for.

Craig stopped typing up his interview with sixteen-year-old Page Three girl Lauren Little. 'What? Your dad's Ussy Bin-Khalid? No way!'

'Yes,' I said with a strange mix of embarrassment and pride. Kadijah and I still couldn't believe that our dad hadn't just stopped at the stand-up Groupon voucher we gave him all those years ago. He was now a 'regular on the UK comedy circuit' and gigged five or six nights a week and his debut stand-up hour at the Edinburgh Fringe Festival had been very well reviewed. He now boasted the same agent as Michael McIntyre. He was actually getting rather good, much to Pamela's dismay.

'Craig and I don't normally like Paki comedians because they just go on about being Paki all the time, but your dad is proper hilarious!' Derrick said, punching me lightly in the arm. It seemed playful but the punch actually hurt. Had I even heard him correctly? My boss couldn't have said the 'P' word, surely not. I must've misheard.

A long silence clung in the air. So, I laughed to acknowledge the nicety and chose to deny the racial slur. I must have misheard him, I thought again. It had been a long first day, after all. And I still had to edit Craig's 'Barely Legal' article where we had a countdown for a child opera singer and a Harry Potter star turning sixteen.

Derrick walked out of the room to go to his meeting with

the producer of *Hollyoaks* and Craig smirked. 'Yeah, Derrick's a bit . . .'

'Un-PC?' I offered.

'Yes,' he nodded, and I wondered when un-PC had become a euphemism for racist.

'But he's a good guy.'

I smiled. I sat at my desk staring at my screen. Despite the toxic racism, I had finally achieved my dream of getting a job sitting down at a desk where my screen could not be seen by either my boss or my colleagues. I opened Facebook.

'Err, Nadia,' Craig sniggered. 'Bit of advice, Derrick can see your screen in the reflection from the frame behind you.'

I turned around, aghast to see that he was right. My screen was being projected onto the glass frame behind me. It was the infamous Salvador Dalí painting with the melting clocks and watches in the desert.

Shit, I thought.

I left the building that day feeling as most people often do on a first day, completely overwhelmed and bushwacked. No pun intended. I began my walk to my new digs in London, trying to disregard the racist comment about my dad from Derrick. I focused only on the positive. I still couldn't believe I had found a place to live for free in London. Of course, my aunt hadn't, given her blatant homophobia, been my first choice, but the deal was too good to refuse. Free accommodation in central London? Like *Bangers* and racism, I would just have to push the homophobia aside.

'Hey, wait up!' I heard a deep voice from behind me. It had a husk to it like gravel on sandpaper. It brought back memories of

Bristol. Various people approaching me from behind, angrily blaming the pain in their trousers on me.

I had come to Shepherd's Bush to get away from these people. I kept walking. Staring straight ahead, approaching the mosque on the corner of Loftus Road, the hustle of Muslims rushing into what looked like a community centre for Maghrib prayer.

I could hear the person running towards me from behind and panting. Someone was following me! My mother had told me London was a dangerous place, it was getting dark too! I had no choice but to duck into the mosque for safety. There my mind started to race. Perhaps it was another person angry at me for giving them herpes. I knew herpes wasn't an airborne disease, but it could have migrated rapidly from the BS1 postcode to W12 simply via the Southwestern Train rail links. 'Bollocks,' I said to myself from the interior of the mosque. A gaggle of young Muslim girls who smelt aromatically of henna looked me up and down, making me feel like I was back at school again. I don't think I belonged in their club, on account of saying 'bollocks' and not 'bismillah'.

I turned back around, hoping that whoever had been following me had now given up. I negotiated the swarm of people entering the mosque, tutting at me as I walked out. The level of dismay was not dissimilar to when I had gone the wrong way up the stairs at a tube station. I was relieved when I finally got out and was back onto the Loftus Road. The last of the day's sun warmed my skin, simultaneously blinding me.

'Hey, Nadia!' This time the voice was right in front of me. I ducked my head out of the light so I could see my herpes attacker. I thought about running. I wasn't fast but I could certainly beat a person that was suffering from a bout of pus-filled cold sores on their nether regions. But something inside me told me to stay and face the music. I couldn't keep running from my problems. I had to take responsibility for them.

'Yes?' I sighed.

Everything started to go in slow motion, as my body went into PTSD, my heart raced, ready for the tirade of abuse I knew I was about to get.

'You left your wallet on your desk,' the girl said.

She was barely a girl, really. She towered over me. Her broad shoulders seemed to shield me from what was in front of me. She had short floppy hair, like a boy's, which parted greasily in the middle of her small forehead. Her forehead was the smallest I had ever seen. The space between her scalp and her eyebrows was minuscule. I wanted to measure it, just like I wanted to measure my epilepsy specialist's nose every time I saw her for check-ins. It was odd this obsession with women's features.

The girl, or rather woman, handed me my purse. I stood, my mouth agape, reading her face. It was oddly unsymmetrical. Her nose veered slightly to the left and her large eyes seemed like they were too close to each other and yet I couldn't stop staring at them. The size of them was disproportionate to the narrowness of her face. There was a lot going on in her face, I realised. Her features were overcrowded, filling every available space.

'I think the word you are looking for is "thanks"? Anyway, my name is Courtney. I work with you at *Bangers*, upstairs in the edit suites,' she said.

'Oh, thank you!' I blustered. 'Sorry, I thought you were someone else.'

'Someone you were running from and had to escape into a mosque for?' she mused. She smiled and showed her teeth, which were as overcrowded as her face. Her unconventional 'ugliness' was somehow deeply charming, so much so that I felt myself blushing.

'Running from let me guess,' she paused for effect, 'Derrick the Racist?'

'Racist?' I pretended I didn't understand.

'Has he talked about our Jewish landlords yet?'

'No!' I yelped, appalled. 'He did say the P word, though.'

'Yeah, Derrick's the most racist, antisemitic, misogynistic man I've ever met, and my last job was at the *Daily Mail*.'

'Crikey.'

'If I have any advice for you, it's this: just think of the money and don't let the bastard grind you down.'

'Isn't that a quote from *The Handmaid's Tale*?'

'Yes.'

'Well,' I said, as I made to leave, 'I won't think of the money because he's paying me minimum wage, but I certainly won't let the bastard, or any other bastard in fact, grind me down.'

Grind. The very sound of the word was causing a fracas inside me.

I was simultaneously scared and excited at the same time. I felt an affinity with Teta; she always described the magazine industry in this way.

Fatiha

CAIRO, 1956

ف

'When I was in Paris, I used to think that Place de la Concorde was Tahrir Square's much more glamorous sister,'
I said to Ali as we followed the crowd to what the English were
now calling 'Liberation Square'. He was a few paces in front of
me with our little Usman on his shoulders. I wondered for a
moment where Aziz had gone. He was with us just a second ago,
but his small body was able to squeeze between the crowds and
run off. We would probably find him later at the square getting up
to some sort of mischief no doubt. I concentrated on holding onto
Yasminah instead of wandering off to find him. Her small hand
was cold like my own. I pinched her fingers to warm us both.

'Mama!' she said, pointing at two women in the road linking
arms and dancing. The crowd passed them cheering and laughing
loudly. So loudly in fact that the celebratory rejoicing drowned
out the small number of hisses from some men who either failed
to understand the true significance of such a day or didn't care.

Ali was in front of Yasminah and I focused on the back of his head to avoid losing him. But I couldn't catch up with him. The sheer depth of the crowds on the street made everything feel so much slower. Cairene people, ordinarily so frenzied and frenetic, were forced to amble, saunter and meander like the Nile. Even though we were all euphoric with excitement there was a calmness to Cairo that gave out an ominous, unsettling air of a new chapter. It was fresh yet somewhat trepidatious and alien. Where would we go from here, we all wondered. Change instilled in some people a great sense of adventure but in others a great sense of fear. It was this mix of emotions that encapsulated the feeling on the streets.

As I clutched Yasminah's hand, I felt as though I was privy to the future. She toddled around, stumbling as she went, her pace of life finally at one with Cairo's, which had a pacifying effect on me. It felt as though I could slowly drift to sleep knowing that my child was in safe, warm hands. We had caught up to Ali and little Ussy now. With my free hand I held my husband's. He responded by kissing the top of my head and winking at Yasminah.

'Well, you probably compared the square to Paris because it was originally called Ismailia Square after the nineteenth-century ruler Khedive Ismail. Khedive commissioned the square to imitate the affluent districts of Paris. Paris on the Nile, he even instructed!' Ali said, more to Yasminah than to me.

'And was renamed Tahrir Square four years ago when we overthrew the constitutional monarchy – King Farouq – in favour of a republic!' I sang sweetly to my children.

'Paris on the Nile?' I questioned mainly to myself rather than to Ali. 'Perhaps that's why Doria is so fond of her walks along the river.'

'Francophone,' Ali said, nodding, and I shoved him in the ribs for imitating her haters. 'Is she coming?' he asked, and I shoved him in the ribs again. I squeezed Yasminah's hand, ever hopeful.

Today was a very big day in all of our lives. It felt like the whole of Egypt had come to the square from every walk of life, men, women, rich, poor, young, old, avid supporters of the cause and perhaps rather more oddly vehement non-supporters too.

Now that we were at the entrance to the square, I could see the journalist Zafarullah Zerdak at the corner of Talaat Harb with his wife. He ran his hands through his greasy, mousey hair as his overtly pregnant wife held a placard which said, 'We Support Nasser No Matter What'. 'No Matter What' was underlined and had the same sarcastic tone that fused his backstabbing propaganda. I waved at him, smiling ironically, and he waved back, his perfectly bright white teeth shining like an oddly friendly shark. These sorts of people concentrated not on putting themselves on the right side of history but on the right side of power. I felt sorry for these sycophants, nothing was absolute to them. They were sheep, not bulls.

I wondered how many other people were as fickle as Zafarullah. Five years ago, one and a half thousand women helped us storm parliament to demand the vote, but now when we had finally secured it, with Nasser's blessing, there were tens of thousands more.

'Yallah!' Ali said, whistling me over to the crowd around the statue of nationalist hero Umar Makram, who famously resisted Napoleon. I ran over to him and the rest of our gang.

'Where is Aziz?' I asked.

'He has found Naila's boys. He said that Naila's husband had given them some money to get us all some candied chestnuts.'

I looked at him aghast.

'Candied chestnuts?' I groaned.

'We thought it would make a good press photo if they caught sight of us all eating them!' Naila's husband Dyab quipped suddenly in my ear. I looked up at him and faked a laugh.

I could see Rashida and Shula with their families and waved. Rashida made a face at me, and I made a face back. We needed no words between us to communicate our despair at Dyab's blatant publicity stunt. He loved being in and out of the papers. It was ironic that they were calling Doria an attention seeker, for it was Dyab who was only interested in the cause for his own fame. And now he wanted us all to stand with some candied chestnuts in reference to the article in *Rose al-Yusuf* magazine titled 'The Leader of Candied Chestnuts Discusses, Love, Dancing and the PhD'. But the article portrayed Doria in unflattering terms, mocking the fact that she was as artificially sweet as the very chestnuts that she served to the *Bint Al Nil* Union. The journalist sneeringly wrote that Doria, serving the delicacy, 'expressed an air of aristocracy, akin to Marie Antoinette, unlike the western publications that she fraternised with who baptised her a modern Cleopatra'. According to him, Doria's politics were solely performative and he questioned, 'was she affirming this aristocracy when she offered candied chestnuts to the board members of *Bint Al Nil* at their long meetings?'

The press had been relentlessly mocking Doria for months now, calling her an attention seeker by going around the world, dressing overly glamorously and speaking out about Nasser's regime. But the worst of it was in one national publication where they released an abhorrent picture, superimposing her head onto a belly dancer's body in an obscene pose. She had phoned me crying, proclaiming it was the 'worst propaganda for a Muslim feminist leader!' Last week she had released a statement telling her haters it is one thing to criticise her but another thing to insult her.

It was all so bittersweet: the very reason we were out celebrating today was because of her demands. Yet no one was thanking her, they were only in gratitude of Nasser. The press was questioning Doria's performative politics, suggesting it was not fuelled by her need for equality but by her own narcissism, when everybody knew that Nasser was only appeasing women by giving us the vote so that he could take control of the EFU and *Bint Al Nil* and realign them with his own centrist ideology.

I saw Dyab rushing towards his sons. And as I waved at Rashida, still holding onto Yasminah, I said to Ali, while smiling through gritted teeth, 'We are not posing with candied chestnuts for the press! No matter how much Dyab insists. OK?'

'Of course not, is he crazy?' my husband asked.

'Yes, he is. Very. Come on, yallah, let's join.'

I tried my best to put political nuance aside and take in today for what it was. A celebration of a step forward into the future. I took in the flags and banners, and the people holding them, this time not marching or storming but dancing and skipping, rejoicing. Traditional Nubian music was playing as well as Saidi and there were even hired professional dancers in the street. These women had been driven in from Upper Egypt, no doubt, in long colourful robes balancing Saidi sticks on their heads, their bodies jaunting from side to side to the beat and their arms above their heads free and flowing. We formed a circle around them, Ali and the kids along with Naila, Rashida and Shula and their families. The crowds were clapping to the beat of the click of the castanets as the high-pitched trumpet and the dreamy simsimiyah played out.

Ali brought Ussy down from his shoulders and I let go of

Yasminah's hand so we could let our children dance. We pushed the two ahead of us, as we got to the front of the performance. 'Look, Yasminah!' I cooed, as her little head gazed up in wonder at the spectacle. I spotted Aziz running around with Naila's twin boys, the three of them conspiring as they always did, Aziz imitating the dancers by putting his hands to his chest mocking their jiggling bosoms and the twins laughing hysterically. I glared at him, and he stuck his tongue out at me. I ran over to him and dragged him back by his ear. He yelped and hissed like a monster.

I crouched down to his level and said firmly into his ears, 'Respect for the women, please, Aziz.'

'Boobies!' Aziz said, and he ran off laughing.

'What is it about six-year-old boys and "boobies"?' I said, coming over to Naila and clapping harder so no one else could hear.

'Six-year-old boys?' Naila said. 'I don't think it stops at that age!' I rolled my eyes and nodded, looking up at both Dyab and Ali, who were entranced.

We came home merry and laughing. I took my shoes off to climb the long stairs up to our apartment. I watched my little family from behind, Aziz boisterously jumping on each stair and sliding down every other banister, Yasminah giggling in delight at her brother but too scared to do the same, and Usman asleep in Ali's arms, his eyelashes, which were even longer than his siblings', fluttering as he dozed in and out of peaceful slumber unaware of the significance of the day. I vowed that he would forever be told of his part in it.

Strolling into our apartment and collapsing on the sofa, the kids climbed all over us. Ali flicked the television on. The sounds of the crowds followed us into our home via the late evening news. I stumbled into the kitchen to make some tea when I heard the words from the reporter:

'Doria Shafik has announced her second hunger strike in protest at Nasser's so-called dictatorial regime!'

'Fatiha!' Ali called suddenly out of his euphoric stupor. I rushed back in leaving the saucepan bubbling on the stove. 'What the hell is she doing? We have got the vote! Kalas!' he shouted. I stared horrified at the television. I had often stared horrified at the television in recent years along with the papers, but this horror felt different. Because I realised in that moment that even I was feeling divided as to whether this was a move which aligned itself with the absolute or not. I dialled her number; perhaps I, her best friend, could make her see sense. Yes, I would talk to her, calm her down; now that she no longer had Nur, she didn't have anyone around to bring her back down to earth. Alone all day in that big house, with only her poetry as company, it didn't do the mind any good. I would speak to her, and it would all be OK again. She couldn't do another hunger strike, the last one almost killed her. And yes, she may have been commended because she only ended her strike upon receiving a written statement that President Naguib was committed to a constitution that respected the rights of women. But Naguib was a pussy cat compared to Nasser and she knew it. This hunger strike would be suicide. Nasser could not be placated and what grounds did she have? He had already given us the vote!

I waited for her to pick up, to hear her sweet voice, "Allo?', but to my exasperation it just rung out until I heard a long beep and then a crushing silence. My mind began to race and I was transported back to when Doria had announced her plans for the first hunger strike two years earlier.

Yasminah

ي

There were many parts to Behesht-e Zahra cemetery. The graves of unknown soldiers were lined up clean and uniform as if still standing to attention, never resting even in so-called paradise. A red lantern on a piece of bark held vigil on each. There was no way to distinguish one from the other. Forever a collective, never an individual even in death. Soldiers are the ultimate Buddhists. For they have foregone their ego, their true souls only existing, not in the cemeteries, but in the hearts of their loved ones. These graves were never touched by familiar faces, only stoic strangers coming to make sense of their own horrors, not to commemorate theirs.

Then there were the Iran–Iraq War victims' graves. These graves had personality. At times you felt like you were in their bedrooms, awash with photos and memorabilia. Next were the tombs of 'celebrated' public figures, even in death able to get a little bit more out of their terminated life. Their statues were supposedly things of beauty and opulence but they had a subtext of vulgarity.

And then there were the ordinary graves. Personalised but not overtly optimised. Not a total ego death of the unknown soldier nor a narcistic installation of a politician or a celebrity or a dictator.

The class system existing even in death was the philosophy I was grasping while walking through Behesht-e Zahra cemetery.

'Zahra's Paradise,' I said, translating the name of the cemetery from Farsi to English, as we sat on the bench opposite Ommy's grave. It was one of the nicer civilian-looking ones, it overlooked a linden tree whose golden flowers smelt like sugarcane candy. The foliage it produced created a secluded shady alcove behind his grave, a place for mourners to grieve in private.

'Hardly!' Farah said. 'This is nobody's paradise!' Her face had aged, like honey. Her sweetness was thicker, no longer pure and smooth; she had texture now.

She turned around to check no one was watching and then she held my hand. They were still as soft as when we danced at Rainbow on the night of Doria's death. It also felt like the first time again with Ommy, when we held hands under the table at Aziz's club. I looked down and felt the impenetrable hardness of her wedding ring.

'I always wondered why you didn't come with me to London that day I stormed into your home,' I told her, my face hard, stoic, refusing to look into her eyes which were still as grey and big as before. Instead, I focused on Ommy. I saw him laughing at us hysterically. Everything was always such a joke to him. The night before I left finally for London, I showed up at Farah's house. I told her that she loved me and that it was only fear standing in her way.

'What would have happened to my children?' she said suddenly angry. 'I couldn't abandon them like . . .'

I got up. I wasn't going to be insulted again like before.

'How is Hany?' she said.

I didn't answer. I sat down again. This time I'd brought her behind the linden tree, I couldn't rely on just words any more. I pulled her into me and kissed her softly as first, then harder. She pushed me away and then she pulled me back into her again. Our breaths were syncopated, in time with each other, our heartbeats finally as one. After several minutes we both stopped, realising what we had to do next, what we could possibly not repress any longer.

'Let's go,' she whispered.

I followed her out of the cemetery like a student on a school trip. We tried to keep in single file, but I wanted to ask her everything and the world. I couldn't stop the pull that was aligning us together. We walked out of the illustrious gates of Behesht-e Zahra and into a taxi.

We sat in silence, only letting the hustle of Tehran speak to us. It was only when the taxi driver drove up a gravel road that we began to protest.

'This is not the right way,' Farah said softly to the driver at first, but when he didn't listen, her voice was firmer. 'No, this is not the right way, I live in Pardis!'

The driver made a sudden stop on a dusty abandoned road. Not saying a word, he opened the glove compartment and casually took out a gun. Farah gasped. 'No, please! Please, I am a mother, please! I have children, babies, please, no,' she wailed while I breathed in, my eyes transfixed on the gun. He turned to us and smiled.

'Shhhh!' he said laughing, flashing his identity card from the Islamic Revolution Committee. I held Farah's trembling hands, turned towards her and tried to tell myself that this was just a warning. We had not previously been caught by the Committee, but I had heard horror stories about other gay couples who had become victims of their hate crimes. I tried to comfort her with my eyes while my head began to quietly explode with mania. Her tears plopped onto the leather seat of the taxi, like the pebbles Aziz and I would throw into the Nile.

We got taken into a large shed. We were both trembling now and Farah could barely walk. She kept stumbling on bits of gravel, falling down and sobbing. Every time she did the driver took his gun out again and I quickly hoisted her up, practically carrying her to our destination. Two shadowed figures came in front of us and kicked us to the ground. The driver put his gun back in his pocket, pulled a small packet from his jacket and lit a cigarette while he sneered at us struggling at his feet.

My stomach felt like it had gone into my heart, I couldn't even gasp. They kicked us again. Farah wailed, her mouth sobbing, her eyes still shocked. I rolled over to see her expression expanding and contracting with pain. I reached out for her hand as I waited for more agony. I prayed to Allah. Please, just a kick. I don't care how many but please, please don't let them do anything else to us. And if they do, let them do it to me, not Farah.

I waited for my fate to be decided. I lay there, the cold stones on my back, picturing my tragic ending, seeing it materialise on the thick iron ceiling before me. Hot tears slithered down my cheeks while I considered the tragedy of my life and how it flowed like a river – the great Nile – rippling into Mama's life, Baba's life, into Hany's life like wretched little tributaries. People pray for a quick death, but in that shed, I would be grateful for a slow one. My body was shutting down, lethargically processing these last few moments of consciousness as we were kicked again and again, my thoughts turning to the tragic beauty of it all.

Then I heard screams, and I wondered why Allah was not allowing me the dignity of a silent death. I wailed at the loudness of it all. I yelped and bawled and cried out to the ceiling. It took me a while to realise the screams were laughter. That the other men had run out, sniggering, yelling, 'Perverts!' I looked up, confused, and saw the driver still standing threateningly over us. He stubbed out his cigarette and walked away. With every crunch of the gravel, I didn't dare believe we were truly free. I wouldn't allow myself to believe it, to be sure that they had gone. I lay with Farah for what felt like an eternity. I had her finally in my arms, in peace at last, but at what price?

Finally, I let myself move. Where I had used my body to shield Farah, I now lay with her side by side. I looked into her eyes to see that they were crushed like walnuts, split open. We would never have our paradise, I realised. Not in the way that we wanted.

Nadia

ن

I liked reciting the Quran. It had a poetic rhythm that soothed me. There was a musicality to its recitation. The Surah Al-Fatiha was my favourite. It had a very similar beat to the 'Hail Mary' that we used to recite every morning assembly at our school in Ascot. That was back when our parents made Kadijah and me pretend to be Catholics because St Anthony's boasted the best Ofsted results in our catchment area. Now that we were pretending to be Muslims in Dhahran I was realising that the two religions had a lot in common. Aside from the obvious, Ramadan was Lent and Eid was Christmas. Friday was Sunday and Catholic guilt was Islamic shame. The only real difference was that I had a touch more respect for Mohammed than I did for Jesus, who was only really famous off the back of his dad. Mohammed was more the self-made man, the Richard Branson of prophets if you will, whereas Jesus was more of a Chelsea Clinton. I had shared this thoughtful observation with my Quranic teacher who promptly told me to go home and kiss

233

the sacred book three times for comparing the Prophet to a man who chose to call his company Virgin.

We were legitimate Muslims now in Saudi Arabia. Kissing Qurans and everything. Although I was also regularly snogging the face off Lee from 911 that I had ripped out of my *Smash Hits* magazine and put above my bed. Uncle Christopher knew we had an obsession with the Spice Girls, so he sent us clippings of them that were in his *Sun* newspaper as well as a copy of *Smash Hits* each month. Receiving these packages from our dodgy uncle was like receiving contraband in prison. We would often find that the magazine had been tampered with by Saudi Arabian customs officers. They had blacked out all the bits of exposed flesh on any articles the Spice Girls were in, so that Posh looked like she was wearing leggings not a miniskirt and Geri looked like she was wearing a turtleneck not a tank top. Fortunately, and with somewhat ironic hindsight, they left 911 alone.

Our Islamic faith was official. Not only were we kissing Qurans and attending a strict Muslim school, but we were wearing the abaya, the hijab, sometimes even the niqab if we travelled further west, away from the more liberated Bahrain. Even my Irish mum had converted. My dad's contract was drawn up on the proviso that they were to have a shotgun Islamic marriage at the Saudi Arabian embassy in Green Park. A Muslim man could not be married to a non-Muslim, for he would be otherwise declared an apostate, the strict laws of Saudi Arabia pertained.

'A forced marriage,' my mother called it, laughing, before adding, 'the only way that any woman would be stupid enough to marry your father twice,' to which my dad would remind her, yet again, that all his earnings would be tax free.

Through our religious conversions I later saw that my parents were only doing what typical immigrants do. They were changing and adapting their behaviour to fit the country they were in. In the UK we were Irish Catholic; in Saudi Arabia we were Egyptian Muslims. What Kadijah and I actually were, although we didn't vocalise it at the time, were agnostic; what we *all* were, I believed, although my parents would never admit it.

This dichotomy of religions was never spoken of. Our Egyptian family assumed we were Muslim, and our Irish family assumed we were Catholic.

'This is music to my ears, my two favourite grandchildren reciting my favourite verse! The Surah Al-Fatiha – it's my surah!' We could hear Teta laughing and crying at the same time, which often confused us.

Kadijah and I shared the phone and made eyes at our dad. He mimed for us to stay on the call a little bit longer.

When Teta got overly emotional, Kadijah and I never quite knew how to react. At least we were on the telephone so she couldn't pinch our cheeks and kiss us at the same time. The mixture of pain and tenderness was again disconcerting to us.

'Emotional abuse!' Kadijah mouthed to me, nudging me hard in the ribs at the same time.

I didn't know how to react, so I just whispered 'so passive aggressive' to show her I agreed. With Kadijah it was always better if you just agreed with whatever it was she was saying, whatever cause she was supporting, whatever person she was slagging off. Even if you didn't believe her at the time, you would always inevitably find out that she was right in the future.

We listened while Teta gushed in Arabic about how we were finally such 'good Muslim girls' now that we could recite surahs but to also 'try and fight against the Islamic patriarchy', which again was somewhat perplexing.

'Women still cannot vote, and they cannot drive in Saudi!' she screamed so loud we pulled the phone away from our ears.

My dad was sitting in the armchair by the television; he was half listening and half watching a football match, Saudi versus Bahrain. He got up when he heard Teta's emphatic protests through the phone. He took the phone from Kadijah and me. 'Mama!' he said, sniggering to himself. 'Women can't drive here, it's no different to the UK, only it's a law not just an opinion!' He ran off like a naughty little child, back to his football.

'Wallahi Ussy!' we heard Teta scream back before laughing and chastising her 'cheeky' son.

My sister and I stood awkwardly, still sharing the phone before looking at each other and nodding. It was time to hang up.

'We have to go now Teta, we are working on our . . .' I began.

'. . . Quran homework!' we said in unison.

Kadijah added, '. . . an essay all about Aisha, wife of Mohammed, and how she learned military skills . . .'

'. . . pre-war negotiations between combatants, conducting battles,'

'. . . and ended wars!' we said together. We could hear her shrieking 'Alhamdulillah!' over and over again. We hung up and Kadijah instantly changed the TV channel while indicating for my dad to get out of her chair.

'Hey!' my dad retaliated.

'They are on half time and *Family Matters* is on! You said if we spoke to Teta, we could watch it . . .'

'OK, OK,' my dad said, scuffing her hair and joining my mother in the kitchen.

We both allowed ourselves to relax, Kadijah on the armchair and me on the sofa. Oh, how we loved Steve Urkel from *Family Matters*. I had even dressed as him for Halloween, which Kadijah had warned me was 'cultural appropriation'. I didn't know where she was getting these terms from, it's like she was speaking a foreign futuristic language half the time. But Antonio had agreed.

'You can't be Steve Urkel, you're not a black American boy,' he'd said.

Antonio was an Italian boy on the KFUPM campus that I regularly rollerbladed with. I had a fairly complicated relationship with him. We had kissed and he had given me a ring (it was a cheap plastic one which I was fairly sure was from a Christmas cracker) but then he had dumped me for Gemma Harris, a Scottish girl he had said he was more compatible with. Probably because they both went to the underground Christian school together.

'Your sister is dressed as a cat. Sami over there is dressed as a wolf. Walid the tiger from the Frosty's ad and your mum has gone as a twenty-two-year-old cheerleader, we're all cultural appropriating,' I said, wondering if I had used Kadijah's term correctly while eyes agog at his mother's exposed décolletage.

All the western women took full advantage of Halloween in Saudi. For it was the only night in the year that they could dress as slutty as they wanted without the Mutawa (the religious police) saying anything. As much as the Saudis shunned westernisation (arts and culture not science and technology), the way they celebrated Halloween was more American than America. 'Everyone on this compound is dressed as something they are not,' I'd rebutted.

'Allah-hu-akbar!'

Kadijah and I groaned. With the call to prayer the television instantly went into the Islamic intermission test card. A picture of the great mosque of Mecca, a stock photo of the Masjid al-Haram, surrounded by crowds. My sister and I amused ourselves during the twenty-minute prayer intermission as we waited for Urkel to come back onto our screens by playing a game called 'Where's Auntie?' It was a game we had made up which was a sort of Middle Eastern version of 'Where's Wally?' To relieve the tedium between waiting for the call to prayer to be over and our programme resuming, we would try to find Aunt Yasminah in the crowded stock photo. We figured she went so regularly to Mecca she would of course be in the generic image.

'There she is!' Kadijah yelled, as we burst out laughing, pointing at a fat woman in a turban headscarf.

'That's Auntie if she let herself go!' I yelled.

'You know, I think Teta is very happy you girls are learning the Quran,' my dad said as he strolled back into the room, scoffing one of my mother's chocolate chip cookies, fresh out of the oven. I could see the steam coming out of the dough and with it my mouth began to water. Since coming to Saudi my mother had become like a Stepford wife and had developed a passion for competitive baking for the brunch mornings she frequented with the other bored expat housewives. We knew full well these brunch mornings were all a ruse for the (mostly British) ladies of the compound to get together and secretly brew their own wine.

I lifted my head up from the sofa, to allow room for my dad to sit down while breaking a bit off the cookie. I felt the warm chocolate goo flood into my bloodstream, like a sudden influx of guests at a house party. With the happy sugar rush placating me, I plonked my head down on my dad's knee while he stroked my head.

'But she told me that she wants you both to read her article in *Bint Al Nil* about the verse 4:34.'

Kadijah groaned. Teta was always talking about the controversial articles she wrote in *Bint Al Nil* with her bestie Doria Shafik.

'Any opportunity for her to relive her happiest days, when she was immersed in the written word, fighting for Egyptian women . . . yada yada yada blah blah blah,' my dad quoted Teta while throwing the last bits of cookie into his mouth, before cracking his knuckles and burping and farting at the same time.

Fatiha

ف

I was frustrated that I was pregnant at such a time when my country needed me. I collapsed into my chair in my office, the phone gripped tightly in one hand while the other stroked the magnitude of what was before me, both physically and metaphorically. Doria began the rigmarole of her latest antics which, inspired by her beloved Mahatma Gandhi's philosophy of non-violence, she saw as an act of defiance that would get her, us, *Bint Al Nil* and Egypt closer to her absolute. Meanwhile, I rolled my eyes to the ceiling. I was deeply embittered, almost to the point of tears, that my physical predicament was preventing me from going on a hunger strike too. I heard Ali muttering at the television in the living room and despaired at the irony of it all. How, ultimately, my body had become incapacitated by a man, which was preventing me from continuing my work for women's liberation. I had not wanted this baby. But Ali saw a child as a gift from Allah. This child, he had told me, would be 'the intelligent one', he had said, despairing at Aziz, who was using his fingers to root around his nose, as if his nasal cavities contained not just yellow crusts of mucus but golden crustaceans of treasure.

'This baby will be the exceptional one,' he had said, looking at little Yasminah with equal disdain who was failing to understand the mechanisms of the building block toy we had recently bought her. She was trying to stick a cubic shape into a circular hole. The phallic nature of it all reaffirmed my wish that if only Ali had had similar difficulties six months prior, perhaps I would not be in this very predicament. Ali. Oh, Ali. He had insisted, this child was blessed. I wasn't so sure. I was so certain it was a boy because I knew Allah so adored introducing irony to my life: here was yet another male causing disarray in my life. This child who hadn't even been born yet, this small yet ever-growing tyrant was declaring his dictatorship on my body. He was disabling me from continuing my life's work with Doria. Hormonal tears began to fall, as I heard Doria's latest explosive plot. I whimpered away my weak, artificial crocodile tears. Tears that I could not trust as they were orchestrated by the uninvited guest chemicals fizzing around in my body. They were not hardened tears, they were flimsy. They were not multi-dimensional ones, they were fickle. I would be laughing the next minute, I knew it. I couldn't even trust my own emotions any more; my body was not my own.

'So, you must come immediately here to me, to Zamalek, habibbti. You will have to pick up the children from school after I have left and to fill Nur in, is that OK?' Doria's words wounded me even more. The ferocity with which she spoke of her plans of protest only stabbed me with paralysis when they ordinarily jolted me into action.

'Yes, of course,' I said cheerfully, while my face contorted with devastation, my lower lip quivering, my tears falling, my cheeks collapsing. I closed my eyes again. It was the only way not to see what was before me.

The very monster felt both a part of me and detached. Like a gigantic pimple that I wanted to squeeze out as quickly as it had appeared. Instead, I left it to grow all the more bulbous so that it would not leave a scar, at least not a mark, psychologically. I had seen first-hand how removing it also removed a part of the self. A self you could never get back. A ghost which I would only be reacquainted with in paradise. Alas, this infliction would merely wound me temporarily. Even if I was like some destitute urban woman from some backward village and wanted more to get rid of it even at the expense of a permanent hell like hem, if I had even suggested we got rid of it in the nascent stages, Ali would never look at me the same way again. So, I let it overpower my body and found myself only at very odd moments contemplating throwing myself down the stairs. I had come close. Claiming I needed the liminality of the communal hallway, where I was both in my apartment but out of it, to clear my mind while I wrote an important article for the magazine. When really the only thing I was writing were the different ways of bringing my current predicament to an end. Just one step off the crumbling cliff, I thought. These things happen, the doctor would say. Such a tragedy, Ali would whisper, while I wept and wept and wept the last of my crocodile tears. But I couldn't do it. Not only because of the fear of my judgemental neighbours witnessing my dramatics, but because Ali would render the entire tragedy as what it actually was: orchestrated theatrics. If he even as much as suspected I put my ambitions for my country before his son, our relationship would be doomed.

So, I convinced myself that this was not merely a bunch of

cells entwining their carnivorous roots into my body like vines on a Venus fly trap, but sacred flesh; full and formed from Allah. I told myself that this new addition to the family was a gift, that he was the chosen one, the special one. But most importantly, in order to accept it, I told myself I would not let it disrupt my work. I could do both: give birth to a future prodigy while righting the past of Egyptian women's emancipation. Doria and I wanted to continue Amin's work, holding fast to our belief that Egypt could only head into the enlightenment of post-colonial independence if all of Egypt's people, men and women, rich and poor, were free and equal. We had begun indeed to unionise, to redistribute the wealth, but the new regime was splintering and splitting. The Muslim Brothers were attempting to take control of our now military-controlled government while the supposed commendable Revolutionary Command Council was pitting General Naguib against Colonel Nasser. Egypt had shed its ties with Britain, but without the reins of colonial rule, a stampede of so-called stallions fuelled by vanity and toxic male narcissism was causing an ongoing state of insecurity, instability and inconsistency. It was the refusal of the Revolutionary Command Council's desire to share seats with women which was the last straw for Doria. I would not allow my pregnancy to delay Egypt's progress into modernity.

Alas, now it was undeniably taking its toll. I was in the latter stages of pregnancy where my rotund swollen belly overshadowed every act of defiance. My bump had sneakily bulged into my eyeline and now the monstrosity was unavoidable, a constant reminder of my physical inabilities. I had been through this before with Aziz and Yasminah of course. While I was still in the last trimester with my daughter, I managed to write, to attend meetings, even to walk the streets, reciting Doria's proclamations as if they were poetry. But now, what she was suggesting was near impossible to partake in.

'I have never let pregnancy get in the way of my protest in the past so why must I now?' I asked more to myself than to Doria. I knew I was defeated, however I couldn't help but try once more.

Doria laughed and continued, as if her chortle alone was a sufficient explanation. She had already made me swear once again on the Quran as soon as I had answered her call that morning.

'You must come immediately to me,' she summoned. Her two girls were at school and Nur was at work. We would be alone for several hours, together planning the practicalities. I would tell Ali I was going shopping, which he knew almost immediately was a euphemism for my secret business with Doria, so much so he had stopped asking for me to pick up his favourite brand of cigarettes and had taken to simply grunting whenever I said it.

I whispered down the telephone, 'Yes, I shall.' I had lost my voice at the very thought of this illicit rendezvous. I could hear Ali tutting and changing the channel on the television, followed by a croaky cough, from my office. He really must stop smoking, his teeth were yellow from tobacco, his lungs dusty. How did Doria remain so glamorous, cigarette in hand practically all her life and my husband looked so old and tired? I closed my eyes and held my heart, thankful that Doria was around to add excitement to my marriage, otherwise I wondered who knows what I would have done. Without Doria's work would Ali and the children have been enough? The doomed thought ticked through my brain as fast as a train running through Cairo station. It was gone before I could make it a tangible consideration. Instead, it lay in the depths of my subconscious.

'Please, Doria, perhaps I can join you? There must be a way. It shouldn't be for long. It's a symbolic gesture anyway, really, they won't let us go more than twenty-four hours before they relinquish . . .'

Doria laughed again at the preposterousness of my proposition that I, a woman in her sixth month of pregnancy, take part in a hunger strike at the Press Syndicate. I could tell that she would be unwilling to relent, however I knew that if anyone had the brains to find some sort of medical, political or logistical loophole which would allow it, it would be my very best and dearest friend. It wasn't so preposterous putting my child at risk. After all, Doria was too. She had already admitted to me that, despite her love for her children, she couldn't worry about the traumatic implications this would forever have on their lives if she did die of hunger. Getting closer to her absolute was more important than being around for little Jehane and Aziza. Perhaps it was all really very selfish, the work we were doing? It seemed, at times, that our legacy was more important than the love we had in our lives in the present. Yet still Doria would not allow it.

'A pregnant feminist on a hunger strike, Fatiha, we would be annihilated in the press! Not only would we be the laughing stock, but it is a deeply flawed philosophy. We would never be taken seriously again, can you imagine? We are fighting for future generations and yet stifling the health of a token foetus of that very generation. Absolutely not! I am taking Naila instead.'

'Naila! She's probably only agreed to it to lose a few pounds!' I retorted as I threw my sweet but simple friend under the bus.

'It doesn't matter. It's a numbers game. The more of us that we get into the embassy, the more influential we will be,' she explained, before emphasising, 'Women who are not in the family way! Now for goodness sake, I won't hear another word about you joining us. I need someone on the ground to talk to the press, reassure Nur and help me with political negotiations should I become deliriously weak with hunger. Now get over here straight away, yallah basora!' I couldn't argue anymore and so I sighed, before hanging up.

'Aiywa.' I let the phone click back into its groove. 'Ali!' I called. 'I'm going shopping!'

∾

A week later, Doria, Naila and seven other women, including the American journalist Charlotte Weller (who had celebrated Doria's plight in the international news and become a symbol that our protest was not just for the rights of Egyptian women but for the rights of women in the west too), were physically removed from their mattresses at the Press Syndicate and taken for urgent medical care. I watched as Nur pulled his wife's fragile body through the stampede of photographers' flashes and the equally critical and congratulatory crowds making a symphony of tuts and cheers, into the car which would take her to hospital. Doria, meanwhile, worried that being in hospital and away from the public eye of the embassy would result in a loss of impact. As much as she hated the press, she needed them. I had come to realise that *Bint Al Nil* could survive the past five days without food, but we couldn't survive five days without the media. Women's liberation cannot be achieved quietly and demurely, we have to be loud. Let them call us hysterical, let them call us ugly, let them call us sluts. Media, fame and her celebrity fuelled her like food. Without it the cause would be starved. I held her in my arms in the hospital bed as she made sure that headlines were still being made about the 'five brunettes and two blondes' and 'Doria Shafik who, even after having two children, still preserves a Marilyn Monroe-type figure'.

'As long as we are still making the front page, as long as we are publicised, we will have progress. We must never become invisible to Egypt.'

And so Doria, despite fighting for her life, continued making headlines from her hospital bed. *Al-Ahram* newspaper published daily accounts of the 'battle of wills' and 'the war of nerves' between her and Naguib and Nasser's unofficial representatives. Even reporting that the hunger strike between what cynics called the 'al-abathat – the irresponsible women' had not only incited debate over gender equality but suggested a potential referendum between a return to civil rule and the re-establishment of parliament or surrendering to the military junta. Seeing the impact Doria was having from her hospital bed, the Revolutionary Command Council finally relented, and our demands were promised to us at last. Doria had asked for women to be represented on the committee which constructed the new constitution. This had been accepted and the Council, after days of Doria shaking up the country, became suddenly sycophantic, even admitting that it agreed with the human rights policies of the United Nations and would 'gladly accord political rights to the Egyptian women'. Three days after that negotiations were finally agreed.

Despite this heroic conquest, she still polarised the nation and, leaving hospital, she was met by a torrent of abuse. Men circled around us hissing and booing, declaring, 'Let the husbands beat these whores, the Quran authorises it.' But what hurt Doria the most was the criticism from the League of Arab and Eastern Women and the National Feminist Union who deemed the hunger strike futile and were reported to have claimed that 'at such an unsettled time in Egypt, demanding women's rights was against the interests of the country'.

Perhaps in the polarisation, the drama of it all, in the last stage of my pregnancy, I saw only what it was to me personally. My best friend had almost died. Now she was a small, frail woman who needed to be carried by her husband. She had lost over 36 pounds, Naila an enviable 25. Meanwhile, I remained a fat figure of gluttony, gorging on glazed dates and fat fig rolls. I ate to feed not only my son but to compensate for the loss I felt at not being by Doria's side during her rebellious act. I stuffed my face to stop the pangs of jealousy I felt as I witnessed not myself, but silly Naila on the mattress next to Doria on all the front pages. All the while as I feasted, I knew deep in the pit of my stomach that this hunger could never be satiated until Doria was returned to me. Only then would I stop such excessive eating. Only then would my belly stop rumbling. And so, when Doria was returned to me, it was only then that I could finally feel the jubilant feet of my son, whose tiny toes protruded my flesh, as if in celebration. A child who had now become in my fantastical mind a reincarnation of Qasim Amin or even Ibn Arabi but perhaps more realistically, a prized token of the next generation of Egyptians.

Everyone at *Bint Al Nil* was deeply changed after the hunger strike. What the girls lost in weight they had gained in empowerment and camaraderie. Meanwhile, despite my growing obesity, I felt significantly smaller, and even months after, I couldn't shake the feeling that through my failure to join these women, to join Doria in one of her 'most irresponsible acts', I had forever lost a part of myself. My failure to join these women resulted in my feeling that I had lost my sense of self.

Nadia

LONDON, 2012

ن

I turned the lock and heard the metallic tinkle of my cousin Hany's simsimiyah, the Arabic harp-like instrument that he was learning to play. Shit, I thought. He was playing the opening chorus of Umm Kulthum's 'Inta Omri'. Perhaps I *should* have gone to my dad's Edinburgh Preview in Soho tonight. I had politely declined. My dad's new hour at Edinburgh, or 'difficult second album' as he called it, entitled *Sex Bomb* gave me the shivers. I don't know what could be worse, listening to an hour of Muslim terrorist jokes or an hour of jokes about his sex life, which is what the blurb promised the show would be. He'd also told me how his entrance music was going to be the Tom Jones track of the same name. Oh. God. No. Nobody wants to see their dad do that. Night in at Aunt Yasminah's it was.

I heard Hany's simsimiyah again, this time accompanied by Rasha's flute, Rabia's oud, Rania's trumpet and little Rahima's tambourine. Hany and his wife were like the Muslim version of the von Trapp family. Only when I teased them about it, they

251

insisted it was to help the children deal with their separation. Music and still living together apparently helped my cousin and his wife (also my cousin) deal with the separation.

I groaned. I was tired, all I wanted to do was watch back-to-back episodes of *Hollyoaks* on E4 (and call it research). All the while saying as little as possible to my aunt in the other room who would be watching back-to-back episodes of *Loose Women*. But when family were round, mine and my aunt's monosyllabic relationship went out the window. It was the only time we conversed verbosely about topics outside of small talk and domestic mundanities. I took a meditative breath in at the door and tried to collect myself. Kadijah had told me that controlling your breathing helped manage your expectations with that of reality. 'Breathe out the expectation and breathe in the reality. Welcome it,' she had instructed.

So, I said goodbye to an evening spent relaxing writing down notable 'hotties' off *Hollyoaks* and googling who their agent was and said a bright hello to an evening of Middle Eastern live music, Arab delicacies and explaining the concept of *Bangers* magazine to my Muslim family. I opened the door with a big dazzling smile, as if I had just entered my own surprise birthday party. Rasha, Rania and Rahima dropped their instruments and came running to greet me. 'Auntie Nadia! Auntie Nadia!' Rahima latched onto my hands and started climbing up my body like I was a tree, flipping herself over when she came to my head. 'Whoa, you've really advanced since those Tumble Tot lessons, Rahimy,' I said.

Rasha and Rania laughed and told me that their little sister climbs everything and that their mother was always yelling at her, fretting about the deposit on the big house that they had recently moved into.

'Oh, be careful, Rahima, your parents worked really hard to afford that house.' By committing benefit fraud, I thought.

I stood for a while in the hallway bantering with the youngest generation of Bin-Khalids, trying to keep my cool, young aunt persona, asking them about school and Rasha's GCSE options. They gazed up at me, their eyes wide. No doubt thinking how very cool and grown up I was, as Kadijah and I used to do with Aunt Yasminah. 'So, er,' I said to fill the silence while they fan-girled me, 'yeah, definitely choose history over geography, Rash . . .' They were still staring. The three of them stood gawping up at me, with a mixture of fear and excitement. It was not dissimilar to their expressions when I had taken them to see Maz play a dead Victorian at Thorpe Park's *Fright Night* a few years back.

'In Year 11 the history teachers take you to Belgium, geography you just go to the Brecon Beacons.'

Suddenly little Rahima jumped up to touch my fringe before running off and giggling.

'Your fringe has got even shorter since the last time we saw you,' Rasha said.

'Oh yeah?' I said, turning to the mirror in the hall.

'I think it's too short,' their mother Rabia conceded as she approached me in the hall. She pulled me in to kiss my cheeks, before pushing me away to inspect. She studied my forehead as if she was a scientist in a lab. 'Yes, too short.'

I could feel myself wanting to cry.

'La, Mama! Daisy Dee has her hair like this,' Rania said, making me want to kiss her. *I looked like a popstar!*

'Yes, and Daisy Doo's fringe is too short too!' she laughed.

'Daisy Dee!' they all groaned.

I followed them into the living room-kitchen area, unsure

whether I had received a compliment or not. I flattened down my fringe and patted my lips to stop them quivering. The kids went back to their instruments. They said I looked like a pop-star; it was definitely a compliment, I told myself.

'Look, Auntie Nadia!' Rahima jiggled her tambourine. I jiggled my body back like a belly dancer. She laughed. I breathed in again, this time taking in the smell of my aunt's feast that she was preparing. I could smell the sweetness of the dates and cinnamon in the oven with the braised lamb shanks, the lemon and parsley of the tabbouleh salad and the pungency of fresh chopped garlic in the baba ghanoush. My mouth salivated, practically dribbling like a dog.

The one great thing about having Hany and his wife and kids round was the food. The worst thing was the insults disguised as compliments or the compliments described as insults. Aunt Yas-minah mostly survived on lentil soup, but when family were around, she went all out. She would make kochari or Teta's breaded escalopes or vine leaves or bamia but my favourite was always her lamb tagine. Perhaps not just for the taste but for the ritual of eating it from a large communal wooden bowl. My aunt would get the cushions out and we would sit cross-legged round the coffee table, a spoon each in hand, held like a sword, ready to do battle on the same field. Our cutlery fighting for the biggest chunks of lamb, the fluffiest bits of couscous. It was a touching way to bond with relatives and the next day I would often feel a new kinship with them. This closeness materialised in the form of a cough or a cold or in some cases a virus or infection which had been transferred via the close culinary experience.

'Salamwaylaykum, Cus!' I said, nodding.

'Salamwaylaykum right back at ya!' Hany dropped his sim-simiyah on the floor and came towards me. I kissed him once on each cheek and as I did so, took note of his snotty nose and croaky voice. The snotty nose and croaky voice that would be my fate this time tomorrow. Great, I thought. Can this night get any worse?

'You put on weight, no?' Hany asked.

My heart dropped. I shrugged.

'Yes, you put on lots of weight . . .' Rabia said. I saw the spoons laid out on the table and were glad they weren't knives. 'You were too skinny, before,' Rabia continued, 'you look, ah, what's the word?'

'Radiant?' I said, collapsing onto the sofa and putting my head in my hands.

'La, ahhhh . . . cuddly!' Rabia said. 'Much better,' she said, rubbing my thigh.

'Cuddly? Do you mean curvy?' I asked.

'No. Cuddly,' she said, cracking into a pistachio.

I got up to go and help my aunt in the kitchen. Without any hesitation I took an onion and started chopping it. I let the tears fall.

'Habibbti, everything is ready, you don't need to do anything,' she said, taking the onion and the knife away from me. I turned towards the window and wiped the tears away, telling myself to pull myself together.

'It smells wonderful, Auntie,' I said, turning around and smiling, my mouth wide and open.

∽

After dinner, Hany and Rabia and the kids played a new song they had been learning. My aunt and I sat laughing and clapping and for a while it made me forget our differences. We were family after all, what did it matter if they told me I was fat with a terrible fringe or that my aunt highlighted homophobic passages in the Quran probably to preach about to her grandchildren later? Our blood was thicker than insults and bigotry, surely? I continued to clap to the beat and found myself taken over by the rhythm of the song; it was starting to sound vaguely familiar and was making me want to get up and dance. So, I did. And to the children's delight, Aunt Yasminah did too, stopping only briefly to run to her bedroom and retrieve two scarves. She wrapped one around my waist before wrapping the other around her own, the act of which I found touching, like she was putting on my oxygen mask before her own. Hany and Rabia laughed as they continued to play. Rasha tried to keep a straight face as she squeaked on the flute. Holding hands with my aunt, we moved our hips to the beat of the music before letting go and gyrating around the room on our own. I began moving my hands in the same circular movements as my hips. My aunt did the same. I closed my eyes and saw Maz and I dancing on the pole at G-A-Y. I suddenly recognised the song.

'It's "Kiss Kiss" by Holly Valance!' I stopped dancing.

'La, mish keda, it's "Şımarık" by Tarkan! Tsss!' Rabia hissed while concentrating on her fingering of the oud.

'Yes, it's Tarkan, not that stupid bimbo off *Neighbours*!' Hany said as he also concentrated deeply on his fingering of the simsimiyah.

'Oh yeah, he did the original. My friend Maz loves the Holly Valance version,' I said.

My aunt suddenly stopped dancing and walked out of the room, saying, 'I must go and pray.'

'Didn't she pray before we ate?' I mouthed at Hany.

Hany, Rabia and the kids abruptly stopped playing.

'Is Auntie OK?' I asked, if only to fill the silence.

Hany sighed; he opened his mouth to speak but then closed it again.

'What?' I asked.

'Mama doesn't like your friend. She thinks he's a bad influence on you. And he stunk the house out with bacon the night he came over when she was doing Haj. She had to re-tile the walls.'

∾

When everyone had left, I began to sulk. I helped my aunt wash up but refused to converse with her. I concentrated only on scrubbing the pots and pans with the metallic scourer with the same precision as an archaeologist. Wanting to uncover the old surface of the pan but not wanting to destroy it in the process. My aunt dried the plates and filled the silences between my one-word answers by humming the tune of 'Intra Omri'.

'How is work going?'

'Fine.'

'Is your boss nice?'

'Yes.'

'Are your colleagues nice?'

'Yes.'

'Have you made any friends there?'

'Courtney. She's nice,' I said, before adding, 'she's gay like Maz by the way.' I stopped scrubbing to watch Aunt Yasminah's expression change from chirpy to sullen.

'Did Maz really stink out the flat with bacon so much the night I had the seizure that you had to re-tile the whole kitchen?' I went back to scrubbing the pan, this time more aggressively and less carefully than before. 'I mean it all seems a little dramatic if you ask me,' I added.

If my aunt was shocked by my outcry, she didn't show it.

'You know the smell of bacon makes me feel very sick. I could smell it after a week of Febreze, the extractor fan on and windows open all day.'

'Well, I'm glad you got the sick smell out, because you know, I know you find the smell very dirty and unclean and that it says in the Quran it is haram.' I peeled off my kitchen gloves and mumbled something about having to be up early in the morning to finish my 'Countdown to 16' article. I flounced into my room and collapsed onto my bed crying, wondering when the word 'bacon' had become a euphemism for 'gay'.

Yasminah

SAUDI ARABIA, 1999

ي

I sat wedged between Mona and her girlfriend Amal on the train to the Al-Jamarat. It was day three of our Haj this year and we were on our way to perform the tenth Dhul Hijjah, the Rami, the stoning of the devil. As usual we were with a group of other women who also had no male guardians to take them. As long as we stayed in this all-female group and didn't go off unattended, the Saudis permitted it. There were six of us, mostly from London, all of a similar middle age. An age so middling that it meant that they were divorced from their husbands, their fathers were dead, their brothers were non-existent and their sons were not old enough to be their mehrams. Mona and I never explicitly lied about our family situations but we, Amal too, I presumed, all gave off the impression that we also had no available male family to take us either.

I looked towards the group organiser, Yusria, a Sudanese woman who lived in Ladbroke Grove. A woman who through-out this trip perpetually held a clipboard and wore a whistle round her neck. She also had a permanent frown from constantly counting us multiple times a day. I smiled at her standing over us, wobbling a little as the train jolted. She tried to smile back, a quick unengaging smile, before checking to see if everyone was in tow again. It was easier for her to count us now, because this year she had introduced a new colour for us.

'Green is the new black,' she had joked, handing us all our new religious uniform at a meeting before the trip. We were dressed now in abayas and headscarves, a dirty lime colour instead of the traditional black. We would stick out amongst the crowds of mostly men in their white sheets draped flimsily around their bodies, like Gandhi.

The train leaving Muzdalifah and heading back to Mina was as packed as the Hammersmith & City line on a Monday during rush hour. I stood up to let an elderly woman carrying a walking stick sit down. Mona moved closer to Amal so that the old lady could sit on the edge and hold the pole. My best friend and her girlfriend were almost snuggling now, enjoying the enforced closeness without raising suspicion. I found myself standing directly under a man's armpit. I could practically smell the salt of his sweat and the thick curly hairs on his arm had the whiff of the waxy Labdanum resin. The scent of this incense pumped through the entire city of Mecca constantly, so much so I wondered if my religious spiritual enlightenment and consequent higher sense of consciousness wasn't transcendental at all but actually just me getting unintentionally high from the fumes.

I dipped my head down so I could just about see over to Amal and Mona, in the crack between his skin and his hair. I felt the ordinary pang of jealousy that momentarily pulsed through my body like a small electric shock each time. The sting that reminded me that they got to share this trip with each other, and that I could only share it with myself. No one would have guessed it, but the way they sat next to each other, their legs both crossed towards each other, their eyes never far from each other's gaze, it was impossible not to see it once you knew it. It was as if they had a shining white aura around them, an aura that was as welcoming as it was alluring, but even when they let you into their sphere, it still felt like they had yet another barrier that couldn't be penetrated; their own world you could never be truly part of. I had longed for this sort of bond my whole life. Always coming to the tips of it, the precipice of it, before it was taken away.

My heart had stopped for Ommy but with Farah it beat faster. I thought of the Behesht-e Zahra Cemetery. I was already hot, but I felt my upper lip beginning to sweat, the space between my thighs beginning to chafe. I tried desperately not to think such impure thoughts but then I wondered were these thoughts really so impure, if they were grounded in love? I focused on the armpit of the man in front of me, in an effort to quell them. I saw a bead of sweat hanging off one of its hairs. We were so crammed like sardines, I couldn't even turn my head to shelter myself from the imminent drip about to cascade onto my face. I closed my eyes. I saw Farah and Ommy dancing.

The train pulled up to the Al-Jamarat stadium. The jolt propelled the sweat from the man's underarm, which was hanging onto his hair for dear life, onto my face. I grimaced and quickly wiped it off my nose with my hand, while trying not to retch. I concentrated on the ethereality of the pilgrimage and not on how another man had violated me once again, albeit unintentionally.

It was only 6 a.m. and crowds had already formed so that almost the entire block of the grey concrete stadium was covered with white robes. There were pepperings of black, where the women walked beside their mehrams and male guardians. Our group was about to add some colour to the black and white scene and sprinkle the place with a dash of our green citrus zing.

As the train began to pull in you could hear people start to recite the Talbiyah. I started whispering it at first, my voice still croaky from waking up with no water, but before long I felt my voice growing in volume until I was spitting out the words as our train arrived at its station.

'Here I am, O Allah, here I am. Here I am, You have no partner, here I am. Verily all praise and blessings are Yours, and all sovereignty, You have no partner.' I was practically singing the words now. My arms began to goosebump despite the heat. I felt like I often did at Haj, that we were all Muslims. Despite being from all different parts of the globe, all different walks of life, all different colours of skin, Sunni and Shi'a, traditional and liberal, saints along with sinners, we were all as One now.

This was the very reason that I paid the three thousand pounds each year to Surah Sights, Yusria's Muslim travel agent on Shepherd's Bush Road. It cost me three thousand pounds each year, but it gave me three thousand reasons to keep going, to forget about Farah and what could have been and focus on the true love of my life – my son. It was worth every penny to feel closer to the divine. The absolute, and to know that every trip I made each year wasn't just for me and my own spiritual connection but for all our friends in Iran who had been robbed of their lives so young, before they had a chance to go.

The train released the doors and with it, Mona, Amal, Yusria, Miriam, Noura and I all stepped back. Miriam was a pale-skinned Lebanese woman from Warrington in her late fifties and Noura was forty-two years old, of Pakistani heritage from Hounslow. They both worked in HR. We all breathed in a collective sigh at the human stampede, all in an anxious rush to stone the devil.

'Let them go,' Yusria said. 'Alhamdulillah.'

When the fracas had somewhat calmed and we felt able to proceed safely, Yusria handed out our stones and pebbles for us to throw at the devil. Once handed to us, we began walking in silence towards the three walls. I counted five in my hand. Five.

'Kamsa,' I uttered, counting them again. It felt like a sign.

The symbolic gesture of stoning the devil was to rid us of the sins of our temptation. Each year I threw stones to rid myself of my shame. The shame of Ahmed, the shame of abandoning Hany, the shame of stealing from Aziz, the shame of, in a fit of rage, almost outing Farah to her children, to her husband, the shame of hurting Baba's heart.

But this year I had five stones in my hand. I felt them in my hand, some smoother, some smaller, some rougher, some more dented. I looked down at them; some shinier, more crystalised, some darker, others paler.

I grabbed the smallest and threw it towards one wall. 'Abdullah,' I said to myself.

Then I grabbed the one that seemed the most fragile, that was beginning to crumble in my hand like sand. 'Aysegul,' I said.

''Minah,' I felt Ommy whispering in my ear, giggling, 'you throw like a girl.'

I threw another, the slightly rougher one that scratched my hand a little with its diamonds glistening. 'Zaki,' I uttered. This time it went further.

'Not bad,' Ommy laughed again.

I breathed in, and I threw the penultimate stone. Perhaps not a stone at all, more of a pebble with its smooth, curved predict-ability. 'Yasmeen,' I grunted.

Then I had the last one in my hand, the shiniest one of them all. I rubbed it between my fingers, holding onto it for just that little bit longer before hurling it, like a baseball pitcher, at the wall.

'For Ommy,' I spat at the devil.

Yasminah

ي

Walking down the street, arm in arm with a handsome man, I swear I could feel my neighbours watching me. Perhaps it was my imagination and that the curtains weren't twitching, that tongues weren't wagging, that my ears weren't burning. I reminded myself that in London people don't care what I do or who I see. In London I was invisible, which to me was a superpower, not a sign of middle-age irrelevancy. I had wanted anonymity all my life and now that I had it, I still felt as though the whole world was watching and judging my every move.

I tried to forget about the imaginary audience inside my head and enjoy having Aziz here visiting me. I leaned into him, taking in the smell of his coffee-coloured trench coat. It still smelt like his club. I breathed it all in, like a fine wine. I smelt the beer-stained wood of the bar, the caramel of the coffee, the pungent acidity of the arak. I could even smell the pool table, the chalk on Ommy's snooker cue and the wool of the baize as he leaned over to take a shot. Then I could hear the click as the cue hit the ball, and I could see his face again. His glorious, perfect face that had faded over the years to just an outline, a silhouette, but now with Aziz by my side I could visualise him again. And with it, the memories both exhilarating and agonising.

It was a frosty night, and I watched the steam coming out of my brother's mouth as he spoke. His lithe body visibly shivered. There was a vulnerability to him whenever he was in England which in moments stripped him of his bravado. He never did quite fit in here. England was far too straight for him, he had said, with its rules and regulations and health and safety and HR legalities and whatnot. I smiled. 'Egypt is freer,' he said. 'For me,' he quickly added. It felt good to reverse the roles: when Aziz was in England, I protected *him* from *himself*.

Aziz nodded his head at QPR football stadium. 'Ussy go here?' I shook my head. My little brother hadn't played for years; his childhood dream of being a professional footballer had faded with each year of puberty and puppy fat.

'Science is certain, football is a fantasy!' Aziz and I both said suddenly in unison. Shaking our heads at our brother's pragmatism.

'But now stand-up comedy?' Aziz asked bewildered.

I shrugged. 'I think the divorce and with everything that happened in Saudi, well, it's a way to let it all out.'

'Wallahi,' Aziz said as he lit a cigarette. We passed the mosque on the corner of Loftus Road. I nudged him. 'This is my mosque,' I said.

He leaned back, taking in a drag of his cigarette along with the building. 'This is a mosque?' he asked. 'It looks like where I took my driving test.'

'You mean where *Malik* took your driving test?'

We laughed.

'Other than in Bradford, a city up north with the biggest Muslim demographic, all the mosques here are just, well, regular buildings. You know, so as not to . . . agitate white people.'

Aziz leaned over to me and whispered, 'That's a shame. Because I love agitating white people.'

We walked down to a dark basement, the size of a large shed, with tables lit by candlelight. At the front of the room was a raised platform with a microphone stand and behind it a banner which read, 'Muslim Men Making Jokes'. I could see Kadijah's fuchsia pink hijab and matching lipstick two rows from the front. The candle on their table was placed at a certain angle so that it shone on Nadia's exposed chest, lighting up the bony skin of her clavicles like an x-ray. She spotted me and Aziz and waved us over. Pamela was sitting across from them on another table with a bald man who looked like a white version of Ussy. My little brother was always getting told by white people that he looked like Ben Kingsley when he had browned up to play Gandhi. Pamela's new beau actually looked like Ben Kingsley when he wasn't playing Gandhi.

Aziz ran to embrace his nieces. I watched as Nadia and Kadijah both screamed in surprise.

'Uncle Aziz, what are you doing here?' Nadia said, punching his arm, her eyes twinkling.

'What. The. Hell. Uncle Aziz, does Dad know you're here?' Kadijah asked, her mouth agape.

'Hello, Aziz, fantastic to see you,' Pamela said, trying to sound as relaxed as she could in front of her boyfriend. 'This is Tony, my partner, he's here for the weekend from Manchester.'

Kadijah and Nadia rolled their eyes and turned their back on their mum and Tony to make lewd gestures with their fingers.

'Well, you know, couldn't miss seeing my little brother play at such, er, a great comedy club.'

Nadia passed my brother over a beer. 'This night is hack, I've been to it before with my dad, it should be called "Muslim Men Making Jokes About Hummus".'

'Or "Muslim Men Making Jokes About Terrorism",' added Khadijah.

'Yes, that's all it is, an hour and a half of Muslim men talking about how in the Middle East hummus is a main meal not a starter and airport security after 9/11. I mean, we might as well go home now, but my friend Maz wanted to come, he loves stand-up comedy. Oh, here he is!' Nadia got up to wave her friend over.

I turned around and with it I turned my back on the present. Everything slowed down, clocks melted, and time zones blurred. Was I dying? My whole life seemed to be suddenly playing out before me. I was transported back to Aziz's club again. When Ommy had walked through the door, his thick black hair catching the last light of sunset, his eyelashes so thick and long I wanted to comb them, to stroke them, to feel them warming my cold fingers. His Roman nose and his broad triangular jawline. His head was a pyramid turned on its point, his face, heart shaped and beating.

I gasped, the oxygen filling my lungs. I held my breath as if doing so would stop time going forward, which it now was. I ached for just one second more of my past. I looked into his eyes and felt him all over me again, the night that we had in each other's arms and then the friendship that followed, the rebelling and the revolting and then the many other days and nights we spent together laughing, always laughing and joking and messing around, being free. So utterly free.

'MAZZZZZZ!' Nadia squealed.

'NADS!' her friend screamed back.

They embraced each other by hugging and slapping each other's arms.

'Babe! That's my BCG arm!'

'I know! Ha ha! Uncle Aziz, Aunt Yasminah, this is my best friend, Maz.'

'Boyfriend?' Aziz asked with a quizzical look.

'God no, I'm not that way inclined if you know what I mean,' Maz said, shaking his hand. 'Uergh, the thought of such a thing, although we did snog at Hetty Ashley's house party when we were sixteen!' he teased and Nadia punched him in the arm again.

Aziz laughed. 'Very nice to meet you.'

'Maz is also a comedian. Well, an actor who plays comedic parts. He wanted to come tonight because, well, he's keen to dip his toes into stand-up . . .'

'You could ask to go on here, you look Arab – are you Muslim?' Aziz asked.

'No, I'm Greek Orthodox, Maz is short for Marcus,' he explained.

'Well, Greeks eat hummus, don't they? Write a few jokes about the blessed chickpea, they'll put you on.' Kadijah winked.

Everybody laughed. I tried to join in, to smile and to laugh; all night I did my best to blend in and to be as merry as the crowd. But I couldn't stop looking at Maz and seeing my dear Ommy. And although it brought back his warmth, the darkness of it all overrode everything. It hung over me all night. I felt as though someone was holding a large rock over my head and it was going to come crashing down on me at any moment. That I was going to relive his death over and over again. I tried to focus on the show, on my brother's performance, on his jokes about falafel wraps and baba ghanoush and how, because his children were half Irish and half Arab, he had inadvertently created the perfect terrorists. But I was living my own terrorism inside my head; sitting next to Maz, I was sitting next to Ommy, except I couldn't hold his hand or squeeze his fingers under the table, I couldn't lean on his shoulder and feel his body shaking with laughter as he made jokes about everyone we ever met. He had been taken away from me once. And now seeing Maz, it felt like he was being taken away from me all over again.

Fatiha

ف

'Congratulations, Fatiy!' My colleague Shareen pinched my arm, confirming to me that this wasn't a dream. Her radiant smile was even more electric than usual. She knew how much I had longed for this promotion; how much I had waited, tactically, hinting, not demanding. Quietly, in the background. Not making a song and dance out of it all like I normally did. Instead, I finally let myself believe in the system. That if I am humble and undeniably good, I shall be rewarded.

I couldn't quite believe that it had finally happened. I forced a smile. Shareen's topaz blue eyes twinkled extra hard. She proved the theory of nominative determinism for she was one of the sweetest women I had ever met. She reminded me of myself at her age. Seeing only the good in things before age had conditioned me into seeing the bad.

'You are not just the only *woman* to take on this role but the oldest *person* to take it on, Teta!' Farouk was always making fun

271

of my age, calling me Teta even before I had become one. And now, mostly thanks to Aziz, I was Teta to, oh, so very many grandchildren.

Farouk had the cockiness of Aziz but none of the charm. He thought he was endearing, when really he was slimy. He might have mocked my age but he knew never to mock my experience. I was aware of his thoughts on my past and my connection to his family; other colleagues had told me so. But he never said these insults to my face, unlike his father. I was thankful for that at least.

Doria said we had won the case. She had said the judge adjourning the hearing indefinitely was the patriarchy's pathetic way of admitting defeat. I wasn't convinced at the time as none of our demands had been met. But five years later, I realised she was right.

What would she make of me working with Farouk, son of our defence lawyer Mufidah Abdul Rahman's bitter rival, I wondered. She would laugh and we'd feel like schoolgirls in Paris again. She'd stop me breathing with her impressions of all the people we found ghastly. And then I'd stop her breathing when I made a face pretending that they were behind her.

'Yes, congratulations, Teta!' Farouk sneered. 'Now you can finally retire!'

'Inshallah, shukran,' I said, ignoring his jibe. I was tired of it all. Perhaps I would have taken his mockery in good will, like Shereen always did, had I not been through what I had been through in the last few months with poor Ebtehal.

I still couldn't believe they had given me her husband Nasr's old position when I had been openly defending his freedom of speech ever since he was declared an apostate. Ever since he had dared to write a paper on the metaphorical rather than literal interpretations of the Quran. Perhaps the position was given to me in order to shut me up. Blood money, I wondered.

The hypocrisy of this university was like a microcosm of the whole nation.

The truth was I didn't want to celebrate, not at the expense of what was happening to poor Ebtehal and Nasr.

'I accept this promotion until Nasr is back.'

The department all smiled awkwardly, unsure what to say. We all knew he wasn't coming back.

'Sure, sure. And you are OK to take over his PhD student?' Dr Abdul asked.

'Well, yes, of course, if Nasr is fine with that?' I said, as if any of them cared about Nasr's feelings.

'Nasr is in the Netherlands now. He's been extradited, so he can't exactly do anything about it!' Farouk piped in, his mouth sneering so much he was almost dribbling.

'What is the student's thesis?' I asked Dr Abdul, ignoring Farouk.

The question seemed to diffuse the whole department, from a solid to a gas; at once particles close and tight, full of energetic excitement, now they were dispersing into the atmosphere, separating and distancing themselves. Appearing interested in different corners of the room, some even leaving it completely.

'Yes, well, I wanted to discuss the student's thesis with you before you meet him. His name is Jamali. I trust you are able to put your own beliefs aside and take on this project objectively. As a professor now, this is of course absolutely essential to the requirements.'

I wanted to scream. Objectivity was not a word this university quite understood when it came to Islamic Studies. If they were objective, they would have not silenced Nasr, and the

Egyptian government would not have made Ebtehal divorce him. Doria and I had fought to eradicate forced marriages, but forced divorces were never something we foresaw.

'You see now, Professor Bin-Khalid, Nasr was working objectively with Jamali's thesis. Given his political disposition, he was a little, let's say unsure as to how he would supervise such a thesis but, actually he did quite a good job and we think you will take over his supervision with a similar, er, zest.'

'What is Jamali's thesis on?' I asked again.

'Yes, well, you see it's on the hermeneutics of Wahhabism with particular reference to Ibn Taymiyyah and Muhammad ibn Abd al-Wahhab . . . hmmm.'

My heart dropped.

'Wahhabism? He knows I did my own thesis on Ibn Arabi's views on gender and sexuality in the Quran and hadiths, correct?'

Dr Abdul's pupils dilated, as men's often do when they prefer you to be passive.

'And that my partner, Doria Shafik, who I worked with alongside for many years, rest in peace, did her thesis on women's rights in Islam?'

'I think the fact that Nasr took on his supervision willingly while he was being deemed an apostate renders the student most open minded. Don't you think?'

I smiled sweetly.

'You see the thing with Islamic Studies is there is never any new ground covered. No new research. It is simply a recital of old knowledge. Even my own thesis was a regurgitation of Ibn Arabi's preaching. I wanted to mould his words of the politics of the thirteenth century and apply them to the twentieth century, but I could only mildly hint. Never demand a new interpretation. Just tentatively imply. It's hilarious we use the word "hermeneutics" in so many Islamic Studies theses, but the word "interpretation" gives the impression that there are different ways to look at it,' I said to Ali later that night, hoping that he would comprehend my complex problem and be able to respond coherently. He continued to cut his toenails on the edge of the balcony. I was almost certain that he knew the clippings dropped onto the apartment below, disgusting the neighbours, but he didn't care. Snobs, he used to call them. 'They think they're better than us because their three daughters are all married to doctors,' he used to sneer.

I'd always tell him when he did, 'Doesn't it count for something that you married a doctor, albeit an academic one, and your daughter, well, she would have been one too if . . .' my voice would always tail off then, thinking of my daughter's remarkable yet unfinished thesis on gay rights in Islam. But it didn't matter because I knew he wasn't listening or wasn't even really there. I just needed to say the words. Words I was never allowed to say in public.

'I did my thesis on Ibn Arabi because I loved what he said about women and gender and sexuality in the Quran and hadiths. I was happy to preach.'

'Yesssss . . .' Ali hissed. He had fallen back onto his chair now and had started cracking his knuckles loudly to the same syncopated beat as my annoyances.

'Ibn Taymiyyah and Muhammad ibn Abd al-Wahhab? What can this possibly mean? He's a Wahhabist, surely.'

'Bismillah,' Ali uttered while belching and farting at the same time, causing me to straddle the line between despair and hilarity.

Nadia

ن

There was a peacefulness to the office before Derrick came in at eleven each morning. Those two glorious hours between nine and eleven felt not dissimilar to when you wake up after some terrible tragedy and for a few moments you have forgotten that anything bad has happened. In Derrick's absence, Craig let me watch BBC Breakfast instead of ITV. There was something soothing about the ambience of Bill Turnbull interviewing a heralded new playwright about his latest show at the Donmar Warehouse rather than working to the sound of Lorraine Kelly interviewing a reality star about their new fitness DVD.

Through the small window in the alcove, the morning sun shone a spotlight on our office that made it almost ethereal. I could see every piece of fluff on Craig's suit, which shone around his body like a godly aura. I felt deeply relaxed even though I knew that the bright light was shining on me too and my upper lip was due a wax. We sat opposite each other, with the ease of two colleagues who had reached a point in their working relationship where they no longer felt the need to fill every silence with small talk about what they were planning on getting for lunch. We had nonverbally agreed to sit in our sweet morning Derrick-free silence and refrain from the efforts of conversation. A quietness, a stillness, a contemplativeness that would fill us with strength, affording us the capability to contend with the rest of the day with Derrick in it.

After these precious hours alone and with our thoughts came the inevitable tirade. We would hear the sound of his motorbike pulling up, which would instigate the start of the proverbial storm after the calm. Then we would be instantly bombarded by Derrick shouting orders before sitting down to unsubtly insult our work by reading it aloud. As he did, he would comment every few paragraphs and question whether we had lied on our CVs. Asking us things like, 'Did we *really* have a GCSE in English Language as we clearly didn't understand the proper use of a comma!' This was almost always coupled with some form of racist, homophobic or misogynistic rhetoric about someone who had pissed him off that day. If anyone dared to confront him or threatened him with HR (five years ago, a guy called Elroy apparently), he would just claim that it was all just 'banter' and that *Bangers* did not have an HR department. 'My magazine, Nadia,' he'd sneer in his cockney twang, 'despite being full of tits is actually bloody ballsy and doesn't pander to mainstream sensibilities', like he was journalism's answer to punk rock.

'You don't have a problem with the language I use, do you, Nads? It's just banter!' he had said to me when he had given a graphic description of what he would do to a particular buxom soap star should he have the good luck to meet her. He had slapped my back as I drank my tea, a strategic move on my part, the cup over my face masking my expression. Whenever he said anything vulgar, I would always find a way to cover my face in some manner and pretend I hadn't heard the unsavoury comment. Sometimes it was as simple as looking away, out the window, becoming fixated on what was happening on Shepherd's Bush Road. Other times I'd leave the room completely, announcing that I was going to make everyone a cup of tea. There in the downstairs kitchen I would stand there, mortified, wondering how I could live with myself working for a man so vile. I'd do the breathing exercises that Kadijah always talked about and visualise my end goal: *Gracious* magazine. I just needed to finish this internship and I would be ready to send my CV in. I also reminded myself that he came in late every day and would often leave early, so I really wasn't subjected to that much of his 'banter' anyway.

Those two precious hours between Craig and I were vital for our mental health and blissfully banter free. Instead, we filled the silence with ferocious typing, voracious clicking and constant scrolling. The sounds of which was how I had originally imagined working in journalism to be. Our expressions in deep concentration, what Kadijah would call a 'flow' state, 'the optimal state of human consciousness' as she put it. Craig and I were totally absorbed in what we were doing, so focused that everything around us fell away. 'Where action and awareness merge,' my sister had told me. I felt well and truly in this flow state before Derrick came in each morning and I sensed Craig did too. Today felt extra euphoric as Derrick had another brunch meeting with the producer of *Hollyoaks*, which meant he wouldn't be back till at least two, possibly later if they both got drunk and decided to go to Oblivion, their favourite strip club.

Every so often Craig would look up at the reflection of the frame of the painting behind me, see that I was on Facebook

Messenger or ordering shoes from ASOS before clicking away on his screen again. His lack of protest was an acknowledgement that he was using these hours without Derrick to piss around on the internet too.

Today I was stalking Zain on Facebook. He was definitely back from Saudi and living in Liverpool. I sneered at all his photos of him and his gran doing the Beatles tour in the album he had posted entitled *Gran and I: Beatles Mania*. I tried to refrain from commenting, 'My vag looked not dissimilar to a strawberry field after you invaded it', on his Facebook wall. I thought better than to accuse him of rape on the internet when the act was only *mildly* non-consensual. However, his selfish actions were responsible for all the tragedies in my life. Zain's herpes was the reason I was bullied out of Bristol and the reason I now lived with a homophobic woman and worked with a racist boss. Not only this but his entitlement to my body that night had instigated a tirade of tragedies for other people too. Poor Fitty McHotty, I had heard rumours from Lydia that the herpes incident had wreaked havoc with his confidence and sense of self. So much so that women didn't call him Fitty McHotty any more, they just called him Ian. Suddenly emblazoned with outrage for poor Ian's penis, I began typing on Zain's wall:

You gave me herpes!

Hovering over the 'post' button, my fingers flirting with fate, my body began to feel weightless. The more I read the four words, the lighter I became. The anger, I realised, was gradually expelling from my body. I read the words again and this time I laughed. They seemed to me to be so ridiculous and on such a preposterous platform. I deleted the comment. *I mean you can't just accuse men on social media, you idiot, who does that?*

As I did so a new notification came in. *Courtney King Wants to*

Be Your Friend. A sudden thrill went through me. Since Courtney had run after me in the street with my wallet on my first day,
I had seen her only a handful of times. Mostly in the kitchen
when I was forced to make tea for the producer of *Hollyoaks* or
when I was escaping one of Derrick's racist rants. Each time I
saw her, she woke me up. In order to get through my internship
at *Bangers*, I had to turn a certain part of myself off. Each day, my
body went through the motions but my mind was elsewhere;
my coping mechanism was to sleepwalk through Derrick's
misogynistic racist abuse, but there was something about the
presence of Courtney that brought me out of this state of slumber. I was back in the room again, fully present.

Her online presence was no different; it jolted me up from
my daydream where I blissfully imagined a world where Zain
and other men like him became accountable for the torment
they caused to women with their penises, vis-à-vis public humiliation on social media. A warm fuzz filled my stomach with the
acknowledgement that she was probably up there in her edit
suite pissing about on the internet too.

I hovered over the *Yes* to accept for several minutes so as not
to seem too keen, before hitting it. The click instigated another
wave of warmness inside me and I realised with sudden alarm
that I very much needed to go to the toilet. I strategically yet
gradually began to raise the volume of Bill Turnbull. I faked
being interested in his guest who was predicting that the millen-
nial generation would eventually stop mocking Gwyneth
Paltrow's eating habits and start copying Gwyneth Paltrow's
eating habits. As the segment came to an end, I didn't restore the
volume to its previous level, instead I got up and mumbled
something about needing to make a cup of tea. Craig looked up
for a second before going back to an article about Prince Harry's

real dad. I closed the door behind me, which was ordinarily left open, and prayed that Craig wouldn't notice. These were the actions I had to go to before letting my bowels loose each morning, for our extractor fan-free toilet was right next door. Sometimes I even feigned needing to go to the shop to get tampons and snuck into the local Costa Coffee where I had the toilet code memorised in order to relieve myself in complete privacy.

I turned on the taps and the hand drier and dropped a large rolled-up ball of toilet roll into the cistern, before finally feeling like I had soundproofed myself enough to let rip. I flushed and washed and tried to leave the scene of the crime as quickly as possible. Thinking I'd made it, I swung open the door, brazenly, only to find Courtney right there in front of me.

My heart started racing and I could feel blood rushing to my face as the mortification began to set in. I mumbled a hello and tried not to look her in the eye as she passed me and went into the cubicle. I prayed to God she had some weird condition which made her have an extremely weak sense of smell and fumbled my way back into the office. Why was I so embarrassed? I only got this way about doing number twos with men. With my girlfriends, I'd stroll out bold as a builder, saying something pithy like, 'I'd give it a few minutes there, love.' But with Courtney I was embarrassed! It was if I wanted her to think I was a little princess who didn't do things like that. It was very disconcerting.

I sat back down at my desk, aghast and slightly unsure what had just occurred between us. I tried to shake it away but staring right in front of me now was her entire Facebook page.

Her profile picture was of her on a beach, holding a massive fish. There was something very alluring about the photo; it made me think very odd thoughts, like, I want to be that fish.

I started going through all her albums; one was called *Road Signs Collected Drunkenly Over the Years*. This mostly consisted of Courtney and her friends standing proudly in their living room next to orange cones and red triangular road signs. It was all so bittersweet. I felt deflated that this was not an original thing to do when drunk and in your early twenties but at the same time felt we had so much in common.

The next album I found was called *Me and Elle: Phuket*. A very attractive blonde girl was with her in all these photos. I looked at the date that she had posted the album and was relieved to find that this was over four years ago. I wondered if they were still together. I was intrigued by Courtney's beach attire; not opting for a swimsuit or bikini, she wore what looked like men's long shorts and a Nirvana t-shirt. Her androgyny excited some part inside me that I had never felt before. I was so enthralled I failed to hear Derrick's motorcycle outside. He bounded up the stairs and strutted in yelling, 'Nadia, get the fuck off Facebook, you idiot! You're supposed to be working on the "Countdown to 16"! What am I paying you for? Craig, go tell fucking Emmanuel Feinstein, he's outside asking for his rent like a bloody Shylock, that we'll give it to him when he sorts the leak in the ceiling in Courtney's edit suite! Clare, where's my coffee? Do you guys do any work when I'm not in, for fuck's sake!' He banged his fists on the table like a caveman and we all jumped.

I minimised Courtney's Facebook page and opened up my 'Countdown to 16' article and sighed.

∾

Derrick fortunately left at 4 p.m. and as we heard him shoot off on his pathetic midlife crisis contraption, I thought I heard the collective sigh of Craig and Clare who were downstairs on reception. Almost immediately I went back online and logged into Facebook to check out more of Courtney's photos before I went home (I was also planning on stalking this Elle girl who I didn't have a particularly good feeling towards). To my surprise there was a red notification in my messenger tab, and I realised with great excitement and trepidation that I had a message from Courtney. I clicked on it, silently praying that it wasn't anything to do with stinking out the toilet.

How's it going? she said.

I looked at the time. She sent it two minutes ago, almost instantaneously after Derrick had left, I realised.

It's going, I typed. I hovered my fingers over the keyboard, rather proud of my sarcastic reply.

Tell me about it! Derrick is ON ONE today!

When is he not ON ONE? I typed back, shocked at how easily I found talking to her. The conversation was just flowing.

LOL, she typed.

I winced. I ordinarily stopped engaging with people who 'LOL', but with Courtney, I found it somewhat endearing.

The most mental boss I've ever had, FOR SURE.

I know. He's bringing his daughter in tomorrow, so don't worry.

What do you mean?

When he brings his daughter in, he's on his best behaviour. The racism, the misogyny it all goes out the window. I guess remembering that he has a mixed-race daughter momentarily makes him stop being a racist sexist! Anyway, fancy a drink tonight?

This time I did not reply immediately. In fact, the idea of going for a drink with Courtney, despite our friendly and easy rapport, scared the hell out of me. I bit my lip and looked out the window onto Shepherd's Bush Market. A young girl and her mother were stroking the cat of a homeless man who was selling *The Big Issue*.

I eventually decided to go for it. I was new to London and needed to make friends.

Yes, I typed.

But as I hit send, I wondered what I had really said 'Yes' to.

Yasminah

ي

I hadn't anticipated the implications of coming back from Haj on New Year's Day. Shepherd's Bush Road was eerily still and yet awash with dozens and dozens of silent partygoers, painfully holding their heads up with one hand, their shoes with the other. Passing the mosque on Loftus Road I saw two women, one holding back the other's scruffy hair, as she threw up onto the road. I saw her eyes, streaming, bleary with tears as she tried to get her breath back, only to vomit up more of the remnants of the night before. In between heaves, she gagged and cried and coughed and laughed with her friend, as if her purging was proof of a successful night out. A man in ripped jeans came to join them, stumbling from the corner shop with a see-through bag of 'Fanta and fags'. He dropped the bag in front of the girls and promptly started pissing in the street. This only made the girls more hysterical; they laughed in that wonderful noiseless way. The convulsions muted; reduced to merely shaking until you couldn't breathe and then, and this is the truly glorious part, you start to feel intense abdominal pain which sets off the panic and sense of impending powerless doom, where you wonder if you are in fact about to die from laughing.

As if in order to experience the joy one has to also experience the pain.

I passed them and hoped my smile was not interpreted as condescending or judgemental in anyway but what it was: genuine. But I was still wearing Mona's old hijab from the trip and dressed in a long abaya. I knew what white people thought about women dressed like me.

I touched the scarf to feel closer to Mona. It still smelt of her.

'Haj, habibbti, it's the only way to make sense of any of this, not the hadiths, not the Quran, but here, in Mecca, you can feel Allah's love for us, right?' she used to say, touching my arm, taking her sunglasses off and readjusting this very hijab. This year was the first year I had done Haj without her. We had been going every year for the past few years to go for all our friends who couldn't go. It was a wonderful, yearly peaceful ritual. After Mona died, I had read that Betty Shabazz, wife of Malcolm X, had gone to Mecca to recover from the assassination of her husband. I had told Mona's wife this, but it didn't seem to help heal her hem. She refused to go with me this year.

So, this was the first year I went completely alone. But the wonderful thing about Haj is you never are alone. You feel the presence of your loved ones all around you. Those who have passed and those who are still here. You feel their love circling around your body, like gas in a soda can. And when you complete the pilgrimage, it feels as though you have opened the can and all your loved ones are celebrating with you. It's better than any party I have ever been to.

The feeling lasts for months afterwards, even when you are

home, in the UK. But today, perhaps it was because Mona was not here, that feeling had drained out of me since landing at Heathrow. The bright terminal lights at two in the morning were overwhelming, not celestial. The whiteness was too exposing. I could see every pore on my face, each one like a crater into my past. I felt an unusual pit in my stomach. The only explanation was the absence of my best friend, Mona.

As I approached the steps into my flat, I chastised the empty bottles of wine on the road, the kebab meat falling out of a pitta bread, lettuce and ketchup like blood on a crime scene. This couldn't just be grief about Mona. Something was off. I looked at my front window. The curtains were open. I remembered drawing them before leaving. I would never have left them open. I had left them closed; I was positive.

I opened the first door into the hallway of other flats. I heard music. I heard groaning. I heard singing. There was someone in my flat. Someone had broken in. I fell to the ground. Reliving the trauma of our Heliopolis flat all over again. This time I would call the police, not ignore it. I got out my mobile phone, my hands shaking, but just as I was about to dial, I heard a man's voice.

'Nadia, babe, do you want a bacon sarnie?'

Nadia.

'Nadia, how are you not up yet, do you not smell the bacon? What are you doing in there? Hello! It's Maz's special recipe! Bacon sandwiches, with Bloody Mary ketchup!'

My niece. Nadia. Bacon. Nadia.

Nadia broke into my flat. Nadia. My niece. In my flat. Eating bacon. With a boy who mixes vodka into ketchup and then puts it into sandwiches. In my flat. Nadia. Bacon.

I turned the key and stepped in.

Nadia

LONDON, 2012

ن

People always say that living in London comes at a price. I hadn't factored on it being an emotional price. I started to question my values. I was working for a chauvinistic, racist, deeply antisemitic man and living with a homophobic woman. I was ignoring it all because I wanted to further my career. I hated myself. But I had no other choice. I had spent my life escaping, fleeing Saudi, Bristol, all because I enjoyed sex. I couldn't bear to uproot again; no one would believe it would be for moral reasons – my friends would tease me and assume I'd done something 'slaggy' again. They would joke but deep down I knew what they thought of me. I was the punchline. I had to see this job through, I had to become a successful magazine journalist. I had to fulfil my lifelong ambition of working at *Gracious* magazine and finally getting myself a job in an office where my boss couldn't see my screen. (I'd heard rumours that every writer sat in their own American-style cubicle at *Gracious*).

Gracious was the classiest of women's magazines. It wasn't like

Hot!. Hot! was no better than *Bangers* – where *Bangers* sexualised women's bodies, *Hot!* scrutinised them, which was arguably more oppressive and problematic. At least when Craig and Derrick were zooming in on a woman's thigh, they weren't checking out her cellulite. Instead, they grunted and groaned and filled the room with a real sense of body positivity towards every shape and size of *Hollyoaks* actress. *Hot!* never had anything nice to say about a woman's body.

Gracious was more in line with my grandmother's magazine, *Bint Al Nil*. It appealed to the intellectual woman, encouraging education through focusing not on frivolous soap stars but on women of substance. Like peace ambassador Amy Layla, who just so happened to be about to marry one of Hollywood's most eligible bachelors. *Gracious* applauded her humanitarian work whilst also outlining where she got her shoes from. I was going to be like Teta, one of those pioneering magazine journalists, and discuss the political implication of wearing a kitten heel at the United Nations General Assembly. That was my dream. And as with all dreams, they all come with sacrifices. I had to tolerate chauvinistic racist abuse from Derrick and live with Aunt Yasminah, a stuffy old homophobic Muslim woman, until I had built up enough magazine experience to apply for a job at *Gracious*.

I couldn't educate my aunt on gay rights; she was too far gone. She would be dead soon, I thought. How had my thoughts got so macabre, I wondered, as I walked towards the flat, passing by the drunks of QPR and saying a silent prayer for Uncle Christopher. I couldn't expect my aunt to understand the gay rights movement. She was from a different time. Although, saying that, I often thought that Teta was far more progressive than Aunt Yasminah. What with not only her antics with Doria

Shafik and her Egyptian feminist magazine but with her support of Nasr Abu Zayd and his wife Ebtehal. In the nineties, he was labelled an apostate for daring to suggest that the Quran could be interpreted in symbolic rather than literal ways. And Teta was one of the only academics in Egypt who stuck up for him! If only I was living with Teta, I would not feel like I had to hide anything about my life. I had done a performing arts degree, for crying out loud, most of my friends were gay, it was a wonder I wasn't gay myself.

I climbed up the steps to the flat and made a silent prayer that my aunt wasn't in. All I wanted was to have a 125 millilitre glass of wine. And another 125 millilitre glass of wine. And another, I thought. I had found a way round drinking on epilepsy medication. It was quite genius really: I had stopped taking my epilepsy medication.

I turned the key in the lock and my heart dropped. I could hear my aunt watching *Loose Women*. I entered the flat and smelt the white sage and cinnamon of her incense. I mumbled a salamwaylaykum and went straight to my room and closed the door. I could hear her laughing at her favourite Loose Woman, Carol McGiffin, describing a drunken night out with her toy boy. If she found that funny, why did she never laugh at my life, I wondered. I sat on my bed and opened the wine. I swigged it from the bottle and felt my rage for my aunt's hypocrisy start to dissolve. When I heard the final credits play, I felt I was inebriated enough to chat to her.

My bedroom door creaked; it sounded like my stomach when I'd had too much of Aunt Yasminah's lentil soup. There was always a vat of lentil soup in her fridge. She was constantly making it. I wondered if it was her attempt to fill me with farts to stop me from sleeping around. Her lentil soup caused me such immense stomach contractions, I felt like I was being eaten from the inside and not in a good way.

'Hello, habibbti,' Aunt Yasminah said.

'Hi, Auntie,' I said, my eyes glowing with tipsiness. I sat down on her bed, a simple single bed. I would have a daily chat with her and then move to the living room where we would ignore each other all night. It was the perfect set-up, really. Either that or she would be at work. Speaking to a homophobe for five minutes a day in exchange for a free place to live in London didn't seem all that bad, I thought.

I saw her annotated Quran on the nightstand and eyed it up as if it were the enemy. A threat that I had to constantly keep an eye on lest it start to attack. I watched the Quran like airport security watches a Muslim at Heathrow. Aunt Yasminah was brushing her long hair, as she scraped it into a bun and stuck a hat on to pray. Kadijah and I often wondered why she chose to cover her hair with a hat and not a hijab. Perhaps now I lived with her I could ask her such intimate questions. We couldn't just get by on small talk any more.

'How come you cover your hair with a hat and not a hijab, Auntie?'

Her back was turned away from me as she adjusted her hair into the hat. She turned around, surprised at my question. Her eyes grew bigger, I could see her pupils dilating. She opened her mouth to speak before closing it again. Then she laughed.

'I lived in Iran when wearing the veil was seen as lower class and a sign of opposition to Shah Mohammad Reza Pahlavi. The last Shah had banned wearing a hijab altogether from 1936 to 1941– the Kashf-e hijab, the decree was called. So there were still repercussions from that time. It was seen as backward and unfeminist to wear it in some circles.'

'Oh. I didn't know you lived in Iran. It's not like that now. It's illegal *not* to wear the hijab,' I said.

'I know. It was very different when I was there. I wanted to cover my hair because I didn't believe in rejecting every symbol of conservatism. I occasionally wore a miniskirt but the more Quran I read, the more I wanted to dress modestly. So, I wore a hat to get round the Kashf-e hijab. And now I do it because it makes me feel closer to . . .' She stopped. She looked at me, her eyes smaller now. She looked down at her lap.

'Closer to . . . ?' I prompted.

She ignored me and instead rooted around under her bed and got out a shoebox full of old photos. She brought out a photo of her with a man with a face like a piece of art. It was a face that was to be studied in a museum or in a science lab for the physics of perfection. I wanted to measure every dimension and write a book on it.

'This is Ommy. He died in the 1979 Iran uprising. He changed my life.'

Nadia

ن

Her name was Jaleela. The first girl I kissed. Her lips were so thin she always looked as though she was holding them in under the weight of her oversized buck teeth. Her skin was as white as the bag of cocaine we were offered as payment for the act. Zain didn't know that we would have gladly done it for free; I did anything for his or any male validation.

When we kissed, I felt like I had discovered a new conversation. As if her mouth was my Rosetta stone. It had been buried inside me all along, unknowingly and now that it had come to the surface, I felt the words of it were in my blood. I understood completely, my newfound bilingualism made all the sense in the world. The natural state of a second-generation immigrant. The equation of my liminality could be solved with one kiss from Jaleela.

I wanted to take it further with Jaleela, after Zain had left and the cocaine had worn off. But she awoke so mortified by our act that her porcelain skin turned as red as her lips. I blushed too but with lust not embarrassment.

'Hey, ladies, salamwaylaykum, that was sick last night!' Zain strode in. I closed my eyes, remembering what I had let him do to me while gazing into Jaleela's eyes. Zain and his harem, Jaleela and I would joke, the only way to defuse the tension between us. Although I could think of a million other ways.

When we were in the taxi home, the driver on the King Fahd Causeway, the bridge that separates the more liberated Bahrain from its conservative cousin, the Kingdom of Saudi Arabia, I realised that something had changed in Jaleela. As we veered into the confines of our Al-Khobar compound, in the heart of Dhahran, where we could not as easily do what we had done in Bahrain, I felt a distance between us. In Bahrain there was laughter and embarrassment, now in Saudi there was silence and shame. The moment she got out of the car I knew I had lost her forever. But then I wondered, was it possible to lose someone you never truly had?

I was almost glad when I didn't get my period so I could ring her, talk to her, go to her house, touch her hand and panic. But she didn't want to know. Told me to stop ringing her, to stop coming to her house, that it wasn't her problem that I was such a drunken whore.

∾

Now I stood in the living room of our Saudi apartment, sixteen years old, hearing the call to prayer while holding a pregnancy test in my hand, got on the black market by Zain.

'It's positive, Mama,' I bawled into her arms. She held me for several minutes as I cried. I could hear her thinking. She wanted to call my dad, but she was scared of the Mutawa who bugged certain calls.

'Do you have any idea how serious this is?' she said, suddenly dropping me from her arms. She leaned forward. 'We could be killed for this! I should disown you! Say she is no child of mine, spit on you while you are getting stoned!'

I yelped out in pain as if she had slapped me hard. It stung all over and the salt of my tears increased the acidity of the pain, like I was somehow in an act of self-immolation. In a way I was.

Mama went out for several hours. While she was gone, I emptied my bag and found a leftover bottle of vodka that I had smuggled back from Bahrain.

It was strange to think that the very substance that got me into this predicament in the first place had the medicinal qualities to get me out of it.

Alcohol contains both good and evil, I remembered reading in the Quran. *But the evil is greater.*

I drank the whole bottle while I ran myself a bath. It felt like I was dying in a fire. My insides inflamed, my brain burning. It felt good, everything going up in flames. Burn everything down, I thought. Not just the thing living inside me. Burn the whole fucking house down, I thought. My mother came back to find me in the toilet with the bath running and bleeding from my legs. I was now too drunk to understand completely what she was saying or what was happening. I wailed, stretching my arms out to her. I wanted to die in my mother's arms, with her holding me, rocking me, loving me. But instead, she threw a packet of pills at me and yelled at me to take them. She screamed that it was the pills not the alcohol that would get me out of this mess and then she stormed out of the room. I took them and started convulsing.

Now I look back on this memory and know that was when I had my first epileptic fit. I can remember the hot water burning my skin but being incapable of getting out of the bathtub. I could feel myself shaking onto the tiled walls of the bathroom, my head banging like a football onto the white surface. I could have drowned. While my mother was trying to save herself. My life was an afterthought. I hated her but I loved her at the same time as my mistake bled out of me, I cried with confused relief. The shock of all the gore making me forget everything else.

A few days later we all boarded a plane back to the UK. Out of all the horror, my mind was a mess, a swirl of constant anxiety that could only be quietened by thoughts of Jaleela.

Yasminah

ي

Of course, Aziz was getting married again at his Alibi club. To me it still felt the same, despite him having bought next door's building enabling him to extend the dancefloor and set up a VIP bar, which he bragged many of Cairo's elite celebrities, politicians, writers and intellectuals now frequented.

'Oh yeah, like who?' I said, expecting him to list a bunch of corrupt Cairenes who were probably responsible for the current political unrest and police brutality.

'Naguib Mahfouz used to come a lot,' Aziz said.

I stared into my brother's eyes, the eyes that always contained a sprinkle of mischief, a pinch of bravado and a pretty big dollop of narcissism. I waited for him to blink. I waited for him to give me the punchline. But he didn't. He was sincere.

I had underestimated him once again. His business was not a seedy, chauvinistic cesspit of masculinity and debauchery, where he could get away with ogling women and getting drunk all his life. It was a legitimate, well-respected and successful club where the likes of Naguib Mahfouz, the Nobel Prize-winning writer, would go.

'Before his stabbing or after?' I asked.

'Both. Once he recovered, his wife organised a big party for him here.'

'Wow,' I said genuinely.

'What are you doing down here, sis? You're not trying to steal from me again? I've changed the code, it's no longer Mama's birthday!' he said, punching my arm.

I scrunched my face. 'I am so sorry about . . .'

'La, la, la, you were going through some pretty terrible stuff back then, habibbti,' he said, putting his beer down on his desk to put his arm around me. He smelt like my nineteen-year-old brother did back then, tobacco, beer, sweat, halowa breath and women's perfume.

'I hope the perfume I smell on you is Reem and not a harem!' I said, trying to defuse the sincerity. We never spoke so genuinely; it was oddly disconcerting.

'I am so deeply sorry about stealing from you, I was a drunk back then!' I pretended I was interested in the lockers by the safe to create some distance between us. I was not comfortable with such affection. We could hear the dancing upstairs and the howls of laughter from Reem followed by melodic stamping and clamping.

'You know what the code to the safe is now?' Aziz asked, squinting at me.

'No?'

'24.04.99.'

My lip started to quiver. I held it in. I breathed in all the air I could. I called out his name, but the word couldn't come out, as if my vocal cords were being strangled.

'Baba,' I said finally. The relief of saying it instigated a visceral reaction inside my body. No longer strangulated or restricted, my whole body opened up, released itself to the weight of my trauma. I fell to the ground, with the same velocity as my tears falling from my eyes. Only they weren't my eyes, they never were, they were Baba's. I had Baba's eyes and Mama's mouth. I saw the world like him but expressed it like her. I was a symphony of both. I never missed them because they were never far from me. They lived in every fibre of myself.

'I wanted to come, I wanted to come so badly to see him all the time, but I was so scared to lose Hany, if I came back into the country. And then his mind went, and Mama said he thought that everyone was somebody else. She said he often thought that Dyab was that terrible journalist, what was his name, Zafarullah Zerdak, and that Mama was Doria!'

'I think she quite liked that, actually!' Aziz joked before sitting on the floor to embrace me. He held me while I let the emotion come, finally succumbing to the sincerity, the vulnerability, the weight of it all. I didn't want to laugh it off any more. I wanted to feel it.

24th April 1999. Heart attack. My mother, after years of caring for him, thought it would be his mind that eventually killed him. But it wasn't, it was his blessed heart. Baba. He had been dead over ten years; my mother had been on her own for over ten years. You could see the decade of mourning on her face, her wrinkles were now deep rivers where they were once light tributaries. I watched her with Nadia and Kadijah as they both stuffed their faces with cake. I could see her trying to understand their attire. She looked quizzically at them both. Trying to make sense of Kadijah's hijab and short skirt, it was as if she was trying to solve an algebraic equation. Then her head turned to Nadia, whose dark hair was flowing freely in soft waves; fortunately it covered her bare chest exposed by her low-cut top. It had the number '69' on. I searched my mother's face to try to get into her thoughts. Was she wondering, was this feminism now? Was this what Doria and she had fought for? The freedom for one woman to wear the hijab and the other to wear a low-cut t-shirt with '69' on and for them both to dance together? When Huda Shaarawi, Doria's mentor, took off her veil in 1923 at the Ramses train station in Cairo, coming back from a feminist conference in Rome, and shocked the world, causing a wave of other Egyptian women to also remove their veils, was this what she envisioned for the future of feminism?

The freedom to choose whether we cover our hair or our faces or our hearts or our souls? Perhaps like I had read in Muslim feminist Fatema Mernissi's heralded book, *The Veil and the Male Elite*, all women, whether they are western or Middle Eastern, wear the metaphorical veil in some form. I know I do.

What had happened? Had we gone back? Egypt was now on the verge of a revolt. Protesting many things that Doria and my mother protested in the Egyptian Revolution of 1952. Police brutality, low wages, unemployment, the unfair distribution of wealth.

It also had parallels with Iran. Conjuring up the memory of being on the precipice of a so-called joyous revolution. I had thought I could be free in Iran but because of politics I could not. I also thought I could be free in London, but I could not. Not because of politics but because of personal circumstances, because of Hany, because of what happened with dear Farah.

As the music pulsated into my heart, I began to clap and

stamp with the whole wedding party. I looked at Aziz with his new wife Reem and all his many children around him. I saw Mama looking for the first time not with disapproval at him, but with love. Her expression had changed from the days of aggravation to that of adulation. She sat next to Usman and Pamela now, holding her youngest and favourite son's hand as he spoke delicately into her ear. Nadia and Kadijah were playing with her walking stick on the dancefloor. Nadia, pretending she was a pole dancer for several minutes before Pamela rushed out to her, telling her to stop.

I looked again at Aziz, who had, despite Mama and Baba's reservations, lived the exact life he had wanted. A life of pleasure. A life of being himself, fuck everybody else's expectations of him. I was in awe of my brother. I had to tell him. I had to make sure he knew how much I loved and respected him. I rushed up towards him on the dancefloor, taking him aside, away from the crowds for just a second to let him know, to tell him what I had never ever said to his face.

I whispered into his ear, what I wanted to tell him, what I needed to tell him, otherwise I would regret it for the rest of my life.

'Brother Aziz,' I breathed, removing my metaphorical veil, 'I'm bisexual.'

He smiled at me, his eyes a mix of mischief and joy.

Nadia

LONDON, 2012

ن

It was only a matter of time before I got sexually assaulted by Derrick at work. He wore his sexual predator card in plain sight, he wasn't like one of those men peacocking as a beta male. The type who would wear one of Kadijah's t-shirts that say 'I'm a male feminist' to throw you off the scent and then stick his hands down your jeans in the staff kitchen as you're pouring your pot noodle. Only to leave casually, blowing on their tea and uttering, 'oooh, sticky rib, not tried that flavour before', as they pass by Carol from HR.

No, Derrick wasn't like that. He knew who he was, and he didn't try to hide it, and in many ways, I respected him for it. In fact, after three months had gone by and I hadn't had anything so much as a few perves on my décolletage and a brushing of my clavicles when I wore my stringy vest top, I started to feel like there was something wrong with me. I started to wonder if it was because I was brown. But Craig dismissed this.

'Don't forget he has a brown wife and a half-brown daughter, a strategic move on his part, so no one can accuse him of being a racist,' Craig had said to me one morning when Derrick was in late, interviewing a disgraced *Blue Peter* presenter.

I was working on the intro to the piece 'Good Girl Gone Bad' late one night, when the sexual assault *finally* happened. If Derrick was younger, better-looking and crucially not a racist, it could have been a scene from a romcom. Alas, Derrick was balding, short and the motorcycle he rode and leather jacket he wore were not in a James Dean way but in an I've-just-turned-fifty-five way.

We both stepped back to admire my word play:

Candace Caketon Caught with Cocaine
The disgraced Blue Peter presenter tells Bangers how she is more likely to be blowing Peter rather than doing Blue Peter after being released from both her seven figure CBBC contract and police custody.

'This is good,' Derrick said, 'really, really good.'

And there it was, his hand on my arse. I tried not to flinch and counted to ten before leaving the room to make a tea and a pot noodle. I smiled to myself as I watched the yellow powder magically transform before my eyes into cardboard-tasting carbohydrate. I was surely due for a pay rise now. Perhaps I could even afford to move out of my homophobic aunt's flat and get a place of my own.

I walked back up the stairs with my pot noodle. I looked at Derrick, wondering if I could broach the subject of my pay rise now or that it would be deemed 'tacky' to do so, so soon after the groping.

'Cor, bloody hell, Nadia, what's that curry!? You smell like a bloody . . .'

I stuck my headphones in and smiled.

~

I stayed for another hour working on the Candace Caketon piece. Derrick left before me and asked me to lock up.

'Right, Courtney is still here, so make sure you don't lock her in, and you need to give her the Candace Caketon piece anyway, but yeah definitely don't lock her in . . . The fat dyke'll probably have a heart attack . . .'

Words. Just words, I told myself. Just stick your headphones in, look out the window and drown them out. They are just words. That's how I got by the last three months working for this sexist, racist, antisemitic, homophobic creep. I told myself it was just words and how powerful were words anyway? Derrick wasn't carrying out violent attacks (as far as I was aware), it was just middle-aged prejudice rants. His racist rhetoric became meaningless. It stopped shocking me. I blocked it out with not only my headphones but my entire mind, which was elsewhere. My mind was in the future at *Gracious* magazine, not at *Bangers*.

But it suddenly hit me with alarming force that my whole life was words. Words were powerful, words were significant, words had the power to change lives, words were magical, words were like pot noodles. Seemingly insignificant with questionable nutrients but could ultimately sustain you through the day by nourishing your soul with warmth and, er, weird little chicken bits.

Words were everything. They were my whole life. Everything in my life was about words. My own grandmother and Doria (rest in peace) had transformed their lives, our lives, the lives of Egyptian women, the lives of Muslim women, through the power of words. And when their words got too much, what happened? President Nasser silenced their words. That's how powerful words are – they have the ability to intimidate grown men.

I looked at Derrick, as he sat picking bits of food out of his teeth, because he's a man and he doesn't need to worry about looking like a sex object every hour of the day. I realised that every particle in my body was repulsed by him. Perhaps what struck me the most, what I most despised about him, was that I was no better than him.

I was writing misogynistic, chauvinistic, anti-feminist articles, reducing women to nothing but sex objects, which is ironically exactly what I had done to myself over the years. I was complicit in Derrick's abuse.

'Right, I'm off then, see you tomorrow, don't forget to send the Candace Caketon piece to the printers and they'll put it in tomorrow's issue,' he said, walking down the stairs.

'Sure,' I managed to muster.

'Oh and . . .' he said, walking back into the room, 'great work today, Nads.' He smiled.

It was the first time he had given me a genuine smile. He looked like a little boy. I smiled back. I smiled like Candace Caketon, who had looked as though her soul had been extracted from her body and the void had been filled with cocaine.

As soon as I heard the sound of his stupid pathetic middle-aged midlife crisis motorbike, I deleted the entire Candace Caketon article and started writing my own . . .

∾

Never before had words made me feel such happiness. I felt the presence of Teta and Doria shining through my body like light through a window on a sunny day.

I took the piece straight to Courtney. She was in her suite watching YouTube videos of cats. Typical lesbian, I thought. Wow, Derrick was really rubbing off on me!

'Courtney!' I yelled a little too loudly. I was still high from writing the piece. It felt like I had just given birth to it, it was my absolute joy. I cradled it in my arms before placing it in front of her.

'Whoa,' she said after she had read it. 'Are you sure you want to do this? I mean you'll lose your job.'

'I think the question is, do you want to do this with me?'

She pushed her hair back and breathed out. Her legs were splayed wide apart, and I realised in that moment that all I wanted was to fall into her lap. I wanted her to hold me. It must have been the sheer exhaustion of the past few hours.

'I have hated Derrick for an eternity. But I'm so drained by his energy at the end of the day I can't bring myself to apply for anything else and then I think maybe my tattoos are too much and no one else will hire me.'

'Don't be silly, I love your tattoos and this isn't 1954,' I said. It was true. Her forearm was a work of art.

'What's this one?' I said, stroking her arm. 'It looks so familiar.'

'It's from Salvador Dalí's famous piece, it's a melting clock. Just reminds me about time and, you know, life and how the clock is ticking . . .' she said.

'Maybe this is the push you need to apply for your dream job?'

We did that thing in romantic comedies where we stare into each other's eyes a little too long. I realised I wanted to kiss her. I think she felt the same because she was looking at my lip.

'Oh god, sorry, but what is that on your mouth? It looks like it's about to explode,' she said.

I touched it in horror. Oh God, no, not now. 'It's a cold sore, I get them when I'm run down.'

'The herpes virus?' she laughed.

'Yes, and I have that too, all right?! Every couple of months I get massive sores on my vagina that I have to rub cream on because a guy I fucked in Saudi who also got me pregnant didn't use a condom, OK?!'

Courtney didn't say anything, she just leaned forward to hold my hand. I tore it away.

'Look, are you gonna have some balls and print this with me and be on the right side of history or are you going to stay with the same racist, sexist, homophobic boss so that he can sell misogynistic rhetoric and imprint in the next generation of girls' minds that the only way to get love and validation is through stripping off and being a sex object to men?'

'Hell yeah, let's destroy this son of a bitch!'

By the time we got to the printers it was almost midnight. Some sad teenage boy called Onslow who was on the late shift was waiting for us so he could lock up.

'Finally,' he said as Courtney and I both handed him the USB stick.

We held his hand for an abnormally long amount of time, knowing that this was the point of no return. Tomorrow we would be fired and hopefully so would Derrick.

Tomorrow Derrick, after twenty years of exposing himself to innocent girls, would finally be exposed himself.

'The truth really does set you free,' Courtney said as she walked me back to my flat. We were standing on Ellerslie Road;

I could see the QPR stadium from the corner of one eye and my aunt's bedroom curtains out the other.

'The truth will set you free,' I repeated. 'Unless you're Derrick Silver!'

'I think I want to set myself free right now,' Courtney said, tickling my ear with her lips. I could feel the coldness of her metallic lip ring slip down to my lower neck. It felt like a butterfly.

The beautiful creature fluttered over my cold-sore-encrusted lips, teasing me, hovering over them, before finding a perfect spot on my forehead. She kissed it gently before going back to my neck again. Each time she touched my flesh, my skin blushed with delight.

'What are you doing tomorrow?' she asked.

'Sending my CV to *Gracious* magazine.'

'Correct,' she said.

'What are you doing tomorrow?' I asked.

She whispered in my ear again and the butterfly came back.

Yasminah

ي

I missed the crickets at night in London. In Tehran they were the soundtrack to our evening. They covered up the sounds of the cheers and eventually the cries of the revolution. I always thought of Lady Macbeth whenever I thought of the crickets, how she heard them creak in the dead silence of the night as the fatal stab to the heart was orchestrated by her husband to the king. How she would only ever see blood when she heard crickets again. How she would struggle to sleep when she heard them, for it was a symbol of when she gave away her soul.

There was about a week in London, in the unrelenting summer of a four-day heat wave, made almost as suffocating as Tehran with the lack of air conditioning and melanin in pale English people's skin, that the crickets creeped in. They would catch me unaware one summer evening, when I'd be watching back-to-back episodes of *Loose Women* after work. I would hear them chirping, "Minah, 'Minah!' and I would smile and cry at the same time. Sometimes I would get out my old photos of Ommy, Farah and the gang and say a prayer for them all.

I heard the crickets that evening. Instead of my usual nostalgic dive into the past, I opened the window that overlooks the QPR stadium and breathed in the husky London summer air. It had a similar heaviness to Tehran air, smog and tiredness. I saw two lovers standing by the stadium entrance wrapped in each other's arms. They were kissing in the way that new lovers do. Shyly and slowly. The larger male figure was kissing the girl's neck. There was a sweetness to his kisses. As if he only had a certain amount to give, so he gave each one out tentatively and considerately. Her body seemed to twinkle in the moonlight. They were at the butterfly stage of love, I thought, as I watched their hands flutter over each other's bodies, from each other's waists up to their breasts. *Breasts*, I thought. I took a step back realising they were two women, and my heart began to skip with delight. I felt as though it was a sign from Ommy. I was always looking for signs that he was talking to me, and this was one. 'Shukran, Ommy,' I whispered to myself.

I turned *Loose Women* off and began to watch the couple closely, not like a pervert but with a certain sentimentality. My accepting city, it felt like I was back in Tehran again in 1970, when there was an innate sense of promise, of progression, of not just tolerance but acceptance. I could feel a tear roll down my cheek; it felt as though it was marking out its territory like contours on a map. The larger girl had tattoos and piercings and the other girl must have been about Nadia's age with long dark hair in soft waves and a . . . I gasped. It was Nadia! I could hardly take it in, I thought she was boy mad! She never stopped reminding us that she was, after all, what with the Saudi saga and the constant need for male validation. She thought I didn't hear her and Kadijah at family gatherings, with their conversations about their nights out, but I did. Not to mention one particular Eid Mubarak where I heard her talking to Kadijah on the stairwell about how a recent smear test had revealed that a boy called Zain had not only given her herpes but HPV too.

Yet, my niece was standing in front of my eyes kissing a woman! I couldn't stop the tears of joy. I wanted to give them the privacy they deserved but I couldn't bear to come away from the window. I was too euphoric! As the couple made several attempts to leave each other, I began to prepare myself for looking like I hadn't been watching the whole beautiful scene. I switched *Loose Women* on again and tried to look natural.

Nadia walked in and said, 'Salamwaylaykum,' and went straight into the toilet. I brought my hands to my face and scrunched up my face in delight. I couldn't wait to talk to her. She was so open about her relationships, I'm sure she would divulge something, which would then lead me to dropping a hint which would then cause her to tell me everything and we could finally be close again. I had missed the closeness that we had when Kadijah and Nadia were small; ever since they turned into teenagers and returned from Saudi, Nadia especially found it hard to look me in the eye. I had hoped that her living with me would rectify this, but she had only ever engaged in small talk with me, and what with my shifts and her work we were the cliché ships in the night. Now that she was having a relationship with a woman, we could bond! The excitement inside me was palpable, I felt like her freedom was my freedom, I felt transported back to Farah when she danced with me in the nightclub the day the Shah announced the same-sex wedding. I felt like I was on the precipice of promise again.

Nadia

ن

U ncle Christopher had requested we play his favourite song as we entered the church for his funeral. The irony of the song, 'Tears of a Clown', was not lost on me but as I stared at the other oblivious funeral guests, I realised I was the only one picking up on this heart-breaking final wish. For Uncle Christopher was always the clown of the family. His song request only highlighted that, despite his humorous drunken antics, his always-the-life-of-the-party status, his criminally hilarious debauchery, he was actually crying inside.

Nobody chooses to drink themselves to death because they are happy, I thought, as I sneakily poured myself more wine in the toilet so that Pamela couldn't see that I was surpassing my 125 millilitre maximum dosage. I was risking a seizure, but I didn't care. Like my best friend Maz, I couldn't go through the grief of my uncle dying of liver cancer and not drink my feelings. Pamela was doing the same, Kadijah too and my dad.

It was odd seeing my Muslim dad in a church, Aunt Yasminah

too. Like seeing a friend from work at Tesco or a teacher at the shopping mall. The last time I had seen my dad in a church was before we went to Saudi Arabia. Months before he had got the job in Saudi, Dad had feigned his Catholicism in church on the day of my Holy Communion which I did to keep us at the Catholic school we attended. I shuddered, recalling the memory. Awkward, unsure and the only brown man in the village, sticking out with his strong Egyptian accent. Watching his hands unnaturally clasped together, as dark as the wood-stained mahogany pew. A sweet potato amongst the Maris Pipers. Watching him make the sign of the cross, tapping his head, his heart, his shoulders, as if checking that he was really there. He followed the congregation with the same level of concentration as he did his Keep Fit with Mr Motivator on GMTV.

Two steps behind, an uncoordinated sweaty mess with no rhythm, he mimicked everyone from standing up to sitting down to bending on his knees. I half expected the priest to come over and put him in the correct position like my aerobics instructor does with me.

Now he seemed more natural in a church setting. After years of being an immigrant your skills at adaptation only grow more Oscar worthy. But perhaps it was because stand-up comedy had given him a newfound sense of confidence I had never seen before. Stand-up had given him everything that I had taken away from him. A job, credibility, humility, respect, a whole new group of friends, fame and a new girlfriend. Karen. Almost twenty years younger than him and with three kids under ten. He had a joke about her in his set, in fact. Something about being more interested in Karen than the Quran, which Pamela mocked for being a cheap pun.

'All through our marriage it was the same jokes, cheap puns, word play, the lowest form of humour . . . and now the comedy world adores him, what is going on?! I think they're in on the joke, I think what your father is doing is like that Andy Kaufman comedian. What's it called again?' Pamela said.

'Anti-comedy,' I said, impressed that she knew about this niche genre of comedy. Although she *had* watched an awful lot of *The Mighty Boosh* while her ex, Tony, had got stoned. My mother was right, though – my dad's act was all just cheap puns about Islam.

'That's it,' she said, ignoring me, 'anti-comedy, where people are laughing because it's not funny! That's why your father is doing so well – he doesn't realise that people are laughing at him because he's *not* funny!'

'Well, whatever it is, it's working out for him. His Edinburgh run has sold out!' I said, before my mother quipped, 'He's sold out, for sure.' I made a face, for the first time not disputing what my mother was saying. She did indeed have a point. Stand-up comedy had infused in my father a morbid desperation for fame.

I loaded my buffet plate with chicken wings, rice balls, a bacon butty and a sausage roll. I could feel Aunt Yasminah judging me for the pig on my plate. But it was what Uncle Christopher would have wanted, I told myself, and today was about him, not about her.

After I had inhaled my food (what is it about grief that makes you so bloody hungry?), I went back to the bathroom, handbag in tow to refill my wine. I had drunk about a bottle and a half by now and I was just starting to feel like I was about to fly. I felt the unease in my stomach, like I was about to go on a rollercoaster. I was dizzy with anticipation and adrenaline. I made it to the cubicle and fell to the floor. I could feel myself coming up out of my body, watching myself from above. My body was throttling back and forth in the small space between the walls, it was convulsing, and my mouth was frothing and splattering like pulling the last dregs into a pint of Guinness. I watched myself for a while as if I was watching a soap opera. I watched until I felt a hotness in my knickers. The heat expanded onto my trousers and liquified. The smell of hot urine filled the room and I felt myself fall into a fuzzy slumber.

I heard the sounds of my mother rushing in.

'Oh Jesus, somebody help, she's having an epileptic seizure, help!' She held me in her arms as I heard Kadijah bursting in and instantly calling an ambulance.

'Come on, Nadia, my darling baby Nadia, come on, come on!' my mother said.

'They're coming, I'll stand outside and wait for them,' Kadijah said with uniform stoicism.

'I love you, sweet Nadia, please, all I've ever wanted in my life is for you to forgive me for what I did to you in Saudi, I love you, Nadia, please stay with me, please.'

I could feel my vision slowly returning as my head began to throb. I could feel it banging and beating as if my heart was in my brain. I looked at her as she held me in her arms, begging for me to come back for us to make up, for her to be a proper mother to me now.

Suddenly I stopped seeing Pamela completely. It was as if a switch inside me had been turned off.

I touched her lightly on the cheek. 'Mum,' I said, 'Mama,' before passing out into her arms. It was then that I realised that the switch inside me wasn't a switch at all, it was a lever which my subconscious in its delirious disarray had chosen to fall on, causing the bit of my heart that had been lost in Saudi to come on again. The light hurt my eyes; it felt good though, really good, to finally wake up.

I was no longer a sad clown. I was like what Maz had written to me on a postcard from the Jacques Le Coq School of Clowning:

Aware and conscious of every emotion, sad as well as happy. Only then, will the true self be revealed, and the clown is no longer a one-dimensional clown but a vehicle of true comedy; an honest mix of every part of what it means to live a life, a culmination of thunderous tragedy and euphoric joy.

Fatiha

ف

J amjam was not how I imagined a Wahhabist to be. While his brows seemed constantly furrowed when female students came into his vision without a hijab, his overall demeanour was open and jolly. I had been surprised to find him in jeans and a *Ghostbusters* t-shirt.

I chewed on my polystyrene coffee cup during our meeting, surprising myself with how nervous I was. I wore my hair back in its usual slick bun and I found myself touching it anxiously as we discussed his thesis.

'The Hermeneutics of Wahhabism with Particular Reference to Ibn Taymiyyah and Muhammad ibn Abd al-Wahhab,' Jamjam regurgitated. His eyes were twinkling. 'I love saying it,' he said.

It's like music to him, I thought. Something he probably doesn't believe in.

I tried to hide a sigh. A small part of me had fantasised about changing the direction of his dissertation, not into a complete opposite direction with, say, a sudden interest in the origins of

Shi'a Islam but perhaps a sidestep out of extremism with 'The Linguistic Methodology of the Zahirites', perhaps? I had practised this thesis title into the mirror several times that morning but now I realised I had to abandon the script and embrace what he was putting in front of me. He wanted to study Wahhabism. In Islamic Studies this meant he wanted to praise Wahhabism.

'So, tell me, Jamali . . .'

'My friends call me Jamjam. Please . . .'

'Jamjam, sorry.' Was I as personable as a friend to him, I wondered. 'So, tell me where you are at with everything.'

I closed my eyes briefly, as if trying to grab a few seconds of micro sleep to gain the energy to take on what could only be described as a debate between my head and my heart. My professionalism and my principles. My life's work and my life's meaning. Supporting a student of the university with his thesis but staying true to Doria and my own research.

By the time I had opened my eyes, Jamjam had stood up on one of the chairs and was asking me to look at Islam from Allah's perspective. Two sides both fighting for his love: the Shi'a and the Sunni Muslims; akin to two divorced parents fighting for the love of their child. I could feel my eyebrows rising and whenever I did that, I felt an affinity with Doria. I remembered back in our university days when our lecturer would get overly theatrical, like Jamjam was now, and our eyebrows would meet and rise together. We would wiggle our brows and roll our eyes and make a mime with our hands expressing how mad and, most likely, drunk our professor was. Then after class, walking back to our apartment block we would entertain each other with impersonations of our lecturers, mocking everything from the way they talked to the way they walked until we were laughing so hard, we couldn't breathe.

Oh, how Doria would have mocked Jamjam! For he was acting as drunk as our old French teachers. 'Typical Wahhabist,' she'd say, 'drunk on power!'

'Get down!' I yelled. 'Who do you think you are? Get down off my chair!' It was as if someone had pressed a button inside of me, releasing all the pent-up feelings I had for the torment of poor Nasr and Ebtehal, forced to leave Egypt for daring to challenge Islam. It was all so confusingly bittersweet; I was elated about my promotion but still deeply perplexed about accepting it. As if I was being disloyal to Nasr by taking his job, and now the stress of the challenge of working with a Wahhabist.

'I'm sorry, Professor Bin-Khalid, it's my presentation . . . I wanted to impress you, I'm so excited to be working with such an experienced academic.'

My eyebrows were so far up in shock they were crawling like thick slugs onto my scalp. I felt myself wanting to crawl back in time myself. 'Anger can be a weakness or a strength,' Doria said right before we stormed parliament. 'If you are in control of it, it's a strength.'

I breathed in, trying desperately to regain my composure.

So, I listened to Jamjam's presentation of his proposed thesis. It was undeniably well researched even in its nascent stages. When he finished, I asked him what he intended to get out of his PhD. He told me that he wanted to uncover new information about the Wahhabists, new interpretations of Islam.

'In Islamic Studies, unlike any other subject, no new ground is covered, only repetitions of what is already known. A PhD in Islamic Studies is unique in this way,' I scoffed.

We were walking out of my office, heading to the cafeteria. Jamjam stopped in his tracks and moved his head and his big eyes methodically towards me like some sort of exotic bird. He touched my arm. I was aghast. A Wahhabist touching my arm! I could not wait to go home and tell Ali. And about his *Ghostbusters* t-shirt! If my husband understood me today, he would never believe it!

'I am going to cover new ground, Professor, I am going to change interpretations of Islam, just like Abu Nasr!'

'You mean you're going to get yourself arrested and declared an apostate?'

He placed his hand on my arm again; we both looked down at it for several moments before he took it away. 'Islam is history. Wahhabism is history. We only see the extremism of Wahhabis in Saudi Arabia, but there are tribes carrying out the Wahhabi faith in non-violent, peaceful ways. I am going to redefine the stereotype of the Wahhabis!'

I laughed. I couldn't quite believe it. I didn't agree with a word he said, but I was at least now ready to listen.

Nadia

ن

It was odd going back to my aunt's flat that night. I could still feel Courtney's breath on me, still taste her scent. My whole body aching to finish what we had started. I was a cocktail of lust, repressed passion, and adrenaline from sticking two fingers up at *Bangers* magazine. I could still feel the blood pulsing through my veins, still feel the heat penetrating from my fingers, clammy and wet, all still fresh from the euphoria of rewriting Derrick's article. Yet now, despite my newly liberated soul, my big act of revolution, as I clicked the door open to the confinement of my aunt's flat, I found myself suddenly stuck and small. After all that I had been through that night, I was now about to come face to face with my homophobic aunt.

Despite the repressive nature of my aunt and her flat, I felt strong. For the first time I felt drunk not on booze but on confidence and self-worth. Like Teta, I had the balls to finally stand up to injustice, instead of being complicit in it. However, by doing so professionally, I had unwittingly enabled myself to be true to who I was personally. Perhaps if I hadn't rebelled against Derrick, I wouldn't have had the courage to liberate myself from the restrictions I had put on my own self. Saudi was the greatest tragedy of my life. But just like Maz had now come to terms with his tragedy, I could no longer mask it with comedy and alcohol. I had to address it. Everything that had happened to me in Saudi was not because I had sex with Zain; it was because I had loved Jaleela. The only way for me to be with Jaleela was for me to be with Zain. And yet by being with Zain, I had got myself pregnant, the repercussions of which had long overshadowed the feelings I had for women.

Courtney had been the one to make those feelings resurface. The high that she gave me was like no man ever did. I wondered, as I stood at her door, whether I would now be able to stand up to my homophobic aunt?

Yes, I told myself. But first I had to deal with what was in my knickers. (I had practically slipped all the way back home.) I strode into the flat, mumbled a quick 'salaam' and went straight into the bathroom.

I showered and cleaned my teeth and listened to see if my aunt had gone to bed yet. She hadn't. I grimaced into the mirror. I did not want to talk to such a homophobe when I had just had my second homosexual experience, my first one since Jaleela. Oh boy! I was exquisite with excitement but dreading the interaction with my aunt. I hated repressing my emotions when I was with her, but I was left with no choice.

I walked out of the bathroom and tried to go straight to my bedroom, but she called out to me. I stood in her doorway as she turned off *Loose Women*, and turned to me, another loose woman.

'How was your day?' Aunt Yasminah asked, her eyes shining.

'Good,' I said.

'What did you do?' she asked.

'Work,' I said, determined to remain monosyllabic.

'You're very late back, did you see a friend after?'

'Yes.'

'What friend?'

'Just a friend.' I clenched my teeth. *God damn it, what is this, an interrogation?*

'A friend?'

'Yes,' I sighed. 'A friend from work.' I started to walk into my bedroom.

'What's her name?' she asked.

I turned around and I could see she was smiling. Not in a genuine way, in a sort of I know something you don't know kind of way. Like she was better than me, she emulated smugness. I started to grow angry.

'Look, Auntie.' I breathed in ready to stand up to her, but instantly a deep fear pulsed into my veins, halting me. 'I'm really tired, I'm going to go to bed.' I relented as I turned back towards my room again. I chastised my cowardice, my inability to put my money where my mouth was, to unashamedly be my authentic self to people who might not ever accept it. I was torn between having the courage to tell my aunt my truth and avoiding confrontation. What if she kicked me out? Standing up to Derrick meant forfeiting my employment but standing up to my aunt would mean homelessness.

'OK, habibbti, but I am just pleased you have made a friend in London, it's good for you to make a friend in London.'

I stared into the mirror above my bedside table as I envisioned myself sleeping rough or – even worse – moving in with one of my parents. I saw my expression going from one of glum contemplation to sudden surprise. My face realising before my brain that she had seen everything from her window. She had seen Courtney and me touching and kissing and making love with our eyes and through our clothes and she had seen Courtney's butterfly flutter over my cold-sore-encrusted lips, healing them with the feathers of her wings. She had seen it all. She knew. She knew I was gay or bisexual or whatever it was I was.

I didn't know what to do but I knew that today had taught me that I couldn't stand for Derrick's chauvinism or misogyny or racism and therefore if I wasn't going to stand for his prejudices I was certainly not going to stand for my aunt's.

I heard her coming towards my room. 'You saw us, didn't you?' I said, my voice cold and trembling.

'Saw what, habibbti?' she said, coming into my room. Her eyes were full of so-called concern but I could see right through her. She couldn't hold down the upturn of her lips, which were forming a crazed smile.

'You saw me kissing a girl.'

'Yes, I did.'

'Well, I guess I'll start looking for another place to live . . .'

'What?'

'Look, Auntie, let's stop with the small talk. I know you hate gays, I've seen your Quran, I've seen the way you look at Maz, and I'm now seeing the way you are looking at me right now with sheer disgust and smugness, that you're going to get into the gates of paradise and I'm not, no matter how much you go to Haj every year for everyone in our family that can't or won't go.' I had accidentally spat on her face. It landed beside her lip; she didn't wipe it away.

'Habibbti! La-ah!' she said, taking my hand and leading me into her room, leading me back to the shoebox of photos.

∾

She treasured each photograph as if it were a trophy or a medallion from a competition she had won second place in. Missing winning by all but a nanosecond, she tucked it all under her bed so as not to remind herself of how close she came to everything. She showed me pictures of everyone, her whole gang, hanging out, goofing around, getting drunk. Not dissimilar to the album on my Facebook account entitled *Uni Bits 'n Bobs: when you're so drunk you steal pub pint glasses 2004*. It was like she was a different person in the same skin as my aunt's, but her heart and her brain were of another person. Another person I never knew, another person I never bothered to get to know. I'd assumed that this person, this open and accepting person didn't exist. I'd reduced this person down to a stereotype. I'd assumed that she was just another oppressed Muslim woman. A victim of the Islamic patriarchy, forever unfree and bound by her piety that her religion expects from her. I was no better than the *Daily Mail* or the *Sun* assuming all Muslims are the same, the women are oppressed and the men are terrorists. I realised with alarming clarity that this was a western stereotype that had infiltrated my blood like a parasite. Not all Muslim women are oppressed. If anything, in my family it was the opposite. Knowing that Teta stormed parliament with Doria Shafik to ensure that Egyptian women got the vote and with new knowledge of my aunt's gay activism with Ommy and Farah in Iran, I saw that it was the Muslim women in my family who were the 'terrorists' – or rather the agents of change – and the Muslim men were the oppressed.

'So, what happened with your PhD thesis?' I asked. We were slumped on the floor, leaning on the side of her bed.

'My thesis was on gay rights in Islam, my supervisor was gay herself and very supportive, but then she lost her job when the Islamic Republic got into power, and she advised me to drop the subject and change to something less controversial.' She sipped on her cardamom tea, seeming to swallow down any bitterness.

'So, what did you write about instead?' I touched her arm, keen for her to continue with the story. I was completely mesmerised, kicking myself that I had underestimated my aunt so much. Still unforgiving of my ignorance that I had reduced her to all but a tired cliché.

'I told them to go fuck themselves.'

I gasped, never having heard my aunt so much as say 'fiddlesticks'.

She smiled at me and continued. 'That if I couldn't research gay rights in Islam with the university, I would do it on my own. And I did. Well, I started it but then Ommy was killed and Farah who had been demoted from a judge to a mere administrative assistant told me to flee. She told me to burn it. Burn the book and flee. So, I did.'

'You burnt it?'

She smiled. She shook her head mischievously. 'I had several copies.'

'Auntie!'

She went under her bed again and pulled out a box with a stack of folders with various Tehran University insignia on. She pulled them all out before unearthing what looked like a first draft of an uncompleted manuscript.

'Oh wow! Auntie!' I cooed.

I flicked through it, greedy to absorb its broken history. She had chapters on different segments of seemingly homophobic segments of the Quran that she had interpreted in not dissimilar ways to the way in which Muslim feminist academics scrutinise the now infamous verse 4:34. Such Muslim feminist academics as Amina Wadud and Fatema Mernissi (who Teta wouldn't stop banging on about) who pertain that the meaning of the time the Quran was written in had a different weighting than it does now and that it is important to consider the culture of the time and the language used and to not implicitly take every word literally.

Not only this but the thesis also had different case studies of gay Muslims being unfairly prosecuted and put to death.

'Can I take this to read through properly, Auntie?'

'La, la, la, it's not finished, and it was written a very long time ago and I don't want . . .'

'Please, just for me, I promise. To make peace with my bisexuality and Islam,' I lied.

She thought for a moment before relenting. 'OK, but please do not show it to anyone else.'

'I won't.'

∾

Of course, the very next day, I showed it to Courtney who was as equally blown away as me.

'It's so refreshing to see gay rights represented from this perspective, it's wild!'

'I know, right, she needs to publish this!'

'Oh, for sure.'

I started tickling her with my slightly less inflamed lips blowing on her ear. 'I know you have a lot of contacts in the publishing industry, right?'

'Yes, babe,' she began to groan with delight.

'Do you think you can get it published for her?' I had my hands down her trousers now, rhythmically penetrating and placating her at the same time. To get her just where I wanted her: to give me the contact of Gracious Publishing House, the subsidiary of *Gracious* magazine.

It seemed to be working, she was groaning and moaning and normally when I did this with guys, they tended to do what I said. But Courtney was a bit trickier to manipulate.

'What the fuck? Are you fucking me to get ahead?' she said, pulling out my arm and settling back onto her dishevelled sofa.

'What? No,' I fibbed.

'Yes, you are! I'm not a piece of meat that can be manipulated into doing what you want merely by . . .' Her sentence hung off the edge of a cliff where it descended to its death.

I didn't know what to say. I was stunned. This was how I behaved in most of my relationships. I used sex as a transaction of some sort. Wasn't that the point of it? An exchange of what you wanted and what they wanted.

I didn't blink. I was shocked. Tears fell and still I didn't blink. I realised I'd been having sex wrong my whole life.

'I think I've been having sex wrong my whole life,' I said aghast.

'Oh babe,' she said, wiping my tears, 'you've just never made love.'

∾

It was remarkable when we had finished. Our phones were going off left, right and centre as if they too were engaging in an explosion of lovemaking. We both had a string of unknown numbers and over a dozen voicemails. I stepped into the

bathroom – I say stepped, I could barely walk – while Courtney saw to her phone.

I sat on the toilet and for the first time I didn't feel like a
drunken whore. Was it because I had made love for the first time
with someone, not for a story to tell my friends, or for male validation or to get ahead in my career or because I was too drunk to
know how to get home? As I stared at the beautiful mess that
was in my knickers, I realised that for the first time I had had sex,
no, made love completely and utterly sober.

I stepped out, declaring my newfound sober enlightenment
with gusto.

'I'm giving up alcohol, completely, not even 125 millilitres
and I'm going back on my epilepsy medication.' I sang the words
and Courtney shushed me, but it didn't matter because I knew
the only person I really needed to hear those words was myself.

I sat on Courtney's lap while she talked on the phone.

'Yes, well, I'm sure we would be happy to come in for a chat,
yes, us both, for sure.'

I made a face at her and she just grinned.

'Well, OK then, we look forward to it.' She pressed the
button to end the call before declaring at full decibel, 'That was
Gracious Publishing! The editor read your article slamming
Bangers magazine and wants you to come in for a chat!'

I couldn't even speak. This time words were insignificant.
This time I basked in a tangible excited gobsmacked silence. It
sounded like an orchestra was playing in my heart and for the
first time in my life I felt like I was the conductor.

Yasminah

ي

They say the truth sets you free. It doesn't always. The truth will only set you free if your truth is agreeable to the culture you are living in. My truth didn't set me free. As free as I am in London I'm chained by the padlocks of my past. Like Doria, who ended her life falling from a balcony, her death a suicide or an accident no one could be ever sure, but one thing we could all be sure of was that her beloved Egypt killed her. It started off by being kind to her, letting her have certain successes, like little scraps you give a dog to silence their bark. She would sit chewing the fat, gnawing the meat off the bone, looking up with her big eyes, those iconic film star looks, and those infamous eyebrows and dare to ask for more. With her blatant audacity, she walked and talked with the entitlement of a man, taking things and expecting to keep them until eventually she was kicked like an animal, gagged like a victim and put away in a prison of her own mind by the press, by the regime, by the dictatorship.

It was only after seeing Nadia that I saw my life had parallels with Doria's and Mama's. How I had been on the precipice of promise in Iran, how I had almost written a book and received the love I so craved from Farah. But I was greedy like Doria and Mama, I wanted so much more so I started to screech and scream, I started to not just do but act, to not just write but research. I was warned several times by the Islamic State; they sent me secret smoke signals, but I didn't listen. It was only when they killed Ommy that I began to understand, that I began not to fight, but to flee. Just like Doria, some cynics said she walked off her own balcony willingly, others will swear that she was pushed. The truth is my fight turned into ambivalence, acceptance of the status quo. I gave up, just like Doria.

I looked in the mirror and raised my own bushy eyebrows and realised it was I, not Mama, who was really the bad tribute act to Doria Shafik. It was I who had started a thesis and not finished it, it was I who started a revolution but never revolted, it was I who stormed into Farah's house, kissed her and left her there to pick up the pieces of her broken marriage and smooth over the cracks with her own tears. Her children now unsure who she really was and who would never ever know the real woman. Farah herself leaving her own mind and letting her soul be controlled by a man she never loved and never would love in exchange for her life, her children.

Perhaps we were all just bad tribute acts to Doria Shafik?

This was why when Nadia and Courtney came storming into my flat, I agreed to finish my thesis and try to get it published. I was no longer going to be silenced.

I decided to dedicate the book to Ommy, along with the inscription 'I sense a revolution coming'.

Nadia

ن

' I TV comedy panel shows are the lowest form of wit,' my
mum hissed into my ear as we queued to watch my dad
film one.

'I thought the lowest form of wit was sarcasm?' Hany piped
in. He was openly holding his wife's hand, despite the fact that
Rabia's home was still registered as a single-parent household.

'No, I think the lowest form of wit is puns,' Kadijah's husband Christian groaned.

We all nodded in agreement.

I was standing holding Courtney's hand, and this was the first
time she had formally met my whole family. I could feel her
palm sweating, so I squeezed her hand to reassure her she was
doing just fine. Aunt Yasminah already adored her. But then
again that might be because she got her a book deal with one of
the biggest academic publishing houses in the country.

We queued for another five minutes before a steward escorted
us all to our seats. A warm-up comedian started riffing with the

341

crowd while the on-screen comedians, including my dad, got their hair and makeup done. Or in the case of my dad just his makeup. He patted his shiny, bald, brown head at the makeup artist and made a goofy face.

My mum and I giggled, squeezing each other's legs to try to stop ourselves from laughing too loudly before filming. I could feel Courtney's broad shoulders shaking right beside me; I dared not look at her for I knew I would burst into hysterics at the sheer ridiculousness of it all.

My dad was wedged between a *Hollyoaks* star and an *X Factor* contestant. The show was called *What's So Funny?*, where a contestant is given three comedy clips to watch and, based on their reactions, the other contestants have to guess which laughter matches the clip. The reactions were pre-recorded and over the course of the filming we saw my dad laughing hysterically with spaghetti hoops bursting out of his mouth, silently chuckling at a bus stop and laughing underwater at a leisure centre, in full scuba diving gear much to Kadijah's delight.

It was odd seeing my dad filming his first TV panel show. Odd for us all as a family who never thought his stupid dad jokes would take off, least of all my mum. I looked at her watching him and despite her bitter jabs at his 'ridiculous comedy career' I saw real love and admiration in her eyes. She seemed to be happy for him, and ever since his split from Karen, and hers from Tony, 'the sixty-five-year-old Mancunian man-child stoner', they seemed to be getting along a lot better. Who knows, Kadijah and I sometimes wondered, perhaps comedy will reignite their marriage? After all, as my dad told me the great Stewart Lee once told him, tragedy plus time equals comedy.

At the after-party, I finally got to introduce Courtney to my dad. Courtney's lip ring was quivering although she insisted it was because she was cold. I knew she was lying because a lumberjack body like hers never gets cold. I found it quite touching how nervous she was to meet my parents. My mother had already given us the nod of approval, so now it was just my dad to go.

'Dad, this is Courtney, my girlfriend.'

'Yes, your friend who is a girl! Hello!' he said, shaking her hand.

'No,' I said defiantly. I was tired of this family pretending all the time and not being honest. 'Courtney is actually my girlfriend. We love each other,' I said, taking her hand.

'Yes, yes, female friendship is very close and intense . . .' he laughed before walking away to talk to his agent who was trying to get him a part in the latest Teletubby film.

I groaned and mouthed a 'sorry' to Courtney.

I started to feel really angry that my dad was not accepting my truth just like he had never let on to us about my aunt's past. Determined to glaze over everything, using artificial sweeteners instead of real sugar, leaving everything with a saccharine aftertaste. Not realising that real bitterness is better than fake, candied emptiness.

If I had learned anything over the past few months, it was that I had to speak my truth and that tiptoeing around people, scared to disrupt the 'peace', was an act of silent warfare that harmed more people than a rebellious act of defiance.

I stormed over to him and his agent. She was short and tiny; she could have played a Teletubby herself. Even though I was looking down on her petite frame I felt like she was looking down on me. She had that typical agent sneer on her face, which seemed to say, *I'm better than everyone because I'm shagging the director of the new Teletubby film*. Annoyingly my dad had told me his agent, Cressida, had appeared in *Gracious* magazine's '30 Under 30', an article which predominantly showcased the children of famous parents 'miraculously' having their shit together before the age of 30.

'Cressida tells me that nepotism is necessary,' my dad said before shaking his head and laughing, 'Ah, Cress. She is always teaching me new things.' I almost threw up a little bit in my mouth at the way he affectionately abbreviated his agent's name. 'She says that nepotism only got her foot in the door, and it was her hard work that opened it!' He looked confused as he attempted to repeat her exact words but it didn't sound quite right. I smiled and nodded. The way he gushed about this over-privileged daughter of a well-known comedy commissioner and cousins to one of the biggest stand-up comedians in the country; I had half a mind to think she wasn't just shagging the Teletubby director but my dad as well.

'Nepotism, you mean people that are only famous off the back of their dad?'

'Yes, like Jesus,' he said, recalling what I had told my Quranic teacher in Saudi. He nodded, as if it somehow cemented his agent's credibility even more.

'You're right, Dad, Jesus is only famous off the back of his dad. But Cressida is just cousins with Michael McIntyre, not sure it's the same thing.'

'First cousins,' he said.

Now I was standing in front of them both, as Cressida was explaining that for most of the film he would be in full Tinky Winky costume, but 'rest assured, I've also got you a small cameo role where we can see your face and you punch all the presenters from *Saturday Kitchen*. I think it's going to be really good for your profile, Ussy.' She had her hand on his arm, and my dad's pupils were expanding, as were her own. *They are definitely fucking*, I thought.

'Hi, Dad. Look, I feel like you're not really hearing me when I say that Courtney is my girlfriend.'

'Yes, your friend who is a girl!'

I rolled my eyes. How was my dad so blind? He thought that my best gay friend Maz was my boyfriend and that my actual girlfriend was just a friend!

'No, Courtney and I are lovers. Lovers.'

Cressida took her hand off his forearm and whispered something in his ear which seemed to change his whole demeanour.

'Habibbti, that is fine. I welcome Courtney as your lover, into this family, no problem.'

'Really?' I said.

'Yes, Cressida tells me that having a gay daughter will be really good for my career!'

Yasminah

ي

We got back from the filming of Ussy's silly comedy show late that night. The crickets were crying, and a black cat followed Nadia and I up the stairs to the flat. It wouldn't stop meowing. We let it stroke our legs before shutting the door on her. But still, we could hear her cries.

'Let's take her in,' Nadia whispered, 'she's so cute.'

'OK,' I said.

Nadia scooped her up and brought her into the kitchen where she found a small bowl and filled it with milk. She crouched down, placing it on the floor. The cat slurped it all up in seconds and Nadia poured more. The cat again consumed it all in a matter of moments and for the third time Nadia poured her another round.

'I think this cat has a drinking problem,' she said, laughing.

Out of the corner of my eye I could see the answering machine glaring in the living room. There were twelve messages flashing at me like a row of exclamation marks on the page.

I could feel my stomach drop. I was used to getting a lot of messages since the book came out, but this felt different. I pressed the button that released all of them, and they played like a song, a melancholic symphony.

It was Aziz. All of them were from Aziz. The symphony was fast at first with a crescendo; his baritone voice had gone up an octave, it was full of panic. Yet, as the messages went on his voice became smoother. There was everything in these messages; it was like reading the great works of Shakespeare – there was both the tragic and the comic.

Once I had listened to all twelve messages, they went back to the beginning again. 'Like life,' I said out loud, 'life is a circle.'

Nadia came towards me holding the cat in her arms, singing 'The Circle of Life'. She held the cat up in the air like it was the Lion King. Nadia looked quizzically at my streaming tears and my trembling body, now shaking with laughter.

She said nothing but her big eyes dropped to watch the answering machine, as if watching it would help her understand it more.

Aziz's words filled the air. 'She had certainly mellowed towards me in her later years, told it to me straight that she had always thought I was a piece of shit but over time she had seen that I brought her just as much joy as I did pain. That's what she said about you too. And even Usman. That's what family is really, your pain as well as your joy. That's what life is really,' he said, sounding as surprised at his sudden philosophical insight as I was with mine. 'She had told me that her life was full of equal parts pain and joy, and that without the pain she wouldn't have been able to relish the joy, that to truly appreciate joy, you must also have pain. Pain brings joy. That's what Doria had always told her. Without pain you cannot have the joy of change. I've had a drink for her tonight at the club, for all the moments of pain she gave me and all the moments of joy. You should do the same, Yasminah. Inshallah.'

My beautiful Mama was gone. I imagined her being met in paradise by Baba and Doria, who would spend the rest of eternity competing for her affections. I smiled through my tears.

'Teta,' Nadia whispered as her tears fell. We looked at each other, our eyes burning. The cat was on Nadia's shoulders, licking both our cheeks in turn, as if our tears were the milk of life, and we laughed.

Glossary

aiywa	yes
alhamdulillah	praise be to God
bardo keda	a phrase meaning 'also like this'
bass	added to the end of a statement to indicate the end of a discussion
bismillah	in the name of God
ful	a traditional Middle Eastern breakfast dish made from fava beans, olive oil and spices
gallabiyah	a loose-fitting traditional gown, also known as 'jalabiya'
gharbzadegi	(Farsi) a perjorative term that translates as 'westernised'
habibbi (m.) or habibbti (f.)	a term of endearment, often meaning 'my love' or 'my dear'

351

halowa	a sesame-based paste
hanan	affection or compassion
hem	slang for being overwhelmed with indescribable problems and chores
inshallah	'if God wills it' or 'God willing'
janabah	sexual impurity or a state of uncleanliness
Kashf-e hijab	a decree issued by Reza Shah of Iran in 1936 which banned all Islamic veils
keda	like this
la-ah	no
mazhar	a large drum with a heavy frame
mesh keda	not like this
molokhia	a stew made from jute leaves
riq	a traditional Arabic instrument; a type of tambourine
sabah al kheir	good morning
Saidi	traditional music from the south of Egypt
salamwaylaykum	a phrase often used as a greeting and meaning 'peace'

shaz gensi	a paedophile or pervert, also used as a derogatory term for a homosexual
shukran	thank you
simsimiyah	an Egyptian lyre
tam'eya	falafel
Umm	mother of (for example, Umm al-Dunya is an Arabic phrase meaning 'Mother of the World')
wallahi	I swear by God
yanni	used as a filler, like the colloquial expression 'you know'
Yallah basora!	Come on, quick!
Yerhmek Allah	a blessing, meaning 'may God have mercy on you'

Acknowledgements

I can't believe my dream came true and I got a job where my boss cannot see my screen! It couldn't have been possible without the wonderful team at Unbound who believed in *Daughters of the Nile* from the get-go. Absolutely MAHOOSIVE thanks to Aliya Gulamani, for not only sending me the most joyously dreamy emails but championing my work and writing completely wondrous letters of recommendation. Equally MAHOOSIVE thanks to Flo Garnett who, along with Aliya, encouraged *Daughters* development into new heights and realms. It simply would not be the same book without you both. Flo, thank you for being the editor of my dreams (basically this criterion meant that you only ever encouraged *more* references to Boots Advantage Card points). To the rest of Unbound – Suze, Ilona, Marissa, Rina et al – thank you for making me feel so welcome. It's not often I go to a big-wig swanky media company in the city, sit in a boardroom and feel like I absolutely *should* be there. Thank you all for quelling my imposter syndrome. And of course, to fellow Unbound Firsts winner, Iqbal Hussain: I can't wait to throw the most nineties-tastic *Northern Boy/Daughters of the Nile* book launch party with you!

Thank you Adeola Opeyemi for your detailed notes and to

Tamsin Shelton for such astute attention to detail. And to both of you for your kind, encouraging words. Enormous thanks go to Jodi Hunt and Mark Ecob for THAT cover which seriously emanates the sass of Nadia and the overall tone of the book (dark as f**k) despite me being in total denial that it was a light-hearted comedy for the duration of the writing period.

Special shout out goes to the Society of Authors for awarding me with a very generous grant to continue to work in my pyjamas each day. Thanks also to Georgia Holmes and the rest of the team at W. F. Howes. A particular career highlight was auditioning for my own audiobook. A part of me wanted to *not* get the part, simply for the hilarious anecdote but thanks for actually giving me the part of Nadia, who is completely and utterly not based on me.

Gigantic amount of thanks to my PhD supervisors, Dr Penny Pritchard and Helen Gordon. Penny – thank you for putting up with my inability to use commas correctly and for being a constant rock of support throughout the last three years, I could not have done this without you. Helen – thank you for making me understand that I needed to do more research than simply watching *Vera Drake*. It's been an honour to be mentored by a writer of your prestige. Thanks to all the other legends at the University of Hertfordshire who helped me along the way: Drew Pautz, Lorna Gibb and to Joe Thomas. Which brings me to thanking Helen Lederer and the team at Comedy Women in Print for giving me the scholarship to go to Herts (like Doria and Fatiha at Sorbonne!) to do my Master's degree and learn my craft. I honestly wouldn't be the writer I am today without this initial 'break'. Eternally thankful to you all.

To my therapist, Ayesha. Thank you.

To Cynthia Nelson, thank you for writing *A Woman Apart* – Doria Shafik's biography – which became my bible/Quran throughout the writing process. I am so thankful to have also had Yousra Imran's sharp eye on all things Quranic and Islamic. Not only this but we have discovered that we may actually be the same person (TBC). Shukran, habibbti. And to Alya Mooro for cherishing the message of this book as much as me. Thank you to Sadia Azmat for letting me title Ussy's show *Sex Bomb*. Not only are you a dear friend but you have been a true inspiration for this book. If you want to know more about Muslim female sexuality, read her memoir entitled . . . *Sex Bomb*!

Thank you to Sherry and Nigel – and your very fun and funny children, Alex and Lizzie.

Thank you to Faye Treacy, for all the very many long voice notes on dating, family and writing. You are a ridiculously talented screenwriter; it's always an honour to read your work.

To my dearest friend Charlie, you are the C to my D. Thank you for feedback with THAT blow job joke too, you filthy animal. To my bestest friend Sophie, I knew you were the girl for me when I saw you in the playground aged eleven. Sorry for always making you play an extra, when I was Sophie Ellis-Bexter and Danny from *Grease* in our home videos. To my sister, Amirah, thank you for being the calming, stable, rational voice in my life and for calling me for help when you accidentally stuffed six tampons up your foof and couldn't get them out. To Ben, the best brother-in-law a girl could ask for, sorry for making that joke about DJs – it wasn't me it was Teta! And to the sweetest nieces in the world, Thea and Eadie, I adore and love you both to the moon and back. To my Mum, and to whom this book is dedicated. Mum, I was actually going to dedicate this book to Rosemary's mum. (Do you remember the woman who told her daughter she could no longer be friends with me after we toilet-papered the Year 3 toilets?) But I thought, nah, dedicate the book to the woman who only ever laughed (not cried) at my naughtiness. I hope this dedication somehow cancels out all the £65s I owe you. To my Dad, I'm sorry you had to read so many sex scenes, but at least I'm not an actress and you didn't have to watch the sex scenes, right? To both my parents, thank you for making me see that writing and academia are in my blood.

Finally, to Doria Shafik and all the other Muslim feminists who inspired this book: I hope I have done you all proud.